SWEET CHEEKS & HER MOB BOSS

MAFIA, MURDER, AND MAYHEM SERIES
BOOK 2

ELM JED

UNDERGROUND EDITION

Sweet Cheeks & Her Mob Boss

Underground Edition

© 2022 Elm Jed

Cover Art by: S.Wolf.Art LLC

EBook ISBN -9781967019014

Paperback ISBN- 9781967019083

✿ Formatted with Vellum

To Moony,

For always being my rock in the storm
And my other half with the arm floaties

CONTENTS

CONTENT WARNINGS

Contains darker themes, gun and physical violence, torture, sexual predatory behavior, explosions, and attempted suicide.

BOOK PLAYLIST

"I Want to Break Free" – Queen
"Ghost in the Night" – The Satellite Station
"Porn Star Dancing" – My Darkest Days, Chad Koeger
"Crazy in Love (Epic Trailer Version)" – J2, Wulf
"We Will Rock You (feat. The Triple Killers)" –J2, The Triple Killers
"Bow- Slowed" – Reyn Hartley
"Dirty Mind" – Boy Epic
"MONTERO (Call Me By Your Name)" – Lil Nas X
"Purple Lamborghini (with Rick Ross)" – Skrillex, Rick Ross
"Flames" – Tedy
"Prisoner" – Raphael Lake
"Without You" – Ursine Vulpine, Annaca
"The Kraken" – Hans Zimmer
"Demons are a Girl's Best Friend" – Powerwolf
"Strange" – LP

BOOK
NERD
:-P

CHAPTER 1
IT'S LIKE LYIN' IN PARADISE

My room smells of bloodlust, dark spices, and sex. My hand drifts to the side, feeling his warmth next to mine as I pick up the faint sound of Vinny's breathing, and smile to myself. The darkness surrounds me with spots of crimson, violet, and a weird green hue speckling my vision. Vinny grumbles beside me, putting his arm over my chest to pull me toward him, and I chuckle at the needy vampire.

Clothes have exploded from my closet, making my bedroom floor a mess. I may have neglected a few of my chores at home this week. In my defense, I am working two jobs between *The Vault* and *Unbound*. It's not the greatest excuse, but I'm sticking with it. I stare up at the ceiling and absent-mindedly move my hand across Vinny's arm to feel his warmth.

It's been a month, and it still doesn't feel real.

My best friend of twenty plus years confessed he loved me, and I did, too. Both of us kind of fucked up not saying it for years, just like the perfect pair of idiots we are.

And Vinny is now my…lover? Partner? Could I get away with calling him my boy toy? No matter the title, the vampire is in my bed now, grumbling in his sleep after last night's sex capade.

I figure I have about an hour until work downstairs, debating how to get out from underneath Vinny's hold. My phone chimes next to my bed, and he groans as I fumble for it, sending it clattering to the ground. Now I'm groaning as I fall naked to the floor and reach for my phone, finally finding it to answer, "I did not order a wake-up call."

"I thought you went by Topside hours," Bill says on the other end.

"Haven't for a month now."

"Must have missed the memo."

"Or you haven't checked any messages from me or your damn email," I mutter as I stand up and reach for my blanket. Vinny has already snatched it, and I can barely see crimson eyes watch me. "Give me the blanket," I warn him.

"But you look divine in this light, sweet cheeks."

"And cold. Hand it over, bloodsucker."

"Blanket hog."

"Thought you realized that our first night together, bestie." The blanket ends up around my shoulders as I sit on the bed. Vinny sidles up behind me, wrapping an arm around my waist.

"Hey, pay attention to me!" Bill complains through the phone. "Hurts bad enough you're having fun without me."

"Never would have invited you anyway," I say.

"Oh, that *hurts*, baby sis. After everything I've done for you."

"Does that include itching powder in my underwear, numb-nuts?" Vinny growls from behind me.

"He kind of apologized," I chuckle while Vinny pokes my shoulder. I swat at the air around him, and say, "And I'm sure Bill doesn't do pranks anymore...on you." I hear Bill's muffled laugh on the other end. Five bucks he's already pulled one today.

William "Bill" Midnight is notorious for his pranks and jokes. He's a young vampire in his 70s, though it seems most days he hasn't reached maturity yet. He taught me how to play practical jokes and "run from the law" at a young age before he ran off to Chicago to join PSB's Midwest division. One of the few vampires we have contact with that doesn't rat us out to the humans.

"Have him come to Chicago sometime. I can show you both around," Bill offers.

"How about no?" Vinny answers as I frown at him, and he kisses me quickly on the cheek while getting out of bed.

"Still a grumpy vampire before 5 PM, isn't he?" Bill asks.

"It's payback for waking my ass up when I was on Topside," I grumble as Vinny chuckles from across the room. "So, what's up, underwear wrecker?"

"Pulled a few strings in New York; you're safe to go back on Topside." My shoulders relax at the news.

After the incident last month with the hospital and most of the NYPD realizing my relations to the Underground Mafia, it didn't seem like I'd ever return safely back to Topside. I didn't necessarily want to go back, but it's nice to have the option.

"Am I in any trouble for getting in the way of their operations?" I ask.

"Got you marked as an *innocent* bystander who won't be filing charges against PSB or NYPD for neglect and almost killing you. Did you see how much anti-venom they administered into your veins? You should be dead; that's impressive."

"Tell that to my parents and see how they react."

"I'd *happily* annoy that best friend of yours, but never Alanzo or Carmen. I value my emotions and hormones." Bill laughs it off, but I can hear the fear in his voice. Good to know the lesson he learned from Pops years ago stuck with him.

"Remind me to destroy his suits the next time he's in town," Vinny comments as he gets dressed.

"Stop eavesdropping, grumpy pants," I scold him.

"*He* woke me up."

"Sucks, doesn't it?"

"I'll tell you what *does* suck...and well, might I add." Vinny is suddenly close, and his face comes a few inches from mine, bringing facial features into view.

"Oh, I know. But *that's* not happening unless you go get coffee."

"Promise?" His red eyes glimmer in the dark as he watches me, fangs fully out.

"Get the coffee, bloodsucker, and you'll find out." I push him away, but the bastard doesn't move.

Bill moans on the other end of the phone. "Stop torturing me with this flirting bullshit."

"All the more reason to do it," Vinny responds, bringing his lips to mine with a searing kiss. His fingers trail through my unbound hair, holding my head in place for his tongue to slip over my lips. I open, lost within his taste until Bill makes another disgruntled groan. I give Vinny another quick kiss and pull away. He relents, leaving the room quietly. I wouldn't be surprised if my family is awake, but neither of us wants to find out the hard way, especially with Ricky and his beauty sleep.

"You prepared for the vampiric backlash being with him?" Bill asks.

"I was blissfully ignoring that until you mentioned it," I say. "Thanks a lot."

"It's good to keep you updated with the Vampiric Society and their need for control. You know about that war they almost started in Russia over a pureblood Mating a werewolf, right?" Why don't phones have a button to punch the person you're talking to?

"I have a Masters in Paranormal History and Literature, Billy Bob. Yes, I know."

"Reminders are always good; sex brain can make things go fuzzy. Bet you've learned that by now with the playboy Vincent is."

I dig my fingers into my temple, and regret picking up the phone. "Why do I choose the worst vampires to be friends with?"

"Far more interesting, and we keep up with your wit. Let's be honest, you'd be bored, baby sis."

"Give me more info, or I'm hanging up and sending a glitter bomb to your office."

"You can still send the glitter bomb; I'll just put it on my coworker's desk, they've lasted two weeks, and that's far too long."

"Bill…"

He sighs, and I hear his chair squeak as he leans back as someone asks for a pen. Of course, he's calling me during work hours. How his boss hasn't killed him yet is beyond me. "You're set to go back to Topside without being arrested for being affiliated with the mob, although they'd never succeed anyway with how deep Vincent's fangs are in the agencies. Even that *Detective* can't put his hands on you."

"Good to know," I say, putting my glasses on, and getting rid of the warped depth perception. "Anything else?"

Bill takes a breath. "The results are in. Pause for dramatic effect…he *is* your father."

"Shit." I'm not surprised. We already did some tests with Charlene, but I wanted a second opinion.

"Did some digging on him, too," he says.

"What did you find?"

There's some rustling of papers in the background. "He's about 95 years old, a young daemon, with no prior criminal records with us or NIIA. I used some contacts in New York to see if they had anything. There's not much on him other than being in New York for like a year. Before that, it was Maine, Florida, Idaho, and Texas. Birth certificate places him in Idaho, but no mention of parents, and he's listed as a full-bred daemon."

"The loner kind of daemon then," I mumble as I get off the bed. "He's been in New York for a year?"

"Stayed in Brooklyn on Topside. Looks like a freelancer, too.

Consultant of some kind, but the records don't say what, which seems *odd*."

"Yeah, not easing my nerves," I say, putting on a tank top. "How'd you track that much on him?"

"Do you really wanna know?"

"Never mind, I don't have coffee yet, which that blood-sucker better hurry up already."

"So happy your relationship is filled with joy and independence."

"I will come to Chicago and strangle you."

"Add joy to my day, *please*," he sighs as papers flop in the background. "He's squeaky clean, baby sis. Other than being a deadbeat father that left you with a mad scientist. By the way, *that* is an entirely different thing."

"What did you find?" I ask as I pull my jeans up.

"Nothing."

"Nothing?"

"Nothing. PSB and NIIA practically made it look like he never existed and may be in a witness protection program. He's in the grip of federal divisions you don't poke around at. I don't have clearance to go further, sorry, my hands are tied and not in the fun way." I let out a groan and fall to my bed. "And since we know you won't pay me for this, tell Vincent he can. I need new suits. He's your sugar daddy, now, right?"

I snort loudly, "Maybe he'll send you a suit filled with itching powder."

"Come on, you owe me something for this."

"How about I let you keep your favorite appendage?"

"Fair, but I still want milkshakes the next time I come into town. As long as you promise nothing *salty* will flavor it."

"Ew, you're gross."

"But endearing."

"Maybe I'll get you a new suit or two without powder." Bill grunts in approval, followed by awkward silence. "What is it?"

Another squeak from his office chair, and he whispers,

"Watch your back. I was threatened more than usual when I investigated Traloski and *daddykins*. Top brasses are acting skittish. Something's not right, baby sis, so keep your back covered if you go searching again."

"Think I already learned my lesson."

"Never stopped you before." Bill laughs as I roll my eyes at the phone. "See you around, baby sis." He hangs up, and I let my hand drop to the bedspread.

The door clicks open, and I reach for the gun under my pillow, aiming it towards the door. I get a whiff of freshly brewed coffee, and Vinny chuckles under his breath. "Little to the right, sweet cheeks."

I adjust my aim, then put the gun back under the pillow as he walks over with the mugs. "Thought I needed to aim for the heart."

"Except you've already captured it, sweet cheeks. Have to protect it now," he answers, handing me the delicious "anti-murdery juicy-juice."

"You're getting mushy on me." I laugh as he sits down beside me. I take a sip and moan under my breath at the taste. Perfectly made by Vinny, as always. "Thank you."

"Welcome." He kisses my neck and trails his tongue down my skin. "What did that prankster have to say?"

"Other than you getting him a new suit or two?"

"Seriously?"

"Better make it four. He may have jeopardized his job."

"He should be better at it then."

"Be nice, vampy."

"What did he find?"

"Edgar's my real father and has no criminal records, traveled a lot, presumably a freelancer of some kind. No red flags," I answer, taking another sip of coffee.

"Anything else?"

"PSB and NIIA are the ones who made Traloski disappear.

No surprise there. Seems like what I found at my old college is all that's left."

"Midnight's gonna get suits for nothing helpful," Vinny mumbles as I stare at the dark liquid in my hands. Vinny places a hand on my knee. "Brenda…"

"I don't want to talk about it yet." I lean my head on his shoulder as we sit on my bed, in my old room in my childhood home that I moved back to after leaving my apartment and library job on Topside. My life was upended due to mob shit and ghouls, and then, deadbeat *daddykins* showed up twenty years after leaving me either in a sewer or with a mad scientist to traumatize me with scars, blindness, and nightmares. Yeah, not ready to talk about it yet.

"Alright. You working in the club today?" Vinny brings his hand up, brushing my hair back.

"Yeah, some of the newbies are transitioning to waitresses. Gotta get ready for any new survivors coming through. What about you?"

Vinny shrugs and sips his coffee. "Blood bank check-ins and imports at the docks."

"Your day sounds more fun," I say, and he chuckles.

"I thought I was the one turned on by blood?"

"You're rubbing off on me."

"New kink to discuss?"

"You wish, you hungry hippo."

"Only for *you*, sweet cheeks." He grins and kisses me again. I hum at the contact, trying to keep my coffee mug steady as he pushes further.

Lips still against his, I mumble, "I'm gonna be late."

He doesn't pull away. "Blame it on me."

"Gladly."

Even with Bill's little warning about PSB and the Vampiric Society, I was going to be blissfully distracted for this moment in paradise.

CHAPTER 2
I WANT TO BREAK FREE

"Bobby, put this away for me, will you?" I ask, placing bottles of liquor on the bar. He takes them with a smile and nods as his light pink skin glistens under the club lights.

It's one of the few days Pops shuts down the club to check inventory, re-evaluate employees, and inspect security systems. The dance stages, tables, and seating are cleaned and sanitized, and the back is organized, ready to return to schedule once Pops and Ricky give the okay. I glance over at Bobby finishing up inventory behind the bar and catch a glimpse of myself in the mirror.

My hair is tied back, showcasing the undercut and two scars running down my face. In the past, I've had varying emotions about the scars that riddled my body and always wondered what I had endured, hoping to find answers. Now I wish I hadn't. The mysterious scars were now a reminder of what Traloski left me with. I trace the ridges on my arm down to my wrists.

A real freaking Frankenstein monster story.

"Baby girl, you all done?" Pops' voice brings me out of my thoughts, and I watch through the mirror as he approaches. I drop my hand and turn to face my father. His deep violet eyes find mine, and his collected expression shifts into concern. His gaze darts from me to the mirror, and he sighs taking a seat at the bar. "He can't hurt you, baby girl."

"I know, Pops," I say as I sit next to him. "And I'm finished, unless you need my help somewhere else."

He smiles a little. "Don't avoid the subject, even if you're being responsible."

I shrug, looking down at the counter. He places his paperwork on the bar, reaching for my hands as his thumbs caress the scars on my wrists. I try to avert his gaze, but I know I'm not going to win. Sometimes it's annoying having a father who's extremely attuned to emotions. Topside wasn't even far enough from his reach.

"Baby girl, remember our deal; you talk when you need to," Pops says softly.

I stare at my reflection, my jaw clenching as I look at the gruesome facial scars. "I always thought I was like one of the kids you saved from the black market or the Paranormals used for parts in the slave trade. I thought they were survival marks..."

"They're still survival marks, baby girl. You survived and flourished."

"You know, I thought being with Vinny, well, any partner really, I'd feel better about the scars and shit, but I don't. The feeling of being out of place hasn't really left or just..."

"Just what baby girl?"

"Insecurity, I guess, because I thought I was...okay with how I looked."

"You're not now?"

I let out a long breath and meet Pops' gaze, gripping his hands. "It's different now, Pops. They're reminders of what I was used for, and it's hard to look at them now without thinking that. Without thinking I lost...lost..."

"Control of your body?" He asks, and I slowly nod. Pops hums to himself as he looks over to the stages. He raises a brow, bringing his attention back to me. "Well, what if you danced again?"

"What?" I ask.

"You used to love it. It always made you feel free and in *control*. Besides reading, it was your favorite thing to do."

"Pops, I don't—"

"You've seen how it's helped the other survivors regain confidence. Everyone needs a reminder from time to time, no matter the background they may come from."

I turn to look at the stages I'd danced on for years. It was a haven during college and even when I was younger, dancing like a lunatic with Ricky and Gina next to me. I stopped dancing completely when I moved to Topside for the library job. Back then, I decided not only would I leave Vinny behind for the better, but other parts of myself, too. Within months, I became grumpy, irritable, and annoyed with life. Shocker. I hid the better parts of myself in a box deep inside out of fear, safe from others and myself. I didn't allow myself to be free, afraid of the consequences. Now, that freedom called again, an odd feeling within my chest yearns to get back on stage.

I swallow hard, thinking about Vinny. No laws are against mixed breeding, but it doesn't stop antique-thinking from aristocrats within the Vampiric Society, who cherish their pure bloodlines. The Dracultellis are one of the last few pureblood families in the U.S. Vinny may be the Blood Mafia Boss, but Bruno calls the shots within the Society, including throwing me into the Hudson River if I cross too many lines. I'm not anything those vamps would allow as a partner, especially a Mate to Vinny; an adopted half-breed stripper who's the daughter of a rival mob family *really* looks bad. Vinny reassured me he'll take care of it, but the odds aren't in our favor. I've read enough about their little loud *discussions* to know.

"Nothing wrong with going back to something you love," Pops whispers. "Especially if it never truly left you in the first place."

I shake my head and say, "I haven't danced in years, Pops."

"Never stopped you before," he argues.

I sigh and bring my gaze back to him. His eyes twinkle in mischief, and a grin pulls at my lips. He wasn't wrong, and I did miss it.

I roll my eyes, and say, "I *doubt* my grip strength is any good."

"Don't believe you a second there, baby girl," he argues. "I know you've been doing other exercises besides those in the bedroom."

"Aw, Pops, don't!" I scowl and wave my hands in the air as he laughs. "Okay, point taken, but I really don't know how rusty I'll be. I haven't worn heels in, like, two years."

Pops stands up and walks around the bar, aiming for the music station just behind it. "Don't do any drops, and only do the moves you remember and can complete safely. Otherwise, just have fun, baby girl."

"Even if I look like an idiot?"

"That's the best part," he smirks. "But you won't."

I look back at the stage, and my jaw ticks as I mull it over. Ricky approaches us, flopping back into a chair and leaning against the bar as he says, "Everything's set backstage. Gina's finishing up in the changing rooms while the rest of the crew is on break. We'll be good to open in an hour."

"Good," Pops says. "Help me encourage your sister to dance again."

"Are you dancing?" Ricky perks up instantly.

"How dare you." I narrow my eyes at Pops.

Of course, he'd want me to. Ricky taught me a good portion of my pole dancing moves. "It'll be a *relief* to see you dance again," Ricky pleads. "Come on, make my week! Joey won't let me into the coffee shop. He said he's afraid I'll paint it neon blue or something."

"You totally would."

"It would add flair," he says with mischievous blue eyes and a wicked smile. "Why *not* dance? It's just us anyway. See if you still got it. I'll even tip you a twenty."

"I don't need the money," I argue. "And I still *have* it. Never lost it."

"Could've fooled me."

"Didn't you say, like, weeks ago that I'm *that* good?"

"Prove it."

"Pops," I whine. Pops keeps his attention to the audio system behind the bar. I give a huff of defeat. I know they're right, but now I want to do it out of spite from Ricky's jab at my pride.

"I'll play your favorite song," Pops says.

My eyes narrow. "You play dirty."

"It's effective." He smirks through the mirror's reflection.

"There's new leather costumes in the back just *waiting* to be broken in," Ricky sings with a wide grin.

Damn it.

I head back to the changing rooms, calling back to them, "This is manipulation!"

"It's called being *very* charismatic!" Ricky yells back. "We've worked really hard on these tactics since you're immune!"

I find Gina in the changing rooms, and she squeals in delight when I tell her I'm dancing. She ushers me into one of the new leather ensembles which is a thin bralette with a tear-away vest, long, fingerless gloves, black booty shorts, and tall, shiny thigh-high boots. The heels aren't extremely high; neither of us wants me to fall on my ass. Gina pulls my hair back into a high ponytail and takes my hand to lead me back out to the main floor. The dim lights in the club set the ambiance for work hours while spotlights point at the main stage, brightly lit for my entrance. Gina pats my back and sits in the front row with Ricky, both of them wearing gigantic grins.

I shake out my arms and legs to warm them up, and climb

the stairs, looking back at Pops still near the music station. "Ready, baby girl?" He asks with glowing eyes.

"Ready as I'll ever be," I answer. "But it's going to be a jumbled routine."

"Wing it like you always did," Gina suggests.

"Did not."

"Did, too," she says, wrinkling her nose at me, and stroking Ricky's hair. I roll my eyes and look at Pops for support.

He smiles and presses the play button. "Just another Tuesday showing off, baby girl. Prove your brother wrong. Again."

My favorite song starts and ushers me to the poles, my steps falling to the beat of the music. I close my eyes and grin when I reach the middle between the two main poles, already feeling bliss ease through my bones. As always, Pops was right.

I improvise the routine at the drop of the beat, falling to my knees and slap my hands to the ground. Gina whoops and Ricky cheers as I sway my shoulders, moving to the harsh bass, and slowly stand. I pull off the gloves with brava and throw them at Gina and Ricky as I saunter to a pole. Taking a deep breath, I grab for it and spin. My legs straighten out in a V as I do a simple move to remind my body of the feel before moving to the other poles. It's like riding a bicycle, but a shit ton more fun.

The next verse sweeps in, and I dance to the first pole again, climbing up to hook my legs and throw my head back as I spin. The slight pain of holding myself up lights me up from the inside, and I feel free. I continue, testing myself with different moves on the pole and halfway through, the leather vest comes off. I climb up elm pole further to the top.

Ricky yells, "Watch your balance!"

"No drops, baby girl," Pops warns.

Since I can't do drops, I decide to do one of my signature moves and grab the pole firmly, letting go with my legs as I swing my body to spin. I hold myself firmly as my legs go into a

V again, then clasp them around the pole into a tight hold. My upper body lets go, and my stomach muscles scream as I lean away from the pole above toward the bottom. My arms open, and I spin down and stop myself just before I hit the ground. Upside down, I look where the audience would be, and my heels slam down onto the stage as the song ends. I breathe heavily and grin as my family applauds.

"Ha! Taught her that!" Ricky shouts as he walks up to me.

"Sure, you did, Ricky," Gina says, rolling her eyes at him. "Good job, baby sis. Like you never left." She gives me a thumbs up and a wink, heading back to the changing rooms.

Ricky tussles my hair as I sit upright, and suddenly I smell dark spices and bloodlust. I reach around Ricky, grabbing the .45 that's tucked into his pants. The safety clicks off as I aim it past my brother toward Vinny's chest. Ricky swears under his breath as he steps to the side, allowing me to see I've hit my target perfectly. Pops chuckles as I click the safety back on.

"Nice performance there, sweet cheeks," Vinny says. "Wondered how long it'd take before you'd dance again."

"Taking bets on me, bloodsucker?"

"With you? Not anymore." His smile glints in the low light of the club.

Pops joins Vinny near the back seating, crossing his arms as he looks at me. I take the hint and give the gun back to my brother. "Don't go using my stuff for your weird hello with Vinny," he grumbles, putting his gun away, and changes the subject. "So, this mean you'll do routines again, right?"

I sit up fully and let my tired legs dangle offstage, and say, "One time dance, Ricky. That's it."

"But you were good!" Ricky pleads. "You know what, now I'm playing dirty. Pops! Vinny! Don't you think she should do routines again?"

"Seriously, bro?" I ask in irritation. Sibling guilt is strong today.

"Only if she wants to," Pops says. "We'll have an opening

for a few stand-alone routines in a couple of weeks. Gina may need another for that one number you choreographed."

"You're serious?" My jaw drops. I thought *he* wanted this to be a one-time try. Wrong.

"Why not, baby girl? You're a seasoned dancer even after your hiatus. You just need some practice before getting in front of an audience."

"Come on, you know you want to," Ricky says with a mischievous grin. "It's in your blood. And it's a family tradition."

I hide the grimace that bubbles up inside me. In the past, I pretended that maybe a part of me was succubus. Now, knowing what I really am, I couldn't play pretend anymore. It wasn't in my blood. At least the family tradition I couldn't argue with.

Dancing and stripping are part of the succubi and incubi culture. They thrive on the pheromones from the activity and sometimes need it to help control their powers. There are many stories of breakouts from succubi or incubi having sexual rampages after losing hormonal control, and clubs like *Unbound* help mitigate that. The culture focuses largely on sharing, whether it's emotions, bodies, passions, or sex, and pastimes such as dancing are a bridge to that. But with that bridge comes responsibility. Consent is huge in the succubi and incubi community. They protect their young until they can control their powers, knowing full well the consequences of an untrained succubus or incubus could be harmful to everyone outside the community. You can't know if someone wants a dance for platonic need through touch or sexual endeavors unless discussed. This has all been ingrained in me since I was little, succubus or not, I was part of their community.

I bring my gaze to Vinny beside my father and remember that as much as he blends in, he isn't an incubus, and that might affect if I should dance again. Vampires are territorial by nature, especially if you're sleeping with them, and mine is a pureblood who doesn't like to fucking share. He's reminded me enough times of that, and Ricky just suggested I dance half-naked in front of a room full of strangers. Not exactly a relationship booster.

Vinny catches my gaze, and whispers something into Pops' ear, who nods and gives Ricky a side glance before heading up to the apartment. My brother takes the hint to leave with him, huffing as he does. Vinny walks over and stops before me as I remain seated on stage. He puts his hands in his pockets, and asks, "Have I ever told you what to do?"

"Long list or short?" I ask.

"The list that doesn't include you endangering your life or mine."

"Bungee jumping doesn't!"

"You can't fly if it breaks."

"No, it's because *you* are afraid of heights and know I'll drag you with me."

"Not the point," he says, deadpanned.

"Fine, going to Florida should be off the list then."

"*You* hate tourists."

"Stealing Anita's red bottoms?"

"That endangered *both* our lives, and it was *my* ludicrous idea, sweet cheeks."

I snort. "Coming from the responsible one who wouldn't let me have ice cream before dinner." I cross my arms, deflecting him.

Vinny narrows his eyes, attempting to hide a smile. "We both know I snuck you ice cream plenty of times, sweet cheeks. My title of best friend will not be tarnished because of your stubborn streak."

He sits beside me on the stage edge, his shoulder brushing against mine. A shiver runs through my body, reveling in the small contact. I stare out at the empty club, and say, "*Fine*, your title is secure."

"The point is, sweetheart," Vinny says. "You don't need to

look at me for permission to dance. I'm your partner, not your father." He smirks as I give him a side glare. "It's your body and life to choose what to do, not mine. Unless you don't want to—"

"I do, actually. It felt pretty damn good being up there and it's better than roaming library halls like a Victorian ghost on Topside."

"Then why you giving Ricky a hard time? Other than the usual annoyances."

I turn toward him, taking in the sheer beauty that is Vinny. He wears a pinstripe suit, dark button-up, and the family ring on his hand which shines like his moussed black hair under the club lights. Those crimson eyes intensely watch me, waiting for an answer.

I gesture toward my mostly naked body and then to the stage. His brows raise up in question, and I say, "I'll be seen by everyone who comes into the club. You're *honestly* okay with me dancing and stripping?"

"Your family is."

"Literally in their DNA to be okay with it."

"Have to compete with that now?"

"You know what I mean, Vinny. Things have changed."

"But you danced for years while we were just friends, no fun benefits, but we're making up for lost time. I think we're doing quite well on that front." I stare at him a little in shock. "Your body to decide what to do, sweet cheeks."

I purse my lips at him. "Your uplifting support can be very annoying at times."

"Because then you have to admit out loud you missed dancing to Ricky?" He smirks.

I try to push away the small smile on my face, but it succeeds. I roll my eyes and shove his shoulder. "More like admitting that Pops was right, *again*."

Vinny's eyes flick down my body and then back up. "I do have one condition."

"Finally, *something!*" I fall back onto the stage.

He hovers over me, tracing a finger down my jawline. "Only I get to touch you. They can all window shop, fantasize, or replenish their emotions, but only I can touch you."

"Club rules haven't changed, Vinny. No touching unless consented. I *may* make an exception for you," I smirk.

"I think I'll win you over."

"You better buy me a drink first."

He chuckles. "That's an easy deal to agree to. And I get to watch whenever I want."

"You already do that."

"Double checking," he smirks. His expression softens as he cups my chin. "Brenda, I knew this about you and your family. And it's good to see you light up like that again. I hoped you would dance."

I sit up and throw my hands in the air. "Well, I thought I left it all behind with a whole bunch of things, and now it's like I'm back at square one," I say, rubbing the shit out of my undercut. "I missed it, but I'm afraid if I go back to this, I'll just go back to everything from before. Did I really waste *years* living on Topside when I could have been down here doing what I love? How badly did I fuck up? I could've been dancing instead of cleaning up after mangey teenagers? And then I wonder if you and I—"

Vinny shuts me up with his lips, and I lean into him, breathing in the scent of dark spices that rise from him. I move my hand up to smooth back his hair even more, letting him keep me quiet, apart from my moaning. He pulls away slowly, and says, "I'm not leaving, sweet cheeks. You took a side road, but you didn't waste anything. All that matters is that we're here now with a new future. So, go back to dancing and rearranging books, you *tantalizing* spicey librarian."

"Keep talking like that, and I'll tell people you're going soft," I say with a smile.

"Only for you, sweet cheeks. It's the price getting to see you naked on a daily basis." He looks around swiftly. "Speaking of, when does the club open?"

"30 minutes."

"We'll make it work." Vinny picks me up and carries me to a private back room. I barely contain my laughter as he closes the door.

WANTED
COFFEE

CHAPTER 3
S·I·B·L·I·N·G·S

I walk into Joey's messy coffee house four blocks east of *Unbound*. Most of it is covered in plastic wrap, buckets of paint, nails, and the smell of freshly cut wood. The main area is bare, with only the oak wood bar taking up half the back near the hallway and backdoor that leads upstairs to two levels; the first for any meetings Joey starts holding in a few weeks, and the second for living quarters. He hasn't said anything about moving here permanently, but I wouldn't be surprised if he did. The shop and rooms are spacious enough from what I could see in the reconstruction.

"Joey?" I ask, easing around the wet bar and searching through the chaos of tools to find the stash of scotch. "Joey!"

Outside the front door, a breeze picks up, and I hear the beat of wings, looking up in time to see him land on the brick pavement. Joey's dark leathery wings fold behind his back, vanishing with a rippling light as he walks in. His clothes are covered in glue and dust as he shucks off his dirtied tank top, and asks, "Thought you were working at *The Vault* today?"

"In a few hours," I say with a shrug and grin. "Decided to take stuff into your own hands? The punks taking too long to renovate?"

He shakes his head. "Nah, just needed a break from business, and it gives me an excuse to avoid Ricky for a bit." He rounds the bar and gives me a quick kiss on the temple, grabbing the scotch and dirty glasses.

"More complicated than you thought the job would be?" I ask, taking a seat on the counter. I swing my legs a bit as I lean back onto my hands. "Mafia shit, I mean."

"Always knew it would be." Joey pours himself a drink and gestures with the other glass. I nod, and he begins to fill it. "It's the frustration part I could live without. I'll feel better when this place is up and running."

"Guess Pops' grumpiness wasn't just due to lack of pecan pie at some dinners," I muse.

Joey snorts, handing me the glass before he leans against the empty wall for the espresso machines. "Doubt you've come to help me renovate. So, what you need, sis?"

"Can't come by to see you? It's been a few days. You've been holed up here as a full-time carpenter covered in sawdust doing mafia shit."

"Not gonna buy the whole 'missing the big brother' spiel," he says, raising a brow.

"But it's a classic."

He sets the drink down. "What's up, baby sis?"

Picasso should take note of the distorted hues and shapes I see with my glasses as I look at him. His scent grows harsh, and I sigh, putting down my glass. I'm not as stubborn or prideful as I used to be, but I feel tired all the time like everything is taking more effort than usual. I look down at my glass, skimming my finger over the rim. "You get any more intel on Edgar? Besides what Bill told me?"

Joey tips back his drink. "He's been here a year as a freelancer. Most of it is under-the-table money, financial analyst looks like. All accounts were associated with gambling firms and racing tracks. Always a *good* sign."

"Does he do the gambling?"

"Nothing to say that he did. He's clean."

"Great," I mumble, knocking back my drink, and I sense Joey's aroma shift into brisk clove and cardamom. "I'm fine, Joey."

"No, you're not."

"Yes, I am."

"Sis, you've literally been through hell the past month." He puts his drink down with a clink. "You found out what the fuck happened to you, lost everything on Topside, forced into a human hospital, almost *died*, and then that damn daemon shows up. No way in hell are you *fine*."

I stare at the ground and rub my hand through my undercut. "I'm home now. Everything's okay."

"It doesn't fix things, sis."

"Well yeah, because none of those *things* can be fixed," I argue, grinding my teeth and refusing to look at him. I just wanted to visit my big brother without having another quarter-life crisis talk. "Just let it go, Joey. I have."

"No, you haven't." He walks over and nudges me as he sits next to me on the bar. He wraps an arm around me and lifts my chin to look into his comforting gaze. I relax a bit into his hold. "Come on. Talk, munchkin."

"Meanie."

"Part of the big brother mafia boss package. Should've checked the fine print."

"Ooh, scary," I mumble with a small smile.

I could deflect all I want, but he's right. It's hard to wrap my head around what happened before Pops found me all those years ago, my life on Topside being over, and my daemon daddy showing up out of nowhere. And now the fear of losing Vinny because of stupid cultural laws hovers over me like a cloud of bloodred smoke. There's so much going on; where do I even begin?

I sigh deeply, and ask, "Does it count if I talked to Pops?"

"Maybe, did you tell him everything?"

"Not exactly," I mumble. Joey takes my hand, rubbing his thumb over the same scar across my wrist. The familiar touch relaxs a part of me, and I lean into his side. Minutes tick by in silence before I finally say, "I'm scared."

"Of what?"

"Everything. Change. People. Losing more shit, apart from my sanity, that is." Joey squeezes my shoulders a bit more, putting his cheek against my temple. "What if Vinny and I are a mistake?"

"That vampire is a pain in the ass, but he loves you. And you love him. You two were practically made for each other, no mistake there."

"Even if half the Underground hates—"

"Who gives a fuck what they think?" Joey interrupts. "With time I'm sure Vinny will concoct some insane plan to keep those vampires at bay. Probably already has. You'll have plenty of time to figure it out."

"Except I lost time by pushing him away," I mumble. "What if I made things worse by moving to Topside years ago? For him, me, and the rest of you? If I had just stayed home...fought a bit harder, maybe...maybe..."

My voice chokes a little, a flash of the past reminding me of Bruno's bloodied fangs and his warning growl as I wince from the bitemarks throbbing on my neck. I clear my throat and try to move from Joey's embrace, but he doesn't let me, keeping a tight hold around my shoulders.

"None of it was a mistake, sis," he says softly. "And you have me, Ricky, Pops, and Ma who will always be here for you. No matter how stubborn you are, we'll always have your back."

I nod and stare down at his hand on mine, his thumb still caressing my skin. "Some days, Joey, I wish I could do it over. Have more time and not feel like such a fuck-up."

"Hey, that's my sister you're talking about there."

"Well, your sister almost started a war between the Under-

ground Mafia and Topside, so I think that falls under fuck-up."
And I may do it again.

"Except you stopped that potential blood bath."

"By sheer spite," I scoff, and lean away from him. "Look, Joey, I'll admit you're right. I'm not over it. But if I had *just* stayed home and not listened to—" I cut myself off before I damn my future any further. If anyone in my family found out what Bruno did, it'd be a bigger shitstorm than before. Fuck, *that* would definitely start another war.

Joey stares at me as I concentrate on the contorted colors and shapes around his head. He tilts his head and asks, "Do you want some advice from someone who left home for years before you came along?"

"Are you just gonna talk about Spain again?"

"No."

"Then I'll take the advice."

"Sometimes we need to look at our lives in a different perspective. Figure things out on our own and what we want. And it's not like you disappeared for years, you always had us… and I guess, Vinny." He grabs my chin gently and smiles. "Just because you came home doesn't mean you wasted time or failed. Home is home. And whatever was supposed to happen, would've happened whether you moved or not. Wars will always start between the mafia and the police. And distance from those we love, reminds us time is precious. It's the whole distance makes the heart grow fonder bullshit. It's accurate sometimes."

I narrow my eyes at him as his scent shifts into something calmer. I knew if I wasn't immune, I'd be at more ease and probably blissful, but advice and the comfort of his voice is all he can give me, and I'll take it. I playfully shove him. "When did you get so wise, and what did you do to my annoying older brother?"

"He became a mob boss."

"What does that make Ricky?"

"A monkey's uncle," Joey grumbles, kissing my cheek before he jumps down from the bar. "And you better tell that monkey's uncle to ease up on the paint job for this place. It's a coffee shop, not a nightclub."

"I'll dance to keep him occupied, just cause I love you." Joey scoffs and knocks back his drink. "He's always ecstatic about teaching me new routines, anyways."

"Good, keep this place taped off from him," he says, pouring himself another glass. "I won't be down here the next few days. New shipment of people coming in tomorrow, and I've got to move them to the safe houses before the end of the week."

"The Bronx clear then?"

Joey pauses and raises a brow. "Vinny didn't tell you?"

"I haven't asked questions since the hospital incident. Kind of learned my lesson to keep my nose out of it."

"For now," he mutters.

"Hey—"

"Sis, you've got a knack for sticking your nose where it doesn't belong. It's that tenacious, researching librarian in you, which we can blame Beckham for." He laughs as I pout at his assessment. "The South Bronx is empty." I furrow my brows at him. "As in *empty*. Mafia cleared out, most of PSB and NIIA are gone along with the NYPD, apart from normal patrols. All that's left of Paranormals are those who own property too stubborn to leave."

"Anyone else disappear?"

"We're good on our side, but you'd have to ask Rodney and Vinny about their own."

"Guess that's…good." My voice is soft, and I think over the other events that have plagued my mind these past few weeks.

PSB and NYPD were knocking on doors and causing more issues than usual, so the Underground Mafia moved their safe houses and routes to other areas on Topside. No mafia or government agency in the South Bronx, and suddenly the mess that was there is just gone. It's too clean cut and doesn't feel right. There's no explanation why NYPD pushed past neutral zone lines or why PSB allowed it to happen. And the half-breeds who went missing are still missing. NYPD and PSB think it was the Underground Mafia, and the Underground Mafia think it's the black market rings, but I know our inside contacts would have said something by now if they saw them. No one knows who or why they're gone. So, where the hell did the half-breeds go?

"So…are you gonna try talking to him?" Joey asks, derailing my thoughts.

"Who?"

"Edgar."

I snort. "I don't see a point. Besides, he disappeared. *Again.*"

"Fucking dickwad," Joey mumbles as he puts away the bottle of scotch.

Another reason why I asked for information on Edgar; the bastard has rarely been seen since he first arrived. We got a sample of his blood, and even after five different tests, Charlene couldn't pinpoint my lifespan. Bill's findings didn't have that answer either. Nothing indicated whether I'd live out the human or Paranormal side unless I start getting gray hairs, but that may be from stress at this point.

Joey leans on the counter and tilts his head. "No matter what, sis, I promise you'll always be my baby sister. I know I've made that promise multiple times before, but I mean it every time. No matter what. Edgar showing up or not, you're our family. Cuorebella through and through."

A smile pulls at my lips. "I know, Joey."

"And maybe tell Vinny how you're feeling."

"Pretty sure he already knows," I say quietly. "But I'll try."

"Promise?"

My chest tightens a little at the tone of his voice. He'll always be my protective brother, and the thought centers me. "Promise."

I jump off the bar and stretch my arms then give Joey a kiss on the cheek. He brings me into a close embrace, holding me to his chest. "I love you, sis. I know things are weird, uneasy, and uncertain right now...but I'm glad you're home again. You belong with us."

I take a deep breath in, allowing myself to melt into my brother's warm embrace. "I love you, bro. And thank you."

"Anytime, munchkin."

CHAPTER 4
GET YOUR ASS UP, SHOW ME HOW YOU DANCE

"I'm not putting that on," I say.

"Come on! Just a bit of lace," Gina pleads.

"No, we agreed on the costumes already. You never said anything about lace."

She pouts with the obnoxious lacey pink bralette and thong in her hand. A few dancers giggle at us, while one of them, Mack, almost falls off their chair laughing.

"The fact you thought you'd get away with it, Gina," Mack says between giggles.

Gina huffs and ushers the giggling dancers to finish getting ready as some leave backstage or return mostly nude from the stage, finishing up their numbers.

"Nice to have you back, baby sis," Mack says as I lace up my boots.

"Didn't exactly leave," I say.

"There's a difference between visiting and getting ready with us. Plus, we miss you annoying Gina." Mack giggles as their bright smile shines against their garnet skin, their eyes like galaxies, indigo and violet swirling together with gold flecks near the iris edges. They have tight curly black hair and are shorter than most succubi but make up for it in heels. Ten years ago, they were sold out of Poland and held captive in Germany before Pops rescued them and brought them to *Unbound*, but they still have a slight Polish accent.

I stand up and almost tower over the succubus, running my hand along their jaw to caress behind their ear, and hand over their gloves. Mack hums at the physical touch, and I smell their elderberry scent lighten. They give me my leather vest, and say, "Thanks." I wink at them as the music vibrates through the walls as dancers laugh and talk.

I take a few deep breaths and shake out my limbs as I wait for my group to head out. I've been practicing with Ricky and Gina for the last two weeks, working on muscle memory as we ran through familiar routines. I knew I'd have some sore muscles tonight, but it'll be worth it to land the routine right. Gina comes up next to me and places a hand on my shoulder. "Ready, baby sis?"

"Ready enough to get tips again," I smirk.

"You may fall short from last time," Gina laughs. We both smile, remembering the money we garnered at my panty cele-bration. I've got to ask Pops for that cash back. "Just keep your top on, otherwise Ricky will have my ass."

"He already has," I murmur, and she rolls her eyes at me.

"Fine, *Alanzo* will have my ass, and not in the fun way," she says, passing me and tossing her long dark hair over her shoulder.

Mack and I are the only ones in our routine who will keep our clothes on, while the others will barely have a thong on by the end. There were two rules' Pops gave Gina and Ricky when I started working as a dancer: no one touches me and no full nudity. Rules I could easily live with. Most of those who danced loved being hired to go to backrooms or give lap dances, but I was with my parents on this decision and content just being a stripper.

The music changes, cueing us to go. Mack and I wink at each other and walk into the darkened mood lighting, heavy music, and swirling scents of succubi and incubi sensuality, which immune or not, you could get high off of. Perfumes mingle with aromas of lavender, musky vanilla, cinnamon, and sweet rose, relaxing the many people seated throughout *Unbound* under the ambient purple-maroon lights glowing as bartenders make drinks and workers serve patrons. Bobby announces our entrance, and I see people cuddling on the couches, kissing, drinking, and reveling in the trance the club provides at its height. The lights dim as we arrive to our spots on stage; Gina, Lola, and I are on main stage, while Mack, Jacqui, and Veronica stand on the smaller stages with poles.

I move my hand over the metal pole, take a deep breath, and look out to the crowd. Pops and Ma are near the bar with proud smiles as Joey and Ricky salute me with drinks in their hands. I spot Rodney at a back table wearing a shit-eating grin with Gunther and Marcus beside him. Then I find Vinny's ruby eyes as he sits on the far-left side in a private area. A wave of heat travels to my core, tightening as he smiles. I grin to myself as the beat drops, vibrating through the club and my body. My hips sway to the echoing bass as I give one last look to Vinny, catching his challenging smile. He winks at me, and it's game on.

I walk around the pole and grab it to spin, holding myself upright with legs spread as Gina strips. Lola and I climb the poles and I cross my legs tight around it and lean back, moving my body to the music as Gina finishes taking off her clothes. I slide down with a tight drop and flip onto my stomach, pushing my hips down and back up. Getting on my knees, I zip down the vest, and toss it after a few gyrations of my hips. The world spins around me as I get back on the pole, and I feel free as each dancer has their solo dance. I take a deep breath and climb to the top like the other dancers, then we all flip upside down and fall spread eagle. We clack our heels together on beat and back to the splits, cueing some dancers to flip around into different drops before leaving the stage. Gina and I are the only dancers left, and she flashes her eyes, smiling with anticipation as she drops to the ground with a spin, elegantly landing on stage to give me the floor. I'm always the finisher.

I grab the pole, hooking a leg around it and use my other to spin me. Once the world is twirling, I let my hand go, pressing my foot against the pole as I ripple my torso down until I become parallel to the ground. Taking a deep breath, I grab the pole and quickly swing my hooked leg out, moving my entire body into a spiral with both legs twirling around me as I descend. I move down the pole with my hands as I twirl around the metal. My foot makes contact with the stage, and I let go, sauntering heavily to the edge, planting my feet, dropping my ass, and opening my thighs as the song ends. The crowd applauds and shouts as I control my heavy breathing and find Vinny's gaze. He wears an absolutely wicked grin and holds a king-sized chocolate bar in his hand, his brow quirking in amusement.

My favorite kind of tip.

I pick up a few bills on stage, partially ignoring the loud crowd as I stand. Gina plants a kiss on my cheek with glowing eyes, nodding for me to head off stage as she does a small number with Mack and Veronica. Lola and Jacqui make their way toward patrons for lap dances while I go to my crying mother.

Ma's blue eyes are filled with tears as she smiles warmly at me, her arms are soon around me. "Take it you liked it?" I say against her hair.

"You did wonderful, baby," she says. "You made me proud."

"Thanks, Ma."

She pulls back and looks me over. "I need to make you new costumes. Are these digging into your skin?" She begins to trace a finger under the seam of my booty shorts, tugging at the material as she checks the fit.

"Ma!" I yelp, swatting at her hand. "Can you wait until later?"

"I just want you to be comfortable, baby."

"I know, I know," I put my hands up in defeat. "Whatever you want, Ma, but how about when the club *isn't* filled with patrons?"

She kisses my cheek. "Alright, we'll do another fitting with Gina."

Pops smiles from behind her and says, "You did good, baby girl."

"I think I did that finishing move better than I have in the past." I put my hand on my hip.

"Constant practice will do that with your brother." Pops looks toward Ricky near the other end of the bar with incubi and shifters. "And it looks like he's off duty already."

"Aww, ease up on him, Pops," I say, suppressing a grin.

"They all worked hard tonight, Alanzo," Ma scolds him, pressing herself against him. "Let them relax." Pops moves his attention to her, his gaze becoming a sensual smolder.

"Are you seducing me, gorgeous?" He traces his thumb under her bottom lip.

"Do you truly want me to, *mio cavaliere?*" Ma's hand runs down my father's chest.

"I think I hear Rodney calling me—bye!" I exclaim and escape my parents. It's wonderful to see them still in love after so many centuries together, but I have my limits.

I walk to the cluster of couches near the bar and lean over Rodney's shoulder. His deep green eyes find mine, and a feral grin spreads over his face as he tosses me onto the couch next to him. "Hey, lil sis, good job up there," he comments. "Like you never left."

I laugh and sit back, propping my heeled feet on the table before us. Marcus stands at the end of the couch, and Gunther sits on the other side of Rodney, suppressing his laughter. I turn my attention to the alpha Wolf Mob Boss and ask, "Where's my tip, Lassie?"

"Thought only the bloodsucker could give you that," Rodney jokes.

"You're terrible." I smack his shoulder, and he chuckles, pulling me into a side embrace.

"Your tip *could* be free drinks next time you're at *Donny's* or in Garrick's, but you already do that."

"I'm thinking ahead."

"Uh huh."

"Obviously, I gotta get it in advance. You may miss a performance or two, which impedes on those *tips*."

"Now who's terrible?"

"Learned it from the best," I say, grinning. "Including you."

Rodney laughs, knocks back his whiskey, and ushers over a waitress for more. As he refills his liquor, I turn to Marcus, whose scowl tells me *just* how much he's missed me. "How ya been, Balto?" I ask.

"Don't," he growls.

"What? It's an honorable nickname. How about Shadow?" He growls again. Guess not. But the fact the big guy hasn't ripped my face off is actually quite telling of his patience around me of late. May be from the incident last month, so it may wear off soon.

"Shouldn't you be *teasing* someone else, lil sis?" Gunther asks between chuckles. Rodney goes still as he gets his drink from the waitress, and I look across the room.

Vinny hasn't moved from his small private section across the club as he watches me with smoldering eyes, lazily swirling his scotch. I shouldn't sense him from this far away, but the idea of him wraps around me as he dips a finger into the glass and brings it to his lips, sliding his tongue over the wet finger. My muscles clench as I notice his open jacket revealing the undone top buttons of his shirt. The heat deep within me stirs as I rub a little against the couch, and the leather I wear doesn't feel like enough coverage as my breath hitches when he smiles, quirking a brow.

"Lil sis?" Blinking rapidly, I look over to Rodney and see a wondering smile on his face. He flicks his eyes to Vinny and back to me. "You done playing hard to get or do I have to drag you over there?"

"You? Doing him a favor?" I smirk.

"If it makes you stop eye fucking him from the distance, maybe."

"And here I thought you'd be happy for me."

"Limits, lil sis. Limits."

"Fine, your safe word is 'Montana,' and you better use it wisely." I stand with a wicked grin, leaning down to kiss him briefly on the temple. He barks a laugh and grins but loses his playfulness as he looks past me. I follow his gaze, and my stomach drops.

The sperm donor, Edgar, leans against the wall near the exit motionless as he watches me with a heated expression on his face, scrunching his brows together in deep thought. His wings are folded in close as he hides in the shadows of the club, gripping his drink tightly to his chest.

"Is that who I think it is?" Rodney asks. Marcus and Gunther flit their gazes to the daemon.

"Yeah," I mutter.

"When's the last time you talked to him?"

"Fucking weeks," I say. "His disappearing act seems to be second nature."

"Any others show up?"

"Only him."

I flip my hair back and ignore Edgar's hardened eyes. I turn to face the wolf boss and his watchful guards, who bring their attention back to me. "I could have Marcus let off some steam *escorting* your father out if you'd like," Rodney offers with a sly grin as Marcus snarls in agreement, looking like he'll rip his wings off. Frenemy or not, I'm still considered part of the Pack, and there's a protective code over their "pups," which I still fall under.

"We'll keep an eye out for daemon sightings up Top," Rodney says. "Just in case he brought more."

"They usually travel in numbers," Gunther snarls.

"Well," I say, patting his shoulder, "so do we."

I salute the three werewolves before walking across the club past workers and patrons having fun with the strippers, while dancers enter their spotlights on the stage. I see one of the new incubi dancers, who looks more open than when he was brought in four weeks ago. Rounding the last couple of couches, I keep my attention on the new dancers, not noticing the human male reaching for my ass until his fingers skim the bottom of my shorts. Before I can turn to smack him hard, someone's already pulled his hand away.

Vinny grips the human's wrist tightly, who can't be more than thirty and judging by his dilated eyes, has either taken drugs or is *that* high from the pheromones in the air. Humans are usually more prone to the effects than Paranormals. Sweat forms on the man's temple as Vinny towers over him with red eyes ablaze and bares his teeth, showing his elongated fangs as he warns, "No one touches her."

The man whimpers, "I'm sorry. I thought—"

"You thought wrong. Darius." I watch as the bouncer intervenes and takes the human from Vinny's grasp.

"Rules were stated when you entered," Darius speaks as he appears, grabbing the drugged-up human to drag him away. "No touching unless consented, even from dancers who allow it. Move it." Darius disappears through the club, Joey joining him as the door opens to the outside and shuts behind them. I almost want to pity the guy, but then again, he did grab my ass, and everyone signs a waiver. No free-for-all. And Pops *always* believed his dancers and workers first.

"Guess you're right about being territorial," Vinny says gruffly as his eyes pierce through me, vicious and cold. Another touch and that man would've lost his hand.

Vinny's sweet like that.

"Pretty sure that's not the first time you've had to do that. Even before the…benefits part."

"Someone has to watch out for your ass. And I qualify." He grins.

"You an expert?"

"More than you realize."

"Really?"

"Certainly, sweet cheeks." Vinny brushes past me, gesturing for me to follow him. He sits on the couch and leans back as I straddle his lap, sitting squarely on him. "Presumptuous much?"

"You're comfy," I argue.

"Ah, yes, something I've *always* dreamed of you telling me," he says sarcastically, and I chuckle.

Vinny brushes back my hair while his other hand travels up my leg, trailing his fingers over scars that contort my skin. I block out the music and voices around us as I stare down at the powerful vampire beneath me. There are still nights I wake up in fear this is all a cruel dream of temptation. Or I'll wake up in the hospital bed again, tied down with leather straps, while Drauper screams in the distance. Or maybe I'm still left with the mad scientist running scalpels down my face or Bruno's fangs piercing through my neck. Although old nightmares haven't returned, new ones take their place. The fear stretches over me, wearing thin and my neck pulsates as a reminder of how real they can be.

"Sweetheart?" Vinny's soothing voice pulls me from my thoughts, and I find his ruby eyes. "You alright?"

"Long night," I say with a weak smile.

"No lying."

"I'm not." More like pretending everything is fine. Not quite lying.

"You're not here right now. Your mind's wandering again."

"I'm a librarian, always thinking about my TBR."

"What comes to mind?"

I grin ruefully. *"Dracula."* He smirks, tracing his thumb over my bottom lip. Then slowly, he wraps a hand around the nape of my neck, pulling me forward. The kiss is slow, warm, and tender as I taste the delicate aromas of dark spices and scotch on his lips and remember he's mine, even if only for now.

I fall deeper into the kiss, hoping for more as heat builds within me. Vinny's free hand drifts up my leg, brushing his fingers under the seam of my shorts. I gasp as his fingers skim across my abdomen, and he takes the moment to deepen the kiss, his tongue making its way past my lips and exploring further. The taste of him burns down my spine and into my core, settling my emotions. The grip on my neck tightens, holding me in place as the scorching kiss makes my heart beat harder. Anticipation builds inside me as his hand moves downward.

"Vinny," I hiss against his lips.

"You need a distraction, sweetheart," he says, kissing the side of my mouth. "I'm here to help."

"Right now?"

"Afraid you'll give us away?" The rasp of his voice makes my body shiver. "I never thought you'd back down from a challenge."

"Damn you," I rasp as his touch scorches through me.

He hums against my neck, and it vibrates across my skin. One of his fingers trail lower as his thumb circles my clit, causing my breath to become shaky. I throw both hands forward, gripping onto the back of the couch, and a vicious smile grows on Vinny's face. My mouth opens, gaping as his thumb continues to circle and press, his eyes watching my reactions with delight as a shiver runs through my body.

A moan escapes my throat and Vinny hushes me, "Careful sweet cheeks." I clamp my mouth shut, meeting his eyes with mine. "Remember I don't share well, and you're supposed to be untouchable."

"Not for you," I whisper as I run my tongue over my bottom

lip and grin as he sucks in a harsh breath. He returns my teasing gesture by pressing his thumb harder against my clit, stroking his fingers up. Inhaling harshly, I try to keep myself steady and bring my head forward as my hair falls forward, covering most of our faces.

He chuckles and says, "You'll have to try harder than that to not be seen."

A finger presses into me and hooks upward and I gasp at the small insertion, rejoicing in the sensation as he continues to rub my clit and thrust his finger into me. Moans try to break through as I concentrate on his hands, my skin warming from the heat of his body underneath me as pleasure rolls down my spine in waves of absolute ecstasy. Sparks flick up from the base of my spine as my legs start to tremble. His thumb remains in place, palming my sex as he inserts two fingers into me. I close my eyes, biting my lip as it takes all concentration for me not to cry out.

"Look at me, sweetheart," he whispers.

My eyes flutter open, and I meet his enflamed gaze. His hand on my neck caresses down my back and grips onto my ass to keep me in place. It may look like a regular make-out session from a distance, but the thrill and fear of someone taking a closer peek makes me shiver; I'm not usually one for voyeurism, but with the heavy music, darkened lights, and smell of heightened passion—damn it's fucking hot.

Carefully, I grind against Vinny's palm, and his eyes flash with burning lust. I push my hips for more contact, and he presses harder, pumping his fingers then joins a third finger. The trembling in my legs worsen and I breathe in short, shaky breaths as I stop grinding, and Vinny takes me to the brink of orgasm. Suddenly, his hand is on the nape of my neck, and he crashes his lips against mine into a bruising kiss as he thrusts his fingers deep inside me. I lose my breath as the orgasm hits, a shock from my nether region traveling through my entire body, fuzzing away my thoughts. A tingling at the bottom of my spine erupts, and my moaning is muffled by Vinny's mouth as the orgasm rips through me. I clench my thighs, holding him in place while the waves of pure pleasure release.

As I come off from the high, I hear the music drift back into reality, and he softens our kiss, bringing me back to earth. I pull away and place my forehead against his shoulder as he massages my scalp in languid, tender movements. He eases his fingers out of me and I gasp from the loss, eyeing him as he brings them discreetly to his mouth, licking them with slow care, contently humming.

"Proud of yourself?" I ask softly.

"Oh, you've no idea how much these last five years I've wanted to do that."

"You've already tasted me."

"Not after seeing you handle a pole so *efficiently*."

"Pervy vamp."

"Seductress."

"Perfect pair."

Vinny smiles and kisses my cheek then reaches to the side and holds up the chocolate bar he had earlier. I lazily grab the candy and fall off him onto the couch, my legs draping over his lap like a blanket. I pry open the chocolate and nibble on the rich taste.

"You going to share?" He asks.

"Nope," I say between bites. "You already got your snack, bloodsucker. My turn." If it wasn't for the loud bass within the club, you could hear Vinny's laughter all the way to Topside.

CHAPTER 5
FATHER'S HERE TO HELP YOU

Fine. I'll admit it, Vinny's distraction worked, but an orgasm will do that to a person.

Unbound eases down as evening hits the Underground, and the human patrons leave for the daytime of Topside. I'm dressed in my usual jeans and tank top, pulling my hair up into a ponytail as dancers switch shifts for the main Paranormal clientele.

Gina saunters past me and picks up her bag, smiling as she says, "You did great your first night back. Knew you missed it."

I roll my eyes as I strap on my guns, placing one behind my back and another inside my boot. She clicks her tongue as the last of the other dancers leave the room. I raise my brow, and ask, "What?"

She flicks her eyes at my guns. "Little overdone for going upstairs."

"Maybe cause I'm not going there."

Gina's eyes flash, and she smirks, "Vinny's turning you into a sex kitten."

I roll my eyes. "I enjoy his company, sex or not."

"Oh, just admit it, you're not a virgin anymore, baby sis," she laughs.

I stand up and give in. "Fine, the sex is fun. I'll take it over the pining after him for years gig."

She leans against the counter as Mack enters with Lola and Veronica, laughing as they change into normal wear. Gina moves closer to me and whispers, "What's the plan then?"

"Plan?" I look incredulously at her, continuing to clean up.

"Yeah, when are you two getting Mated?"

"What?" I almost screech. Mack looks over at us for a moment and I press a smile at them. They go back to talking with Veronica and Lola. I whisper, "We're figuring it out. We don't need to be thinking about that yet."

"Except...you should."

"Why do you sound like my parents when they worried I'd die alone?" I hiss.

The dancers leave the room finally and I put my costume away. Gina crosses her arms, pushing up her breasts with gusto in my face. "Because, like me, they know this is for real, and should be seen seriously by everyone else."

"Look, Vinny and I know it's real," I say, grabbing my extra pair of glasses. "But at the end of the day, we're best friends... partners figuring out what's best for us. We don't need the answers yet." Why'd that last sentence feel heavy on my tongue?

"Oh, like how you were 'figuring it out' when you called Vinny the first night living on Topside? *Supposedly*, moving on?"

"Because he's my best friend, and I had just moved." Totally not because of a vampire threatening my life. "And how did you find out about that?"

"I didn't," she smirks with victory. "You two are just that predictable."

"This goes towards your argument how?" I ask, moving past her.

She stops me, pointing a finger at my chest as she speaks, "You two spent three years separated by Topside, playing a terrible game of chicken, until life hit you hard. Where you were almost *permanently* separated. You can't wait for another event for you two to finally—"

"Why are you so concerned about—"

"*Fucking* get Mated, so no one can take you away."

My eyes widen and my jaw drops. "What are—"

"Your daemon father was here tonight and fucking watched you dance with a disgusted look in his eye. After all that's happened, I don't trust outsiders right now, *especially* that bastard. The way he watched you, I wouldn't be surprised if he hates the idea of you being with a vampire. You know daemons don't like anyone outside of their own."

"Vampires aren't much better," I grumble. "Which is why Vinny and I are taking our time."

I walk past her to the counter, putting my make-up away as Gina crosses her arms. "He seems old school, Brenda. He could bring others—"

"Wolf Mob is already looking out for any more," I tell her, but her hard gaze doesn't relent. "And by international law, I'm under Pops' protection as *his* daughter. Neither human, Paranormal, or half-breed can break that."

"Like that hospital on Topside?" I stop, staring at my reflection in the mirror. "Pretty sure he'll have as much respect for those laws as them."

Daemons, like vampires and werewolves, are territorial. Due to centuries of abuse, they hid away from the rest of the world while the rest of the Noctis Immortalis blended into society. They're known for their hidden communities and disappearing from *everyone's* sight, including the NIIA. Historians and anthropologists don't even know where they disappear to entirely. When daemons find out about someone who has their blood, they come in groups to whisk them away, vanishing with the rest of them—it's all they know how to survive. If Edgar wanted to keep his line protected, he could bring more daemons to take me. International law or not, they could be more brutal than my ambulance ride.

"He's a loner, Gina," I whisper. "He'll have to go through the entire Underground Mafia, my parents, and Vinny. And I'll shoot him in the kneecaps first."

"Better safe than sorry," she says, turning on her heel to clean the rest of the counter space. "But if you two get Mated, then no *being* can touch you."

I touch the bite marks on my neck and a quick pulse moves under my skin as I recall the memory. The marks feel cold as I drop my hand, shaking my head. "We'll figure it out when the time comes."

Gina scoffs, looking at me. "Like waiting for the Vampiric Society to accept you? Those pureblood, aristocratic bastards won't give up one of their last males without a fight."

"Could happen," I lie through my teeth. "But I'm not gonna push Vinny to deal with them, which could cost him *everything*, Gina. I'll take what I have, and hopefully, things get easier in the coming years. Worked with the werewolves."

Her expression falls. "Not the same, baby sis."

"It'll be fine." I say the words, repeating them as a mantra in my head. Over the last few weeks, it's been harder to believe it.

She sighs and comes over to hug me. "I just don't want you going back to being that angry, miserable female again, baby sis. If you two can't be together, it'll break you both. We all know you mean too much to each other." I hold onto her as she whispers close, "You've already lost enough."

I think of Drauper and our severed friendship. I remember the ache to leave him behind, but I know she's right that I wouldn't survive without Vinny. It's why I left for Topside, to make sure I didn't fully lose him, and I can't fail now. I grip her tight and pull away to look at her. "We'll figure it out. We always do."

She nods stiffly as I step away, grab my bags, and head for the door. "Just don't let those dickheads tell you what to do, including that daemon," she calls after me.

I nod with a smirk and walk out, weaving past people in the club and slipping out through the back door. I lean against the brick of the building as the door shuts away the loud music. The Underground moves into twilight as the damp, muggy air hangs still while lights shimmer above and I take a deep breath, rubbing my undercut roughly.

Shit, this feels like such a mess. The worry of Vinny and I being a mistake creeps into my bones. Between vampires and daemons, I wasn't sure who was worse to deal with. Gina and Joey are right, I need to talk to Vinny and find a way to make this work with the least amount of bloodshed. I kind of miss the days when I only had to worry about one father intervening.

I sigh and decide to ignore the lingering fear and head to Vinny's for a drink and another "distraction." I readjust my ponytail when I suddenly smell a combination of patchouli, beard oil, and worn leather. I turn toward the aroma and see Edgar at the end of the alley, his wings open a little as his gray eyes watch me.

"Being a creeper part of the resume?" I ask.

"You put on quite the show," he says, sauntering towards me with an unflinching swagger.

"It's a *family* tradition," I say as his burnt oil stench invades my nostrils. Please tell me I don't smell like that.

"Of course, it is," he scoffs.

"You got something to say about it?" I move away from the wall and face him, taking in the sight of his dark, peppered beard as he stands a few feet away from me. "Don't like the shows, don't come back."

"Aren't you supposed to encourage patrons to return?"

"Not part of my job criteria, but the show I gave is enough to keep them coming back for more." His scent and scowl deepen as he narrows his eyes, furrowing his brows. Oh, *look*, I hit a nerve. "If you didn't want me to be a stripper, you shouldn't have left me. Got a problem with it? Maybe, *you* should rethink your actions."

"I didn't leave you there. But then, *you* never asked."

I laugh and gesture at him. "I was still left in the sewers to die. You couldn't even succeed in helping me. You failed."

He straightens and glares at me. "I did what was needed."

"Doubt it."

"Do *not* question me," he snarls. "You don't—"

"Fuck off." His eyes widen, and I grin.

He steps forward and points at my chest, but I don't back down from his close proximity. "Watch your language. I am your *father*, whether you like it or not."

"Jerking off into a tube or fucking some random human doesn't make you a father."

A growl emanates from Edgar's chest as he bares his teeth, and I match his energy; like hell I'll back down from him. His gray eyes harden, and his breathing becomes more ragged as he looks down at my attire and back up. "I see being around those *devils* have influenced you, including how to respect your elders."

The son of a bitch is about to get lead in his kneecaps. "All the more reason for you to leave, huh? So, fucking go. It's what you're good at, running away."

"I will not. I care more about you than anyone in *there*," he says, jutting his thumb at *Unbound*. The smell of gasoline mixes with his worn leather scent. "They know *nothing* about being a daemon or being respectable. I'd never allow *my* daughter to dance like that." I keep my mouth shut, clenching my fist at my side. "But I can't imagine they'd ever have that kind of self-respect or dignity. They're deviants; it's in their nature after all."

"But not in mine?"

"Daemons are more refined than that. You'd know—"

"If you hadn't *left* me."

"Don't blame me for what they've done," he says.

I glare at him and curl my lip. "You know what? We're done. Not like you fucking cared in the first place." I grab my bag and shove past him.

His scent heightens and he calls after me. "If I didn't *care* about you, why would I come find you? I'm the only one who can keep you alive, or you'll end up dead like the rest of your siblings."

It feels like a cannonball hits my chest, the air suddenly thin as I stop in my tracks and slowly turn back to face the daemon. I'm unable to form words as I stare into his hard gaze and press my arms to my side to keep from shaking.

"Did you really think only *you* lived past the program?" He asks in an undermining tone.

"They died a long time ago," I rasp. "You saying they didn't?"

He tilts his head, furrowing his brows. "Many others survived, leaving the program."

"What do you mean they 'left?'"

"You were...*born* into the program, like the others. I can't get into the details, but I was told *all* my children would be safe once they finished their series of testing. Unfortunately, I was forced to leave early, and they refused to tell me where I could find you. Traloski was...*possessive* of his subjects. I tried to go back but he disappeared after the government found him. Everyone involved was either arrested or taken, including you and your siblings. I had *no* idea you were left in the sewers, that was *your* assumption."

I fumble for words and manage to say, "I saw a picture of me and other kids—"

"Your half-siblings."

"Why? What was it all even for—?"

"The program was supposed to help Paranormals from contagions caused by—"

"Bullshit."

His eyes flash as his scowl darkens. "All the tests were

meant for medical advancement to aid Paranormals against human warfare."

"You really believe that?" I question, stalking back to come face to face with him. His expression turns into a disgusted sneer. "Then why wait this long to find me? To tell me the truth?"

"Do you know your number?" He asks and my chest constricts. "There were dozens of you, and I looked for your siblings, but..." he pauses, looking down, "...all of them were dead by the time I found them. The drugs had slowly deteriorated their bodies, killing them." I freeze, staring at him in horror. "I *tried* to help the others, but I was too late. You're the last one alive."

"Why were you in the city for a year before coming to find me?"

His brow quirks. "I was trying to help two of your siblings. *Obviously.*"

A tightened ache wraps around my heart at the thought of being so close to my siblings, and never knowing it.

His wings shiver behind him. "All of that immunity testing came with a high cost. Traloski talked about having a serum to awaken Paranormal abilities within the body to keep the side effects from killing you. He couldn't administer them until you reached a certain age, but the program was disrupted too soon. It's why your lifespan can't be calculated. You're near the same age as them when they died...who knows how much time you have left."

"How would you—?"

"You're experiencing symptoms of fatigue, aren't you?" He asks a bit too calmly, and it feels like the world is crumbling beneath my feet. "Your body will slowly shut down until one day you just won't wake up. It could be months before that happens, but you looked quite exhausted after your...*dancing.*" He tilts his head, and I swallow hard. "You'll start having more difficulty sleeping and concentrating, but we can find Traloski to help you."

"He's gone," I retort.

"He's not," he says darkly. "Half-breeds disappearing is his MO."

I glare at him, sneering with a shaky breath. "You've known this entire time that monster is alive?"

Edgar's jaw tightens while his lip curls. "Unfortunately."

I take a threatening step toward him, making him back up as I growl under my breath, "Where is he?"

"I don't know."

"Are you fucking—"

"Why do you think I ran from you at the center? I wanted to find him before confronting you, because I knew he was still here after finding more of *my* children dead."

My bullshit meter was going off. The fucker landed me in a sting operation that forced me into the hospital.

"You know what? How do I know any of them are even dead?"

Edgar pulls out small pieces of newspaper, unfolding the small squares and fanning them out in his hands. I peer closer, and a tightness develops around my chest as I struggle to breathe. Obituaries. Ten of them. Pictures of those with noses, mouths, eyes, and scars exactly like mine, their ages ranging from 27-29, and one of them stating they were an amputee. My memory flashes back to the picture I'd found in the paperwork from Columbia, another who had survived, but had lost their legs to the testing.

I reach toward the newspaper clippings, but Edgar pulls them away, folding them back up and putting them in his pocket. His scent disappears entirely, and he looks at me with a somber expression. "It's all I have left of them," he says. "*My legacy.*"

My jaw tightens as a cold chill moves up my spine after seeing a glimpse of my future, and I step away from him.

"You'll have a better chance of finding Traloski than any of them," he says grimly. "You were one of his favorites."

"Don't I feel special?"

"I'm trying to help you." He reaches for me, but I step further from him.

"Oh, like the others?" I scoff gesturing to where he hid away the clippings. Fuck me. I could deal with having a human lifespan, but having an expiration date that could be next week? Would I even make it to thirty? I grab my bag, swinging it over my shoulder as I walk down the alley away from him. "Thanks for the unhelpful warning."

"Brenda," he calls.

"If I have to find that damn scientist, then I will. Without *you*."

"I could help—"

"You've done enough!" I scream as I sprint.

My head spins, and my stomach churns as I run to *The Lounge*. There's no way I could trust him, even if he lived through the program, but Charlene still hadn't gotten a read on my blood, and there's no other way of knowing. There's nothing left to trace, no one left to ask. Everyone who was like me...gone. And I'd share the same fate.

My mind spirals as I barrel through *The Lounge's* front doors. The staff is setting up for the evening with a few vampires in booths, necking each other in the shadows. The familiar aroma of brandy, cigars, and leather hits me to my core and makes me choke up. My emotions run wild as I rush past the bar through the backdoors to the foyer and see Samuel sitting at his usual spot. He grins, but it quickly fades as he speaks. "Baby sis?"

"Anyone below?" I ask, walking to the elevator.

"Nah, all clear," he answers as I slam the button. I don't look back at him as the doors open. "Do you—?"

"Let no one below. Don't wanna blow someone's head off." The doors close, and I hit the down button.

Fear and rage boil in my blood, making me want to destroy

something since I can't wring Traloski's or Edgar's necks. My siblings' obituaries haunt my vision and I gasp, clutching the side of the elevator. The elevator dings, and I pull my Glock out as I kick open the doors to the gun range, checking my ammo just before I aim for the nearest target. The gunfire echoes in the room as I fire at every plastic target within five minutes. My gun empties, including extra ammo, and my ears are ringing.

It's not enough.

I pull the 9-Mil next, aiming at a singular target near the far end, imagining it's Traloski. And Bruno. And the doctors who strapped me down. And those damn cops from weeks ago. And whoever fucking left me in that damn fucking sewer. And finally, *Edgar*.

The target's head blows apart. I reload, and a scream rips out of me as I fire away at the next target, whose head falls off with the final bullet. Tears stream down my cheeks as I try to regulate my heaving breaths. The gun clatters to the ground, and I pull out the one in my boot and fire at another target without looking. The gun pops off, echoing throughout the room until I hear the empty clicking sounds. I'm shaking as I debate grabbing a gun from the armory when his scent rushes over me.

I keep my eyes on the beheaded targets and aim in his direction, knowing I'm off by a few inches. His shoes scuff the ground quietly, but I bring my head down as tears roll down my face. The gun rattles in my hand as I shake until his hand grasps around mine. Vinny carefully pries the gun from my hand, clicks on the safety, and drops it to the ground before moving his hand up my arm. His other hand cups my cheek, and I close my eyes, leaning into his touch as his thumb strokes my skin. He says nothing as he brings me in close, wrapping his arms around me into a tight embrace and cradling my head to his chest.

The dam breaks and sobs tear out of my throat as I clutch onto him. "I'm here, sweet cheeks."

[illegible]

CHAPTER 6
UNTIL MY DYING DAY

"And then I shot up your range," I finish with a heavy sigh sitting next to Vinny on his bed, while he stares at the ground.

After sobbing on his chest for thirty minutes, he brought me three floors above *The Lounge* to his two-bedroom apartment with a living room, kitchen, two bathrooms, and well-stocked weapons room. I rarely come over because I don't want to see his family, including Anita. I didn't need another set of prying eyes into our relationship.

"You think he's telling the truth?" He asks.

"All of them looked like me, Vinny," I say softly. "Those obituaries...none of them made it to thirty."

"There has to be another way to keep you from ending up like them."

I shrug and stand up, my eyes itching as I head for the bathroom. "There's no way to be certain unless I find Traloski."

"And he has no idea where to find him?"

I pull out my contacts and rejoin him on the bed. "I don't think so. Otherwise, I think he would've dragged me to him."

"Because he needs you alive," Vinny mumbles. "You're no good to him as a dead daemon."

"Probably why he was looking for the rest of my siblings..."

He scoffs, "So, he uses you to find the monster that experimented on you?"

"His list of qualities is rather short."

"And why haven't I ripped his throat out?"

"Wait your turn in line," I mumble as I bring my legs in close. "And you're a goody vampire." I smile weakly, but his ruby eyes become sharp in the darkness surrounding him. "He's not worth your energy, Vinny."

He gets off the bed, and I hear clothing rustle as he drops his jacket, tossing it aside. I can barely make out his figure through my warped vision, concentrating past the dark hues of color. "You gonna tell your parents?" He asks.

"I don't know."

"The last time you went looking for Traloski, you almost got yourself killed."

"In my defense, I had no idea what I was looking for then, and now I do." Kind of.

Vinny sighs heavily. "What do you want to do, Brenda?"

"Must be serious, you used my first name."

"Not the time."

"It's always the time."

"Brenda—"

"Well, I don't know, *Vinny!*" I raise my hands in agitation. "All I know is if I don't find that fucker, I'm dead. If I do find him, I may still be dead. I'm fucked either way, but I can't…I have to find him, whether or not Edgar's lying of knowing where. If Traloski is out there, he'll make more like me, and they'll suffer like I did. I have to at least try to not let anyone else go through what I did…or die the way I might."

It's quiet as I put my face into my hands and let out a shaky breath, until Vinny murmurs, "I'll help you look for him."

I drop my hands and search for his ruby gaze. "What?"

"I'll help you find him."

"Vinny…"

"If you're right, he's probably linked to the disappearances.

Half-breeds go missing, you find the files, and your biological father shows up; it's too much of a coincidence. You mentioned something weeks ago about a wild card trying to make us leave the zones on Topside. This might be it."

"Vinny, you don't need to endanger yourself or—" The burning scent of dark spices and bloodlust invades my nostrils. The aroma making my heart clench, and I hear the crunching sound of wood as Vinny's nails dig deep, crushing it beneath his hands. I know it's his dresser he's destroying in his grip.

"I want the bastard who did this to you," he says with a lethal tone. "I want his head for scarring and blinding you, stealing parts of your life. I want his blood drained and dumped into the sewers because the life I had planned with us will be gone. *You'll* be gone," Vinny growls, and the lights in the room flicker. "Taking away your chance to live…and the idea of you… you…"

I stare at him as he struggles and walk tentatively off the bed toward him as his scent deepens. My mouth goes dry, and I wrap my arms around myself as my stomach clenches. "Vinny, we knew there'd be a lifespan difference—"

He growls low, "*Not* the fucking same. I was going to convince the Society to allow us to Mate, Brenda." My heart aches as I stop where I stand. "I have members of the Blood Mafia who were going to vouch for you against my father's wishes. They'd defend my decision to Mate outside the pure-bloods. It would've taken a few years, getting everything together, but it would've *worked*. If they find out the truth, all of those vouchers will be gone. My father, the Society, even fucking Anita, will do *everything* to make me leave you. Forcing me to move on and not waste my time."

"Maybe it's for the best," I choke out.

Vinny stills, and his aroma dampens a moment before it enrages into a burning storm again. "You are worth more than anything to me, whether you're here for less than a fifth of my life or its entirety. And I'm not going to let a mad scientist, vampires, or that fucking daemon take you away from me."

"Vinny—"

"I meant it when I said I wasn't letting you go." Ruby eyes blaze across my vision, the irises a fire through the darkness filled with certainty.

If Vinny fought the Vampiric Society, he could lose his title as Blood Mafia Boss, giving it back to Bruno. Him being one of the few pureblood vampires on the eastern seaboard wouldn't be enough to save him from their retribution of "betraying" them by Mating a non-vampire.

I rub my palm into my temple. "You could lose all of it, Vinny, and if I'm dead in a few years, fuck months, it's not worth it. I'm not worth losing over two centuries of work and your position in the mafia—"

"You are worth more than any of that, and I will toss it all away for you. All of it."

I freeze as his words pierce through me. My heart pounds heavily, and I long to touch him and crumble in his embrace as he approaches me. I can't let him. I'll have failed him, and I love him too much for him to potentially lose everything. I shake my head, "Vinny, no, you—"

"None of those things matter if I don't have you, sweetheart," he says, stopping a few inches from me. "I've lived a long time alone, thinking this shitty life of mine was just death and pain. I was convinced kindness and love weren't meant for me, and I didn't care because my mother was gone, and my father didn't give a damn. I was raised to be a mafia boss. Nothing more." He touches my cheek and holds my face gently. "Until a young girl looked me in the eye, grabbed my hand, and led me out of that darkness despite what I was. *You* proved me wrong and became the starlight I didn't know existed."

Vinny leans forward and presses a kiss to my forehead as tears stream down my face. I swallow hard as he pulls back, wiping away the tears gently. All I see are his ruby eyes as he says softly, "You've always said I'm your best friend, and we've been almost inseparable for over two decades. You're everything to me. *Everything*. I've wanted to be someone you could always love and trust at your side. And for the last few years, I held onto a string of hope that there'd be something more than just friendship." His voice falters and grows coarse as he declares, "The very thought of living without you is like drowning in blood and ripping out my lungs. I have loved you with *everything* that I have, and am completely, utterly bound to you."

I look down, staring at his chest, unable to speak.

"I don't give a shit about the Society," he says roughly. "I'll never want what they want. I want...I want you as mine forever. A bond that no one can break. If we only have so little time left, I want us together until the end. I want you as my Mate if you'll take me."

I bring my hand up, clutching it against his cheek while I place the other on his chest, feeling the beat of his heart I joke he doesn't have. I feel the warmth that I tease he knows nothing of. Except Vinny knows it far better than I do, being able to say the words that I struggle to find. I whisper, "They'll never agree to a ceremony in time."

"Then we don't tell them."

"Vinny, they have to be present for it."

"Not the Mating I'm talking about."

I still at his words and look up wide-eyed. "Claim Mating?"

There are two paths to Mating within the Noctis Immortalis. The first is by ceremony recognized by the community of the Paranormals involved. The second, Claim Mating, is discouraged because those involved don't need permission of any society, making it dangerous because *no one*, by Noctis Immortalis Law, can divide them. It is an eternal oath that can only be separated by death.

He grips my hand against his chest. "We won't tell them. It'll be between us."

"Vinny…if anyone finds out—"

"Then we deal with it *together*. We keep this secret. Just us." He leans forward and places his lips against mine tenderly. My chin quivers as I taste him, falling further into the touch. He pulls away and strokes his thumb over my lips. "All I want is you. And to keep you safe by my side until the very end."

I stare into his crimson eyes, faintly seeing the black freckles in them. I concentrate on the warmth of his hand and the hard beating of his heart pulsing under my touch. The air is thick, filled with his aroma and scent as I take a deep breath. "You'll be mine?"

"I already was, sweetheart." His voice is husky and deep.

Mine. He'd be mine. The fear of losing him washes away as I stare into his gaze. For however short or long, I'd have what I've wanted with so much of my being for so long.

"Do you want this?" He asks. "Because there's no going back if we do."

Vinny's laughter, smile, touch, dumb jokes, angry glares, tears, joy, everything I've loved, hated, adored, and been annoyed with would be mine. All of Vinny the Vampire and his over-the-top care would be mine, whether for months, years, decades, or centuries. Mine. And I'd be his. It's all I've wanted. Because I was already his, too.

"Yes," I breathe.

"What?"

"Yes, you deaf old bloodsucker, yes, fucking be mine."

Vinny clutches me close and slams his mouth to mine, his hand at the nape of my neck. My breath hitches from the sudden bruising kiss, and I inhale deeply and taste the wanting desire and need from his lips. He reaches down, not breaking the kiss, and grabs my ass, lifting me as I wrap my legs around his torso, holding my body against him as my back presses against the wall. He keeps my head from banging into the hard surface, kissing me like it's the last time and rasping out, "Say it again, *please*."

I hold his head and speak against his lips, "Yes, Vinny. Yes."

I pull him to me, and our mouths collide as my tongue moves across his top lip, taking my fill of him. A deep guttural moan escapes him as he grips my ass harder, causing me to gasp as he plunges his tongue further. We frantically clutch the other as he pulls my tank top off, breaking our scorching kiss before he dips his head down to my chest and between my breasts. I lean my head back, focusing on the caress of his lips, his tongue sliding up over my skin, and I feel him trace my scars with reverence and care. He stops over my heart and kisses the spot sweetly. I choke back a sob, clutching to him for dear life.

Deep in the pit of my stomach, I feel it, the want from years of being so close, yet so far. The yearning to touch him, the loneliness that engulfed me, dreams of longing, and nightmares where he'd never return. Mine. Vinny the Vampire would be *mine*.

The want drives deeper as he carries me over to the bed, taking my pants off, and lays me down. Inhaling deeply, I can almost taste Vinny's darkened aroma, the burnt spice that reminds me of mulled wine and clove, whiskey barrels dipped in honey. His pants drop, and then his hands travel up my legs carefully to my underwear, his fingers skimming under the seam before slowly taking my panties off at an agonizing pace.

"How long are you going to drag this out?" I moan.

They're finally off, and he drops them as he traces his fingers back down my thighs. "Long as I can, sweetheart. Now, turn over."

I flip over, and he unclasps my bra and takes it off. I try to turn around, but he stops me and pulls my hips up so I'm on all fours. His fingers trail down to the apex of my thighs, heat rising within my core while he grips my hips. A finger comes up and circles my clit while another sinks into me. I moan at the sensation, and my breath quickens as he does it again and again.

"Playboy tease," I groan at the slow penetrating movement.

Vinny nips at my backside and thrusts two fingers into me, pressing onto my clit. My body jerks as I try to keep my arms up beneath me. I clutch the bedsheets as my head hangs, breathing heavily as he continues to torture me, pumping his fingers into me. An orgasm builds inside me as his other hand grips onto my hips. The slight pain jolts my body, and the heat grows, trickling over me as his mouth presses against my back, sending a warm breeze across my skin. The sensation of his plunging fingers inside me, his thumb circling and pressing, and his nails biting into my skin collides into a pleasurable release.

The orgasm rips out of me quickly, and I scream, "Vinny!" He doesn't stop as he strokes over the sensitive part, easing me back down as bliss pulls at my muscles. I breathe heavily as my head falls onto the bed. His fingers leave me, and he turns me back around as he licks my juices off his fingers. The bed dips as he carefully moves over me and caresses my breasts with adoration.

"Sweetheart," he says quietly. I hum and hazily look up at his dark ruby eyes, which call me forward through the darkness. He chuckles and touches my cheek. "Do you know how this works?"

"Hey, I may be new to sex, but I'm not that new," I mumble.

He laughs harder and shakes his head. "How Claim Mating works, what you and I have to do." I stare up at him and nod. "Do you trust me?"

"Vinny, if I didn't fucking trust you, I wouldn't be doing this. I trust you with everything," I say as I grab his head, and pull him down to me. "Now, *please*, Mate me and get all territorial, you adorable bloodsucker."

"You think I'm adorable?"

"*That's* what you—" His lips crash against mine, shutting me up gladly.

I wrap my arms around his neck, pressing his body close to

mine as his erection nudges at my entrance. His hand travels down between us, stroking my thigh and into the apex of them. It feels like forever, holding him this close just on the cusp of penetration as our breaths become steady. Vinny finally enters me at an alarmingly slow rate, and I gasp at the fullness when he enters me. Although my body has grown used to him, I'll never tire of the sensation of his cock inside me. He moans into my mouth, moving steadily with his hips as my nails dig into his back as I lift my hips to meet his while he thrusts harder and harder into me. Pure pleasure rushes my senses as I tighten around him and stifle my screams from the glorious feeling, a heat overflowing from me as he continues his punishing blows.

Arms wrap around me as he pulls me close to sit up. I wrap my legs around him as a growl vibrates from his chest, sending a shiver across my skin. I grip his shoulders, driving him deeper as my muscles begin to shake and the ecstasy drives higher. He grabs my hips forcefully, and I gasp, "Vinny!"

I find his crimson gaze, and for a moment, time stands still. My erratic breaths calm as I stare into his ardent gaze and hold tightly to him, our skin nearly fusing together in our hard embrace. His heartbeat slows with mine as our hips move together and tears form in my eyes, my heart aching for the vampire before me. Vinny's gaze softens as he brings his forehead against mine, and I whisper, "I love you."

"I love you," he says, dipping his head down to sink his fangs into my neck.

A scream catches in my throat as his fragrance of bloodlust, dark spices, and aged whiskey fills my nostrils. The piercing of daggers shoots through my neck, sinking deep into my flesh. I feel the blood pulled from my vein as Vinny thrusts into me hard, and I finally cry out, digging my nails into his shoulders. He pulls away from the wound, his tongue sweeping over the blood. My skin burns, tightening as an orgasm builds, pleasure roaring from my core up through my body as sparks encase my spine, gradually climbing to the base of my neck.

I tangle my hands in his hair, pulling his head back to look into his fervent, passionate eyes as I declare in Noctora, *"My eternal, Claimed Mate."*

Vinny kisses me and repeats the binding oath. *"My eternal, Claimed Mate."*

My orgasm releases through me, and I cry out, digging my nails into Vinny's skin as he growls against my throat. Ecstasy barrels through my body, leaving me in euphoria as I grip him close and inhale his scent deeply that now covers my skin like a protective barrier. I bring his lips to mine, kissing him deeply as relief trickles through my veins.

Mine. Vinny's Mine.

SWEET
CHEEKS
LOVES

CHAPTER 7
UNDER MY SKIN

"I'll need to go to Topside if I want to find Traloski," I murmur against Vinny's chest.

"At least Midnight took care of that." I poke his shoulder, and he grumbles, pulling me closer to him as we lay in his bed. I snuggle within the nook of his shoulder, and gently run my finger over his skin under the covers as he kisses my head. "Go up during daylight hours. If you go up at night, Samuel or I go with you."

I'm kind of surprised he relented so quickly for me to even leave the Underground so soon. "Not that dangerous, blood-sucker. I did live up there for three years."

"The NYPD, PSB, or Traloski could be looking for you despite Midnight's magic tricks. I know you can take care of yourself but investigating on your own is dangerous."

"Wasn't really planning to go alone…." I mumble. He shifts to better look at me, but I avert my gaze, and throw out my idea. "I could have Drauper—" Vinny growls as his head falls back. "Well, tell me how you really feel, vampy."

"He almost got you killed."

"Accidentally."

"Sweet cheeks," he warns.

"Look," I say, sitting up a little. "He and I kind of made a good team." Okay, even I'll have to convince myself a bit more on that, but I need a contact during daylight hours who can walk in the sun without a hoodie. "He knows the Bronx enough and was able to contact Doddard, which tells me he knows *how* to find contacts. Bill can't do anything more, Chicago's too far, but Drauper could help. We *need* someone in the NYPD."

His fingers tap my shoulder in agitation. "I could find you another contact."

"You could do with one less person after your ass, Mr. Bossy."

"Only one I care about going after my ass is you."

"Not helping."

"Wasn't trying to."

"You said you wanted to help."

"Not with him."

I pause and tap his chin. "Are you jealous?"

"No." His voice is flat, and his fingers stop tapping my shoulder. I narrow my eyes, then fall back to lay down next to him. At least Mated life hasn't changed anything when it comes to territorial tendencies. I guess I'd be worried if he wasn't annoyingly protective.

We sit in silence together as I try to think of a way to convince him this is a good thing. I'm not exactly excited myself to work with Drauper, but he's been helpful in the past. He's the only person I know on Topside that *may* help me in law enforcement. The one human who wants to make a damn difference. I hope.

What does Ma always tell me when it comes to relationship building? Oh right, compromise. "What if I update you where I am and don't go into the Bronx without an escort?" I offer.

Vinny is quiet as he looks over at me, and I can smell his scent darken with worry as he says softly, "I trust you, Brenda. It's him that I don't."

"I'll be careful and take my extra pair of handcuff keys."

"Sweet cheeks."

"I'll tell you where I go. No going into neutral zones unless you, Samuel, or Rodney are with me. I can even send you nakey pics at exactly 5PM so you have something to wake up to."

He finally laughs and strokes my cheek and neck, his thumb pressing just above where his father bit me. The tension eases from him as I press his hand in place, and he lets out a long breath. "Tell me when you go to Topside, no matter the time," he relents. "If you're there at night, I'll join you. No neutral zones unless me, Samuel, Joey, or Rodney go with you. Fuck, Anita can be on that list. No repeats of what happened." He kisses me briefly on the lips and sighs. "I trust you, sweetheart, but this could be the calm before the fucking storm."

"We don't need you having a heart attack worrying, you old male."

"You just Mated this old male, you grave digger."

"Cradle robber."

"Perfect pair."

"From hell," I chuckle. "At least we become lovable when fed our favorite snacks."

"And less grumpy after naps," he says, grabbing my hand to kiss it. "I'll look into things from my side and tell you what I find. And if I go back into the South Bronx."

I sit up fully, throwing my leg over his torso, leaning down as I place my hands on his chest to get close to his face. "When did we get so reasonable? Was there something in that Mating scent, bloodsucker?"

"No, although sex has a way of making things more... *agreeable*."

I chuckle and lay on his chest completely. Vinny strokes my back gently, holding me against his warm torso. This is the most relaxed I've felt in over a month. The bleakness of my short life ticking away subdues as hope flickers deep inside.

Vinny's that hope, as always. The thought of living feels possible with him next to me.

I take a deep breath, inhaling the Mating scent that now clings to my skin. Only he and I would be able to sense it, but the more powerful Paranormals may still smell something heightened between us. If I had active Paranormal abilities, my own scent would be clinging to his blood just as strongly. We'll attribute the change to sex, lots of it. Mating scents are almost identical to raised sex pheromones. The only true way for someone to find out is by tasting his or my blood. But I know someone who will know instantly when I walk into a room.

"Vinny?" I murmur, and he hums in repose. "I need to tell Pops about us."

He kisses my head. "Remind him I'm Ma's favorite before he threatens to cut my dick off."

<hr>

I SPENT the entire night at Vinny's, getting up early to head home before beings wake up. He grumbles and falls back asleep as I get dressed and kiss him on the temple before getting on the elevator. *The Lounge* is deserted of any clientele as I walk out, and the bartender waves me off as I go. The Underground is still dark with lights twinkling above like starlight as I move down the path.

I don't feel any different after the Claim Mating with Vinny. Some who Claim Mate will find certain abilities or senses heightened, but given how immune I am to everything, no surprise nothing's much changed apart from his scent infused with mine. Yet, everything has changed. The moment anyone in the Vampiric Society or the Blood Mafia finds out what we did, there'll be hell to pay. And I may still have to pay it when I get home to tell Pops. He wanted us together but going behind everyone's backs to do this is an insult to most Paranormals.

It's one thing to date, another to bind ourselves to each other without telling anyone.

The neon lights of *Unbound* pulse as I slip through the front door and tread my way through the darkened club to the apartment. The slumbering ambiance continues into home as I slip off my shoes and enter the foyer, smelling fresh coffee. I quietly make my way through the shadowed apartment and peek into the lit kitchen to see Pops at the table with papers spread in front of him.

"Carmen, love, go back to—" He stops and softens once he sees me wave slightly. "Baby girl, you're up early."

"Back at you," I whisper, and grab myself a mug of coffee. "Paperwork?"

"Gathering documents for the survivors Joey received recently. Rodney's handling the ones going out west to that ranch in Montana."

"The one owned by the female alpha?" I ask.

"Keir. Smart and cunning werewolf, I'm told. Some werewolves and shifters are going to her for the winter to recover." I sit next to him, and he suddenly tenses up, flooding my nostrils with the scent of cinnamon and cigars. He places the papers down, and his hands come into a steeple before him. "Something to tell me, baby girl? Or do I need to have a *discussion* with that vampire?"

I take a deep breath, sip some coffee for nerves, and meet his violet gaze. "Edgar saw me after the show." I explain what daemon daddy told me, the newspaper clippings, how I shot up Vinny's gun range, and the decision Vinny and I made to Claim Mate. Pops moves to the kitchen sink, his scent dampening as I finish telling him I need to go back to Topside to look for Traloski. The air intensifies, feeling heavy as the quiet falls over the kitchen. I wait, sitting as I clutch my coffee mug anxiously.

"He could be lying," Pops finally says. "Anything to make you—"

"They looked just like me, Pops," I rasp. "And you know I've been feeling fatigued lately and always seem to need naps these past few months."

"You're not dying, not this...not this soon...." His voice cracks, and I quickly move toward him, wrapping my arms around his torso. He holds me against his shaking chest. "You deserve a life, baby girl...with us. You can't be..."

I hold him tighter, burying my face into his shoulder. "I'll find him, Pops. We'll find him in time."

Pops clears his throat and kisses my head, stroking my hair back as he places his cheek against my temple. He breathes in deeply, attempting to regulate his breathing. "Don't tell your Ma or brothers. Not until we have answers. Until we know for sure."

"Okay," I whisper. We stay there for a few minutes, and I feel two tears fall from him to my shoulder. I swallow a sob, clutching him closer as the scent of cinnamon coats the room. "You not mad about the Mating thing?"

Pops loosens a breath, pulling back from the embrace to look at me fully as he pushes some of my hair back. "I told you I wanted you to be happy, and that vampire has always tried to do right by you. Should've known you two would've gone the route of asking forgiveness before permission." He sighs, and I wipe away one last tear on his cheek.

"We have a brand to keep up with," I say with a half-hearted shrug.

"Can't be mad at fate, can I?" He asks quietly, cupping my face with one hand. "There'll be dangers being with him, baby girl. I know you understand Paranormals, especially vampires because of him, but it's not the same as reading about them in your books."

"I know, Pops," I swallow hard. "But it's Vinny...you know?"

He smiles faintly and nods. "Yeah, I know. And your Ma and I will stand by you. You know that. The Vampiric Society, Blood

Mafia...they can't necessarily keep you apart, but they'll find ways to break you. Both of you."

"We'll be fine, Pops," I say with a small, forced smile. "We'll figure it out like we always do."

He nods again and embraces me, kissing my head before letting go. We move back to the table, sitting in silence and I hear Ma wake up with her light footsteps moving across the hallway to the bathroom.

"You'll have to do a proper Mating Ceremony for her," he whispers as she shuts the door. "After we find Traloski, that is."

I reach for Pops' hand that covers mine, his thumb stroking over my scars gently. I watch him through my lenses, and he suddenly looks aged to me. I can sense the centuries he's lived through in the soft touch of his hands, a stillness that hovers with the darkened scent of cigars and cinnamon. Pops is over six hundred years old, and he'll have hundreds more. My entire family, Vinny, Rodney, and even fucking Edgar, will have those years.

The hope that flickers deep inside me feels faint at the thought of losing time on this earth. In comparison, my life-span would be a blip on the screen, while theirs would stretch on. Vinny said he'd have nothing when I'm gone, but in reality, he may have to live hundreds of years without me. Not just him. My Pops, the one who found me, bathed me, fed me, loved me, and called me his "baby girl" could watch me die soon. My heart clenches as I grip harder onto his hand as the weight of reality presses down on my shoulders. Pops' violet gaze meets mine, comforting the best he can as I see the glistening of tears again. I don't want to leave him behind, especially when it feels like I already lost time being on Topside away from them. I steel myself, conviction driving deep into my gut as I will myself to not give up. Not yet.

"I'll be going up tonight to talk to Drauper," I say.

"Will you ask Edgar for help?"

I shake my head. "His track record for saving children isn't comforting. And his attitude is somehow worse than mine."

"There's nothing wrong with you," Pops says with a strict tone. "You've grown up to be a resourceful, strong, and confident female that a father *should* be proud of. You're the daughter who he *never* deserved."

He smiles softly and places his hand against my cheek. I lean into his touch, inhaling his relaxing scent. I'm thankful it was him who found me, grateful that I had that stroke of luck in my life. I remain steady as his eyes harden, the tears now gone as he warns, "And if that daemon tries anything...he'll wish he never came to the Underground."

CHAPTER 8
MISSION...POSSIBLE?

I look up at the Manhattan Entrance I used so often in the past. The last time was almost two months ago when I chased Vinny for taking my panties. I smile at the image of him hiding behind Ma, then shudder, remembering the events that happened after. I press the button, and my phone pings with a text message from Vinny: *Leaving?*

I reply, *Manhattan Entrance. You'll get your nudes later, vamp tramp.*

I'll be waiting. Try lace for once.

I scrunch my face. How about no. I'd rather *he* wears the lacey things. I chuckle at the amusing thought and put my phone away.

The elevator door comes down, and I climb in, glancing at the clock. 8 AM. Good enough. I dial the familiar number as I ride up into the daylight. As it rings, I wonder if he'll actually answer or if I'll have to force him to talk to me by going to the precinct station. My gut twists at the thought of going back there until he finally picks up.

"Detective Drauper," he answers. Okay, I should've put more thought into *when* he picked up instead.

The elevator stops, opening the doors to the sunlight, a

marveling sight I haven't seen in almost two months. I step out into the late summer air and say, "You miss me?"

He pauses, and I wonder if I've lost him. "Brenda?"

"The one and only." Did he delete my number?

"I thought you left," he says in a low tone. Oh, he *definitely* deleted my number.

"I went 'down in the Underground' not 'country roads take me home,'" I say with an offkey tone.

He lets out a harsh sigh. Relief or annoyance? "Why are you calling me?" Annoyance.

I step into the sunlight, away from the shadows of the Entrance, and inhale the air of the late hot summer day. The city bustles around me with mixing smells of cement, booze, cigarettes, and gasoline. Damn, I miss the New York City air. "Brenda?" Drauper asks.

"Sorry. Been a while since I've felt daylight."

"You're on Topside?"

"I seemed to have missed out on the rain, but I'll settle for a sunny day."

"And *I'll* settle for why you're calling me. I figured I'd never hear from you again, so getting a call from you at 8-fucking-AM is odd."

"We can discuss my oddities another time."

"I'm hanging up—"

"Wait, I need your help!" I yell over the phone and glare at a few humans who look my way. Who in New York *actually* looks?

He grumbles to himself, and asks, "What do you mean?"

Time for business. I'm a ticking time bomb and only have so much daylight to play in. "I can't explain over the phone, but if you want to catch the bastards stealing people off the streets, meet me at Central Park around noon." I walk down the sidewalk in the opposite direction of my old apartment.

"You know who it is?"

"Guessing you don't?"

"Are you just fucking with me—"

"I don't have time for that. And I *do* need you, Shaggy."

He exhales sharply. Yup, *definitely* annoyance. "Seriously?"

"You didn't want Scooby," I say, and he scoffs. I stop at a crosswalk, looking towards the coffee shop across the way. "Drauper? You in?"

"Where in the park?"

I smile to myself. "Near the Balto statue. It's pretty over there."

"Little out of the way," he grumbles. "Fine, I'll be there at noon. Don't bring anyone. Just you."

"Thought you knew I traveled alone."

"I *had* thought I knew you. But, then again, we all have our secrets, don't we?" The call shuts off, and I stare at the dark screen. Well, at least he said yes.

I put my phone away and head into the coffee shop bustling with people and order a coffee, snagging a seat in a corner away from the other patrons. It's not quite "Vinny Coffee," but it'll do. I contemplate what to do until noon, when my phone rings again. I glance at the unfamiliar number and answer in hopes of scaring off a solicitor, "Unless you're offering a mission, giving me an option to accept it, then I don't care."

"What happens if you don't accept it? Does your phone blow up?" The familiar sensual voice makes me almost spill my coffee.

"Michello?"

"Is that how you greet people nowadays?"

"Only if I think they're trying to tell me about my car's warranty." He laughs softly. "How did you get my number?"

"Joey. For emergencies, but you know, I don't think your family dotes on you enough."

"No giving them more ideas," I warn in a teasing tone. "If I find out you're part of any of my brother's plots to embarrass me, I'm tattooing a werewolf on your ass." Michello's laugh echoes over the phone as I smile at the sound. "So, what's the emergency? Or do I need to prank my brother?"

"Heard it's been…chaotic since I've left," he says. "I recently helped Joey with a group of survivors, and he mentioned you hung up your panties. Congratulations."

I lean back in my seat, slumping with the coffee in hand. "Yeah, and they're still hanging on the wall. How long did yours stay up?"

"Two years."

"Shut up."

"My parents were in charge of a workshop for the abused. My mother was elated and thought it would encourage others to reclaim themselves. They were tighty-whities and hung up next to my sister's socks, which stayed up for three years. She came out as ace before she was twenty. I was forty-five."

"Tighty-whities, really?"

"They're comfortable."

"Something tells me I'm gonna have to steal mine back," I mumble, and Michello chuckles over the line. "You laugh, but you met my family. Ma may keep them up for years.…" I stop myself, remembering what may not be, and my stomach twists. Would she take them down after I'm gone?

"Brenda?" Michello asks.

"Sorry, it's been a long day and an even longer night ahead," I say, looking out the window. I forgot how bright the damn sun was. "It's good to hear from you and know you're okay."

Before it's too late, scratches at my mind.

"Hate to lose a friend so quickly, and Joey said you could use a reminder."

"For what?"

"That you still belong where you are," he says quietly. I clutch my coffee close and laugh a little. "So, baby sis, tell me what's happening in good ole New York City?"

CHAPTER 9
LIKE...ZOINKS!

I finish off my coffee, tossing it in the garbage as I approach the statue. I spent the rest of the morning catching up with Michello over the phone. He said he'd be heading out west to help the new group of people at *Silver Paw Ranch*, the rehabilitation ranch Keir runs. He commented how she reminded him of me from their phone conversations, and we both decided if she and I ever met, the world would be doomed. He suggested I visit the mountains out west some time and see something taller than skyscrapers for once. I've never left New York, and I may never still.

I come upon a statue of Leonardo Marressi, a shifter who stopped two terrorist attacks in the 80s, costing him his life. After the attack, protocols were put in place that whenever a presumed terrorist attack happens in the city, all the Entrances shut down until deemed safe by the NIIA. If bombs ever got underneath, the island would fall away into the ocean. There's a collection in *The Vault* detailing Marressi's life as an NIIA Agent and how he changed the agency for Paranormals. Beckham knew him and suggested I learn his story. I pat the statue's foundation as I pass and come up to my meeting spot.

I sit near the Balto statue and look at the time. It's exactly noon. I bet he'll be late. Again.

I watch people stroll through the park, the sky spotted with clouds barely providing coverage from the hot sun, and I'm thankful for living below ground for most of the summer. My leather jacket is sweltering around me, but I don't want to show off the scars today. I check the time again, and ten minutes have already passed.

A familiar aroma of deep musk and shampoo invades my senses, and I look up to see Drauper approach at a leisure pace. He's clean-shaven with a short fade, dark sunglasses covering his eyes, his badge hanging loose over his t-shirt, and dark copper skin glistening with sweat from the midday heat—no signature brown leather jacket. Smart man. My eyes flick down to his tight jeans and back up. It seems the last of the pining I had for him is gone. My body thrums in want for Vinny, hating he's below and not nearby.

Drauper stops a few feet from me, taking his glasses off. "What do you want?" He asks gruffly with a piercing stare. Great start.

"No coffee this morning? If I'd known, I'd have brought you some."

He frowns and crosses his arms over his chest, not moving from his spot. Damn, okay, worse than I thought it would be. I sigh and lean back on the bench, patting the spot beside me. "You gonna come closer, or do you want me to yell state secrets across the park?"

He walks off the path and stops to stand in the grass, a few feet from the bench. I knew he'd be a little cautious, but this is kind of ridiculous. Was I that much of a bitch? Wait, wasn't I the one who almost died? Unless Joey threatened him more than I thought, which is a high possibility.

"I'm a half-breed, not contagious," I joke, and he remains silent, jaw tense. I sigh, and ease back on the sarcasm. "Look, I said I was sorry, but shit isn't easy on Topside being what I am. I had to take precautions with *everyone*."

"I understand why you did it." He looks away, keeping his arms over his chest.

I mimic him, folding my own arms. "Then why are you—"

"Just because I understand doesn't mean I'm not upset. You used me."

My mouth drops. "Fucking did not."

"You used me to help the *fucking* Underground Mafia. The beasts who—"

"*Stop calling them that.*" The growl in my voice makes his head snap back to me. His dark brown eyes widen at the sudden change. "I already told you, *they're* not the bad guys."

I stand up, my lip curling as defensive mode switches on, bubbling under my skin. Quickly, I suppress the rage down, focusing on why I'm here. Sure, my mafia family does things a little unorthodox, but so does the government and the rest of the world behind closed doors. *Everyone* does. I inhale deeply to calm myself, and exhale, "They're trying to protect their people."

"Because they *act* like family?"

"They are *my* family."

He scowls. "Then I can't help you. Not again."

"Why can't you try to see it from my side? I've seen yours for over a year now and even helped you bring in the bad guys— *actual* bad guys that not even my own family can touch. *I* helped you with that big break against the group of half-breeds who were running laced weed to humans. *I* helped you find that serial killer using Renaissance shifter paintings as his calling cards."

"And how many Paranormal mobsters escaped us because of you?"

"They are not *your* jurisdiction."

"They're fucking dangerous!" The anger boils deep inside me, and my glare darkens. "They're *criminals*. Their illegal activities make it unsafe for people to walk outside their damn homes. Jurisdiction or not, I'm not going to look away when people are in danger." Drauper's eyes pierce into mine as his jaw tightens.

I groan in frustration and start to pace, rubbing my undercut harshly. Did I really need him? Yes. Otherwise, I'm stuck with the daemon sperm donor. How can I convince him we're on the same damn side with a common enemy?

I pause and look back at him, his gaze penetrating mine with frustration. There's a piece he doesn't know about our operations, and if he did, he might actually help. Fuck. Joey's gonna kill me.

I take a deep breath carefully, and tell him quietly, "My father, Alanzo Cuorebella, as you know him, controls operations that rescue people from the black market; those forced into slavery or the sex trade, bought or taken and simply forgotten by the world." Drauper's face remains passive, but his jaw relaxes. "He saves *all* beings, Paranormals and humans alike; that's what my family does. And I *will* defend my own family. They do the dirty work risking their lives to save others from torture and pain. Those 'beasts' have spent centuries undoing the cruelty of others."

My voice becomes coarse by the last sentence as I stare him down. He looks away toward the running path, silently watching joggers pass and people rush to work.

"Look," I sigh, "I won't pretend they do it in a completely legal way, but sometimes that shit isn't black and white. Maybe you don't approve of the methods they use, but maybe you should think of the overall picture. People getting their freedom back."

Silence fills the space again, and at this point my final wish is to have music blasting during my final moments alive.

After what seems like a millennium, he asks, "What happens to those who are freed?"

"Relocated for healing and rehabilitation, most to different states, countries, or, just, where they find their peace. They're given better starts."

"Those apartments, the tempies? They were—?"

"Safe houses until we relocate people to a better destination."

Drauper narrows his eyes. "That shifter who gave me info, he worked for Alanzo?"

I shift on my feet. "Used to." I flick my gaze up and he nods, understanding enough. He doesn't need to know the specifics of Doddard's "resignation" or that he's now a permanent decoration in Brooklyn buried neck-deep in cement with his teeth burrowed in metal pipes. Pops doesn't take kindly to those who jeopardize his survivors.

Drauper's arms relax a little across his chest. I have an in; I can feel it. At the end of the day, he's a compassionate person who wants to help people. My hope flickers a bit brighter.

"We can't locate the half-breeds that disappeared months ago," I continue. "Most weren't part of the mafia but paid for protection from cops patrolling neutral zones, gangs, or smaller factions outside the main families."

His brows scrunch together. "I thought the human mobs—"

"I can't give full details, but the Underground Mafia keeps them in line."

"By letting those bastards do what they want? They *are* my jurisdiction; do you know how much death they cause—?"

"They'd cause more if it wasn't for the Blood Mafia and Wolf Mob." His eyes narrow as I debate what amount of information I can share to get him to trust me without losing trust in the families. "It gets complicated with the politics, especially when you factor in each Paranormal society that plays a role in how the Underground Mafia operates. The Blood Mafia and Wolf Mob are good at keeping smaller mobs in line from doing more harm already, but we can't get rid of them completely; rats always find a way back to the surface. Without the Underground, the mob *you* have to deal with would be worse."

"They don't work with the human mobs?"

"Not how you may think." His head tilts. I won't rat out the Underground Mafia, but I'd throw the human mobs into the Hudson in a heartbeat. Or for a stick of gum. "You know the DiNardi family?"

"As in Antoni DiNardi?"

"He attempted to blow up four police precincts four years ago. Wolf Mob stopped them, while the Blood Mafia made assets disappear. DiNardi got greedy, and the Paranormals put him back into his place. Human and Paranormal mobs are mostly acquaintances, but the humans learn to stay in their lanes or they'll get a visit."

"From whom?"

I smile mischievously. "We both know I don't need to tell you that."

Drauper lets out a long breath and takes a moment to think, scratching the top of his head as his brow furrows. "Why are you telling me all this? Because you think the human mobs took those half-breeds?"

"Doubt it; they're not that dumb." Usually.

"Black market or slave trade, then?"

"Still cold."

"You say you need my help but have nothing to go off of. I thought you said you knew who was behind all the disappearances?"

I take a tentative step toward him. "You know parts of Topside I don't and have connections in the NYPD and other agencies. I can't get that, but I know the Underground."

Drauper steps closer, cocking his head to the side. "Who's behind all this?"

People pass us on their cellphones walking their dogs, and I wait before they're gone to say, "They're someone I may not be able to stop on my own."

"What does that mean?"

"He's human; under your jurisdiction."

His brows raise. "Who?"

Now comes the tricky part: I have no proof that it's Traloski who took those people, which is why I'm stalling. All I have is a disgruntled bio dad, a shit ton of ghouls that appeared from nowhere, and messed-up routes. My Velma Dinkley hunch is that a mad scientist convinced someone to help steal half-breeds off the streets to start a war between NYPD and the Underground Mafia by using the ghouls. I've heard theories more stable about Shakespeare's sexuality than this.

"Who is it?" Drauper asks again, and my face scrunches, trying to think of a way to explain.

I take a deep breath in, wishing for a bottle of whiskey as I throw out my idea. "Would you believe me if I said your theory about ghouls being brought in to hide shit is correct, but for Dr. Frankenstein's newest experiments?" I'm not proud of the octave my voice reaches as his brows raise in surprise. "Look, I know I don't have any proof I'm right or how the ghouls play into this—"

"Clearly."

"*But*," I say, narrowing my eyes. "I *do* know the mafia had nothing to do with it, and neither did the NYPD, PSB, or NIIA."

"How do you already know about the other agencies?"

"You have your contacts; I have mine," I smirk, and he scowls at me.

"Right," Drauper grumbles under his breath as he paces.

I exhale harshly, feeling exhausted and wanting another coffee. Realizing the tired sensation, I quickly flick it away. What felt like simple reasoning in my head sounded crazy as fuck out loud. And the ticking clock in the back of my mind isn't helping.

"Does this *Dr. Frankenstein* work for someone?" He asks.

"He might," I shrug.

Drauper looks at me and purses his lips. "Okay. You gonna tell me *his* name?"

"Depends. You gonna help?" I quirk a brow.

"If it means finding those people and saving others from the same fate, then yes. But I'm doing this because it's my *job* to protect. Nothing more."

"Which is why I came to you; *you* give a damn."

Drauper watches me a moment, then steps closer and talks under his breath. "Look, my superiors told me to back off after what happened in the South Bronx and threatened my badge. I got a lot of heat for almost *ruining* a federal operation. They said PSB was handling everything, but from what you're telling me, they aren't, and now we have *no one* patrolling there. There's definitely something going on."

"We agree we're both right, in some sense?"

"Sure."

"Gee, your enthusiasm is overwhelming."

"I'm not gonna jump for joy over people being taken."

"How about imagining revenge? That always helps me sleep at night."

He places his hands on his hips. "You're gonna be like this the entire time, aren't you?"

"You missed it, admit it," I smirk.

Drauper's expression softens, and I see a glimmer of my old friend again. "What do we look for then...*Scooby?*"

I smirk and nod, "Look up 'John Traloski.' He was in the Bronx twenty years ago in the medical field. Maybe there were human disappearances during that time. You'll have better luck finding any reports since you can access them. Only problem is we don't know where this fucker is now. He could be anywhere in the city or just outside state lines to cover his tracks."

"You want me to find anything that could link him to the disappearances? If it *is* him?"

I know it's Traloski deep in my gut; there's too many coincidences to ignore that lineup. A memory crosses my mind of burns, scalpels, and screaming. The thought of him putting more people through that makes me nauseous, my facial scars pulsing from faded memories. I run my hand through my hair to calm myself, concentrating on the luscious trees nearby. "It's him, Drauper. I know it is."

He nods. "What are you gonna look for? If we're gonna be a team, I need to know what you find, too."

"I'll check my contacts for any recent disappearances in the Underground. You see if any reports show up for Traloski from twenty years ago and if Paranormal beings were involved. Both of us should check in with friends who do patrols of any kind, see if there's *anything* that's fishy."

"And the ghouls? Do you have a contact to look into them?"

I snort loudly in amusement and shake my head. A half-breed with a ghoul contact? Even I'm not *that* good. "Whoever finds something first on them buys the other a double shot of whiskey, the good shit. Deal?"

"Deal." He puts his sunglasses on and adjusts them. "I'm not helping because we're friends, by the way. I give a damn about those people."

I don't give a retort as he turns, walking down the path. I watch him disappear around the bend before I press the speed dial on my phone, hoping he's awake.

"How'd it go, sweet cheeks?" Vinny asks on the other end.

"He agreed. That's something."

"Hates you, huh?"

"I can practically smell it on him," I say as I walk in the opposite direction Drauper left.

"Don't need to like each other to achieve an end goal, should know that from Rodney and me, sweet cheeks."

"Yeah..."

Vinny sighs, and fabrics shuffle in the background. "Look, I don't trust the human, but I won't pretend you two used to have a...*friendship* at one point. It hurts to lose that, no matter how short it may have been."

"You can't just let me pretend I'm fine?"

"Not how *this* relationship works," he says as I scoff. "And you'll stew on it."

"Will not."

"Will, too."

I groan in defeat. "You know what? Go to bed, bloodsucker. It's late, and you need your beauty sleep. You're getting crow's feet."

"This is your sleepy time now, too, sweet cheeks, and since you finished your meeting, you should come down and warm this bed. We both know you jumpstart my cold, dead heart."

"Careful how you talk about my Mate," I say, smiling over the phone.

"You say it all the time."

"I earned it, that's why."

"How so?"

"Years of sexual frustration." I hang up on him, heading for a smaller Underground Entrance. I'm all wound up, which means I'm off to my other favorite place besides Vinny's bed.

Drink
Water

- Vinny
xoxo

CHAPTER 10
DAEMONS AREN'T A GIRL'S BEST FRIEND

"Slipping back into old habits, Little Sister?" Beckham greets me as I walk into *The Vault*. I already smell the peppermint tea brewing, along with brambleberry. He's either having a late night or somehow knew I was coming down. For my dwindling sanity, I'm saying late night.

"Thought I'd make up for lost hours," I say.

Beckham laughs low, and his golden eyes gleam, assessing me carefully. "You're not here to work, are you?"

"Researching counts, right?" I ask, leaning over the counter with a grin. "Let's be honest, Beckham; you don't really need my help. You've got enough people, I'm not needed."

"Ah, that's where you're wrong. You're quite the useful being," he muses, gracefully handing me a mug of peppermint tea. "And you'll always have a position here if you so choose when the time comes."

"One day, my dream of being a stripping librarian will come true," I say and sip the warm beverage. He chuckles.

"What are we investigating today, my little librarian?"

Before I can go forward with anything, Drauper needs to find what Topside has on Traloski, Vinny needs time to get information through the Blood Mafia, and Rodney's ass won't be up for hours to speak to. While I play the waiting game, I can try my hand at another puzzle to figure out—why Traloski chose daemons for his experiments or why daemons worked with him at all.

"What sections cover daemon lore and history?"

Beckham tilts his head, looking up as his long white hair falls over his shoulders across his pale green skin. Humming to himself, he steps toward a catalog machine and flicks a few buttons. He speaks with a faint smile, showing his pointed teeth. "My library is one of the last places with accurate descriptions of daemons. If you wish to understand the capacities of medical experiments on daemons and their societies, may I suggest the third floor, second aisle to the right? There are braille materials as well for any recorded historical references pertaining to cultural rules if you wish to practice your reading."

Times like these I'm glad he thinks of me as a granddaughter slash protégé.

"Are you implying I'm slacking in my studies?" I ask, picking up my mug to walk upstairs.

"You? Slacking? I'd be disappointed and surprised to hear such things, Little Sister."

"Between you and Pops, I don't know who I'd hate disappointing more."

He chuckles deeply. "I doubt Alanzo would ever feel disappointment with his favorite child."

"Don't tell my brothers that. They'll complain for the next decade," I joke, and my stomach twists. *If I'm here for that.* "I'll practice my braille; my contacts need to come out anyway. These new ones are irritating."

I walk up the spiral stairs silently, and his voice carries up to me, "Daemons are tenacious with their own agendas. Be careful listening to the words of a desperate being."

I pause and look down, finding him gone from his seat. I shudder before continuing up. There's something ethereally eerie with beings who reach past a thousand years, which makes them dangerous—a warning Beckham himself gave me when I was young. I'll stick to just reading about them.

I enter the third floor and follow his instructions to the section I'm looking for. I set up camp at one of the reading areas with a stack of books containing daemon myths, anthropologies, literature, and historical recounting. My favorite kind of research.

I place a stack of braille books next to me for whenever my eyes decide to give in, move my gun around, take my seat, and settle in with my tea. Scanning over the materials, I suddenly regret not prying further into their history during my masters when I focused on vampires. All the main Paranormal Species of the Noctis Immortalis have enough information to keep anyone busy for decades. I review, remembering snippets of history and literature.

Daemons are solitary beings who remain in their own private communities, only becoming receptive to mixed breeding in the last century. For generations, they wanted to keep within their own kind, developing the well-known tradition of stealing away anyone with daemon blood in the 16th century. In 1835, the treaty that protects Paranormals from inhumane procedures was enacted. The NIIA wasn't created until the 1850s, so the treaty wasn't well enforced in the beginning, but shortly after being founded, the NIIA created neutral cities, the Underground, and neutral zones under their watch for Paranormal safety. It wasn't enough for the daemons, though. Humans and Paranormals struggled to get along, but daemons barely gave humans a chance to change. Their distrust was deeply rooted in the genocide that almost wiped them out in the late 15th century across Europe and Asia and the abuse that followed.

I put down the history book, pull my hair back into a messy bun, and grab a book on Paranormal abilities, skimming through the historical accounts of powerful daemons, vampires, and werewolves. Daemons are considered the third most powerful species, with long sharp titanium claws that extend out of their knuckles or fingertips, strong feathered wings, and the ability to create lightning or fire in their hands. There's some literature describing a daemon who could control blood by contorting the liquid into a solidified shape like a whip or chain from their wrist. My *Paranormal Genetics and Biology* professor had a theory that the daemon was half vampire, the first to be known with combined abilities, but it was never proven.

Yet out of all the Noctis Immortalis, daemons resemble humans the most, the only trait differentiating them being their ever-present wings. They prefer open skies, and the Underground isn't exactly a great place for flyers, which is why any daemon sightings are usually in mountain ranges in Africa, Canada, or the Swiss Alps. Places far away from humans. Wings or not, their biogenetics may be why Traloski and other scientists consistently used them in experiments. I can't blame daemons for hating humans, but then again, they hate everyone. Ghouls may be classist, but daemons are vengeful.

My fingers trail over lines recounting wars between daemons, vampires, and werewolves. All three are considered the most powerful within the Noctis Immortalis, and a war between them could be catastrophic. I don't even want to think about adding a furious incubus to the mix. I set the book aside, pulling my thoughts away from that outcome and concentrating on the pieces of the puzzle so far.

Edgar said he spent years looking for me and my siblings, which lines up with typical daemon behavior. He could be the last of his community, trying to rebuild it with his own bloodline. Maybe that's why he worked with Traloski, in hopes of rebuilding a community he lost by spawning his own through the program. I pick up another book, staring at the cover about daemon lore, and my gaze narrows at the sketching of daemon claws. Edgar's full daemon; it should be ingrained in him to steer clear of medical professionals, especially humans. If working with Traloski was a last-ditch effort to preserve his bloodline, then where were the other daemons?

I trace a finger over the etchings, the faces of my siblings flashing over my mind and the way Edgar wouldn't let go of the newspaper clippings. Vengeful. What would a daemon do if they went against everything they knew to recreate their blood-line, only to discover their children would be short-lived and left to die? Or that they forfeit daemon traditions?

My stomach twists as I place the book down, rubbing at my chest as the pit of my stomach feels like lead. Something isn't right about this and I'm missing a piece. I could set aside my pride and ask Edgar, but a sick feeling wards me away from that idea. A headache forms, and I decide to take out my contacts and trash them, blinking a few times, I lean back in my chair and sigh in relief. I sit comfortably a few minutes, but then my phone rings loudly. I fumble to pick it up and answer groggily, "Hello?"

"Drinking already?" Drauper asks over the phone. "It's not even 5PM yet."

"Then it's not even 5AM down here," I grumble as I lay back down on the couch.

"Right. Time difference," he says. "How did you deal with that before?"

"Caffeine, naps, and tinted glasses." My glasses were good for two-fold: blindness and dark circles.

"Explains a bit." Watch it, detective, I've got vamp and I'm not afraid to use him. "You awake enough to hear what I found?"

"That quickly? Your detective skills are better than I remember, Shaggy."

"Choose a new nickname," he warns.

"Alright," I clear my throat. "Your detective skills are better than I remember, *Sherlock*."

He scoffs, "Better. You want this intel or not?"

"It's late, give me a break," I mumble. I think I hear a breath of laughter, but my mind might be playing tricks on me. "*Yes, I'm awake enough.*"

"There's nothing on Traloski. I'm checking other sources, but you sure he's still around? Seems like he's just...gone." Traloski's apparently a magician, too.

"Either he's back, or someone's continuing his work."

"Copycat?"

"Or apprentice."

"Even worse."

"Only a theory, which is better than nothing since all we have left are ghouls living in the Bronx. Vanished people aren't great leads." Drauper scoffs and I glare at the bright thing in my hands. "What? You think vanished people *are* good leads?"

"For a moment, I thought they were."

"Is your contact the Grim Reaper? Because most vanished people turn up dead, statistically."

"Or undead."

"Excuse me?"

He sighs into the phone. "The ghouls are gone, Brenda."

"What do you mean gone?" I ask, sitting up, and nearly knocking over my tea.

"Meaning...gone."

"Like gone, *gone*?"

"Yup, gone."

Okay, *this* little game is getting annoying. "When?"

"I was looking into recent arrests by NYPD for those that crossed the zone line, and the latest report says they're gone. All of them. Those apartments are empty, and I double-checked with some buddies who patrol just east of the South Bronx." I hear a door shut, and city noise from Topside rises. He gets quiet. Great sign. "Rumor is the Wolf Mob took out the ghouls for reassurance. No more info than that. I called a buddy at PSB who said don't worry about it. 'No ghouls, no problems.' So, I thought it's a little odd they disappeared around the same time *you* came around asking questions about someone who may have planted them there."

"Okay, so the Grim Reaper isn't your contact," I breathe out. "I'll ask around down here. Stay away from the Bronx, just in case, even if it was fun the first time."

"I worry about your idea of fun."

"Not the only one. Thanks for the update." My voice softens while my mind goes reeling. How do almost two hundred ghouls just disappear?

"Brenda?"

"Yeah?"

"You really didn't know about them?"

"No," I whisper. "They may seem creepy, smell bad, and hate half-breeds, but that doesn't mean I want them to...I mean, I don't think..."

"Yeah," he says softly. "Their society is protective, right? And have a hive mind person...being? Maybe that's who decided they needed to leave."

I quirk a brow. He remembered. "Not wrong, and something to keep in mind."

"I'll call tomorrow if I find more. And maybe...get some sleep." He hangs up and I drop the phone onto the table.

My mind races from the new intel, and the fact Drauper *actually* remembered what I told him about the ghouls months ago. Exhaustion swarms me as I text Rodney for a meet-up soon before I fall onto the couch completely, covering my eyes with my arm trying to think, but fall asleep instead.

B*right light.*

Crimson stains the walls, dripping with thick liquid. Leather straps hold me in a chair as I scream, my voice hoarse as needles prod into my skin. More and more the light becomes brighter. Harsher. My screams echo into the bright void. Horror caught in my throat.

Another prick. Blood continues down the walls.

Pain travels through my veins as I pull at the leather straps.

*Not again. **Please** not again.*

Not this kind of red.

Familiar crimson eyes hover above me. The flash of fangs crosses my gaze, and I feel hope. And then I turn cold.

It's not his eyes.

It's not his hands on my throat.

Not his fangs ripping into my vein.

It's not his scent.

It's not—

*"I warned you…**whore**."*

DARK SPICES, bloodlust, and coffee swallow my senses, pulling me from the nightmare.

I reach for my gun, snapping it into place as I aim in the direction of the scent, clicking the safety off. My eyes remain closed, knowing I won't be able to see him without contacts or glasses anyways. I click my tongue and move the gun a half-inch left. "Damn it," I mutter.

"Not bad for waking up," Vinny says, moving toward me. "But I know you can hit my heart easier than that."

"Hand over the coffee or I try with a bigger gun." I click the safety back on.

"Then you'll spill it."

"True. A causality not worth losing." I put the gun away.

"Especially since I made it with love for you."

"Aw, you're disgustingly sweet. Quit it." He hands me the mug and sits beside me. "What's the time?"

"Seven."

"Underground morning?"

"Yup."

"Fuck," I grumble. One nap and a horrible nightmare, great. And I lost time reading.

"Maybe not now." Vinny drapes an arm around my shoulders, and I allow myself to lean back into his warmth. The coffee is perfect as I moan, taking another drink. "Meant it, sweet cheeks," he says shifting beside me. "I don't want to know what Beckham will do if he finds me deep inside you amongst his books."

"Then don't make this nectar of the gods that could make me forget my name."

"Apart from other ways?"

"You just said not now."

"Well, now you've piqued my interest."

"You're insatiable."

"Coming from the one who jumped me last week in my office."

"You were wearing your leather jacket."

"So?" He hums, taking a sip of his coffee.

I smack him lightly. "*Only* your jacket, you fucking tease."

"It worked," he smirks, and picks up one of the books I stacked. He flips it over as I hold my coffee close. "Daemons?"

I shrug. "Thought it might help."

"I doubt you'll find why your father is a wretched fucker from these," he mumbles, putting the book back.

We sit silently as I let the warmth of him comfort me, trying to forget the nightmare. My body shivers at the thought of waking up alone again, covered in a cold sweat and choked breathing. Damn those nights sucked. I bring myself closer to him as he slowly trails a finger down one of my facial scars.

"What was the nightmare?" He asks, and I shake my head. "Sweetheart, don't keep it bottled up."

"Am not." He lets out a long sigh and takes away my coffee. "Give me back my 'anti-murdery juicy-juice!'"

Vinny ignores me, putting our mugs down and pulls me

onto his lap. I straddle him with my hands on his shoulders and keep my eyes closed. Once I see his eyes, I'm done for. I wait for him to urge me to look at him and ask again what's wrong. Suddenly, his lips press against mine tenderly. I ease at the gentle touch, falling into the kiss as he strokes my back with care. My thoughts slip away as he kisses me, and the nightmare and fears dissipate into smoke. It's just us.

We're fine. He's mine. Bruno can't take him. None of them can.

I pull him closer, my tongue tracing his lips as I clutch the back of his head. The kiss deepens, turning into something needy and bruising with want. Vinny wraps his arms around me, his embrace almost making me unravel. He pulls away, breathing heavily as he catches a tear running down my cheek then kisses where it was. Damn it.

I whisper, "You were gone...."

"I'm right here, sweetheart."

"I couldn't get to you."

"I'm not going anywhere." I bury my head into his neck and shoulder, inhaling his scent as he holds me close and caresses my back. A few minutes go by, and I take a deep breath in, the last of the worry leaving me. For now.

"I really hate nightmares," I mumble.

"More than decaf?"

"More than decaf."

"I don't blame you."

"Do you ever get them?" He nods. "What about?"

"You being gone."

"Aren't we a fucking pair." I laugh lightly as he pulls me back to kiss briefly. A smile slowly spreads on my face.

"Feel better?" He asks, and I nod, finally opening my eyes to see a mixture of blues, greens, and deep violets. His bright, ruby eyes shine clearly in the mess of colors. "What are best friends for?"

"Coffee, sleepovers, and terrible jokes," I say, and he snorts.

"And coming with me to meet with the Wolf Mob to see what the fuck happened to two hundred ghouls."

Vinny stares at me and groans, trying to hide his laughter. "We get Mated, and already you're trying to give me a heart attack."

PUPPY
CHOW
→
THAT WAY

CHAPTER 11
SIN CITY GOT NOTHING ON GHOULS

"Any way I can separate you two? You're starting to smell like him," Rodney grumbles as I go to hug him.

"Watch it, McLycan," Vinny growls. "You're the one who stinks up the entire block when you're wet."

"Stand in the sun and tell me that." Rodney gives me a full hug and places a kiss on my head. Vinny lets out a threatening snarl as Rodney whispers in my ear, "He's worse than usual."

"Not fucking deaf."

"Vinny, calm down before I shoot you again," I warn the vampire. My bloodsucker pulls back his fangs and folds his arms over his chest as he looks back at his closest guards, Samuel and Matty. Last thing we need is others discovering our secret because he's getting territorial. Again.

We're a few blocks away from the community center I investigated with Drauper weeks ago. The apartments are empty, along with the rest of the area, cleared out an hour ago by the Wolf Mob the only noise being the distant sound of cars, taxis, and sirens. Rodney arrived with his crew, including my two faves, Marcus and Gunther with werewolves positioned further down the street, much like their vampire counterparts across the street.

Two major mafia bosses meeting on Topside is enough to warrant that kind of firepower, and the weapons hiding under their jackets. They only play nice because of me. Otherwise, I'd shoot them in the leg, which I have *officially* done to both.

I look back at Rodney, taking off my glasses to clean, and ask, "What's the stitch?"

He rumbles a low noise in the back of his throat, his scent of pine and whiskey intensifies, and his hackles rise. "The ghouls in the Underground are still there. Marcus confirmed they weren't with the group on Top."

"I thought you said in the elevator they came together?" I ask Vinny, referring to our conversation coming to Topside.

He lifts his hands and walks toward me, keeping at arms length away from Rodney. The closeness prompts all the were-wolves to twitch for their guns. "I told you what Joey and another shifter told me. Unless you're lying, Kujo," Vinny accuses Rodney.

"Careful, Dracultelli," Rodney rumbles. "No one knew the Topside ghouls from our side. We heard rumors they'd be moving again, but in late autumn. We didn't know they left until lil sis contacted me."

"I know routes shifted," I say. "What about neighborhood watches on the outskirts of zones? Did they see the ghouls then?"

"No," he replies shortly.

"No, there aren't watches there anymore, or no, they didn't see them?"

Rodney adjusts his stance. "I don't think that info—"

"Fucks sake, Rodney! You *both* know each other's territories through the city. Stop acting like fucking children and play nice, or I'm shaving your fucking body. And *you*," I threaten, pointing at Vinny smirking beside me. "I will tie you up under the sun and see how long you last without aloe!"

"I didn't say anything!" Vinny protests.

"Good. Stay that way, *Lestat*," Rodney grumbles, and Vinny snarls.

I pull my gun out, waving it between the two of them. "Seriously, play nice or no *playdates* for the next month. Got it? Get your heads out of your asses and act like damn responsible bosses."

I've had enough of their testosterone boasting for one night, and it's only been five minutes.

Guards move toward us and draw out their weapons, halting when their bosses snarl at them in warning. Rodney and Vinny silently glare at each other until Rodney looks at me, and says, "I get four brunch dates this month."

"*Donny's* or the Underground Waffle House?" I ask, putting my gun away.

"Both." Rodney cocks his head at Vinny. "And I'll work with the Twilight reject *nicely* if your next birthday celebration is at *Mountain Edge*."

My stomach sinks, but I don't betray my expression. I flit my gaze to Vinny, whose scent gets stronger, and I poke him in the arm. "Deal," I say, and Vinny grumbles in protest. Rodney smirks and turns, gesturing for us to follow him toward the center with Marcus and Gunther beside him.

I jab my elbow into Vinny's side as we follow with Samuel and Matty close behind. Vinny lightly punches my shoulder as I growl at him, shoving him again. He growls back and mumbles, "I don't like sharing."

"No shit. Behave, or I'll shoot you. Again."

"Will it be foreplay like last time?" He smirks.

"If you play nicely, bloodsucker, maybe you'll get candy this time."

We snicker, and Rodney complains from ahead. "How are you two worse than usual?"

"You find me adorable," I answer.

"Only when you're not around him," Rodney comments. "I only tolerate his presence for you, lil sis."

"I thought it was for my *charming* personality," Vinny smirks.

Rodney grumbles as we cross a street. The scent of muddy water, sewage, and trash invades my nostrils. I slow my pace as the others move on, staring at the empty street, recognizing the eerie quiet, similar to that night. I inhale harshly as the memory flashes of screams and gunshots ring in my ears, my skin crawling as I absentmindedly rub the invisible leather straps on my wrists.

"Baby sis?" Samuel asks. I blink, looking ahead to find the others have stopped. Samuel is beside me with his hand on my shoulder. "You good?"

"Yeah," I respond hoarsely, shrugging Samuel's hand off as I walk toward the center and catch a glimpse of Vinny and Rodney sharing a look. "Not waiting on you," I say, moving past them, smelling the heightened scent of bloodlust and pine.

Rodney clears his throat, moving to keep up with me. "We cleared out completely, including neighborhood watches. No point in staying. Ask Dracultelli; he's probably done the same. Easier to move closer to Brooklyn, away from any frequent patrols. That's why we didn't notice the ghouls were gone."

"You, too?" I ask Vinny.

He shrugs. "Basically."

"The human mobs move too?"

"They're sticking to Queens, Staten Island, and the Upper Bronx," Rodney says. "After that shitshow sting, they want nothing to do with this place."

"Two hundred ghouls disappear and no one notices?" I ask, as we stop outside the front of the abandoned center covered in trash and grime. It stinks worse than a bad orgy of wet werewolves and drunk humans slathered in lube, and we all gag a bit from the rancid smell.

Nothing like leftover ghoul in the morning.

"I thought those things could hide their stench," Gunther groans.

"At least take it with them," Samuel adds.

"Those *things* can't control it even if they tried, not their fault," I snap. "Get bit and see how it feels."

Both stiffen as I walk up to pull on the locked doors. My memory flashes again from the last chaotic encounter here and the knot tightens in my stomach as shivers travel down my spine. I take a deep breath, realizing it does smell worse than the usual ghoul leftover. "Any way inside?" I ask.

"With me," Vinny says. "Want me to go in rough or with tender care?"

I roll my eyes at him. "I want you in and out quickly."

"Never said that before, sweet cheeks," he murmurs, running a thumb under my chin as he passes me. His guards protest, but he holds up his other hand. "I'll be fine. I'm the only one with a key," he brags, and disappears through the doors.

"By the rings of hell, he annoys me," Rodney murmurs beside me. "Why'd you betray me like this again?"

"Really? We going there?" I say, crossing my arms and keeping on high alert toward the closed doors. I try to concentrate past my mind screaming that Vinny shouldn't be in there. Either the stench is getting to me or something else is very wrong right now.

"I mean, I'm not really surprised with how he's looked after you all these years, especially when you moved to Topside. He was a complete whiny sore-ass during your college days." Rodney scoffs.

"Careful, McLycan," Samuel warns. "He may be inside, but we're not."

"Oh, fuck off, vamp," Rodney says. "He wasn't boss yet back then, and he was a belligerent pain in the ass." I punch him in the arm, and out of instinct, Marcus warns me with a growl. Rodney snarls at him before nudging my shoulder with his. "All I'm saying is *someone* needed to keep him in line."

"Like Balto over here?" I catch a glimpse of Marcus rearing

back his teeth, but I just smile back. He's an alpha like Rodney, but his instincts are to immediately obey the alpha of the pack, AKA the Wolf Boss, Rodney, which means automatically responding to anyone touching him disrespectfully. The responses I get are similar to warning a "pup" for misbehaving, which is something I've perfected. "And no one controls Vinny."

"But he listens to *you*. Probably more now since, well, you got *closer*." Rodney roughs up my hair, and I swat at him.

He has no idea how much Vinny may listen to me now. Mating is coveted for all Paranormals, and Claim Mating is a step up, where my word to Vinny can be law. Except, our power dynamic isn't technically balanced, there are some pureblood genes in Vinny that even as a Mate I may not be able to influence. Here's hoping we never have to find out.

Vinny returns, choking out some coughs as he rubs his hand over his mouth and nose. "They're dead," he reports, shaking his head.

"How long before they wake up?" Rodney asks.

"No, like dead, *dead*. Most of their skin has rotted off into puddles, hair fallen away, and limbs look chewed off. Never seen anything like that, and there's brown sludge everywhere," Vinny says in disgust.

"Thought ghouls decomposed like humans," Gunther comments.

"They're supposed to," I answer.

"Must be why it smells worse than the dump and sewer combined," Samuel says. "How many bodies, boss?"

"Couple dozen," Vinny answers. "Maybe more further into the building. Bodies are just everywhere."

"They wouldn't leave their own here," I whisper. Ghouls have specific funeral rites when one passes completely, and it includes fire. If those inside were part of a singular hive mind, turned from the same bite line, no way would they have been left like this. "Could they have been here during the sting?"

Everyone's scent dampens, and there's a slight hush across the group. Marcus gives a deep-throated snarl while Vinny moves his gaze to the center, back to me, and answers, "No. Freshly dead, two weeks tops. Longer than that, and they'd look worse."

"Could someone be trying to hide the rest of the ghouls by fouling up the trail with this stench?" Samuel asks. "Or would they just leave the bodies behind?"

"It's not normal for them to do that," I say. "And it shouldn't smell this bad, even being completely dead."

"Shit, then this all points to them going Feral," Rodney snarls, and the guards all murmur in unease as my stomach knots in fear.

There's not much difference between a human or Paranormal snapping from reality, Paranormals just have a name for it.

A Paranormal turns Feral when they have a total psychotic breakdown and lose all sense of self. Vampires turn to their most basic nature draining beings dry, ripping apart anything with blood in its veins, dead or alive. Werewolves turn rabid, foaming at the mouth and becoming more carnivorous. Incubi and succubi turn towns into orgies and make *any* species do unspeakable things, not just sexual. Daemons rampage and become almost impossible to kill due to their claws and powers. As for ghouls, those zombie films got their inspiration from something. Entire countries have quarantined in the past due to Feral ghouls—another reason why people don't like them in cities. Feral ghouls lead to ghoul outbreaks.

"We need to clear out the area. *Completely*," Rodney states.

"By at least twelve blocks, and make sure there aren't any ghouls roaming," Vinny adds.

"What about inside the center?" Marcus asks.

"In a few days, they'll rot into nothing. Might as well leave them and let the smell keep people away until there's nothing left of them. We'll find a way to burn them when its safe. PSB could still be watching, and we don't need them making this worse by coming down here." Vinny gestures toward Samuel, who walks up with phone already in hand.

Rodney turns toward his crew. "Gunther, set up a perimeter. Won't be hard with how much it's already cleared out." They head off as Vinny passes me with Samuel at his side.

Back to square one, no, *worse* than that. Instead of having a lead, there's only more dead bodies. I rub my head as questions fill it. How did they die? Where are the others? Why leave them behind, even if they were Feral? Ghouls usually kill off the Feral ones; they're undead, not dumb. If they left due to dry weather from the summer, we would've heard something, especially through Pops and Joey if they moved out of the city.

A drifting scent of oil passes by, and an idea sparks as I look down the road where I first saw Edgar—the young ghoul. *They* were looking for half-breeds. Drauper thought the ghouls could have been taking the half-breeds, but what if they were disappearing *with* them?

I turn back to the others when an unfamiliar scent of burning flesh and gunpowder slithers under my nose. Safeties click off, and there's a scratching noise as I yell, "Vin—!"

Vinny slams me to the ground as shots ring out, and I smell blood. A deep guttural growl rips from him, "*Stay.*" He runs off among the shots, destruction unfolding around me.

I hear Rodney and his crew shift into hybrid forms, limbs tearing as bones snap and break with the scent of old blood invading my nose. They're fighting ghouls. *Dozens* of them.

Snarls rip out as rancid fluids hit the pavement. I stand focusing on the chaos around me that shifts with darkened colors and shapes, using sounds to count the over four dozen ghouls coming from the shadows smelling half-decomposed, bitten recently. Vinny growls, and I hear two ghoul heads get ripped off and tossed to the ground.

Firearms echo with growls, anger rising under my skin as the smell of fresh blood swarms me. I inhale the spilled liquid and recognize the scent, looking down at the sticky substance on my fingers where I held onto Vinny.

They shot Vinny. They *shot* my Mate.

Something snaps inside me as fury rips through my veins. Ghouls scream and hiss as they attack the others, aiming for the mob bosses. Pulling my gun out, I sprint towards them and aim. I place two shots into a ghoul's chest and find my next target as a ghoul launches towards Vinny's back. They hit the ground when my bullets find them, and I shoot another aiming for my Mate, then quickly reload and unload into two more ghouls.

Adrenaline pushes me as I body slam a ghoul to the ground, and they sink their teeth into my skin. I loosen an infuriated scream, twisting and shooting the ghoul in the chest three times. I quickly grab my other gun and hit another ghoul headed for Samuel. As I try to stand, another pair of teeth sink into my shoulder. Anger drives through my veins, and I turn silently to glare at the wide-eyed ghoul gnawing on my shoulder.

"Nice try," I say. The barrel of my gun goes to its head, and I blast it. I shake my left arm as the venom passes through, and a headache forms. I'm overwhelmed by the aroma of rancid blood, hearing the crunch of bones, and tearing of muscles, pain trickles into my system. I focus past the throbbing as another ghoul approaches my left, and I shoot without looking, hearing them slump to the ground.

A groan escapes me as I fall hard to my knees, the gun clattering from my hand as my body starts to burn and the headache worsens. It smells like a sewage plant erupted, and I puke all over the sidewalk, my body fighting off the venom surging through my veins.

Vinny is suddenly beside me. "Fucking hell...I told you to stay."

"*You can't get bit; I can,*" I growl in Noctora. I'm in pain, but the rage still kicks at every fiber of my being. *"They almost bit you."*

His hand moves across my back as another round of hurling takes over. I shudder and groan as my head pounds. I focus on breathing and inhale the familiar scent of dark spices and bloodlust; our Mating aroma spilled on the ground. My jaw clacks open in a silent snarl, and my hands fist at my side, feeling like knives are pushing through my knuckles. Fury comes back full force, and I growl lethally, *"They made you bleed."*

"Breathe," Vinny hushes, stilling beside me. I hear the clink of two bullets falling to the ground beside us, the distance of the sound informing me they were the ones in his back. His hand caresses me as I puke again, moaning as I inhale deeply the scent of his blood.

I suddenly remember the first time I smelled Vinny's blood, memorizing the aroma as I had with others—each unique like coffee, whiskey, or perfume. Bruno had sliced Vinny's face in front of me with two long gashes across it like mine, except he healed without scars in minutes. I was fifteen the first time I saw his face drenched in his own crimson blood.

Another defensive snarl tears from my throat as I dig my nails into the pavement beneath me. The sound is louder than last, and I feel two beings still nearby.

"Take care of this mess," Vinny orders someone as he grabs me. "She's been bitten and will have aftereffects for hours."

"Take care of her, Dracultelli!" Rodney yells after us.

"When have I not?" Vinny warns, carrying me away from the others.

I inhale the scent of his blood again and continue to snarl deeply. What the hell is wrong with me? *"Vinny,"* I groan.

"Right here, sweetheart."

"What's...why am I...?"

"Hold on." He signals someone once we reach a vehicle, and he sets me inside, taking off my glasses. He gets in next, laying

me across his lap as the doors slam shut and the car gets moving. Vinny keeps his arm around me, holding me close as I try to clear my nostrils from the putrid scent and bloodshed. My head throbs as my body shivers, and I still can't speak in fucking English.

"*What's wrong…with me?*" I ask weakly.

"*Welcome to what I go through most days,*" he whispers in my ear, putting up the divider between the driver and us as the car swerves into a spiral toward the Underground. "It may be a side effect of Claim Mating," he switches to English.

"*I turn into you?*"

"You always joke about me being territorial. Sometimes I can't help it; genetics of being a pureblood."

"*Excuses,*" I groan as my stomach churns. "*Never heard of it for mixed Mating.*"

"Because it's rare, such as you snarling like a vampire," he says, brushing back my hair as I go still. "I didn't tell you about it because it shouldn't be possible. I've heard of it happening to normal vampires, even shifters, but not for half-breeds, and you're dormant."

"*Daemons are territorial….*"

"Not enough to rip into other ghouls for their Mate bleeding; *that's* a pureblood vampire response." Fuck, he's right. "Reverting to Noctora may be a sign your daemon side may not be as dormant as we thought."

I shudder and feel a cold sweat move over my body. My eyesight darkens, and his ruby eyes start to fade from my vision. Shit. I touch his face gently, and ask, "*Mating may awaken my dormant side?*"

"You shouldn't be this reactive, sweetheart. Then again, it is *you,*" he scoffs lightly.

I attempt to jab my elbow into his side, and he kisses my head gently. I hum at the contact as the anger that raged inside me trickles away. Damn it, I'm gonna turn to putty in his hands, and he's never gonna let me live it down.

My eyesight finally goes, leaving me in complete darkness. *"Eyesight is gone."*

Vinny swears under his breath. "And now I have to explain to your parents why their daughter was bitten by ghouls... again."

I laugh and hold onto his shirt. *"Remind Ma you're her favorite."*

CHAPTER 12
KITCHEN OF SECRETS

"Keep still, baby," Ma says, checking my shoulder bite in the kitchen while Pops, Vinny, and Joey talk in the living room. I brace myself as she begins to stitch up the larger wound. Damn ghoul tried to chew on me like a piece of jerky. At the time, it didn't seem so bad, but adrenaline can do that to you.

My parents were just short of livid when Vinny brought me home. Pops almost threw Vinny into a stripper's pole, prompted by Ricky's shriek in horror at the sight of Vinny carrying me through *Unbound*.

I hold my head as Ma stitches my skin together and wince as the needle goes through my skin again. Ma massages my arm, and whispers, "You should've learned the first time."

I swallow hard, unsure what to tell her because I don't have the heart to confess the real reason. I also promised Pops I wouldn't tell. "I'll be more careful, Ma."

"You sound like there's going to be a next time," she says in a soft, worrying tone.

"I can't promise I won't go back—" She gives a quick exhale, finishing up the stitches then turns away. I hear her move across the kitchen, then come back to clean my shoulder and I place my hand on hers, holding it against my skin. "I can't tell you why yet, Ma, but please trust me."

She stills and asks, "Does Vincent know why?" I nod. "Your father?" I nod again. "Should I assume it's business then?"

"Maybe."

"Baby, I don't want you—"

"Please, Ma," I plead with her, trying to find her in the darkness. "Trust me."

Ma huffs continuing her work, then finishes cleaning my arm placing some cotton on my wound. She pauses, kissing my cheek. "Okay, baby. I'll trust you. Just be more careful."

"I'll do my best, Ma."

She wraps my shoulder with gauze carefully. It's all she can do for me since I can't use antibiotics to ease the healing, due to my immunities. Vinny can help speed up the healing process later when the stitches settle in place, using his sealing abilities on the wound. At least I don't have that immunity.

I carefully search for my coffee on the table, but my hand bumps into a container, making me swear under my breath. "Two inches to the right, forward an inch," Ma gently instructs as she walks away.

I'm temporarily blinded, more than usual, from the aftereffects of the venom. This would've happened the last time I was bit, but the anti-venom given to me by the hospital stopped the blindness, giving me muscle spasms instead. A cruel replacement, I think, but my eyes may always be a mystery.

I find my mug and carefully drink from it as Ma kisses my head, leaving the kitchen as she calls out, "*Mio cavaliere*, we'll need to...."

Her voice trails off into the darkness that surrounds me, and I take a deep breath to remain calm as the all-consuming abyss doesn't relent. I'm used to not having sight, but there's at least other colors or shapes, not just a black hole. I remind myself it's not bright light or walls dripping in blood, focusing on the taste of the coffee instead. Pick your battles, Brenda.

I smell cinnamon and cigars and turn my head just as Pops places his hand on my good shoulder. He pulls me in close for a steadying hug, and I breathe in his calming presence and warmth, yanking my thoughts away from the darkness.

"Told you to be careful, baby girl," he says.

"I was. I swear," I mumble. "Couldn't let Vinny or Rodney become roadkill, neither would look good with ginger hair." Pops suppresses a laugh, not letting go while his hand strokes my hair and I lean into him, refusing to move from his touch.

These past few months outdo the shenanigans I got myself into when I was seventeen and burned down two restaurants. *Accidentally*. In my defense, Joey shouldn't have dared me or told me where the human mobs kept their money laundering. Rodney thought it was funny.

"At least you didn't go alone," he says.

"Getting shot up with friends is more fun," I joke quietly.

Pops pulls away and sits in the chair next to me. I reach for my mug again, and nearly knock it over before Pops snatches it and puts it in my hands. "You're out of practice."

"Yeah, got used to having sight there," I mumble, bringing the mug to my lips.

"Did you start wearing the new contacts?"

"Yeah, but I think they're giving me headaches."

"We need to talk to Charlene again."

"Pops..." my voice trails off, and he shifts in his seat, "... maybe it's not worth getting checked out. Since I may not live to—"

"Don't you talk like that."

"Pops, we may need to face the inevitable," I whisper harshly, my stomach churns at the possibility of Feral ghouls within New York City and the answers I may never find in time or Traloski. Odds weren't in my favor right now.

"Until you're lying in my arms completely lifeless, I won't entertain the idea of it," he says in a shaky tone, which makes my eyes form tears. "Do you understand me, baby girl?"

I blink harshly as my cheeks become wet. "You may have to fight Vinny on who gets to—"

"He'd lose," he says, wiping away my tears.

I almost laugh as I put my mug down without much spill. Pops grabs my hands and kisses them briefly. "We'll find that bastard, and you'll have to deal with me doting on you for at least another two hundred years."

"You mean three, don't you?"

"Only if you agree not to move in with Vincent until you're past a hundred." We laugh as he squeezes my hands.

The scuff of shoes grabs my attention, and I whip a hand behind my head, reaching for Vinny's gun. I pull it out and press the barrel to his inner thigh. Pops chuckles under his breath while Vinny grunts, "Careful with the goods, sweet cheeks."

"Not out of practice with some things," Pops comments.

"Cause he drilled it into me," I murmur, letting Vinny take his gun back.

He walks around the table, sitting in the other chair. Pops hasn't let go of my other hand as I turn toward Vinny's direction. I squint through the darkness for any shape or color, but nothing. Not even ruby eyes. Damn it.

"Got an update from Rodney," Vinny says quietly.

"Joey's in charge now, Vincent; go tell him," Pops says.

"I understand and I did, Alanzo. He's off to inform his crew nearby. We all need to clear out completely from the area, including those not under our protection. I actually had to call Midnight."

Fuck, not a good sign if he willingly contacted Bill. I turn toward Vinny and ask, "Why? Did they attack again after they revived?"

"None of them revived or regenerated," Vinny says softly.

"What?" I rasp.

"They were going Feral then," Pops says low, gripping my hand.

"Apparently," Vinny mutters.

"The entire Underground will be in danger if they keep grabbing people to turn," Pops talks in a gruff tone. "NIIA will come down and cause a shit show."

"The Wolf Mob's clearing out the bodies we took out tonight, and my crew will secure the area," Vinny explains. "*No one* is to go within five blocks of that center. It seems all those dead ghouls left behind were Ferals that didn't make it. Probably a dumping ground by the Hive Mind. We keep it quarantined, and any ghouls left behind will die off, especially with this heat. Just can't give them any new bodies."

I shake my head, pulling my hands away from Pops' grasp. "Even if the Hive Mind is Feral themselves, they wouldn't leave behind their dead. They're connected and wouldn't discard them like that."

Vinny shifts in his seat, and the scent of whiskey sharpens. I hold still, narrowing my eyes as Pops asks, "What is it, Vincent?"

"Rodney identified some of the ghouls who attacked us. He checked dental records and markings, and...they were the half-breeds who went missing."

It feels like a stake has been driven into my heart. I stare into the black hole as horror sinks into my bones. You've gotta be fucking kidding me.

"Gunther tried to capture a few who escaped, but they disappeared," Vinny continues. "There's probably buildings they're hiding in. Joey's already taking the lead on warning as many mixed couples and half-breeds in the area."

I shake my head. "All those who disappeared weren't just in the Bronx. If it gets out they were turned into Feral ghouls—"

"We'll try to keep humans out of it. If the media gets hold of this, the NIIA will be the least of our worries. We'll do everything we can to keep people safe, Brenda."

"It doesn't make sense," I murmur.

"You know how much they can hate half-breeds," Pops says.

"Turning people isn't something ghouls do because they hate you. And why not the humans or Paranormals in the area? Why specifically half-breeds?"

"We'll find out," Pops says, touching my hand. "This isn't the first time ghouls have lashed out."

I stare at the nothing before me, my chest beginning to ache as I force back tears from coming down. Vinny touches my hand lightly and the hope in my chest becomes dim. "Say it, Vinny," I choke out. "Just fucking say it."

"I don't think we'll find Traloski through the ghouls. This is something a Hive Mind would do for a vendetta or overtaking a city. We need to find them first."

"Meaning we're back to nothing, other than a mad scientist that *could* exist and *if* he's still alive." I stand up, knocking over my chair as they reach for me.

"Baby girl—"

"Sweet cheeks—"

"No. *No.*" I click my tongue, stumble out of the kitchen, and make my way through the living room. Ma's touch brushes against my arm, but I shrug her off and continue down the hallway.

Pops calls out, "Baby girl…."

"No, Alanzo…." Ma hushes him as I slam my bedroom door behind me.

I fall onto my bed, pulling my legs in close. Fuck. It feels like the walls are caving in as the bleak reality crushes me. There're knocks at my door, but no one enters as I lay in silence with tears streaming down my cheeks. Exhaustion tempts me, but I try to fight it off as worry creeps into my bones. I clutch my pillow, trying to put together whatever pieces there are together, but the exhaustion wins, placing me into an uneasy sleep.

THERE'S ONLY DARKNESS.

No smell. No sounds. No sight.

Not a single scream can break through as I pull at the invisible restraints. Warm liquid trickles down my limbs as I writhe in the nothing.

Gone. Everything is gone.

Piercing daggers thrust into my sides. Noiseless screams tear from my burning throat.

Sharp nails drag down my face. Needles stab at my arms and legs. I thrash. And thrash. Metal thuds against my back, forcing me to my knees in the dark.

A sinister voice, unknown with its mocking tone whispers, "You'll never see them again."

I try to scream. Pulling at the restraints as the daggers cut through my skin. The voice cackles, "Your Mate is dead."

There's only darkness.

I WAKE UP SCREAMING, *"VINNY!"* A cold sweat covers my skin as I tremble, clutching the covers. I open my eyes only to find darkness, and I panic, shrieking as I reach out into the desolate nothingness, unsure if I'm still in the nightmare. Terror fills my lungs as I scream, *"No!"*

My door slams open, and I'm immediately engulfed by Vinny's scent as he pulls me into his chest. "Shhh, I'm here... I'm here, sweetheart. It's alright, breathe," he whispers in my ear, rubbing his hands over my back as I clutch him in the darkness, sobbing against his skin.

Cinnamon tickles my nose for a moment before the door shuts quietly. I heave strangled breaths, searching for crimson eyes, struggling as I realize I can't find him. I can always find him, why can't I see him?

"I can't see you...Vinny, I can't—"

"It's only temporary, sweetheart," he murmurs calmly, cradling my head against his shoulder. I tremble in his arms as he rocks me lightly, caressing my back. "Breathe deep, catch my scent. I'm right here. You're okay."

"You were gone…everyone was gone…I don't want to die. I don't want to—"

Vinny strokes my hair gently, kissing me on the forehead. "I know, and I promise with everything I have, I won't let you."

A whimper escapes me as he holds me tightly, tethering my soul back to earth, making the lasting terror from the nightmare disappear. I inhale his scent, reminding myself I'm still here as I regulate my breathing past the soreness in my throat. I stay in his arms for what seems like forever as my tears dry on his shirt. He kisses me on the cheek, nuzzling into my neck as he breathes deeply.

"Stay here. I'll be right back," he says, placing me on the bed gently. My body begins to shake at the lack of touch as I listen to him walk over to my bookshelf. He comes back, and I instantly scramble to him, clinging to his side. Vinny sits up against the headboard, settling me against him. "Reading always helped you after nightmares."

"Vinny, I'm completely blind and I can't stop shaking." I show him my trembling hand, and he kisses it, then keeps hold as he opens a book on his lap.

"Let me know if I'm going too fast," he whispers, adjusting his hand over mine and placing two of my fingers on the bump dots next to his. He guides my shaking hand over the title page, *The Secret Garden*. He laughs lightly after we read the first page, and I tap him. "Sometimes I thought *you* were the most disagreeable-looking child, especially when you had to leave after our playdates."

I smile at him faintly. "Pot calls the kettle black." He chuckles again as we continue to read in silence.

CHAPTER 13
THE INCUBUS, THE STRIPPER, AND SWEET REVENGE

"Sis, catch!" Ricky shouts, tossing a wrapped muffin at me. I catch it easily and narrow my eyes at him, and a large grin beams across his face. "Just checking your hand-eye coordination."

"You're a dick," I say, and munch on my muffin as he shrugs, going back to rearranging furniture.

It's been a week since the attack on Topside. My eyesight returned to *my* normal after two days using old routines to navigate the house. Charlene checked my eyes again and prescribed new contacts, hoping they'll work better than the last few. Thankfully, no itching today.

The uproar with the ghouls forced Rodney and Joey to reconfigure their movement, with Joey ultimately deciding to shut down half the tunnels we use for moving people. That's where he's at today. This leaves Ricky and I by ourselves to set up the new furniture in the freshly-repaired coffee shop. Apparently, I'm to keep an eye on our middle brother from "destroying" Joey's shop with his artistic endeavors.

"Joey may be able to open the place in two weeks at the rate we're going," I say, leaning back against the bar, watching Ricky move tables around.

"I hope so," Ricky grumbles. "If I have to move more shit for him cause he's gotta go play 'mafia boss,' I'm soaking his socks in vodka."

I laugh. "It's his job, Ricky. And come on, with your strong muscles? Should be easy enough."

"Flattery does you no good, sis."

"I *could* be cruel and say those jeans don't do you any good," I tease, and Ricky gasps, turning his face toward me with a smirk.

"We both know I look excellent in them." He places a table down, stretching his back and allowing his wings to flare open suddenly. I lean back from the small gust of wind they produce.

"Little warning before you go peacocking!"

He waves me off, putting his wings away as he wipes his hands over his jeans and sits next to me at the bar, taking a muffin from the basket Ma left us. I look over the assortment of furniture, boxes, machinery, and utensils lying about in the coffee shop. The place has a lo-fi ambiance thanks to Joey's final decision; a cluster of deep browns trimmed with gold and bronze metal furniture and scattered lights hanging from the ceiling give that warm amber glow. No neon blue in sight. It's homey, reminding me of novels that depict old detectives sitting at the window, watching the rain fall as they contemplate life and investigations—a habit I've picked up after my hell week.

No more information about the ghouls, apart from the more dead ones found in apartments. Vinny and Rodney reluctantly worked together to get everyone out and relocated, even tipping our inside people at PSB that Feral ghouls may be loose and we're handling it. Bill Midnight was the first to know, but unfortunately, he can't make it from Chicago to New York to help, even at the prospect of Ferals loose in NYC. I left Drauper a message about the situation, though I haven't heard back. I thought about talking to Edgar, but he disappeared *again*, and there's no way to contact him. I guess me getting bit wasn't enough for him to care. He better have a good excuse like almost drowning in the East River, otherwise I'm throwing him to the ghouls next.

"How you doing, sis?" Ricky asks, eyeing me with large blue eyes.

"Oh, now you're trying to be sweet?"

"I'm sour, then sweet like gummy worms." He bites into his muffin and pushes my shoulder lightly as I roll my eyes. "Come on. The past week has been shit."

"Let's go with *months* on that."

"Not that bad. I mean, your return debut to the stage was fantastic!" He exclaims, wrapping an arm around my shoulder. "Speaking of which, when you doing another show?"

I shrug. "I don't know."

"We have a slot open tonight, right before Gina or after Mack." I quirk a brow at him, trying to hide a smile at his excitement. "We could do that sister-brother act again!"

"Definitely don't remember the routine."

"It's basically a samba, so I'll just lead you through, and then we hit the poles! It'll be fun. Get the jitters out of us and something fun to do. Better than moving shit around for the bossy brother." Ricky pouts playfully.

I giggle and ask, "Are you actually annoyed that Joey's boss?"

"Are you?"

"Nah. He's still our overprotective, loving older brother. Don't evade, answer my question."

Ricky slumps into his chair, finishing his muffin. "No, I don't. Always knew it would happen, and glad it's not me. I always wanted to take over *Unbound*."

"Well, you're good at managing it and *encouraging* dancers," I tease, and he flashes a wicked smile. "Sometimes, I just...I don't know how you do it."

"Do what? Be wonderfully suave and ooze confidence."

"Topic for another time," I chuckle, lying down on the long

bar. "I mean, dealing with the business stuff, like knowing family is out there, but not knowing where. Or being okay that they may not be okay coming back. Or not knowing when to cross a line to find out or back away. You always seem to bounce back after shit goes down, and I don't know how you do it. You make things appear fine when they…aren't." Or, in my case, act like you're not potentially dying.

Ricky pushes my hair to the side. "I need to shave your head soon."

"Like that," I smirk lightly.

He props his chin on the bar next to my head and smiles faintly. "Life goes on, sis. We can either live it with a smile or a frown, but it doesn't mean we're ignoring the bad things, just concentrating on the good. Ma taught us that." My stomach drops as I remember how she and Pops started a life together, and it wasn't pretty. "We both know some days are harder than others, but we make it through as a family. I can't change what happens, but I can choose how to react. I'd rather laugh and have fun with people and not dwell on what I can't change."

"Maybe it's cause I was away from everything for a few years, but I don't remember it being that easy."

"Never said it was. And being as old and wise as I am…" he says, hopping off his chair as I scoff at him, "…I know it's okay to be sad sometimes, too."

I stare at Ricky, realizing he's being serious. Focus on the good, been a while since I've done that. He tilts his head at me, and I nod stiffly before shoving his arm lightly. He gasps dramatically and messes up my hair with a grin. I grab his arm and say, "Come on, let's blow this popsicle stand. I need my head shaved, Mr. Barber."

Ricky puts his arm around my shoulders as we leave the coffee shop. "A fade is gonna cost you extra, along with a hot towel."

"Does giving you my dessert this week count as a tip?"

"Only if it's Ma's tiramisu."

"Not pie?"

"She makes four a week, sis; it's hard to keep up. Did you know there's a brandy brambleberry pie with whiskey in it?"

"No, but now I want it. It better be real, Ricky."

"Cross my devilish heart," he says, locking up the shop. I roll my eyes at him as we walk to the club with him braiding strands of my hair behind me. I weave a bit more than usual, giving him a hard time to play with it.

The club is mostly empty with regulars dispersed across the place. Ricky takes me back to the changing rooms and sits me down to shave my head while dancers get ready. He makes small talk with the strippers, commenting on my sex life, which I punch him for. All the dancers beg me to dance with Ricky again. After he finishes shaving my undercut, I leave to get a snack from upstairs as Ricky holds up a leather two-piece with fringe, and I have to make sure my jaw doesn't drop. Damn it, I love it. The black outfit looks like a cut-off jacket, revealing an underbust corset. It's not bedazzled, which is a plus. I keep my mouth shut, rushing out of the room as he laughs at me in victory.

"Didn't say yes!" I yell as I walk out to the main area. The lights are dim as Esme, a petite succubus with light pink skin accentuated by her glittery outfit dances on the main stage in her small heels. I smile and hand her a five-dollar bill, and she takes it with a wink before twirling around one of the poles.

As I make my way to the apartment, Bobby waves me to come over and nods toward the back wall. I follow his gesture to see Edgar leaning against the wall with a drink in hand, swirling it as his gray eyes watch Esme on stage with a tight jaw. His lips curl a little as he sips from his drink. How the fuck did I not smell him when I came in?

I approach Bobby at the bar and ask, "When the fuck did he get here?"

"Two hours ago," he answers. "Just stands there, pays for

drinks, and watches. Alanzo said to give a warning if he showed up again. I've waited to see if he'd do anything."

"I'll tell him, thanks," I say, peeling my gaze away from Edgar and head toward the apartment. He doesn't show up when I get bit by ghouls, but he will so he can angrily watch dancers. Ricky may get that dance.

The front door closes behind me as I rush up the stairs, dumping my shoes with the others as I enter the foyer. "Ma!"

"She's doing errands, baby girl," Pops enters from the kitchen with papers and an unlit cigar in his hand. "What is it?"

"Edgar's back. Bobby says he's been downstairs for a couple of hours, just watching and drinking."

"You think someone who hates our way of life would stay away," Pops grumbles as I join him out in the living room. He throws the papers on the coffee table and lights his cigar. "I'll tell Darius to kick him out. He's already making other dancers uncomfortable, and I'm not gonna let him do the same with you. Maybe have a conversation *father to father* on boundaries."

I smile mischievously. "Or I could just make *him* uncomfortable and maybe he'll make his own."

Pops pauses with the cigar in his mouth. "What you talking about, baby girl?"

"The club is our home, Pops," I say, walking toward the bathroom. "If he leaves, I want it on *our* terms, knowing full well what he'll get if he ever comes back."

"And that would be?"

I poke my head out of the bathroom with a wicked grin. "My ass on stage disappointing our daemon ancestors. I'll make him redder than you, Pops."

I do my usual clean-up with a wet rag and soap, quickly washing away the leftover hair from where Ricky shaved, then running to my bedroom and pull on a tank top and light sweats to make changing easier downstairs. Joey's walking into the living room with a pissed-off expression as I walk back in.

"There a reason that bastard's downstairs?" Joey questions.

"Technically, *I'm* the bastard," I joke, and they glare at me. Not the time. Noted. "Kidding!"

"You're in a better mood than I thought you'd be with him being here."

"He's already brought enough grief into my life, not giving him more chances," I respond with a quick glance to Pops.

"We need to toss him out," Joey growls.

"Your sister apparently wants to do that her way," Pops answers.

"How? Shoot his kneecaps?" Joey asks as he crosses his arms.

"I am *not* wasting precious bullets on him," I scowl. "No, I'm scaring him out for some sweet revenge because my soul needs it."

Joey raises a brow. "Want to elaborate?"

Pops speaks around his cigar. "Your sister's gonna strip in front of him."

"Did that ghoul bite affect your thinking skills?" Joey asks me.

"He hates me being up there, so all I gotta do is get on stage to make him uneasy and throw his prejudice back in his face. He'll run right out and won't come back. Besides, if he even tries to touch me, Ricky or Darius will throw him out."

"What do you think about this?" Joey looks over at Pops, who takes a long inhale of his cigar. "Shit, you're agreeing with her."

Pops shrugs, blowing out the smoke. "She knows daemons."

"And what does—"

"If we throw him out, he'll see it as having the upper hand," I explain. "If I get him to leave on his own, he admits defeat and relinquishes control back to me. I get to make the bastard queasy, and we *earn* our space back."

"And if he doesn't leave?" Joey asks.

"*Then* I shoot him in the kneecaps."

"Pops," Joey pleads with him again. Pops' violet gaze glows as he flicks his cigar in the ashtray. I remain steady, hoping he'll go with the plan.

Was it a little petty? Yes. But the sperm donor only seemed to show up to cause me pain or disrupt my life because *he* didn't like it, not to help me. Then again, his track record for *helping* his children, fucking sucks worse than sitting behind someone puking on a roller coaster. I just wanted him far away from my family at this point, who didn't deserve his uptight, judgmental attitude.

Pops sighs and nods. "Have Ricky add you to the roster, baby girl."

"You've gotta be kidding me." Joey presses his fingers into his forehead.

"I'll be fine and on stage with Ricky if you're that worried," I say.

"You will?" Ricky asks, entering the room with a large smile.

"Yeah, just no crazy spins," I warn him with a scowl.

"Deal! Just make it to the pole, and no death drops." Ricky points at my chest, going to his room.

I meet Pops' gaze again, and he nods with a long draw of his cigar. Joey sighs, holding his hands up in defeat. "I'll stay out of it," he says to Pops. "Since you seem agreeable today to her antics. Then again, you've never been able to tell her no, Pops." He walks into the kitchen, shaking his head.

"Not always," I mumble, looking at Pops wearing a guilty smile. "You said no to the machine gun I wanted for my birthday."

"You were twelve, baby girl," he says, patting my head.

"And yet, still no machine gun." Pops scowls, and I quickly kiss him on the cheek before joining Joey in the kitchen.

"Probably won't get that gun for another twenty years," Joey chuckles and grabs some whiskey. "Maybe if you're good, I'll gift you one in ten."

I pause near the fridge, my chest aching as I rub at the freshly shaved part of my head and open the fridge with a sigh.

"You alright, sis?"

"Yeah, sure."

"Look, you don't need to do this. You've got nothing to prove by going out there."

"It's not that," I force a smile. "Just been a while since I've danced with Ricky. You know he always takes the spotlight."

"It's the legs."

"Got them from Ma," I smirk, patting his shoulder. "It'll be like old times like when Ricky and I would see how long it took until Rodney or Brock blushed."

I leave the apartment and snack behind, heading downstairs to the changing rooms, and meet up with Gina. Her eyes glimmer as she holds up the leather number Ricky showed me and purrs, "Let's get ready, baby sis."

I spend the next hour prepping to do my old routine with Ricky. As I warm up my limbs, I check my phone and see a text from Vinny: *My place or yours?*

Smiling, I text him, *Yours, but I'll be late. Family business.*

Got a meeting. If I'm not done by the time you arrive, wait at the bar.

Ricky comes over with his hair braided, a leather speedo, fishnet stockings, black heels, and a bull harness with silver rivets. I stand up and cross my arms, looking him up and down. "Should I be mad you wear heels better than me?"

He smiles, and says, "No, cause I'm the cute one in the family."

"Don't push it."

"You wanna redo that wrestling match again to see who's right?" His face lights up and I roll my eyes at him. I recall that more of a tickle submission from vice-grip arms, but to each their own.

We head over to the door and wait for Mack and a few others to finish their sets. The bass thumps against the walls, and the lights dim to a heavenly violet and maroon as the heightened pheromones and perfume waft in from the club. It's a Friday night here, which means more humans than usual.

Ricky trails a finger across my arm, and whispers, "I need to color your scars again."

"What colors?" I ask, watching the door.

"Violet, blue, and some green. No, wait, pink."

"You get new paint?" He's quiet, and I glance over to see him giving a half apologetic look. "Get new paints first; then we'll talk."

No way is he painting my scars with that old stuff. I'll be the rainbow fish for weeks, and with no library job he won't get into trouble as much as last time. Ma would just make me a new costume to match the paint.

The dancers finish, and people cheer as the music switches. Ricky walks out toward the stage as Mack passes us for the changing rooms. I notice the scent of dampened lavender as they clutch their top close to their chest. I stop them and ask, "What's wrong?"

Mack peeks past me. "He was watching the entire time like he wanted to—"

"Who?"

"The *daemon*. I'm used to vampires and werewolves looking, well, *hungry*, but that was...different."

Anger boils in my gut as I tighten my jaw. Daemon daddy's attitude toward this life was getting beyond personal at this point. "We'll talk to Pops. Don't worry about it."

I must be part daemon, because vengeance drives through my veins as I join Ricky on the main stage. I catch sight of Edgar near the back of the club with his jaw tense as he clutches his drink. His gray eyes sear into mine as I glare back at him with a sultry smile. I turn to Ricky, and I flick my gaze toward Edgar. "Let's make sure he *never* wants to come back."

Ricky finds him and smiles wickedly. "Don't have to tell me twice. Come on, sis. Let's show him how much of a succubus you are." I smile at him, and the lights darken as we get into place.

I'm about to be the biggest disappointment in "daddykins" life.

The Latin-style music starts and vibrates through the club, seeping into the ambiance as the lights shift. Ricky grabs my hand and leads me through the many body rolls, twists, and turns, showing-off each other in the dance. Near the middle of the song, Ricky spins me out, and I stop, landing my gaze on Edgar as I slowly undo the zipper down my vest. His body tenses, and his eyes flare as the vest slips off, revealing the underbust corset and black pasties on my nipples. The rise of burning, aroused scents and cheers erupt in the club. Edgar's gaze blazes and the glass shatters in his hand.

I grin, leaving the vest behind as Ricky spins me into more dancing before separating and moving toward the poles. He climbs up and flares his wings as he spins around, and I climb up and spin with my legs split above me. I twist and climb further up, crossing my legs and spinning back down until my knees hit the ground. I slap the stage with my hands as the song finishes.

The crowd applauds, and I look up with a smile to see Edgar gone and pure freedom from the dance mixes with victory of reclaiming *Unbound*. Score for me, fucker. I stand up and pass Ricky, who's leaning forward for money and giving out pheromone boosts with his enticing smile. I trail a hand along one of his wings, and he looks back at me with a wink.

As I'm leaving the stage, the scent of gunpowder and burnt wood trickles toward my nose. I pause to look out at the crowd and find familiar crimson eyes. The victory I felt shatters as Bruno stands with two guards beside him, his blood-red gaze branding me with hatred as his fangs elongate into a snarl. His long fingers clutch the bar, and his head cocks to the side like a mocking predator as he mouths, *"Whore."*

I quickly leave the stage as my breath gets shaky and two dancers pass me to join Ricky on stage. A shiver runs down my spine as I remember my nightmares, his bite marks on my neck pulsating. I disappear into the back, concentrating on the one good thing that happened.

I scared one terrible father out of here.

CHAPTER 14
HE'S NOT SOME PAPER GANGSTER

There's a sour taste in my mouth as I finish getting dressed, packing my things as dancers make their way to the backroom. I walk out past Gina, who stops me with her piercing gaze. "Why the face, baby sis?"

"Bruno's out there," I whisper. "Can you just tell Ricky I needed to see Vinny?"

She purses her lips, nodding as she hugs me quickly. I kiss her cheek, and she heads back into the crowd. Her demeanor changing immediately as she sways her hips provocatively, approaching patrons near the stages with a sultry smile. I slip out through the back door, texting Joey that I'm going to *The Lounge.*

He responds, *Already?*

Need to see Vinny about something. More like I want to sink into his arms and pretend everything is fine. I add, *Sperm donor is gone now.*

Course your plan worked. I respond with a winky face and walk down the path.

The Underground sparkles with twinkling lights high above in deep blue and violet hues through the darkness. Humans who've ventured down here gasp at how "non-spooky" the Underground appears, while outdoor seating glimmers with low-lit lanterns against the dark brick. It has its own beauty, and it's a far comparison from Topside, where everything is made of metal and steel. Views like this make me forget the LED lights and boards that cover Topside.

Although the beauty of the Underground isn't enough to keep the sensation of drowning away. Every time I'm alone it feels as if an ocean of emotions and troubles engulf my senses. I try to ignore it as I weave through crowds and approach *The Lounge*. I feel more relaxed and in control seeing the familiar sign flashing its neon glory as two of Vinny's guards stand outside and nod, opening the door for me.

The Lounge is hazy with smoke and smells of tobacco and brandy. There's a handful of vampires inside, most of them in booths, necking and sipping glasses of blood that Vinny has shipped in. No humans. No werewolves. No incubi or succubi. *The Lounge* is open to anyone, but only those with particular tastes ever come inside.

Vinny's still in his meeting, so I head to the bar and nod to the bartender, noticing he's new; a well-built vampire with light skin and dark hair pulled into a braid and has an unamused expression. Great. Why does he never warn me when he's got newbies?

"Double whiskey; Red Label," I order.

"How you paying?"

"Vinny's tab," I say, and he stares at me unflinchingly, cocking his head to the side. I mimic the movement. "Trust me. I'm the only one your boss likes to share with."

He narrows his eyes. "You think you're *that* special?" I'd like to go back to dealing with Adrian again.

I huff in exasperation and close my eyes, debating whether I need Vinny's signature coffee or his dick. And right now, I want them both saturated in alcohol. With sprinkles.

I decide not to get into it with the way my nerves are tonight and pull out my damn wallet. The doors suddenly open, and the two vampires with Bruno from earlier walk in. My body stiffens and a chill runs over my skin as I place my hand carefully near the 9-Mil hidden at my side.

I wonder how badly they need their dicks.

They sit one seat away from me at the bar, and the pretentious bartender leaves me to serve them. Their sneers pointed at me is a lovely touch. The air stills and the scent of blood hovers, the vampires having paused in their feeding. I look over, and one of Bruno's guards shows his fangs at me while the other snarls lightly. I flick my gaze to the patron vampires sitting in the booths, watching with curious red eyes. Fuck their prejudice bullshit. I leave my seat, heading to the back to avoid kicking the crap out of some vamps or shooting up Vinny's place. Again.

"Half-breed slut," one of them jeers rustling behind me. I stop, debating catching hell for putting lead into Bruno's guards as my hand twitches over my weapon.

The other says, "What? No response from the sharp-tongued whore?"

"She's only uppity when those skank brothers are around. Or that *damn* mutt." The other sneers.

"That 'damn mutt' could rip your head off as a Sunday treat," I growl back. The patrons begin to leave the bar area. Pussies.

"How does it feel knowing you're like the rest?" The bartender taunts. "Another notch on his bedpost? A side piece. Fuck toy."

"He'll finally get a *real* female when you die like the pitiful human you are," one of the guards says.

My breathing slows as my fingers brush over my gun. Maybe I *could* shoot up his place again. I turn slowly toward them and grin with malicious sass. "How does Bruno's asshole taste? Or do you mix his crusty cum into your drinks to lubricate your throats for him to fuck you slowly?" They snarl and step away from their chairs.

Sometimes I think I take it too far with comebacks. This is one of those times.

They move forward, and I remain where I am, ready to pull my gun when the back doors open. The guards straighten, and I turn to see Adrian and Samuel enter. Samuel's smile fades when he sees Bruno's guys, and he looks at me and asks, "Get your drink, baby sis?"

The guards' scents sharpen behind me as I say, "Not yet. Vinny done?"

"He wanted a minute." His voice is low, looking past me. "Thought the boss told you two to fuck off and scram. You fucked up your shipments *twice*. Find somewhere else to wet your fangs. Sawyer, you were given *orders*."

There's some grumbling behind me, and one of them mutters low, "Deformed skank."

The back doors crash open, and Vinny's scent hits me like a tidal wave. I flinch for my gun but stop myself as he passes in a blink of an eye, slamming the two guards against the wall. A growl from him shakes the walls and the lights flicker making everyone in *The Lounge* disperse, leaving me, Samuel, Adrian, Sawyer, and the two guards under Vinny's grip. I smell blood as his nails flex into their necks, holding them up into the air with ease. They whimper as he lets loose another snarl, lights flickering, and I see Samuel and Adrian pull their guns out, pointing at Sawyer to remain still.

The glasses and mirrors shake as Vinny commands, "Repeat what you told her. I want to hear it."

Shit, I forgot about Vinny's cameras that he moves around every month. That's why Samuel came out before him. It would've been a mercy to shoot them first. They choke against his hold, gasping as blood trickles down their necks.

"No?" Vinny says darkly, throwing one of them into the wall and flipping the other onto the bar, crashing through barstools.

Everyone freezes in obedience as Vinny lets out another rumbling growl and straightens his jacket. They bow their heads stiffly, including Samuel and Adrian. "Next time, *if* there is a next time, I won't be so easy on you. Now, get out before I *permanently* dismiss you."

Bruno's guards immediately obey and scramble out of the place. Sawyer tries to join them, but Vinny catches his collar and slams his head to the bar. He pulls out his gun, pressing the barrel to the bartender's temple, who whimpers as Vinny threatens in a sinister tone, "You were informed to serve her anything she wanted, and you refused and served those degenerates instead."

"Boss—" Vinny crashes Sawyer's head to the bar, putting the gun to his throat as crimson coats his forehead.

"You ignored orders." My eyes widen as Vinny clicks back the safety. Sawyer starts to whimper and plead.

"Boss," Samuel interjects, but Vinny ignores him. "Boss."

"You know what happens when orders are disobeyed deliberately in *my* lounge!" Vinny thunders.

I know he's about to shoot him, his scent rising, burning through the air. Adrian and Samuel stir behind me but do nothing more to stop the Blood Mafia Boss from killing his bartender.

So, I do.

"Vinny." He pauses and slowly turns his gaze toward me, ruby eyes blazing with anger. "Not worth the dry cleaning."

His crimson eyes glow as he lifts the gun away and clicks the safety back on. "Crawl back to my father, Sawyer, and don't fucking come back."

He lets go of the dumbass vampire, who gasps and runs out of the joint. Vinny flicks his gaze past me, and the guards behind me put their guns away and leave through the backdoor silently. Locks click in place, the neon sign flicks off, and the smaller lamplights flicker on. Vinny places his gun on the bar and prowls towards me.

"What were you thinking, bloodsucker?" I ask, backing away slowly.

"Reminding them who I am."

"A fuming, territorial bat?"

"Why'd you stop me?"

"Why'd you listen?" I ask.

He smirks with a devilish gleam. "Because I wanted privacy to remind *you* who I am." He keeps in step with me, towering over me with leftover fury and hunger. His scent grows, and I inhale the burning perfume of spices, whiskey, and bloodlust. I shiver, keeping my gaze on his. "You danced without me, sweet cheeks."

"Last minute thing."

"Encore later?"

"You gonna throw out more clientele or shoot your bartenders?"

"If they disobey orders or refuse you drinks again," he says with a growl. I continue backing up until my back presses against the wall. He leans in and places his hands above me on the wall, bringing his face against my neck, inhaling deeply.

"Where'd you put the cameras this time?" I rasp.

"Not telling," he whispers darkly.

"But I could smile for the camera next time."

"There won't *be* a next time," he growls against my throat. "Apart from sharing, I also hate disrespect towards *my* Mate. Thankfully for them, you're merciful."

"You must really love me then," I rasp.

"You have no idea, *Mate*." Oh, fuck me. Literally. *Please.*

Pleasurable heat blossoms from my lower body, tingling up my spine as I struggle to breathe steadily as he holds me in place. The soft touch on my arms causes me to shiver, enflaming my skin as his overwhelming scent, husky voice, and tender caress put me on the brink of being undone. I reach forward, pulling at his shirt and jacket to remove them.

"In a hurry, *sweet cheeks?*" The tantalizing whisper against my ear sends another shiver down my spine.

He presses his groin against me, and I moan at the touch, instinctively pushing further against him. He swiftly takes his shirt and jacket off, giving me the full glory of his torso. My tongue skims over my lip as I look into those deep ruby eyes.

"Fuck, what you do to me," Vinny breathes before crushing his mouth to mine. We become lip-locked as he holds me against the wall, his tongue entering my mouth, and I groan as we continue the passionate kiss. I taste him and want more, barely catching my breath as he bites my lip and lifts me up against the wall. I wrap my legs around his waist, pressing my groin against him, moaning when I feel his erection. Fuck me, I may already be undone.

Vinny carries me over to the bar and sits me down on the surface. He pulls away from our fervent kiss, his eyes hooded and hungry as they roam down my body and back up. "Clothes off," he commands, and I nod.

He walks away briefly as I slip off my clothes and put my guns away. The steel shutters close with a click, and the last of the locks fall into place, setting us into the darkness of *The Lounge* with only the faint glow of a few lamps. I sit back on the bar as Vinny comes back, stripping the rest of his clothes off. His muscles ripple in the low light, shadows dancing across his skin. Moments like this, I'm glad I can see and remember every detail for the day I may lose my sight forever. I lick my lips and stare at the enticing sight of him.

Vinny stalks back toward me with slow ease, and I tense at the anticipation. When he reaches me, his hands stroke up my thighs and over my torso, stopping at my breasts. He caresses them with familiarity and care as I push them further into his touch. I groan when his thumb circles over my nipples, biting my bottom lip and leaning back as my hips push upward for contact. His lips meet my skin, his tongue following my scars down my body as he lays me down carefully onto the bar. My head hangs over the other side as he sweeps my legs over his shoulders.

He pulls me forward, my neck now having support beneath it, holding my lower half up toward him as I reach to clutch the edge of the bar. Without warning, Vinny's thumb presses my clit gently, the sudden touch rippling through me and emblazing my lower region. "Oh, fuck!"

He continues to play, circling his thumb over and over and pressing until a finger moves down, entering me. A long groan comes out of me as his other hand reaches forward to knead my breasts, pinching at my nipples. Vinny nips at my inner thighs, and I refrain myself from bucking at the contact against his mouth. I whimper loudly as a second finger joins the first, thrusting into me as his tongue moves across my skin then sweeps over my clit with a searing heat. He sucks lightly, my grip tightening on the bar as he pumps his fingers and presses his tongue against me.

"Do you know the first time I wanted to fuck you in my place?" He breathes against my skin. "Claim you in a place I built on my own? Make *you* my own?"

I shake my head, focusing on how his fingers press and knead into my body. His tongue moves over my clit again, and I moan with a begging tone. All I can do is watch him, hear him, and feel his skin against mine. My control is gone, given completely to the Blood Mafia Boss who has me at his mercy. Long shadows cast over his body, dark hair, and glowing eyes— the bloodthirsty vampire of urban myth.

"When you came running in to tell me you made it into Grad school," he rasps, and my breath hitches. "The look of accomplishment on your face. Your joy. Happiness. I wanted to give you something to show you how fucking proud I was of you. To properly congratulate you." His fingers scissor inside me, then hook, causing my body to convulse.

"Vinny," I gasp.

His mouth leaves my clit behind to nip at my hips, breasts,

and neck, kissing upward and along my jaw, raking his fangs along my skin. He comes to my lips, thrusting three fingers into me and pressing his thumb. I pant as Vinny chuckles darkly and continues, my entire body burning like fire as my orgasm climbs and becoming engulfed in ecstasy. I grip onto the bar for dear life as my muscles shudder, and I scream as the orgasm tears through my veins, and my spine tingles, exploding with heat as Vinny kisses me deeply. I shake and breathe hard against his mouth, tasting what's mine.

He eases me down from the high, working me delicately before pulling his fingers out of me. Vinny breaks the kiss to lick his fingers and hum while I touch his chest, feeling the heat of his skin and pounding heart. He pulls me up to stand, turning me around and bends me over the bar with a commanding force. I gladly clutch the bar surface as he spreads my legs further apart, gripping my ass and trailing a finger down my spine toward my…

"Fuck me, Vinny!" He thrusts his finger back into me, my sensitive clit pulsating. I melt at his sinful chuckle, and he suddenly replaces his finger with his cock. Both of us shout as he enters me fully, and I whimper at the invigorating sensation of him inside me, filling me.

His hands stroke over my skin, tracing over scars and curves of my body as he thrusts harder into me, and I grip onto the bar for strength. My legs tremble, already shot from the orgasm I was given moments before. I concentrate on him filling me up, and already another builds as he pounds into me. His scent scorches my senses with pleasure, and he growls low, rumbling from behind as he continues to thrust his dick deep enough to throw all thoughts from my head. All that's left is Vinny as he claims me from behind against his bar. He grips my hips, pulling me back onto him harder, and I let loose a scream. He snarls as pleasure overwhelms and heats me to my very core, and I scream again.

"*Mine. You're Mine,*" he growls near my ear. Hard chest

muscles encase my back with fiery heat and sweat. I gasp at the relentless pounding of his cock, wanting more of him with each thrust. I forget everything outside these walls as he fills me, gripping my hips with a demanding want, and the heat of his skin against mine. All I have in this moment is Vinny. *Mine.*

"Always," I rasp.

"Fuck...sweetheart."

Vinny thrusts again, and I scream as the orgasm crashes like a tidal wave. He roars as his own rages and explodes, making the lights flicker and glasses shake. We come together and breathe hard as the euphoria hits, and it feels like my entire body has shattered as he grips me against his body.

I shiver as the last sensations travel through, my legs trembling to keep myself up. Vinny's body remains pressed above me as he takes long breaths against my neck and kisses it. "And it was worth the wait."

———

"Was I nineteen or twenty-one the last time someone threatened to drain me?" I ask Vinny.

"Twenty-two. A damn newbie who wanted to fuck you, too. I wanted to kill him."

"Did you?"

"Transferred him to Atlanta," Vinny snorts, drinking straight from his bottle of whiskey.

We sit naked on a couple of rugs behind the bar on the floor, leaning against each other and drinking from our own bottles of liquor. He's already been through two. Damn vamps and their high tolerance. Never was fair when it came to drinking games.

The lights glow dimly as we sit and drink after our "ruining" of his place—it only took two hours amazingly, but now I need a nap. Vampires are going to be smelling our aftermath everywhere for days, spanning from the tables, walls, floors, and the bar. It's exactly what Vinny wanted, being the territorial vampire he is. At least he's not a werewolf, who I'm told are much worse. No wait, hearing Ricky's stories, incubi and succubi may beat that.

Vinny grumbles, "I may send their asses down there, too, if I catch them fucking—"

"You know it's never bothered me. Gotten used to it."

"Don't act like it doesn't hurt when they say that shit," he mutters, and takes another swig. "And it bothers me."

"Would've never guessed," I smirk at him. He narrows his eyes playfully and kisses my head. "How long had they worked for you?"

"They were in the game long before I was boss, and that dipshit Sawyer knew what he was doing by refusing you a drink." He shifts next to me, leaning further back into the shelving of bottles behind us. "All Blood Mafia vamps know you drain my dregs."

"Your alcohol you mean?"

"That and then some."

"Smartass."

"Only for you, sweet cheeks," he muses.

I sigh, taking another swig of scotch. "Samuel mentioned them fucking up shipments. Had you already kicked them to the curb?"

"Yeah," Vinny growls. "Lost a couple of shipments from Europe and blood drives from Chicago due to their belligerence. Cost me fifty grand. And now they're working for my father and following my Mate into my lounge." He stops and takes another drink. "Bruno's become very vocal about his... *disapproval* of us. It's bleeding into my fucking crew and the Vampiric Society faster than I thought it would. Probably why they had the guts to come back in here."

Silence drifts over us and I take another long drink, letting the scotch burn down my throat. I lean further into Vinny's warmth, his fingers tracing scars along my arm and shoulder.

The only noise for a few minutes is the occasional yelling outside or slamming of doors. If it's this bad already with vampires thinking we're only fucking, then I don't want to think what they'll do when they realize the truth. Unless…

I take a steadying breath. "You don't think Bruno knows we Claim Mated, do you?"

"No. No one does, don't worry."

"What about the blood you lost in the Bronx?"

"Had Samuel burn it. Rodney already commented on our scents, so I guess we'll have to try harder to convince them it's due to new sex positions and fetishes. How do you feel about fireplay?"

I snort loudly and shove his side. "I'm gonna need recovery time, bloodsucker." Vinny kisses my head and nuzzles into my hair, taking a deep breath in. "Hey, Vinny? What do I smell like?"

He inhales deeply, then sighs in contentment with a wicked smile. I roll my eyes at him. "Dragon's blood and honey." My brows shoot up in surprise. I was half expecting to have a similar scent to the sperm donor, but I guess not. I hum in satisfaction, and Vinny chuckles, stroking my hair back.

"You know, I've always wondered if people smell differently to each other," I muse. "Ma says Pops reminds her of Tuscany summer breezes, fresh grass, and wine. Never got that for him."

Vinny grunts, staring at the bottle in his hand. I poke his side to talk, and he looks at me with a sigh. "At least we have one father's support. I'm just relieved Alanzo took us being Mated well…enough."

I chuckle to myself, knowing he wouldn't have been worried if he knew certain kitchen conversations I had with my parents. Vinny raises a brow, and I pat his chest. "He had other things to worry about, and these last few weeks have sucked ass exceptionally. The Mating excluded."

"You're telling me. Didn't we talk about running away a few years back? Why didn't we?"

"Something about you needing to be responsible and me missing my family kept us from doing it. And I had homework."

"That's what I get for being supportive," he says, finishing his bottle and tossing it into the bin. He reaches behind us and grabs number four, popping the cork as I watch him silently.

I hesitate to ask, "Bloodsucker?"

"Sweet cheeks?"

"When Bruno finds out, cause someday it's gonna happen, how bad is it gonna be?"

He stills a moment and says, "Manageable."

"Don't fucking lie."

"You always said you wanted to see Brazil, right?" I punch him in the arm, and he doesn't flinch. "Alright, it may be *pretty* bad."

"Like-*you*-going-into-hiding, *me*-into-hiding, or being-sent-to-Davy-Jones'-locker bad?"

He sighs as I climb onto his lap, and he strokes my hair back to look me fully in the eye. His thumb trails down my facial scars, stopping just below my lip. "I told you I'll give it all up," he whispers. "If they cause enough havoc and threaten to destroy the Blood Mafia, I'll hand it back. Not like I need the mob to survive."

"Leave the mob?" I ask, and he nods. "We both know that's basically impossible. You'll be a target without the support. Your blood is practically worth hundreds of thousands. And that's just in the U.S."

"Not if I give up the position, hand it over to someone else, and relinquish my entire hold on it. I'll focus on what I built here with *The Lounge* and other venues I own. Go legit." I scoff at the idea of it, and he pokes my nose.

I mull over his words, knowing there's only two options for him to relinquish power to: Anita or Bruno. With his sister, we'd be safe enough and less likely to start a war *if* she takes the position and *if* the entire Vampiric Society doesn't protest. Anita has a high standing within the Society and taking on the duties of Blood Mafia Boss would shift allegiances. But if Bruno reclaims that role...not a happy thought. It's not just the Blood Mafia that will change, but the entirety of the Underground as a whole again. I shiver at the thought of the Underground Mafia breaking apart if Vinny steps down, dismantling what he's worked on over the years.

"Hey." Vinny cups my face, bringing my thoughts back to him. "We'll figure it out."

I lean further into his touch, my heart feeling heavy, and everything that had temporarily slipped my mind from sex comes roaring back. Unease and melancholy creep across my skin, my thoughts spinning to search for answers out of my grasp, but all I see is darkness.

Vinny brings his forehead to mine. "Best friends forever, right? We tell each other everything, so talk to me, sweetheart."

I let out a shaky breath, pulling back to meet his gaze and start rambling. "I'm overwhelmed. With *everything*. I'm angry about what happened to those half-breeds being turned the way they were and that it could've been me weeks ago if not for my immunities. I'm frustrated with *everything* happening on Topside and feel like I lost precious time being up there because I was fucking scared. And I feel guilty for leaving, and not staying." My throat hurts as I suppress a sob, and Vinny cups my cheek. "I don't know if I should make every day count since I'm a ticking timebomb or take a break and *try* to enjoy what's left of my life. But no matter what, it won't be enough. Rodney will go back into mourning because of me, and I promised him I wouldn't let that happen again. My parents will still have to mourn their dead child. Beckham will have to watch family die again. I'm *fucking furious* that I'll have to leave everyone behind so young, knowing you'll have hundreds of years more. Every time they talk about years down the line, I want to hurl. I want to throw something. And there's a list the size of *The Odyssey* of people I want to shoot. And I'm *angry* that I *finally* have you after so fucking long, and it could hurt our families, start a mob war, or tear us apart forever. I don't want to lose you."

I breathe out once I finish, tears forming in my eyes as relief swamps me for getting everything out. I shake a little as the weight lifts from my shoulders and I shut my eyes trying to make the tears stop. Vinny wipes away my tears gently and kisses me, his lips tender against mine as he slips his hand behind my head to hold me against him. A small sob breaks in my throat as I clutch him, gripping his hair. He pulls away, placing another chaste kiss on each side of my mouth. "No one's broken us apart for over twenty years, sweet cheeks. We're too stubborn, right?"

"I guess," I sniffle.

He kisses me again on the cheek. "I can't make your fears go away, but I can listen and sit with you when it gets hard."

"I don't remember that being in the fine print of Mating."

"Mated or not, Brenda, you're still my best friend." He smiles and cups my cheek. "And I was told that best friends aren't scared of each other. That means you can't be scared to tell me when you need to talk."

"Fifteen years later, and you use my words against me."

"You were destined to be a smart librarian, while I have to use what I've got."

"Yeah, the antique, hot vamp."

"Only for you, sweet cheeks." He kisses the side of my neck up along my jawline, hugging me close to his chest.

I shudder, and admit softly, "I can't fail my family or you, Vincent. I can't."

He clutches my head, hugging me tightly. "You won't, Brenda. And you never will." I hold onto him harshly hoping his words are true.

I kiss his neck, inhaling the comforting aroma as he kisses my head. We stay there a few minutes and I take a long breath, the last of the tears disappearing. "Sweet cheeks," he says. "Never call me by my first full name again."

I chuckle lightly. "Don't like it?"

"Little unnerving."

"Fine, I'll stick with 'bloodthirsty vamp tramp.'"

Vinny adjusts, bringing his gaze to mine with a gentle look. "Come on, it's late, and this *bloodthirsty* vampire mob boss needs cuddles."

I grin lightly, kissing him briefly. "Thank you and I love you, vamp tramp."

"I love you, sweet cheeks," he says. "Come on. Naptime." Vinny lifts me into his arms, and I relinquish all control to him as he heads for his place above *The Lounge*.

"Wait! My clothes!" I yell.

"I have clothes upstairs."

"Not mine. Down." He grunts and lets me down reluctantly. I scramble to gather my things, check my phone, stop mid-walk when I see a notification.

"What is it?"

"Hold on," I say, gesturing for him to wait as I listen to the voicemail from Drauper.

"Brenda. Probably not awake…time difference. I found something on Traloski, not much but it could be something finally. Look, I don't know if you're willing to come up to Topside at night, but can we meet at the bar we went to together last time…tomorrow night? If you get this in time, let me know. See you later, Brenda."

I stare down at my phone. Honestly, I thought Drauper ghosted me this past week. Okay, maybe I should have more faith in the detective. I look up at Vinny, and his brows furrow. He heard. I glance down at the time, and I see I have half a day before Drauper wants to meet up.

"You can't come with me," I murmur, looking back up at him.

"I know."

"It may be the only—"

"Sweetheart." He walks over and cradles my face. "Take the damn gun, make sure the emergency system works on your phone, and the moment you see police or Feds, you fucking run. Got it?" I nod, and he kisses me ardently before lifting me up into his arms. "Until then, I'm getting my fucking cuddles."

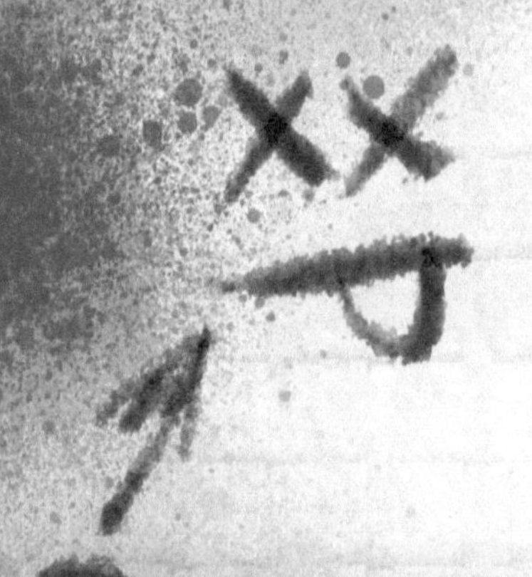
Drawper

CHAPTER 15
CSI: PARANORMAL EDITION

Twilight had just passed as I walk out of the elevator onto Topside with people riled up, ready to party. Some run past with a group of angsty teen werewolves. The heavy dusk doesn't help ease the muggy, heated atmosphere, and I regret wearing my suede jacket. It's the only item I have that isn't heavy leather and can hide two guns at my back.

I don't wait for Vinny as I walk down the sidewalk, fixing my glasses as he comes up beside me adjusting his cuffs. We compromised on him "dropping" me off to see Drauper. "You're a micromanager," I taunt, shaking my head in exasperation.

"It's called being a gentleman to walk a *lady* to her destination."

"And here I thought you'd be more irritable if I was up here during the daylight. Thank goodness you proved me wrong." I tease as we turn a corner onto the street that leads to my old apartment, and I ignore the old tug towards it with mixed emotions. I focus on the busy city noise reverberating off the walls of the buildings from horns honking and taxi drivers yelling obscenities to other people.

"Never did understand your desire of living up here," Vinny mumbles as we cross another street.

"Needed peace from your grumbling, *grandpa*."

"How you *wound* me with your words," he clutches dramatically at his heart.

"It's a talent, Gomez."

"And now I'm your grumbling, *grampy* vamp tramp." I stop and glare at him as his ruby eyes shine against the array of oranges and blues. He smirks in victory. "You started it, *Morticia*."

"Can I return an orgasm?" Vinny snorts in reply, but at least he shut it. Noted for future nicknames, I'll need to conjure up a new vocabulary.

Evening shifts over completely as the last shade of the sunset streams through buildings as we approach the bar. We come upon where Drauper kissed me, and my stomach sinks. I shake my head at the memory, turning to Vinny to send him on his way. I cross my arms and tilt my head, flicking my gaze for him to go.

"Call when you're done?" He asks.

"Yes, worrywart."

"That's a new one."

"Apparently I need to be more creative due to vocab circumstances," I grumble. "Go get your afternoon blood with biscuits. Don't want to come back to a hangry vamp."

I turn toward the bar, but Vinny grabs my arm, making me pause to look back at him. His gaze inquires, dipping down at my mouth and back up again. I grin and sigh at my Mate, kissing him deeply. He breathes in as his tongue briefly slips over my lips, clutching me close a moment until I separate us slowly.

"Go frighten people into the night, bloodsucker," I say, lightly punching him on the arm and walking away, hating each step. I'm not sure if it's the Claim Mating that yanks at my heart or just being back here.

I enter the bar as televisions play sports, neon signs flicker, and it smells of fried food and beer. I search for Drauper, expecting him to be punctually late, but I see him sitting in the back where we'd been last. My stomach drops like lead. Great.

I slip past a shifter and werewolf before I reach the table and notice Drauper's halfway through a pint of beer. He turns his attention to me from the TV, shifting as I take a seat across from him. I order a whiskey neat, quickly, and it's delivered as Drauper watches silently.

"Thought you ghosted me," I say, taking a sip. I need some liquid courage right now.

"Not the one who does that, am I?" Ouch. Okay, I kinda deserved that.

I knock back my entire glass and wave down the waitress for another, which she brings promptly. Could I get away with ordering a barrel? I look at Drauper through my tinted glasses. "What did you find?"

"Straight to business."

"Odd being on the other side of it, huh?" He looks at me, perplexed. "You were like that with your cases."

"I still asked how you were."

"And for whose benefit? Mine or yours?" I lift a brow, and Drauper scoffs, pulling out a manilla folder and placing it between us. "Hit a nerve?"

"You want to do this or not?"

"You're the one who decided to meet *here* and went on about this being purely business, but now you want to make small talk like nothing—"

"I'm trying to be nice here, Brenda."

"And I'm trying not to drink this bar dry," I grumble into my drink. He grabs his beer and takes a long gulp, placing it down hard on the table. We stare at each other for a moment, and I release a long breath. "Look, we don't need to pretend this is anything more than a *work* relationship. Nothing more for both our sakes."

His jaw clenches a brief second before he relaxes and leans back in his chair, nodding at the folder on the table. I reach across and open it to squint at the sea of wrong colors my eyes are playing on me, dark green lettering on light blue paper.

"That's what I got from my contact in NIIA," he says, pointing at the folder.

"Wait, really?" It was a thickish folder, and more than I thought NIIA would have after what Dr. Rhonda told me.

"Captain found out I was looking into some…old cases and *graciously* gave me some days off to 'clear my head.' My guy in NIIA handed that off to me before I was given the impromptu vacation."

"Why something that drastic?" I ask, flipping through for anything new on Traloski and his background. Most of the pages are darkened, covering studies and results.

His voice drops. "Something's going on with the federal agencies. They're not talking to the NYPD and taking over cases that should be in *our* jurisdiction. My captain didn't want me to get involved or 'ruin another sting' as he put it. Especially since…" I look up, and he frowns, leaning forward, "…those missing half-breeds, who fall under human law, showed up dead as ghouls near the Hudson."

A trickle of worry travels over my skin as I trace the rim of my glass. Vinny and the others knew to burn the bodies, they wouldn't have dumped them to be found by anyone. I look away from Drauper, flipping another page. "Cause of death?"

"Acid burned them from the inside out, leaking out of every crevice."

"What color was the acid?"

"Brown-like sewage."

I go still and stare down at my drink. Back to the brown sludge again. It's gotta be a symptom of dying as Ferals, but I'd need to see an autopsy report or the dead body itself to be certain. Haven't had luck with that lately. "How'd you ID them?"

"Dental records; teeth were still intact," he says, drinking his beer. "Why is their cause of death a surprise to you, but not them actually *being* dead?" I meet his narrowed eyes. "You gonna tell me what you already know, or do I need to play the 'bad cop,' *Scooby?*"

A small smirk rises on my lips. "Oh, right, you do this for a living."

He raises his brows. "You actually forget, or just hoping I wouldn't notice any tells?"

Touché. Right, this is a joint operation. "I came across my own group of ghouls in the Bronx. Some were taken out by bullets and others were *long*-dead covered in that supposed brown 'acid.'"

"Where are the bodies now?"

"Burned." And they better be, or I'm tying Rodney up and dunking him in a vat of earwax.

"Why the fuck would you do that?" He asks suddenly, tensing up. "We could have—"

"It was to honor their deaths," I say. "Ghoul traditions dictate burning the bodies of those who have stopped regenerating. Fire is their way of paying respect to their final deaths. And let's be honest, *Sherlock*, if I asked to see the ones you found, would you let me?"

His mouth tightens. "No." I scoff. "Because *I* can't even see them or their autopsy reports. Their bodies belong to PSB."

Fucking wonderful.

We stare at each for a long time until we reach an impasse, and I break the silence. "When were your bodies found?"

"Five days ago," he says with a sigh.

"Around the same timeframe then," I observe, taking a sip of whiskey to numb the growing worry inside. "Anything else found at the scene?"

"That's all I have on them," he sighs. "There weren't enough bodies to equate the number of ghouls that went missing. Not even my contacts in NIIA and PSB know where the rest are. Most told me: 'good riddance' or 'they went back South to escape the hot weather.'"

"Mine are more perturbed not knowing when they left." I flip another page in the folder to find more blackout.

"Do you know the acid that killed them?"

"Presumably aftereffects of going Feral, the undead brain tissue can't keep functioning, overloading and destroying itself from the inside out. Much like how a bad change can happen from being bitten. I'd have to look at the stuff firsthand to make a proper diagnosis."

"What about the ones you found?"

"I got distracted." By getting bit, hurling my breakfast on the damn sidewalk, and temporarily going blind. It's been a long week.

Drauper tenses, tapping a few fingers on the table and coming in close. "There were rumors going around about Ferals being here, but PSB said not to worry. It's true then?"

"All we know is that none of this is normal behavior. Only thing that makes sense is them going Feral. Except, a singular death due to a ghoul going Feral is one matter, entirely another when there's hoards dying. My contacts think it's a vindictive Hive Mind."

"So, basically, everyone's worried while NYPD and PSB are keeping it quiet. And your contacts are…?"

I scowl at him. "Keeping ghouls contained, so don't worry."

"Just checking," he says, and I huff, knocking back more of my drink. "You still think that Traloski character is connected?"

"Do you?" He shrugs. "Careful with your enthusiasm there; you'll cause a tsunami."

"You said ghouls don't change well from the living; the change fights itself. None of them showed signs of that. From what you're telling me, they would have already been ghouls *then* went Feral. And you said they're a classist society. It doesn't make sense to turn humans, whom they hate, to their side. Why turn them into ghouls for a few weeks, but have them die off, rotting from the inside out? It all seems really counterproductive."

Once again, the detective surprises me with the knowledge he retained. Maybe being on Topside wasn't a waste. "Great memory, Sherlock," I comment with a half-smile.

"And as I said in the park, people aren't looking into these disappearances. It's infuriated me that they'll let people just be...gone."

I pause and look over my glasses to see Drauper partially illuminated by a neon sign nearby. I can smell a trickling of his scent as it dampens in worry. "You thought I was going to be a victim, too."

"Would you blame me?"

"Not really." I look down at the folder, coming to its end with nothing more to help us. Damn it.

The waitress comes back, and we order another round of drinks. I lean back, swirling the whiskey in my glass. "We can agree this is something more than just the ghouls?"

"Unless you think they're twisted enough to force half-breeds to rot from the inside out to torment them."

"No, they'd just kill or maim who they don't like. Not make them part of the Hive."

"So, then why not just kill them?" Drauper asks a similar question that's been going through my own head. "Why put in so much work to make people disappear, then have them die months later as ghouls?"

"You're the one who works with 'Unsubs' and murderers, so what would your next step be?"

"Finding their motive."

I hold the folder up, then drop it on the table. "That's why I think Traloski connects. Kidnap, keep for experiments, and then let them die off to get rid of the garbage as it were."

"I'll take that theory over Feral ghouls running around," he grimaces.

"Same. This all you found?" I point at the folder.

"On paper? Yes. Gossip?" He takes a drink and comes in close, flicking his gaze around the place. I gesture for him to continue, wanting the dramatics to end. "NIIA Agent I know worked with a guy who worked the Traloski case and said all official reports state he's in prison. No follow-ups or paper trail on *which* prison. And he's not in the databases officially. They think black ops took him for his...*medical skills.*"

"Oh, we *love* that."

"It's all hearsay, but he did experiment on half-breeds, and the Feds got rid of almost every piece of information on those involved. The guy who was attached to the case doesn't even know why."

"Maybe original mission went wrong?"

"What the fuck was the original mission then?" Oh, I don't know, maybe torturing children and crocheting on Sundays for his breaks. "Unless..."

My skin prickles at the low tone of his voice, and I tilt my head at him. "Unless what?"

"I got my little 'vacation' for more than one reason."

I quirk a brow at him. "You destroy a library?"

He snorts, and I smirk. "You ever find out who did that?" I recall the memory of the entire *Noctis Immortalis* Section being ripped to shreds and Drauper spending a few hours helping me clean up. I shake my head. "The section was cleaned up by the way, but I was told most would stay in the basement."

"Better than trash bins," I mumble, remembering the books I didn't get to save. Another loss from the past few months. "So, what'd you do to piss off your boss, Sherlock?"

"I ran background checks on the people who disappeared to see if there was a pattern besides being half-breeds. Captain didn't like that and said they all fell under PSB jurisdiction, but only some were claimed by Paranormals. I thought it was bullshit and looked even harder since PSB isn't looking into it." He sounds like Midnight. Same shit, different city, I guess. "I found some connections."

My brows raise. "Such as?"

He points at the folder between us. "All the missing half-breeds had immunities of some kind to Paranormals ranging from vampire and werewolf bites, mind manipulation, or healing. Some even against ghoul bites. So, how the fuck does someone with an immunity to ghouls turn into one?"

Son of a bitch, the detective found our connection.

My eyes widen and my facial scars pulsate as the small breakthrough hits me. "Their immunities were public info?"

"Public hospital records and when I talked to a few families, they gave me some personal family history," he says in a distant voice. "I found the others through records of past demeanors from traffic violations, drugs, and prostitution. Almost all those people were in the areas of *your* beings." I snort at the implication of crime influence. Should I tell him about Vinny almost shooting the head off someone calling me whore? Bad example. "Did Traloski look for people, back then?"

"No, they used to go to him."

"So, people are searching for this guy again, ending up as the undead or this time he's stealing people off the streets *then* turning them into the undead. Either way, two decades is a long-ass sabbatical. But *why* ghouls at all this time around?"

"Valid questions," I mutter and finish my drink. What were the ghouls' placement in this? "We need to find those ghouls. Find out how they're connected to the missing people and if they're working for Traloski or a copycat."

"Except all trails are cold. Even recent missing reports aren't of any help."

"How far is the range of those that disappeared?"

Drauper twirls his hand in the air. "Bronx, Manhattan, Brooklyn, Queens, and even Staten Island. Entire fucking city." Fuck and we thought it was gonna be hard looking for the undead. "And there's a higher percentage of those disappearances earlier this year, Brenda. Most are unclaimed by either side and weren't reported missing until weeks after."

"So, no one noticed," I murmur as I shiver, thankful for Pops taking me in. Suddenly, I really, *really* want to give my family a long hug. "Can we track any movement of those who disappeared before they did?"

"Maybe as far back as May, but it won't be easy with how much time has passed. Footage will be a nightmare to scrounge and get, but I can ask around."

"And what about your...*vacation?*"

Drauper shrugs and leans back with his beer. "Long as I don't ask PSB or NIIA for help again, captain won't know." I raise a brow at him, and finally, Drauper smiles. "You've got your contacts; I've got mine."

I stifle a bit of laughter. "You do suck with authority."

"It's called getting the job done."

"Fine. We'll look into footage for any clues to those disappearing. It's better than ransacking every building in the South Bronx far into Manhattan." Not counting the tunnels or subways, which'll take months.

"Sounds delightful," he answers sarcastically.

"What? You've never upturned a building before?" I lean back, crossing my arms, and he snorts. "We find any footage of the missing people; we find the crazy scientist."

"Before they turn into ghouls or go Feral?"

"The Death Star was easier to blow up, but yeah, that too."

He rolls his eyes. "And find out what the hell he's doing to them?"

"*That's* the golden ticket, Charlie." Drauper sighs as I salute sloppily and grab my drink. "We're probably gonna hate the answer to that."

"Newsflash, it comes with the job." He finishes his beer, pushing it to the side.

We stare at each other as the bar fills with cheers, an announcer declaring a goal on the televisions. Even with all the noise, it feels quiet between us, and I sit there unsure how to proceed, my jaw tightening as I think of just getting up and walking out. He'll call me if he finds anything, vice versa, hopefully before the next century. Or me being dead.

The waitress comes over, and Drauper barely turns to her to say, "We'll take one more round." She smiles and walks away.

"Got more to discuss?"

"Thought we could…talk."

"Thought this was only business." He sighs and keeps quiet as the waitress brings our drinks. Damn, they're fast this evening. Either the universe is trying to get me drunk or knows I need alcohol that bad.

"Maybe we could try the friendship thing again. We worked pretty well as a team before. You get the info; I get the…bad guys." I snort loudly. "And maybe I did ask how you were for my benefit, but even talking about undead people and crazy doctors, it's been…nice talking to you again."

"You telling me you only want me for my brains?" I smirk.

"I'm telling you I miss you."

I stare at the man I once called 'friend.' There's a part of me that missed him, too. My days at the library were always better when he came by, whether to talk or joke around, but I saw him as a friend before anything else. The old Drauper I knew sits before me, the inquisitive detective asking questions about Paranormals with his blinding smile and charisma. He's giving me a second chance like I had given him.

I reach for my drink and nod toward his. "You have shit taste in beer, Drauper.

Draper
Stop
That!

CHAPTER 16
101 PARANORMALS

Girls scream nearby, prompting Drauper and I to flinch, but relax when we see it's just a group of humans, succubi, and shifters having fun. I ease my hand away from my firearm. Drauper does the same. Why does the city seem louder tonight?

He chuckles low. "Brings back memories of college."

"Maybe for you, but my experience wasn't anything close."

"What about the rest of your family? I heard they can be… loud." The slight pause makes me wary, but he didn't say beasts. I don't think he's said it all evening. Interesting.

"Loud, but not quite…*that*." Unless for special occasions when the strippers and I get drunk, but that includes pole dancing games. Different reasons.

He hums, draping his jacket over his shoulder. The heat from the late summer hasn't relented into the evening. I shift on my feet, looking out toward the hugging females as Drauper catches my eye. I'm unsure how to say goodbye, given the last few times hadn't gone well with ending in arguments, me running away, ambulances…

"I'll call you?" Drauper asks.

Or we could end the night like that. "Sure." He waves once

and walks down the sidewalk, vanishing through the crowd of people as New York City lives out its "unsleeping" reputation. I exhale harshly once I can't taste his scent anymore.

We spent the last hour sharing life updates. No questions about the mafia, Underground, or my family until just now. It was, honestly, good conversation, if not awkward at first, but we talked. And the hole that had been inside me felt less.

I walk toward a Manhattan Entrance as the noise surrounds me, trying to help my thoughts as I think over everything we discussed. Pieces were clicking together, but the damn puzzle was just the same shade of blue at this point. I reach the elevator, which opens for some shifters and incubi to exit. The shifters change into larger human beings, one of them flashing me a smile. I loosen my hair around my shoulders, scratching at my head as I enter the small space.

I inhale deeply, recognizing the familiar scent of mulled wine and tainted roses as the doors close. I turn and murmur, "Anita...*darling.*"

Anita's long black hair is loose around her shoulders, and she's wearing a dark buttoned vest with billowy pants, complementing her dark lips. For once, no glass of blood is in her hands. Instead, she has a long cigarette propped between two fingers. How she got away from her driver and bodyguard, Brock, is an accomplishment.

"Looking for lost puppies?" I ask, pressing the button to go down.

"A cultural reference I don't know, I presume," she says.

"Yeah, only ones who keep up is Vinny and Ricky." She snorts, leaning against the wall as the elevator descends. "Get tired of the nightly bullshit? Do I need to tell people to hide their puppies or did Brock fuck up?" I mimic her movement, leaning against the opposite wall.

"I'm taking a page from Vinny's book, trying to move around without the constant yapping of people."

"Wondering where you've been lately." She snorts again. "Okay, I didn't give a shit where you were."

"There's our *lovable* baby sis."

"I'm working on my manners," I smirk, looking outside the windows as the daytime of the Underground comes up with glittering lights. The air chills as we move downward, and I'm ready to remain silent for the entire ride. Anita presses the emergency button, halting the elevator. Wonderful. Hopes and dreams up in smoke.

"I wanted to talk in private," she says, lighting her cigarette and inhaling the first drag.

"Were the confession booths booked?"

"You and Vinny seemed to have...escalated your relationship of late."

I don't look at her, keeping my gaze on the Underground below us. The last thing I need is Anita finding out Vinny and I Claim Mated. She won't try to take a bite out of me, but I don't want to become fifty shades of fucked up from cigarette burns.

"When depressing things happen you cling to things to keep you warm and cozy. Vinny's my warm and cozy," I muse.

She tilts her head, staring at me as she takes another long drag of her cigarette. She blows the smoke into the elevator until the smell of burnt, sweet tobacco covers my nostrils. I'm half-tempted to throw her out the window. Pretty sure she'd survive.

"Not saying I'm against it," she continues with a suave and calculated tone. "I'd prefer you two together. He's insufferable when you're not around, and you may not believe it, but I do care about what's good for him."

"So, this *isn't* an intervention? Damn, should've left my banner at home."

"For now."

"Care to elaborate?" I attempt to keep my tone calm, knowing where this is already going. Vinny did almost kill his bartender over me. And two guards. *And* we had sex basically on every surface in *The Lounge*.

"Our father is creating some dissonance within the Society, bleeding into the Blood Mafia through those still loyal to him. He's on the warpath to keep his bloodline pure, and the entire Vampiric Society will side with him when the cards are on the table. Or did Vinny not tell you that before spreading your *scent* everywhere in his lounge?"

Her words pierce like ice, chilling me to the bone and reminding me of my nightmares; fears that kept me from the Underground these past few years. I could handle them with Vinny around, but right now, I struggle not let it consume me.

"What do you want, Anita?"

She steps toward me, crowding me against the elevator glass. "Be more fucking careful, and don't let Vinny nearly tear out the windpipes of his crew."

"They disobeyed him."

"Not good enough this time," she hisses. "Bruno is being more deceptive and using my brother's anger against him. If Vinny looks at *any* crew wrong, Bruno will twist the knife deeper."

"Must be bad, you said the fucker's name." My sass rears its head in frustration.

"Fucking hell, this is serious!" She slams her hand next to me on the window. "Ever since you *interrupted* the Mafia Head meeting, Bruno's had it out for you. If you weren't Cuorebella's kid, you'd be locked up on what's left of Ellis Island."

"I need the vacation."

"I mean it, Brenda," she hisses again.

"I knew what I was doing back then, just like now. Vinny and I will take care of it. We *both* know what we're doing. We're not children."

"Even if it means you'll cost him the entire Blood Mafia? Or start a war?"

"Do you want us together or not? Make up your damn

mind!" I yell in her face, and she takes a step back. "Cause it definitely sounds like you're protecting Bruno, not Vinny!"

"I'm telling you what the Society believes," she sneers in Noctora. *"They think you're corrupting Vinny and the Blood Mafia."*

"Nothing new there! Been told that for years."

"This time it matters! They'll back Bruno and destroy my brother in the process! I won't let you destroy what he's built! He'll be exiled or worse. And with them, it's always worse."

I widen my eyes at her. "That hasn't happened since the Magix family. It's been centuries, and the international laws state—"

"You think they fucking care?" She finishes her cigarette, tossing the butt. "Natalya was one of the last females from the pureblood families in Russia and helped establish half the East Coast, and they *still* banished her and her Mate. They will see this as a betrayal to their bloodlines, so you both need to tread carefully and slowly and stay the fuck away from our father. You need the Blood Mafia to speak for you, but you need more of them on Vinny's side, and they won't if you're spreading your scents everywhere."

"If you don't like us being lovey-dovey, just say so," I snap.

"Don't make Vinny throw out clientele from *The Lounge* or beat his guards to a pulp or *fucking* shoot them because they called you a name. *Again.*"

"Hey! *I'm* the one who made sure he didn't put a bullet in their heads." I jab a finger at her chest. "Besides, it's his fucking lounge. If he doesn't want someone there, he can throw them out. It's a perk for being the owner and Mob Boss. Or have you and the rest of those bloodsuckers forgotten *he's* the Blood Mafia Boss?"

"Doesn't matter. Bruno will find a way to tear you apart."

I snort under my breath. "I fucking dare him to get through my parents first."

Anita brings her face close to mine. Her voice is a threatening calm that almost freezes the last of my blood. "Alanzo won't be able to save you. If he intervenes, a war *will* start between the incubi and vampires. The Underground will be a war zone. I know what your father is capable of; I've seen and *felt* him in action, knowing he's the only one able to destroy this city entirely. Except, I doubt he'll destroy the entire fucking Underground for you two."

My voice darkens. "You underestimate how much my father loves me."

She quirks a brow. "Maybe, but are you willing to live with the guilt and consequences if he defends you?"

A pain stretches over my chest, her words sinking in as I back up against the window. Anita pierces me with a glare, stepping back as her scent of burning roses intensifies, and she warns, "Take. Your. Damn. Time." Her crimson eyes blaze with careful threat. "Act like you have been for years, *friends*. Give it time for the Vampiric Society to see what Bruno will do to them, and in a few years; most will give their fealty to Vinny. Your relationship isn't some *cute* friendship to them anymore. They'll hunt for blood if you threaten his bloodline. You two can be 'lovey-dovey' in the future when it's safe."

I want to tell her I don't have the time. We can't wait for the antique bloodsuckers to get with the program. All because of a demented scientist and judgmental sperm donor. I keep my mouth shut, slamming the emergency button to get off this fucking ride.

It's silent in the elevator as we go down, while it feels like a raging storm is inside me beating to get out. We reach the bottom, and she walks out, pausing to say her parting words, "They exiled a pureblood royal for Mating a purebred werewolf. What do you think they'll do to a replaceable mafia boss who chose a half-breed over...*us*?"

Us. The word clangs through my body as I watch her walk away. I shake in rage as I sprint out of the elevator down the path, dodging random pedestrians. People yell as I run past, warning me to be careful. I don't know where I'm going, but I just run as my breathing grows ragged, and my thoughts churn with unbridled anger and frustration. After some time, I stop outside a coffee shop, breathing hard.

Damn it. DAMN IT.

I push my hair back, adjusting my glasses as I catch my breath and realize where I am. I walk down the street to *The Vault* shakily, blocking out the noises and melding colors of people on the paths, focusing on the brick beneath my feet. I come to the marbled steps and enter, escaping the noise of the Underground. For once I'm here during normal hours and people are milling about through shelves and reading nooks. I nod at a librarian, making my way up the spiral staircase to the empty third floor where I was a week ago, seeing the books still there.

"Sneaky shifter," I mumble, grabbing a few books and heading to put them away.

I find solace as I arrange the books where they should be, running my hands over leatherbound spines, each with their own personality as I move from one to the next. The sweet scents of aged paper, leather, and ink calm my nerves. A smile grows on my face as I feel more peaceful within my element, and I end up sitting in an aisle and start reading. Time passes as I try to find answers, struggling against the steady blurring of my eyesight until I finally lean my head back, take my glasses off, and close my eyes.

The books don't ease me.

Mating will only keep us safe to an extent, but I hoped there would have been some kind of fucking loophole in the Vampiric Society's laws. We could show them I have vampiric traits, maybe convince them I have *some* vampire in me, but it probably wouldn't be enough because I'm a fucking anomaly. Pureblood vampires are another breed of vampire, their genetics functioning at a different level of control and behavior, few have been known for transferring powers to other vampires, but never humans or half-breeds. There's nothing to help explain how I've taken behaviors of a pureblood.

Fuck, I don't want to talk to daemon daddy to find out if I could have vampiric DNA from the testing. I may have no choice if I can't find Traloski.

I sigh, secluding myself into darkness as exhaustion overwhelms me. I'm too tired to fight the sleep that could be my last. It'd be really shitty if my last thought, going into a "forever sleep," was about John Traloski.

SOMEONE'S SCREAMING.

The smell of sewage consumes the darkness, and creaking metal vibrates against the echoes of screams. Pain. There's only pain.

The smell worsens, deepening its sour, rancid scent. A familiar, thick aroma trickles into the air.

Blood. Deep, pure blood clings to the aroma. Familiar. Why is it familiar?

I know that scent.

The screaming stops in the darkness. A whisper far in the distance, shadowed through the haze, "Leave her."

Agonizing shrieks rattle the metal, jolting my body.

I WAKE WITH A START, my arms flinging out to steady me as I feel like I'm falling into a chasm. Something crunches under my hand, and I heave in long breaths, raising it to feel the remains of my glasses beneath my palm.

"Fucking hell." I carefully pick up all the pieces and stand up, easing my way down the aisle to dump my ruined glasses on the coffee table. I rub my eyes, and I'm face to face with my contorted blindness. Bemoaning that I've broken another pair of glasses, I head back down the aisle.

I have *The Vault* aisles memorized, but not the books I've strewn about, which I find by almost tripping over them.

"Damn it," I mutter, closing my eyes in frustration. So much for an uplifting nap.

I crouch down, stacking the books back on the shelf, feeling the indentation of the titles, knowing where they go. I guide myself down another aisle, trailing my fingers over the books until I find the braille section of history and literature. I search for some books and find two that may be worth looking into. A heavy maybe.

I hold them close and smell the familiar scent of my older brother. "Shouldn't you be working?"

"Shouldn't you be wearing your glasses?" Joey retorts as he approaches and grabs the books from my hand, looping his arm with mine. "Come on, you blind bat."

"Hey, be nice to the visually-impaired sister." I poke his shoulder.

"Okay, first off," he begins as we walk down the aisle. "Your blindness has rarely held you back, and you have better hearing and sense of smell than the rest of us. Secondly, you'd love being a bat. Hide in the dark, hang around screeching at people, and maybe take some blood for kicks."

We plop down on the couch, and I take the books back from him. "You know that rumor started because a vampire pleaded a case of bloodsucking on his 'animal instincts' in the 1300s? Poor vampire bats didn't know what hit them with that nickname."

"Did you have that in your dissertation?"

"No…wrong century."

The pieces from my glasses clink across the coffee table. "Shit, sis, what did you do to your glasses?"

"Victims of a bad dream."

"Was it the usual?" I'm about to tell him no, but stop, thinking about the oddity of it. It wasn't the usual nightmare and something about that rancid smell caught me off guard. Not ready to dive into that mess.

"Same old, same old," I respond with a shrug. "Don't worry about it."

"If you say so." He lounges next to me as I open the first book. "By the way…Vinny thought you'd be down here since you didn't tell him you were back from Topside."

"Aw, shit." Wonderful, I forgot.

"And he found out from Anita."

"Double shit."

"He called me to see if you were home or at the coffee shop. Figured you'd be here when all other options were moot. He bet you were distracted by books again."

"Can I add a triple shit to that list?"

Joey chuckles, shuffling next to me as he grabs the books in my lap. "What rabbit hole made you forget to contact him?"

"Dangerous curiosity," I answer as he skims his fingers over the covers. My entire family can read braille, so I can't hide what I'm reading. This may be the first time I wish it was *Paranormal Digest*.

"Find out why Edgar's a dickwad?"

"No," I scoff lightly. "And nothing much of anything that's been helpful or new, and I'm beginning to think reading all my life has bit me in the butt. I know most of this already."

"Because you know everything about Paranormals?" He teases slightly.

"I mean, I did get my master's in it."

"We can blame Pops for all the books," he chuckles. "Although your master's was in literature and history. The rest you took upon yourself to know for personal reasons."

"Well, *someone* needed to know how to keep Vinny and Rodney from killing each other."

Joey moves back on the couch, putting his arm around the back as I continue to find mostly fairytales about daemons and nothing about recent events, living conditions, or behavioral changes. I huff, putting it aside and start a book on everyday family life for daemons.

"We've been worried about you, sis."

"Already talked about this, Joey—"

"Just because we talked once, doesn't mean it's fixed or has gone away. And something shook you up," he retorts. I continue reading, trying to ignore him since that tactic has worked wonders today. "Gina told me about Bruno visiting the club."

Shit. The last fucking being I wanted to talk about. "It's fine."

"It's not fine. He makes you uncomfortable, and everyone knows he *hates* you and Vinny together. Especially after that intervention of yours at the Mafia Head meeting. Is Vinny at least—?"

"Leave it be, Joey."

"I'm worried about you."

"I know, and you're the best big brother for doing so," I sigh, putting the book down and turning toward him. I open my eyes to shades of dark blue and violet, black outlining most of him; everything's so dark and heavily distorted. Damn sight's getting worse. "We're figuring it out."

Joey cups my cheek, stroking his thumb over a scar before pulling me into a hug, resting his chin on my head. "Everyone's been...testy lately. And it feels like you're hiding something, sis."

I go still. My chest aches as I hold him closely, willing all tears to stay down and my breathing to remain steady. I want to tell him and let him know everything that's going on and the pain I feel thinking of not being here anymore. The pain that someone, either daemon, vampire, scientist, ghoul, or death itself will take me from them and I'll fail. How much it hurts to hide and how scared I am of what's happening. And for once, I can't tell my brother my secrets in the dark.

"I need you to trust me, Joey," I beg him like I had begged Ma. "Please."

He tightens his grip, and after a moment, nods against my

head. I snuggle further into our hug, staying in the silence as the library fills the quiet with its ambiance. I breathe in his dark musky, clove scent, wishing I could stay in the comfort of my brother's arms.

"Supposed to get you for dinner, too," he says. "Ma made fettuccine alfredo."

"Your favorite," I murmur.

We remain where we are, our arms staying around the other, neither moving to leave. Joey shifts his face next to my ear, and whispers, "I have a dark feeling I'm gonna lose you, sis. It terrifies me, and I don't wanna think about losing you."

Tears escape from my eyes, running down my cheeks as I hold him, and lie through my teeth, "Not going anywhere, Joey. Can't get rid of me that easily."

Except, my brother is a powerful incubus, and I know he knows...I'm lying.

CHAPTER 17
INCUBUS TIES

Joey's arm is hooked through mine as we leave *The Vault*, the streets far quieter than before. We walk in silence for the first few blocks, and I shove him lightly to rile him up. "You trying to start a fight or something?" He asks.

"Maybe," I tease. "Is it working?"

"It'd be an unfair fight."

"You saying that cause the world looks like Picasso's paintings for me right now?"

"Exactly," he scoffs. "You're more dangerous when you're blind. Seen you shoot a werewolf from fifty feet away without looking. Rodney told me about your recent one." He sounds amused, and it makes me feel better after our half-hour hugging session. He needed the physical touch boost, and I needed a break from books.

I shrug. "It's a talent."

"Seriously, your other senses scare me sometimes."

"Maybe it's from growing up in a strip club like I owned the place."

"Because you did," he snorts.

"Did not."

"Did, too."

"Did not."

"Did, too." His hand covers my mouth before I can argue. "Ask everyone who worked during those early years. Pops shut down the club *daily* for you."

I mumble against his hand, the slobber not enough for him to move it just yet. "Be fankful you got time uf."

"Time off? I had to babysit you, and you were worse than the dancers." He finally pulls his hand away, wiping the saliva off on his pants. I give a genuine grin, and his scent heightens in delight.

We enter *Unbound* just as the staff starts cleaning for the changeover. Shapes shift weirdly, and I blink rapidly hoping my vision will adjust, but it worsens forming a headache behind my eyes. I keep them closed as Joey walks us to the apartment, and I click my tongue guiding myself up the stairs to the foyer, kicking off my shoes as I smell Ma's fettuccine alfredo from the kitchen.

"Ma, do you want the bread out now?" Ricky asks.

"Both baskets, center of table, darling," she answers.

Joey kicks his shoes off and steps around me toward the kitchen. I blink again, but the headache worsens with the blurred shapes and colors. A groan of frustration bubbles up in my throat as I click my way to the living room to sit on the couch's arm. I'm used to shitty vision, but this was making me nauseous. It feels like a funhouse of mirrors with Monet's paintings as the background.

"Hey, sis!" Ricky says from the dining area. "What time is Vinny getting here?"

"Didn't know he was coming." That'd be a first. I snort to myself.

"I'll ask Ma," he says, pattering away into the kitchen.

I rub my temple when the scent of cinnamon and cigars drifts by my nose past the thick aroma of garlic, pasta, cheese, and fresh bread. "Hey, Pops," I say as he rests a hand on my shoulder, and kisses my aching head. I dig into my jacket pocket and pull out the remains of the glasses. "Sorry."

"You haven't destroyed a pair like this since you were in college," he says, taking the pieces from me.

"In my defense, I was asleep this time. Not victims of finals."

Pops places the pieces aside, tracing a light comforting touch over my cheek. He rubs my arm, and I can sense him doing his assessment over me, like he used to when I visited home from Topside. "Nightmare again?" I nod. "Need to talk about it?"

"Not really."

"Why your eyes closed?"

"Everything is really off. And I don't want to end up hurling on Ma's pasta."

"That bad?"

"Remember when Beckham took me to the Underground Metropolitan Museum of Art to see the immersive Pollock exhibits? *That* was tame."

"You try wearing your contacts today?" He asks, and I shake my head. "Go put them in, see if it helps. Otherwise, Ricky can have you borrow one of his blindfolds to keep light from hurting your eyes." He kisses my head and pats my shoulder to head off.

I make my way down the hallway to my room with a few tongue clicks, closing the door behind me. I stumble over some clothes with a grunt. Okay, don't remember leaving my room as if a hurricane came through.

"When did I get so messy?" I whisper to myself, smelling the stale air of my room. Was I really that depressed that I didn't clean up?

I scoot some clothes to the side, planning to clean up after I find my contacts and rummage through my dresser. As I search for my contact case, I breathe in his scent and hear a creak in the doorway. Not stopping my search, I pull out my gun, point it behind me, and click the safety back. "Where the fuck is that case?"

"Four inches to the right." I adjust my aim. "Little lower." I follow instructions. "There. Losing your touch, sweet cheeks," Vinny says.

"I'm hunting for wabbits."

"Is that why you sound like a drunk college student looking for their weed and ribbed condoms?"

"Your flirtation skills are immaculate." I click the safety on and toss the gun on my bed.

"You're losing your touch with your aim; I'm lacking in flirtation skills. Perhaps we both need ice cream or a good screw. I suggest the latter."

He walks up behind me, and I ignore his advances, kneeling down to the next drawer. "Not now, Vinny."

He moves around me, and opens a different drawer, and I hear something open. He comes back, lifting me up to stand to show off his find. "Looking for these?" I frown and swipe the case. Of course, he knew where one was.

I pop both contacts in, blinking roughly at the dryness as I shoot my hand out. Vinny places a bottle of solution in my hand, and I place a few drops in my eyes, blinking until my sight comes back. The distortions and discolorations are gone, including most of my headache and motion sickness. I've escaped the funhouse.

"Thank you," I say, putting the solution and case away. I look around, groaning at the mess I made, and go to clean some of it up.

"I don't remember your apartment ever being this dirty," Vinny comments, and moves out of the way.

"That's because I worked all the time and didn't have a boy over every other night," I smirk. "If I find your underwear, I'm hanging it up with mine."

I toss some clothes into my laundry basket, put my gun away, and remake my bed as he stands quietly. I'm not completely ignoring him, but I'm surly, agitated, hungry, and most of all…guilt ridden. All aspects not attractive to any partner.

I'm tucking my bedsheets when he murmurs, "You didn't call."

And now I officially feel like shit for not keeping my promise. "I forgot."

"Sweet cheeks—"

"I fucking forgot, Vinny," I snap. "I'm sorry. I was distracted by what Drauper told me and then Anita cornered me in the elevator. I was so wrapped up in my own head, I went to *The Vault*, fell asleep, and broke my glasses. So, I'm sorry."

I walk over to my bookcase, sinking to the ground to reshelve some books, pausing when I come across some old children's books. The normal ink-printed ones were what Pops would read me, but most were in braille, like *Frog and Toad*, *Cinderella*, and *The Secret Garden*. I run my fingers across the spines slowly. Every year on my birthday, Vinny would gift me a first edition in braille.

"I've got to be the worst Mate ever," I mutter.

"No, you're not."

"Then worst friend ever."

"Quit talking about my bestie like that," Vinny warns sarcastically.

I set the books down and look up at his ruby eyes peering over at me. He sits on my bed, tilting his head with a half-smile. "You didn't tell me how bad it's getting," I whisper. "I knew the Society may consider exiling you, Vinny, but from what Anita told me, they may actually kill you. They're already this angry and don't even know we're Mated. They'll destroy you."

"Won't come to that," he says, and I shake my head, putting books away. "We're going to keep the Mating a secret, and when the time is right—"

"I may already be dead."

I stand, keeping his gaze with mine as I watch pain lace his expression. He slackens a little, then takes his jacket off, running his hand through his hair and lets out a long sigh. "I'll give it all up before that happens. I'm not leaving you alone."

"I have my family..."

"You're not getting rid of me."

"When I die, Vinny, you'll have nothing," I argue. "My family will have each other, but you'll get thrown away. You'll lose everything. You'll have fought for a dead half-breed and end up losing important—"

"When you're gone, then I'll have lost everything that's important," he says. "The rest doesn't matter and can sink into oblivion for all I care."

I walk up to him, pointing my finger at his chest. "Don't act like you don't care about the others. About your sister or Samuel or your crew...they matter, too. I *know* they do to you."

"Not as much as you." His expression hardens while his tone darkens. "I've told you and *will* tell you again and again; I'll give it all away for you. *You* are the most important being to me." He stands up, cradling my face in his hands. "I love you so fucking much, and I'm not letting you go. I'll live with the consequences, but not without you beside me."

Tears spill down my cheek. "You may not have that choice. I'm getting more exhausted each day..."

Vinny wipes away the tears, kissing both of my cheeks. "Not giving up until you're unmoving in my arms, sweet cheeks."

"You sound like Pops," I choke between tears.

"At least he agrees with me."

"And unbelievably hasn't castrated you yet."

"I still have a decade to win that old bet."

"Oof, you may not make it. Pity. Liked your dick," I tease through tears.

"Liked? Thought you loved it?"

"Don't get cocky."

We laugh quietly, and I stroke his hair back, placing my hand against his cheek. Vinny leans down and kisses me tenderly, bringing me into a close embrace. The warmth of his chest and safety I feel sweeps through my body. I fall into his arms, inhaling the rising scent of spices and whiskey as his tongue traces over my lips. I clutch him harder, deepening the kiss as I press against him.

"You have two minutes to get clothes on!" Joey interrupts from the hallway. "Five to get to the table. Otherwise, I'm sending Ricky in after you. He's got glitter today, so you've been warned."

We break the kiss, and Vinny snarls lightly at the doorway. I kiss him briefly on the cheek, bringing his attention back to me. "I love you, Vinny. I just want you safe, too."

"That's why I have you."

"And who will protect you when I'm gone?" His gaze softens. "I don't want you getting hurt."

He smiles, caressing my face. "Only one capable of that is you, sweet cheeks."

"You sure? I've seen Rodney pack a wallop on you."

Vinny pulls me in close, kissing me harshly and stealing my breath away before saying, "As long as you're here, I'll fight to keep you beside me. The danger is part of the fun."

Suddenly, he feels gentler as his touch brings forth a loving tenderness across my skin. I breathe in deeply, calming myself with his scent and touch remembering what he said weeks ago, *"You calm me."* The flicker of hope ignites dimly, and I hope what we've done wasn't in vain. For his sake.

Vinny kisses me one last time and grabs my hand, leading me out of my room. "Come on, before your brother unleashes that sparkly shit."

We join my family at the dinner table as they converse like every other meal we've had together before. Vinny sits beside me, stealing my bread, Ma asks about my glasses, Joey and Pops talk shop with Vinny, and Ricky discusses new routines I should return to the stage for. I jam my foot a couple of times into Vinny's shin for TMI comments while my brothers laugh at us.

It's normal.

The ticking timebomb that seems ever present feels faint in my chest. I hope and pray to whoever above or fucking below that this isn't one of my last nights with them.

RED
EYES

CHAPTER 18
PAIN AND PREJUDICE

I toss my phone onto the makeup counter, banging my head on the surface and grumbling from my recent phone call. After six days of searching, Drauper hasn't found any videos, witnesses, *nothing* to explain how the missing people vanished. Wonderful. He's still going through footage, but my hope is dwindling for *something*.

I breathe in Gina's scent as she softly walks up behind me and massages my neck and shoulders. A moan escapes me as she works her expert hands over my skin, and she asks, "Ricky suggest the pink G-string again?"

"After this past week, I may say yes."

"Do you just need some snuggles?"

I scoff, "Plenty of that."

The nightmares have continued to the point where I've woken up every night screaming in a cold sweat and can't sleep without Vinny, Joey, or Ricky. Even Pops had me fall asleep on his lap in the living room. One of the few times I wished I wasn't immune to his powers just so I could sleep.

Gina stops the massage and sits on the counter next to my head. I move to lay on my cheek as her long dark hair falls over her shoulders, covering the t-shirt she wears before we open up for our evening clientele. I was supposed to dance tonight, but now I want to curl up under a pile of clothes.

"Anything I can help with, baby sis?" Her tone is cautious like everyone else lately.

It reminds me of when I first arrived. Pops kept me in the apartment for over a month, away from other Paranormals. I wasn't open to other beings if they weren't my family until he started to bring me down to the club, keeping me close to him. He warned everyone to be gentle with me, and Gina was one of the first to hold me and get me to say something other than "Daddy." They all knew that I'd gone through hell and was patient with my healing from what I couldn't remember.

I shake my head and sit up. "Did Edgar come back?"

She sighs, slouching against the mirror. "Two nights ago. Darius and Bobby kept him toward the bar away from the stage. Didn't do anything other than order drinks and stare. He freaked out Mack and Esme. It's the way he stares like he wants to burn the place down and everyone in it. Maybe it's because we haven't had a daemon here in like a century, but he's a little unnerving. Even for me."

"Technically, you've been around one for twenty years," I smirk, pointing to my head.

Gina laughs. "No, baby sis, you're succubus through and through. We raised you right."

"Still doesn't change genetics."

"That's all it is." She strokes back my hair. "And it doesn't define you."

"But it—" I hear his footsteps and reach for my gun but realize I don't have it on me and grab a pair of underwear and slingshot it at him. Surprisingly, he doesn't catch it, allowing it to land on his shoulder.

Vinny stops and looks down at the pink lacey thong and grins. "These aren't yours, sweet cheeks."

"How do you know?" I smirk.

"It's pink and lace, two things you hate." He picks it off,

bringing it close to inspect, and raises a brow. "And they smell...flowery."

"Pervert."

"Don't slingshot stripper panties at me."

"I don't have my gun."

"Pocketknife?"

"Great idea. Leave and come back. I'll check my aim when you return." We both smile at the meager challenge.

"Is it silver?" Vinny asks, and my smile grows into something wicked. "Maybe next time."

Gina gets off the counter and sighs, "At least you two haven't changed much."

"He'd die of a heart attack if I was sweet all the time," I say, taking her seat on the counter.

She laughs. "And those are *mine*, Mr. Pinstripe."

"No offense, Gina." He says with a devious smile.

Vinny hands the thong back to Gina, and she places a quick kiss on his cheek. A snarl rises in my throat, but I force it down as my nails dig into the counter. My eyes pierce toward Vinny, who flicks me a warning look, and I concentrate on his dark pinstripe suit, family ring, and slicked-back hair—the perfect portrait of a gangster.

"I'll leave you be," Gina says, tossing the thong with the rest of her costumes and pausing at the door. "I don't think we'll need you tonight, baby sis. Maybe take a break. We have new females anyways."

"They ready?" I ask, relaxing my hold on the countertop.

"Just young. Some have scars they're scared to show, but they want to overcome that. We'll take care of them. Maybe we'll discuss you talking to them soon?"

"Sure."

She leaves the room, and I turn my attention back to Vinny, who's extremely still in the middle of the empty room. I cock my head, and a small smile rises on his face. His scent blossoms and welcomes me as he begins to take his jacket off.

"You were about to growl at Gina," he says, keeping my attention with his slow movements like draping his jacket over a chair and uncuffing his maroon shirt. "Quite territorial there, sweet cheeks."

"Coming from the one who doesn't like to share," I scoff.

"At least I admit it, but you..." he stops before me, his eyes sweeping over me with wicked delight, "...not so much." His hands grip my knees and spread my legs open on the counter. He steps between them and brings his hand up to place a finger under my chin, then gently strokes my bottom lip.

"Why you here, bloodsucker?" The bite in my voice is gone and replaced with rising want. My body has already become putty in his hands, willing to do anything he asks of me. All he had to do was take the damn jacket off.

He takes a deep breath in, searching over my face as his other hand trails down my facial scars. "I needed to see you."

"How much of me?" He raises a brow. "Give you that dance finally, perhaps?"

He chuckles, moving his hands to my sides. Damn it. "Not here, sweet cheeks. Never here."

I scrunch my brows at him. "Why?"

"This space is meant for recovery," he says gesturing around the changing room. "It's a place to feel safe, recover, and being comfortable. I'd never forgive myself if someone walked in or heard anything, taking that safety away from them."

My chest constricts as I realize he's right, appreciating his awareness of this space. It's always been somewhere people could openly be themselves after tragedy without worry. It never mattered the species, body types, sexuality, gender, or abilities, because being a dancer at *Unbound* meant overcoming trauma and being in control of your body again. It's why Pops created this club in the first place, for those who needed it. I just never thought of Vinny's side of things, being seen as the aggressor. I never saw him as that.

I glance past him and ask quietly, "What about you and Gina?"

"Never did it back here. Always her personal room or one of the other private rooms."

"Somehow that's comforting, but...odd." I try to shake off the old, unwanted feelings.

I couldn't be mad at either of them for being adults when I wasn't at the time. They knew each other for decades before I came along. When I was in my early twenties, it had been agony to see them disappear to the back together. It's been over five years, yet my stomach twists a little at the thought of them....

"Sweet cheeks," Vinny says, reaching for my face to bring my focus back. "We're long done. It's only you, sweetheart."

The loving tenderness and guilt in his eyes make my heart ache. I may have jealousy leftover from years past, but I'm not the only one who hurts. Vinny's already shown me how much guilt he feels from time to time, over past decisions and his old lifestyle. He's always been respectful of me, protecting me from harm in more ways than I can count. The least I can do is remind him I don't blame him.

"I know, Vinny. I know." I reach up, holding his hand against my cheek. "What did you need to see me for? Panties and jokes aside."

He kisses me briefly on the mouth and pulls away before it fully registers in my brain that he had. He wraps his arms around me, holding me close as he nuzzles his face into my neck. I wrap my legs around him and hook them behind his knees, hugging the vampire to me. Vinny breathes in deeply and becomes a little shaky, prompting me to tighten my grip on him.

I stroke his hair, and whisper, "Do you wanna talk about it?"

"Long day of politics and mob shit. Close to getting those heart palpitations again."

"Well, we don't want that," I say against his hair. "Do you need—"

"Only you." He squeezes me tighter as the shaking in his arms worsens.

"Vinny…"

"Few more minutes," he whispers. "Just need a moment with you."

We hold onto each other in silence, and tears prick my eyes as I stroke his head. Fear trickles down my spine as I think about not being here when he's had a rough day. I can see him going back to old vices like drinking or destroying *The Lounge*. I don't want him to be alone.

"Hey, bloodsucker," I say, and he hums against my skin. "I'm getting more territorial, and you're getting needier with physical touch, is this more Mate shit? Or does life really suck right now?"

"Third option?" He murmurs.

"We're slowly switching bodies. I'm becoming a vampire, and you're becoming an incubus."

"Do I get wings?"

"Only if I get fangs…and better eyesight. Otherwise, I'm returning the Mating. There was a money-back guarantee, right?"

"No return policy, all sales are final." Vinny chuckles, and I kiss him softly, my lips pressing warmly against his. I bring him in tight, almost trying to fuse his body with mine, hoping it'll keep him safe. Vinny breaks the kiss and smiles softly. "So, my day was shit; what about you?"

"No heart palpitations on my end."

"Lucky you. No news from up Top?"

"Not really. You?"

"Just more dead ghouls," he murmurs. Vinny steps back, grabbing hold of my hands and laying them in my lap as he stands between my legs. The shaking in his body has stopped, and there's a happier glint in his eyes.

"Feel better?" I ask.

"I'd feel even better if you took your top off."

"I thought you said—"

"Just to look," he says with a shrug and mischievous grin.

I roll my eyes and pinch his hands. "Oh goodie, you're back to being a cringey bloodsucker. Had me worried there."

He smirks as his gaze flicks over my features slowly, taking his time like he's memorizing every bit of me. I understand the feeling. He asks, "The detective call?" I nod. "What he say?"

I sigh, leaning back against the mirror. "He went through footage and still hasn't found anything helpful. He's using what contacts he has."

"No other connections than the immunities?"

"No. Unless you found something with the dead ghouls?"

He shakes his head and pushes back his already grease-slicked hair, pausing as the family ring brushes over his temple. His scent darkens as he stares at the piece of jewelry, and his gaze becomes a haunting glow before quietly, shoving his hands into his pockets. "The half-breeds taken from our side span from the Bronx, Brooklyn, and Queens. No connection, and none of them were looking for 'medical care' either."

"That how we're putting it?" I smirk.

"If someone's outwardly looking to become immune to Paranormals or make money as a test subject? It's the nicest way I can call it."

"Lovely, we're running out of options *and* time," I murmur, closing my eyes as I knock my head into Vinny's chest.

The air feels thick as I remain silent, thinking as I listen to the light thudding of Vinny's heart. He places his chin on my head and caresses my lower back. My gut twists a little, knowing I'm stuck with my own terrible version of *Finding Nemo* as I remember what Gina said.

"Edgar was here a couple of nights ago, making dancers jumpy," I say.

"He was seen at *Deviant Endeavors* and *Lovers Reborn* these last two weeks."

I lean back and furrow my brows. "Two other incubi clubs?"

"And apparently a few bars in the werewolf territory. Rodney asked if he was free game to hunt, but I told him he'd have to wait in line."

"What was he doing there?"

"Scaring the shit out of patrons," Vinny mutters. "Both owners threw him out when he got too close to the dancers. One of them mentioned he had this furious look in his eye, trying to grab her. Seems you pissed him off last time."

I snort. "Good."

"Rodney also overheard a few female wolves say he smelled off, although the wolves haven't had a daemon in their area for decades."

"What the fuck is his agenda?"

"Guilt you, make Paranormals uncomfortable, or maybe scare anyone who's part of the lifestyle in general. You said daemons hate most Paranormals."

"They hate vampires and werewolves the most due to power struggles. So, that makes sense for the female wolves being on alert, but not Edgar's disdain toward succubi."

"You speak to him since you talked in the alley?" I shake my head. "Not that I want you to, because I don't trust the bastard, but why not?"

I stare down at the scars on my wrists. The trickling worry from *The Vault* creeps back up my spine again. "I don't see a point. He has an endgame, and I don't think I want to know what it is. But I'm sure it involves vengeance for losing his children."

Vinny places his hand against my cheek, and I look up at him. His eyes narrow. "What aren't you telling me?"

I release a long breath. "He's here for personal gain, not me. Daemons don't trust humans, yet he worked with Traloski. He got something out of that program to go against centuries worth of trauma, and it may be why he's back. I think he wants Traloski more than me, but I need more info before talking to him again. I can't let him get to Traloski before I do."

Do I think Edgar knows where Traloski is? No. Do I think he's using me to get to him? Definitely. He wants what Traloski has. Why else would he come back to New York after twenty years, apart from the last of his children being alive? He's playing his own game, and I plan to figure it out. From a distance. And frankly, I don't want to talk to the being who left me to be tortured as a baby.

Vinny nods, pacing down the mirrored counter as he taps his fingers along the surface thoughtfully. He stops a few feet away, turning and approaching me with a soft murmur, "There's still another option in Alanzo's desk." I moan, leaning my head back, knowing what he's implying. "It's just paperwork, sweet cheeks. Not dangerous."

"Got me to shoot you, so if anyone's in danger, it's you, bloodsucker."

"Not really complaining, long as you lick my wounds this time." His eyes shine as he grins at me, and I chuckle under my breath.

"You heal too quickly. Maybe I'll use silver bullets this time. You find pain kinky, right?" Vinny laughs and helps me off the counter. "You're gonna make us do it now, aren't you?"

"Better late than never. If nothing helps, we can burn the pages and throw them at Edgar. Little fireballs into his feathered wings, and we can nickname him 'phoenix.'" I laugh loudly at the image he's conjured up.

———

"IT'S NOT GONNA BITE, baby girl," Pops says gently.

"Says you, Pops," I grumble, holding my mug close and staring at the folder on the kitchen table. The last time I saw it,

I was throwing bottles of scotch into my kitchen sink. It's been over two months since I last looked at it.

"There's only one thing in this room that can, and he's forbidden to do so in my presence," Pops says, and we both look over at Vinny behind him, who's quietly drinking his whiskey, leaning against the counter. He was smart to choose liquor.

Ma and Ricky are downstairs working in the club while Joey is off for business in the tunnels with some shifters. Vinny and I told Pops our plan to read through the folder, so he made sure it was just us to go through the paperwork.

I sigh and place my mug down, flipping open the folder. The agony of my past pours back over me as I stare at the top sheet, the labeling mocking me. Suddenly, I hear the rain and thunder again that shook my apartment and the shattering of glass in my sink as I screamed. Liquor burning my throat as I read the horrific paperwork that detailed where every scar came from, like I'd been an animal. My stomach twists as I stare at my original name.

#37.

Merely a number. "Baby girl."

A science experiment. "Sweet cheeks."

My mind falters into nightmares, hands trembling as I shakily turn the page, reading the details of my reactions to anti-venom. Milliliter after milliliter. I'd been given so much of it. I was a baby. A *fucking* baby.

Memories flash of leather restraints and cold metal. I hear voices call for me, but they're drowned out by the roaring terror inside. My lungs ache as I remember screaming, bright lights burning into my retinas as needles prod into my skin. I'm back in the hospital, struggling to be let free. Everything comes crashing back like a rampaging tsunami and my vision blurs as I read, *"Subject tried to struggle against the restraints but was sedated with infused ghoul blood and succubus secretions. Larger doses were given—"*

I barely make it to the sink to throw up, heaving out the contents of my stomach as warm hands rub my back. My hair is swept from my face as someone talks to me, but all I can focus on is puking up everything I ate today. The faucet is turned on, washing my vomit down the drain. I breathe heavily through my nose, concentrating on the sweet aroma of cinnamon and whiskey as it calms my muscles and stomach.

"Right here, baby girl," Pops soothes, rubbing my back in gentle circles and I grip onto his other arm. "Daddy's right here...you're safe. Deep breath in through the nose, back out the mouth. There you go, baby girl."

My panic attacks were similar in the past but weren't this devasting in memory. He hums and brings a hand to my forehead to steady me like he did when I was younger. I lean into his touch, listening to him hum a serene lullaby as the panic drifts away. He kisses my head lightly, allowing me to fall into his embrace.

"You're not reading those papers again, baby girl."

"I need to...I need to face—"

"Fucking nothing," Vinny interrupts. "You already lived through it; no point going through it again. You've got nothing to prove."

"Vincent," Pops says sternly, and I smell cinnamon burning stronger. Vinny shuffles a few feet back.

"Leave him alone, Pops," I murmur.

Pops' scent eases back, and I look up to see his violet gaze. "You got nothing to face, baby girl. Healing doesn't require staring at your trauma again, especially if you're not ready."

"Pops," I rasp.

"Vincent and I can look through it without you. Nothing wrong protecting your mental well-being."

"One would think this was your job for the past three centuries," I say with a weak smirk.

"Then you should listen." He helps me stand fully, turning me to look at him. My eyes burn, and he wipes away the stray tears on my cheeks and pulls me into his arms to rid the last of the shaking. "There's no need to face it again if all it brings is pain. We can try again in the future when you're ready, but it's *your* choice, baby girl. You're not weak. And you're not broken. Let us do this for you."

I nod into his chest as Vinny says, "We'll see if we can find something. I'm sure with Pops, we won't miss anything."

"Well, yeah, he's more literate than you," I mumble.

"He has age on his side."

"And wisdom."

"Alright, enough flirting, you two," Pops says, pulling away. "Go to the living room and lay down for a spell. Watch some television and get a slice of Ma's brambleberry pie, it's alright."

Father knows best.

CHAPTER 19
SECRETS I'VE NEVER SAID

A soft hand on my shoulder wakes me up as another gentle touch moves across my forehead. I blink my eyes open, seeing only deep violets and blues swirling with orange. I took my contacts out after Pops' suggestion of pie had worked, lulling me into sleep. I take a deep breath in, recognizing Ma's sweet cherry perfume as she wakes me gently and whispers, "Let's get you to bed, baby."

"Where's Pops and Vinny?" I ask groggily, rubbing my eyes.

"Your father's in bed, and Vinny had to go for some business. He told me you can talk with him tomorrow evening." She helps me up as I stagger from the couch, wrapping an arm around my shoulders. "We tried to move you earlier, but you were finally asleep, and we wanted you to rest."

I lean into her touch as we walk down the hall. "They say anything to you, Ma?"

"Your father mentioned paperwork, that's all." She leads me into my room and helps me to bed, pulling the covers over me as I snuggle into its warmth. She pats my head and kisses me goodnight. "Love you, baby."

I can hear the pain laced within her tone that only she can hide well enough. It's the calm worry of a mother helping me bathe, soothing me after a nightmare, or telling me the bullies meant nothing. The air dampens from her controlled pheromones, trickling into a worried scent of fallen rain.

"Ma?" My voice is quiet as she stops near my door. "Did... did you read the paperwork on the table?"

She pauses, but her scent doesn't waver in the darkness. "Go to sleep, baby," she hums softly. "You can help me make breakfast in the morning." She leaves the room, closing the door gently behind her.

She knows.

———

MA and I clean up the kitchen silently after breakfast, which was quiet with only my brothers and Ma since Pops left early this morning. Joey left halfway through the meal, asking Ricky to take care of everything downstairs. Ricky then left, grumbling about the family business and scheduling downstairs.

Ma sets aside snacks for the dancers, puttering around me, and asks, "Are you working today, baby?"

"No, I kind of owe Beckham a clean-up on aisle six in *The Vault*. I made a small mess the other day," I say, putting dishes away and sensing her unease again. The paperwork was gone from the kitchen table this morning, and I found it in Pops' desk drawer in his office, wrinkled with rips, whiskey stains, and a flour thumbprint.

My phone goes off in the living room, and I rush to pick it up without checking the I.D. "If you have free alcohol, you'll be a candidate for my new BFF."

"Of all the ways to answer your phone," Drauper groans over the line. I walk further into the living room, away from Ma's ears. "Is that all it takes? Alcohol?"

"Considering I can drink you under the table, yup."

"You haven't though."

"Could. Will. Give it time." I lean against the wall and peer into the kitchen. I know in my gut she's read the paperwork, but I wasn't giving chances for more of the truth to be out yet. "What's up, Doc?"

"I think I found a lead."

"Don't yank my chain."

"I don't have that kind of time. Or patience."

"Oh, you're testy."

"And you're lively this evening."

"Morning for me, Topside," I muse.

"You wanna know what I got or not?" He asks, and I wait for him to continue. "Alright. Three of the half-breeds went missing about two months ago outside a club on the edge of a neutral zone on the western side of the Bronx."

"Same neutral zone as the—"

"Center? Yes, but on the far side of it. Took me this long to find it because of all the drug-running through there. Tapes go missing when the FBI takes hold or when *others* you probably know get involved."

I need more coffee before dealing with prejudice in the morning. "Careful detective."

"Just saying."

"What's the club—?" I hear honking and chatter in the background like he's coming up from the subway as a conductor voice thrums low. Oh, but *I'm* the impatient one? "You're already *there*?"

"No judgment from you. After weeks of nothing, I'm not waiting around."

"I was about to yell at you for not waiting for *me*. Rude. Have you learned nothing from the Mystery Gang? Don't split up." I rush to my bedroom to change my clothes and grab my guns. "Send me the address. It'll probably take me around thirty minutes to get there."

"I can check it out myself."

"You're on the cusp of a neutral zone, *Fred*. Your jurisdiction and safety are finite. Send the address," I say and hang up.

I throw on a tank top and jeans, hiding my 9-Mil behind my back, my Glock inside my jacket, and another gun hidden in my boot. Better safe than sorry, what with the last few times I've gone to Topside. I take extra clips from Joey's room and aim for the front door.

"I'm leaving, Ma; I'll be back later," I call out as she steps out of the kitchen, drying a dish in her hands. I walk over, kissing her quickly on the cheek.

"Be careful, baby, and aim straight," she says softly.

I pause, seeing her eyes gleam for a moment before she turns away. My jaw tightens as I head out the door. Yeah, no way was I fully hiding shit from her.

I slip down the stairs and through the club, disappearing out the back door and take smaller alleyways toward the Manhattan Entrance to Topside. I'm determined to take the subway when I get above but stop when I look down at my phone to see the address Drauper sent. My gut clenches, and a twinge of fear moves through me as I gather my courage and spite to keep walking.

It just had to be Bruno's club.

Twilight
Reject

CHAPTER 20
I COULD'VE BEEN AN ENFORCER

Nighttime covers Topside as I weave through the crowd out of the subway. Neon lights flash as other clubs blast music, clashing with the noise of screaming humans before I approach a darker and more chilling block where Bruno's club sits, *BloodScape*.

It just *had* to be Bruno's club. I'm uneasy at the thought of him being more involved as I send a quick text to Vinny that I'm on Topside with a lead, sharing my location within a block. If I tell him I'm at *BloodScape,* there *will* be bloodshed. I silence my phone, already feeling like this may be a mistake, again, and see Drauper up ahead. He's wearing a black tank top with dark slacks and his signature brown leather jacket. No badge.

I notice a large quantity of vampires bustling beyond him outside the club, which flashes bright green lights with red lasers. I approach Drauper, noticing the street that divides into the neutral zone and my jaw tightens as I check the gun at my back.

"You know this place?" He asks as I join him on the sidewalk.

"Unfortunately," I grumble, checking my Glock inside my jacket. First time I wished I carried silver.

"Wanna share with the class?"

"You gonna make assumptions or actually listen?" I quirk a brow as his gaze stays level with mine. Alrighty, Drauper, let's see how far you're willing to go down the rabbit hole. "Owned by Dracultelli. Older one."

"Bruno?" His eyes widen, glancing at the club.

"How much you know about him?"

"We're given basic backgrounds for each major mob boss on the East Coast, Paranormal or not. You get more in-depth training about them if you're a liaison officer with PSB or NIIA. How does he own a place *outside* the neutral zone?"

"Paranormals can own businesses wherever, but most decide to stay in neutral zones for protection under the NIIA if things go south. If you have a business in a non-neutral zone, the paperwork's a bitch. And they'll do whatever they need to avoid being persecuted by human feds and police at all costs."

Drauper crosses his arms. "Why?"

"Remember that incubus from months ago?" I ask.

"What about him?"

"He was in a non-neutral zone when those officers attacked him." Drauper stares at me as his jaw tightens. "His name is Michello by the way."

His arms drop as he adjusts his stance, moving his gaze away toward the club. He clears his throat, "So, others own places outside the zones?"

I straighten and clear my throat. "Bruno's one of the few Paranormals who owns a place outside the zones, but as you see, he's right on the cusp of it. Safety net. If anything goes down, you just cross the street to the neutral zone right into the arms of NIIA or PSB. Risky, but Bruno's never cared about others anyway." I scowl at *BloodScape* with a simmering distaste.

"You don't sound like a fan of his."

"Cause I'm not," I scoff, and his brows raise in question. "Most in the mafia are like family, but not everyone agrees with each other. You ever see those gangster films? They got that shit right."

"Good to know."

"That's my neutral zone spiel. What did you find?" My stomach starts to twist, knowing it's wrong to be here. Bruno's not around; he's never on Topside. His goons run the club for him, but it still makes me wary. I'm fearful of the vampire's power, but he's gonna feel my rage if I find out he's behind people missing and dying.

"Camera on the back door caught all three missing people leaving with some vampires. The vampires came back. They didn't. There's a camera closer to the street, but there's no footage showing what happened. They go in the club, leave, and don't come back."

"Classic tale." I could try checking on that camera, but it may get wiped before I do. It's probably being rerouted to the Blood Mafia as a fail-safe.

"This is the only place where three separate times they've disappeared, all in the last four months. And now you're saying it's owned by the Blood Mafia—"

"Bruno. There's a difference."

"Brenda, you just said—"

"He doesn't run the Blood Mafia," I say with a warning glare, hoping he watches his tongue. "I know that mafia well enough."

"*How* well?"

The accusatory tone almost kickstarts my spite as a snarl grows in my throat, but I push it down. I walk toward *Blood-Scape* and Drauper catches up as we approach the bouncer out front, and I put my arm through his. My eyes flick to the crimson gaze as the smell of blood, alcohol, and musk rises. "Don't stare; play along," I whisper. "They can smell fear, especially in humans."

He adjusts his arm, holding me closer as I smile lazily at the bouncer, winking at him and licking my bottom lip. The vampire looks to me, then Drauper, and back to me with a half-smile as he opens the door for us, probably hoping we'll give blood later.

The operation of this place runs similar to other Blood Mafia venues, but it's seedier than what Vinny oversees. It's a regular club with diverse clientele, but in the back is the "donor" area. Unless they're purebloods, vampires can't bite others without turning people, so they set up IVs or other forms to collect blood. People can get addicted to donating, especially with the incentive of drugs, money, or sex. A part of the Blood Mafia I was taught well to stay away from by Vinny.

"Got in easy enough," Drauper murmurs in my ear against the deep bass vibrating the club. Everything's overwhelmingly loud in noise, color, and smell. *BloodScape* is filled with more drug induced people than anywhere Underground.

"We smell like humans," I say.

"Should that make me worried?"

"No, because it's one of the few laws they follow," I say against his ear. "No turning humans. Even the mafia doesn't want that kind of flack. Again, paperwork's a bitch."

Our arms stay locked together as we move through the sea of people. I scan the boisterous place, noticing vampires grinding against each other on the dance floor with elongated fangs as their own foreplay. People disappear through the back as vampires return with bloodied lips and euphoric humans behind them. Yeah, reason one why more people "donated" to the mafia more than the government. Two female vamps flash their fangs at me as I head us toward the bar, past a couple of vampires necking each other against a wall. A couple of humans watch them, dancing close as the music drops.

We get to the bar, and Drauper orders drinks, putting his arm over my shoulders to lean in close. "See anything unusual?"

"Not really. This is the norm for them."

He glances around us at the people nearby, holding me tighter to make us look like we're together. My skin pricks at his touch, the foreign contact making my body scream in revulsion. A snarl grows in my chest, but I yank it down to continue our little act. I focus on the mirror in front of us even as my territorial side creeps up my spine.

"How do we spot half-breeds or *shady* characters?" He asks, bringing my attention back.

"You're kidding, right?" I snort, grabbing my drink and easing away from him as he takes his. My muscles shiver at the release, relaxing with his touch gone, the defensive growl settles in my chest.

"You got a plan of any kind?" He asks, frowning down at his drink. I double-check mine with a sniff, recognizing the stupid cranberry cocktail. Vamps and their damn jokes. I knock my drink back for the liquid courage as he pushes his aside. Ick, it takes like sugary shit.

I scan the dance floor mostly filled with drunk humans. "Ask where Blade is?"

Drauper glares at me. Well, shit, guess we're going straight for the kill. Not at *all* dangerous. "Let's find regulars and ask if they knew the victims."

"Bet you five bucks the bouncers won't help."

"You take the dance floor," he says. "I'll check the other bar area."

"Just don't offer your vein to anyone."

"I'll do my best." He grimaces, walking away.

I watch him move through the club saturated in green and yellow light. The obnoxious lights are reason #25 why I'm not happy about being here. #1 is just being here in general.

After there's enough distance between us, I make my way to the dance floor, asking around where to find the best drugs. Most try to share their personal shit for other compensation, which I *politely* decline. Fun as they sound, not my cup of tea.

Lights shift and darken as the music changes to a harsher bass as red lasers stream across the club. I continue to ask around, getting nowhere, and search for Drauper at the other bar. Not there.

Shit. I look over at where we were before. Nada.

Double shit.

"Fuck," I mutter, changing my mission to finding my human detective before the bloodsuckers do. My dumbass really went along with being split up in a mafia vampire club.

Haze spills in the club as people scream, while the heavy dance beats vibrate through the club. Great fucking timing. I wind my way through the thrall, and the tang of iron hits my nostrils as vampires become friskier. A vamp gnaws on another as they moan in pleasure. Humans lick the leftover blood on their skin, grinding along with them. Everyone has a kink and bloodplay is closer to being a hard limit.

I push past them and catch the scent of familiar shampoo, turning to see Drauper near the back doors. He looks drunk as he's "escorted" by two vamps.

Triple shit.

I shove past the crowd and grab my 9-Mil at my back as I reach the door, kicking it open with a thud. I'm greeted by a trashy alleyway with pavement speckled with dirtied puddles, dumpsters, and, lastly, Drauper being dragged by vampires down the alley to the left. His head lulls to the side as he stumbles alongside them. Motherfuckers are mind-drugging him.

I click back the safety, and yell, "Hey! Vamp trash!"

They stop to glare at me, and Drauper's eyes widen as their mind manipulation slips on him. He starts to struggle, but they hold him harshly, barely moving from his efforts. I aim the gun at the vampire holding Drauper at his throat, stalking toward them as they cock their heads.

"Nothing to see here. Go back inside," one purrs, his eyes flash bright crimson.

"Nope. Give back my human, I had dibs," I say, grinning

maliciously. The vampire who tried to influence my mind looks at his cohort and back to me. "Release him or you're gonna find out what lead tastes like, period licker."

"What the fuck did you say?" The vampire at Drauper's throat snarls as the other steps towards me.

Puddles splash behind me, and I smell drugs, grease, and vodka as the door clicks shut with a creak. Three more vamps have entered the chat. Their scents drift with a heaviness, and my body becomes fully aware of all five of them.

Trust your senses, not your eyes. Vinny's advice from over a decade ago echoes in my head. Guess it's exam time.

I ease my other hand inside my jacket as the vampire approaching me, grabs his weapon. I grip my Glock, and snarl to Drauper, "Don't move."

I shoot the vampire holding Drauper, and the bullet sinks into his throat. He gargles as I shoot another henchman in the knee while pulling out the gun around my back, hitting the vampire behind me in the chest. Without looking, I aim the 9-Mil at the vampire coming from the right side and pull the trigger. Screams fill the air as they hit the ground, lead sinking into their flesh. I turn to hit the third vamp but misjudge by an inch with my Glock, and he dodges it, sinking his teeth into my shoulder.

I snarl as unfurled rage rumbles in my chest and twist to shoot him in the gut twice. He unclamps his fangs and falls to the ground in agony as I shoot his friend, trying to stand back up. The vamp who attempted mind control on me gets two more shots in the chest as I speed reload the other gun. I aim at the henchman who held Drauper and blow out his kneecap. All five vampires lay on the ground, bleeding and writhing in pain.

For good measure, I walk to each of the bloodsuckers and place a bullet in their kneecaps. They howl in pain, and I roll my eyes at them. Wimps. Vinny didn't even flinch when I shot him.

"It'll heal in two hours, stop griping," I growl, kicking their guns away.

I walk toward the Megamind reject, who snarls at me, so I shoot him in the groin. *"You bitch,"* he screeches.

"You bet," I respond in Noctora, stepping over his groveling body. Drauper stares at me as I approach him, scanning him over and asking, "Didn't fucking bite you, did they?"

He shakes his head, stunned as I turn my attention to a nearby vampire on the ground holding his neck as blood leaks out. Their eyes flash with hatred as they sneer, *"Who the fuck are you?"*

"Who do you work for?" I ask.

"Fuck you—"

"Another bullet to your throat, and your vocal cords are gone," I threaten, aiming my gun at him. "So, *who do you work for?"*

He looks past me to his fallen comrades, his breathing shallow as he concentrates on healing his bullet wounds quicker. I fire off another round into his shoulder, and he roars out in pain, *"Dracultelli will have your head!"*

"All I needed. Thanks." I shoot him in the groin, matching his little partner. He garbles out a scream as I put my guns away.

"Bitch! Fucking BITCH!" He swipes, but I step back casually.

"We need to go," Drauper whispers, glancing toward the street. The club's music hasn't relented, but my other senses heighten as I catch sight of the security camera.

Territorial anger pulls a devilish smile on my face as I look up, knowing who'll watch the footage. Fuckers tried to take my detective. *My* detective.

The vampire hisses between breaths, holding his junk. *"He'll kill you...he'll fucking kill you. You human trash..."*

Sirens sound off in the distance as I crouch before him, adrenaline racing through my body with vengeance and spite. My calm fury blurs everything out as I grin indifferently, facing the wheezing vampire closely. *"Make sure you tell him the scarred-up bitch took you down. And that I say, 'hello.'"*

He's seething as Drauper grabs me, dragging me behind out of the alleyway toward the zone boundary. We race down a few blocks and come to a deserted street before he stops and gasps behind me, "What the fuck just happened?"

"Vampire snatching, obviously! I said no vein-giving!"

"I was talking to someone at the bar, and the next thing I know, you were pointing a gun at them," he pants. They saw him as an easy target or figured he was a cop, both scenarios being terrible. "What the hell were you speaking?"

"Noctora."

"What?"

"The fucking Paranormal language. Fucking hell! They really teach you jack-shit about us, don't they? How the fuck don't you know that?"

"I didn't need to know it," he snaps back, and I snort. "Although, I'd like to know where you learned to shoot like that. Something else you're not telling me?" I grin slyly, and he deepens his frown. "Another time then. What did they tell you?"

I've made some mistakes on Topside, but this takes the cake. Those vampires are either workers at *BloodScape* with a white-van side gig or they're carrying out Bruno's orders. Either way, they'll use the Dracultelli name to cover their asses, but in my gut, I know Bruno is involved somehow. Unfortunately, the bastard will drag Vinny into it, he always fucking does. Worst of all, Drauper was caught on that camera.

I look over at his questioning gaze. Damn it. They're gonna remember his face, putting him in danger if he ever walks into a neutral zone again, with or without me. And I just outed myself with my shooting skills to Drauper and the vamps. I can picture Drauper's bloodied body on the ground with Bruno standing over him. Guilt consumes me that I may have just signed his death warrant.

"No good, it's a bad lead," I say in a strict tone.

"Bad lead? You shot them all in the groin and kneecaps, after they tried to kidnap me, *how* is that a bad lead?"

Vinny and my family can stand against Bruno, but not Drauper. Laws be damned, that bastard will drag Drauper's body into the Hudson because he isn't protected by the Underground Mafia. I won't be enough to protect him. I have to end this or Detective Louis Drauper will only be a memory.

I take a small step back, not ready to break this friendship beyond repair. "This is where we part ways. This just became more complicated and I'm not gonna let you get dragged into it."

"You already did."

"I know, and I'm sorry." I take another step toward the street, realizing human scents change when they're angry, because Drauper's rises into burning passionflower. He takes a few steps toward me, but I match him inching closer to the zone line.

"Tell me what you know," he demands. "Were they working for Dracultelli to nab humans?" He stops in his steps and stares at me. "Or was it actually the Blood Mafia? Is that why you're—"

I shake my head as Drauper reaches for me, jumping back past the neutral zone line. He stops, realizing I've crossed the invisible boundary of the zone. The nonexistent wall thickens between us, and his eyes darken as I step further away. I see it in his face I'm gonna lose him, but he'll be alive and that'll be good enough.

"It's the Blood Mafia, isn't it? And you're protecting your little *family*, aren't you?" Drauper accuses me.

"It's not like that," I say. "This just got more dangerous, and I can't let you be—"

"Part of it? Even though I was almost kidnapped because of you?"

"You agreed to help."

"Not to be used like bait!" He yells from his side of the

zone. He looks back where *BloodScape* is, then sneers at me. "It was the Blood Mafia all along, wasn't it? It was always them. Were you just hoping it wasn't? It's the fucking mafia, of course, it is! Why did I believe you?"

"It's not like that," I snap back. "For once, trust me fully and walk away. I'm giving you the chance right now."

His expression becomes one of disgust, scoffing as he paces. The sirens in the distance become louder. "I should've known. I always wondered why *Vinny the Vampire* showed up at the hospital. This is why."

My stomach drops as he mentions Vinny, forgetting how they met. I freeze, staring at him as my chin quivers, allowing his train of thought to play out. One more break is all I need, and he'll walk away...he'll be safe.

"You're protecting him," Drauper sneers.

"You don't know what you're—"

"Don't I?"

"This was about the half-breeds, nothing else!" I yell in a cracked voice. The sirens come closer and there's flashing bright blue lights against building walls.

"So, you were just working for them the entire time? Turning your back on justice knowing what they're doing. You're *human*! They're not!"

"They're more than that!" I scream. "You know *nothing* about them!"

Drauper takes a step back, glaring at me as he straightens his jacket and says, "Guess we weren't that good together, huh? Since you'll *always* go running back to the Underground."

"Drauper—"

"It's where you belong, right? With the fiends and beasts who lurk in the night?" He gestures toward my guns as shouts rise a few blocks down, lights flashing. "*You* get this one chance to leave, Brenda. After tonight, if I ever see you outside a neutral zone, I'm taking you in." He turns and walks back down the street toward *BloodScape* and the sirens.

"Drauper." Nothing. "Louis!"

He disappears, and I feel our friendship fall into the gutter. A part of me is screaming to step across the invisible line and tell him the truth. Instead, I take a few long breaths, fighting back tears and spinning on my heel, hightailing out of there for an Entrance to the Underground. The one thought that keeps me from turning back is that he's safer away from me.

CHAPTER 21
SAY HELLO TO MY—

I focus on my breathing and fall back against the wall as the elevator jerks. I try to remain calm as it feels like knives are pressing at my knuckles as my blood boils. Too much, too much anger as a snarl finally releases from me in the empty elevator. Bruno was taking people; I knew it deep down. He couldn't be working with Traloski. No way he'd do the bidding of a human or anyone else. It was either for his own blood supply or to work the black market. The wild card. Fuck, this couldn't get any worse.

I groan and reach for my phone, scanning over the messages left from Vinny telling me to come back to the Underground. And two missed calls from Anita, the latest from ten minutes ago.

"Fucking great." Suddenly my phone lights up with Anita's name, and I answer, "What?"

"*What the fuck did you two do?!*" She screams.

"What are you—"

"*Go to* Unbound *and stay there. You two have fucked things up enough.*"

She hangs up abruptly. I stare down at my phone in confusion, my heart racing. There's a throbbing pulse at my shoulder, and the drying blood on my neck cracks. Shit. I touch where I was bitten tonight, and my chest feels like it's concaving as realization sinks in, they tasted my blood.

The Claim Mating.

Fucking hell!

The elevator halts and I bolt out through the crowds for *The Lounge*. No way was I going home. Not only did I shoot Bruno's lackeys and had a human detective with me, but I was bitten, and they got a full taste of what Vinny and I had done. Now I really wished I carried silver bullets.

As I come around the last corner, I see Anita, Brock, and another guard outside *The Lounge* with lights turned off as a roar shakes the atmosphere. I halt as a chair crashes through a window and glass shatters. Fuck.

"Vinny!" I yell, running for the entrance. For a split second, I see Anita turn and, suddenly her hands are on my throat, slamming my back against a wall. Her fangs elongate in warning as she seethes. "Watch it, Carmilla," I rasp under her grip.

"What the hell have you done?" She snarls in Noctora.

"I had every—"

"When did you Claim Mate?" My eyes widen. The news had already found her. *"I went on Bruno's behalf to deal with his* shot-up *guards on Topside, when one of them tells me he tasted the Bond. In a few hours,* everyone *will know."*

"Let go of me," I growl against her grasp.

"You shot five vampires on camera! What were you thinking?"

A loud roar echoes from inside *The Lounge*. *"Where's my Mate!?"* Vinny thunders, something pulling at me to get to him.

"And then I come back, and he's screaming that!" She snarls, and I struggle against her hold. *"You just started a shit storm."*

There's another crash inside, like wood splitting and fabric ripping. My body rages to get to him, wrath piercing through my veins as each breaking sound echoes to the outside. I can't let him tear apart his place, not his lounge, not again. I try to move, but Anita keeps me in place. *You need to fucking leave while I clean up this mess. I don't know what's worse; you shooting five of Bruno's crew or Mating my brother in fucking secret!*

"*It was* our *decision, no one else's!*" I snap back as Samuel yells from inside. I try to slip past Anita, but she slams her arm in the way.

"*Oh, no, you don't. I don't care how much he screams for you. He's being contained.*"

"*He's not an animal!*"

"He's a pureblood," she snarls. "He was on edge all day, and finding out about you getting bit sent him over that damn cliff." I snarl at her, and she growls back, baring her teeth and shoving me away from *The Lounge*. "Leave. We'll keep him contained until he calms down, then we'll have to deal with five vampires filled with your lead."

"They tried to kidnap a human detective!" I scream. "What was I supposed to do?"

"Call us! Don't fucking *shoot* them!"

"*They* bit *me*! If it was anyone else, they would've turned, and you'd have NIIA down here, too! So be fucking glad—" Glass shatters, and I try to move past her with no luck.

"No way in hell am I letting you near him," she warns. "He'll fucking kill you. Claim Mated or not, so *leave*."

"He won't calm down until he sees me."

"We'll sedate him."

"The *fuck* you will!" My eyes flash to Brock.

"He's *my* responsibility."

"He's *mine*!"

"No! He's not—"

"You're not protecting him by doing this!"

"I'm protecting him from himself!" She shoves me further from the entrance. "I won't let my brother live in agony because he killed you. This is the part where you walk away, *baby sis*. And *this* is the part where you understand there's a line between vampires and Paranormals. *Leave*."

Her words cut into me, and I stagger back. I glance at Brock again and the guard keeping their eyes on us as Anita holds her ground. She's between me and Vinny. My Mate.

My limbs shake in outrage, and I take a deep breath, slowly pulling out the guns I used on Topside. I bring them to the ground, crouching down to lay them on the brick in surrender. Anita scoffs, and in that half second, I grab the gun in my boot and shoot her knees, then Brock's and the guard's. All three go to the ground, yelling in shock as I quickly pick up my Glock, emptying it into Anita's thighs to keep her down long enough to get past. I run past her to the entrance as she screams, *"Damn it, Brenda!"*

"Not sorry," I respond, kicking the door down. I'm not leaving him. I keep repeating in my head that it's Vinny and that he'd never hurt me. He promised.

The Lounge is a mess with parts of the bar ripped out, glass shattered everywhere, and the mirrors smashed. There's yelling in the back, the doors wide open, and I catch a glimpse of Samuel and the other guards trying to keep Vinny away from the entrance.

I toss the Glock to the side and empty my last gun, taking out the bullet already in the chamber. I double check, pulling back the trigger to hear the empty click as I move toward the back, where Samuel and the others try to talk Vinny down as he rips into the wall.

The air shifts rapidly when I enter and what used to be a mixture of alcohol, blood, and wood all I smell is Vinny. His darkened scent of spices and bloodlust slam into my nostrils, burning as I watch him freeze from tearing off more wall. The others halt as Vinny slowly turns to look at me.

Samuel says in horror, "Brenda, get the fuck out of here. He's not—"

Vinny snarls so loud the walls shake, a very primal sound

that vibrates through my bones. His smoldering eyes lock onto mine, crimson glowing in a devouring rage as his fangs elongate. He towers over the others as he heaves long, deep breaths of my scent with his face twisted in fury and hunger. Pure hunger.

"Brenda!" Samuel yells, reaching for Vinny, who throws him against the wall.

Two other guards race to stop him but halt when Vinny freezes. They look over at me holding the gun to my temple, still hot from its last shot stinging my skin. Vinny's eyes flare as he takes a step forward.

"No," I say sternly, keeping my gaze on his. He stops completely.

Purebloods can't become Feral because their most primal self is the definition of it. During my dissertation on Vinny's grandfather, Dracula, I learned what happens to purebloods who let that instinct rule over them. There were three possibilities to get them back into control.

One—Blood, lots of it. Vinny would need to drink dry dozens and dozens of people before coming close to calming his rage. It's why they're containing him here, away from others.

Two—You let them destroy everything in their path until they wear out, but that can take days. It's what happened to Dracula, who destroyed cities.

Three—You allow another primal urge to quench their bloodlust rampage. It's why Anita didn't want me inside, knowing I'd take this third route to stop him. I'll give myself over to him, body and all—*anything* to protect him.

No matter how fucked it is, I keep the upper hand with the gun to my head until I have him where I want him. Mates are the only ones who can be part of the third option, engaging in sex until the frenzy for blood and destruction stops. In the past, Mates have been killed during these violent outbursts, even pureblood Mates, bled out to nothing. It's what killed Vinny's mother.

And I'm about to offer myself to the most powerful pureblood vampire in New York City, who looks ready to devour me.

CHAPTER 22
E.T. (EXTRA TERRITORIAL)

The gun stays level at my temple as Vinny's muscles ripple with fear and rage. His eyes watch my every movement like a predator waiting for a chance to pounce. He's still Vinny, pure-blood berserker or not, I didn't spend twenty years of friendship to lose him like this. His breathing becomes ragged while his hands flex at his sides.

"Brenda..." Samuel whispers.

"Let's make a deal, bloodsucker," I say, taking two steps toward Vinny, his glowing gaze intensifying. "You go into your office and stand beside your desk like a good vamp until I say otherwise, and I'll pull the gun away."

"Brenda." Samuel's voice is shaking. "What are you doing?"

"Protecting *my* Mate," I snarl, and Vinny growls lightly at me with a glint of amusement.

"He'll kill you," Samuel warns. "He's doesn't know—"

"You're gonna close the doors behind us."

"The hell I—"

"Close them once I step through, or I'm wasting a bullet on your knee," I warn, glancing at Adrian. They meet my gaze and nod.

I gesture to Vinny to move, and he backs up steadily into

his office. I wait as he moves, keeping my breathing leveled and then he gives me an impatient growl the moment he bumps into his desk. I walk forward, stopping just past the doors, then nod to Adrian. There's shouting out front, and the guards move out of the foyer with Adrian slamming the doors quickly behind me. I click the locks shut just as Samuel beats on the doors in protest, yelling persists as I hear the others drag him away and I hear Anita shriek, *"NO!"*

I ignore the commotion outside the doors and stare at my Mate, who's assessing my every movement with a hungry gaze. Each twitch or flick of his eyes reminds me of a predator and human instinct screams for me to run. The basic human instinct claws harder as he growls lightly.

"Alright, bloodsucker," I say calmly, standing firm. "I'm gonna move this gun, but nothing's gonna happen until you calm your tits." He breathes raggedly, focusing on the gun pointed at my head as I slowly bring it down. He steps forward, and I instantly place it back against my temple, clicking back the safety. His eyes widen in horror as his body stills, his fangs shrinking back.

"Your patience fucking sucks, Vinny," I grumble. "Don't think I won't do it. I'm already close to death's door, might as well speed it up. It's better than you destroying yourself for the next few centuries."

"I won't...last that long," he rasps, forcing himself to speak against the snarl in his throat.

"Remembering your words?"

He snarls again, then asks, "Is...is it loaded?"

"You wanna find out?" I tilt the gun a bit more to my head.

He remains still, his gaze flicking between the gun and my face. "You wouldn't."

"I don't think you understand the lengths I'll go to protect you," I warn. "And that includes holding a loaded gun to my head, so you don't go full Predator on my ass. I love rough sex with you, Vinny, but I'd like to keep my throat intact. I know you'd never, *ever* willingly hurt me, but if there's one thing I know…it's vampires. *You* made sure of that."

Vinny cocks his head, a small tilt to his mouth like he's trying to smile. Walls are breaking down and he's calming, which gives me a better chance of survival. His hands flex at his sides, gripping into his skin.

"Vinny, what spurred this on? You'd be grumbly about what happened on Topside…" he growls, and his gaze darkens. Case in point. "…but it's not the first time with me. Why was this different? What made you…lose it?"

Pain contorts his expression as his gaze becomes shadowed, his scent warping into something bitter. He gasps between strained growls. "I read everything. What he did to you."

My chest constricts, knowing he was already unsteady and needed my comfort, then he spent hours reading about the torture I went through as a child. On top of it all, I was attacked on Topside. Fucking hell, he'd been a ticking time-bomb and I wasn't nearby to help him. Damn it, why did I go to Topside?

"What they did to you…you were a baby. A fucking *baby*, and he—"

"I'm fine now, Vinny," I say softly, clicking the safety on. "Only scars are left."

"I want to tear him apart. *All of them*," he snarls. "Any who's touched you. I can *smell* them on you."

I glimpse at my new wound, then bring my gaze to him as I lower the gun carefully. Vinny remains still as I drop the gun, clattering to the ground. His muscles tremor, and his jaw tightens as he watches me. "Let's help change that, shall we?" I say, peeling my jacket off and then my top.

"No…" He rasps, forcing himself to look away.

"Vinny. Look at me." His gaze snaps to mine. "You've calmed enough, and you're talking. Good sign," I soothe as his breath hitches, while the fury in his eyes churn into pure desirable hunger. He licks his upper lip as I lean down, taking my boots off and then my jeans.

"Sweet cheeks." He rasps in a dark tone as I stand in just my bra and underwear.

"Vinny, I know you and trust you. If I don't let you remark me, you'll relapse, and we don't want that." I pull my hair tie out, allowing my hair to cascade around my shoulders. "Just remember, if you break me, you'll have a line of people waiting to castrate you."

He tenses, then relaxes as his eyes rove across my body and back to my gaze. Ruby eyes stare into me as he stalks forward fluidly and silently, the most lethal predator. His hand is instantly at my throat, and my back presses against the door. He leans forward, inhaling deeply at my neck as a dark, territorial growl rips from his mouth, his fangs elongating again. It shakes through my body, all instinct orders me to get as far away from him as possible, but I concentrate on his burning scent and warmth over my neck.

"They fucking bit you," he snarls against my throat, grazing his fangs across my skin. He quickly captures my hands, placing them above my head. My breathing becomes erratic as his body heat, scent, and voice stir a warmth in my core. I try to focus, but it's hard as he takes another long breath in and growls. The heat ripples through my body, my sex clenching as tingling sensations run over my skin, and his thumb caresses over my bite wound. *"They tasted what's* mine."

"Take what's yours then."

His head rips back, staring at me with his deep ruby eyes as he inhales sharply. I'm feeling déjà vu from months ago; my back pressed against a doorway as Vinny pins me with his body and hands, roaming over my skin and feeling every tremor that courses through me. This time, it *is* going to be about fucking.

"It's alright, Vinny," I whisper. "You have my consent. It's okay."

Something clicks through him as he moves back to my neck,

tracing a hand down my clavicle, touching my scars as a growl rips from his throat in a possessive nature. His muscles tense and shift as his tongue licks up my throat with a scorching heat. The very movement makes my insides almost melt, sending my mind spiraling as I gasp for air. Anticipation scores through me, and I'm about to yell at him to get on with it, until he grips my neck and bites down. *Hard.*

I stifle the scream in my throat as his fangs pierce my flesh. He's bitten me during sex in the past, but this is different. This is a vampire claiming, pulling at my blood in a violent manner. He keeps his hold on me as my veins feel like fire as he drinks, and I want to shriek against the fiery ice traveling through my veins, but I keep my mouth shut. My mind kicks at me to escape, fear scratching at me as the blood is pulled from me. I don't move. I don't fight. He needs this. He needs *me.*

I remain still as he continues to pull blood from my vein, and I grow lightheaded, and my body instinctively pushes against his for release. My hips press against his groin and at the contact, Vinny lets go of my neck, gasping for air. He runs his tongue over the puncture wounds in a sensuous manner, then gently licks along my jaw, and his lips soon cover mine. The tang of iron hits my tongue along with burnt spice as he presses harder into the kiss, with his hand tightening around my throat. Vinny keeps me in place, deepening the kiss with frantic desire, washing away any leftover pain from my neck. I shiver as the sharp pain dissipates replaced with drowning lust and the heat within becomes hotter and hotter as he presses into me.

"Did...did I hurt you?" He asks against my lips, and I shake my head just enough. "I can't...I don't know if I can stop...not until..." I swing one of my legs around his hip, pulling him closer to me, and I grind against him. A snarl grows in his chest, his hands clutching mine above my head harshly. "Sweet cheeks..."

"I trust you. Now...*fuck me*, bloodsucker," I rasp out.

His chest rumbles as he swiftly releases my hands above my head, ripping off his clothes and then the last of mine into shredded messes. Vinny then grabs my ass, pulling me up against the door forcing my legs around his hips. The hand around my throat goes down to the apex of my thighs. His fingers roughly move over my clit, and then through the folds before he thrusts two fingers inside me. I shout in surprise as he scissors them, hooking upward causing more of my insides to tightly coil in flames.

"Wet for me already..." His voice is guttural, a groan like a male on the brink of starvation.

His fingers leave me, and he licks them clean before I'm slammed into the door with his hips, his cock thrusting into me. I shout again as Vinny delivers punishing blows at a frantic rhythm as he pounds forward. One arm holds me against him while the other goes back to clutch my neck. He keeps me firmly in place, but the grip is comforting around my throat, a gentleness hidden underneath the tight grasp. He holds my neck like he's afraid to break me, yet he thrusts his cock inside me with a roughness that makes me scream.

A dark growl leaves him, vibrating from his chest onto mine. He inhales my scent deeply and trails his tongue up my chest and jaw. I feel my body tense, taking the deep plunging blows while the heat still grows inside me. He lets out a roar near my ear, his body convulsing as he comes already, letting loose within me. I gasp for breath, my own body not at the precipice of orgasm, the rippling sensation only just shy of it. My muscles clench around him as my body tries to gain more friction.

Vinny's orgasm doesn't slow him as he pulls me close, keeping me attached to him as he moves us away from the wall. He's still deep inside me as he takes his hand from my throat to my clit, circling his thumb in slow, agonizing movements. I moan loudly as I feel my orgasm start to rise, but I'm interrupted once again.

Suddenly, I'm placed down and turned around roughly to face the desk, his hands on my shoulders, shoving me down before running them down my back. I lay my chest against the desk surface, hold onto the other edge, and scream as he thrusts his cock into me again. The pain and pleasure swirl together as Vinny takes me roughly, gripping my hips to slam into me again and again. My entire body convulses as he presses his hands on my back to keep me in place, pounding into me. I feel lightheaded, and my vision blurs as I'm swarmed with overwhelming sensations as he fucks me unforgivingly.

His scent ravages my nostrils as it coats over my own sweat and skin. All I feel is him around me, consuming me with each punishing blow and erratic breath. The crack of wood pierces the air as Vinny rips off part of the desk as a low growl thunders behind me. He grabs my hair tightly, pulling me back as he thrusts his dick into me severely. I let out another scream, calling for him in a garbled mess and spurring him on more. Somehow it feels like he's gotten deeper, hitting my inner walls with a ferocity that makes me give in to the pleasurable pain as he stretches me to the brink.

I whimper taking in each vicious thrust, clutching the desk for any bit of support before another piece breaks off with a crack in his hands. My muscles clench around his dick as the heat grows, and I feel the orgasm come back full force, consuming all thought. The pressure builds, and I sense Vinny ready to come again. He grips my hair harder, pulling me back with a roar as my body screams at the pain. I shout for him and explode with ecstasy as the orgasm rips through my body, lightning licking up my spine.

My knuckles go white as I hold onto the desk, mentally preparing myself for the next round. He's not going to stop, not yet. My entire body will turn to jelly from the orgasms, and he'll fuck me raw. I already feel raw and spent as a moan escapes me. He massages my scalp where he pulled, and he presses his cock further into me. His breath hitches as his other hand runs down my back and grips my ass before pulling out completely. I continue my mental prep for the next round, until he wraps his arms around me and lifts me from the desk. I try to stand against him, but my legs have already thrown in the towel. He keeps his arms around me, pressing my back against his heaving chest while one hand clutches my breast and the other moves downward.

Oh, fuck me. Death by orgasm, honestly, is better than any other end waiting for me.

He inserts a finger slowly, his thumb circling my clit. I gasp in short breaths as the soft sensation entices a moan. In a slow, torturous pace he pumps his finger into me and then joins another as he massages my breast, pinching at my nipple gently. My body melts against his as he caresses me, and I lean further back into him for support. I start to lose focus on reality. The pressure inside me builds as a tingling heat forms in my nether region, and I grip his hair and shoulders as he continues.

"Vinny," I gasp as a third finger is added, and I whimper loudly.

He kneads my breast and flicks my nipple, then pinches it hard. I let out another soft scream as he nips at my skin, my hips instinctively grinding against his hands while he works the artistry that is his fingers inside me. Vinny takes a long, steady breath at the crook of my neck, his tongue tracing up my jaw to behind my ear. A shiver runs over my body, and I cry out softly. He kisses the side of my jaw, throat, and shoulder, coming back to my ear to whisper darkly, *"You are mine. Always. You're fucking mine."*

"All yours, Vinny, yours," I pant.

His fingers pump faster, and his thumb presses harder against my clit, causing my body to jolt. I moan, enraptured by the feel of him, when abruptly he takes his fingers out of me, and I'm filled back up again with his cock. A shout catches in my throat as he clutches it with his cum slicked hand. He pumps into me, stretching me at the tight angle as he growls against my skin. Everything builds, heat coiling and tightening at the change of pace. The orgasm grows as my spine pulsates upward from my tailbone and I writhe against him, but he keeps me pinned against him. Closer and closer I'm taken to the edge until he brings his hand back down, presses my clit, and thrusts upward. I scream as the orgasm lets loose, seeing stars as my head spins and my legs tremble and go numb.

Vinny eases me down gently and pulls his cock out of me. He brings his fingers up to his lips, licking what's left of me on him. My breathing slows as I look over to see shining ruby eyes. It's him again. My Vinny. The harsh edges and unbridled fury are gone. My cunning, sarcastic, territorial vampire.

A smile pulls at his lips before he kisses the side of my mouth. "Needed to make up for the first one."

I swallow against my dry throat. "Didn't know you were good at fake orgasms."

"Meant you, sweetheart." His other nickname. Another good sign.

"I didn't destroy a club."

"But I am destroying—"

"Don't finish that," I say in a breathy rasp.

"Too late for that," he says and turns me around, picking me up and holding me gently against him. I anticipate him pushing me back down for another rough round, but he sits me on the desk and cradles my face, his thumbs stroking over my scars and cheeks. He kisses me with a sweet tenderness, caressing my lips against his, and I melt against his touch. Tears form in my eyes at the gentle sweetness, a contrast of the last few rounds.

"I'm okay, keep going...." I whisper against his lips.

He pulls back, leveling crimson eyes with mine before he looks down my body and back up with a careful, worried look. I hold his hands against my cheeks, grinning a little as his expression softens, and he says, "I'm fine."

"You're not done, bloodsucker."

"Sweet cheeks."

"Vinny."

"I won't make you—" I crash my lips against his, and he shudders under my touch. Fear of hurting me or even accidentally killing me is holding him back. I know it. This is supposed to take hours, not a few position changes. I'd keep going to make sure he's alright. He *needs* to be alright.

He pulls away, keeping me in place as he stares hard at me. Hunger lines his gaze as he grazes his sight over me again, then slowly and carefully lays me down on the desk. My back presses against the hard surface, and I spread my arms out to hold onto what's left of it. He stands to his full height, tilting his head at me.

"Close your eyes," he commands, and I do. My muscles tighten as I wait for the next set of vicious pounding of his hips.

His fingers trail down my body, tracing over every scar that distorts and riddles my skin. The slow process continues as he goes from one arm to the next, down my chest, and across my torso. I sigh as the gentle touch soothes and relaxes my body as he lightly presses my skin, running his hands fully over me. I revel in the softness that lulls me as his hands shift down my legs, around my thighs, and back to the apex of my thighs. His thumbs trace just outside my sex, and I wait. And wait.

Vinny leans down over my body, placing a longing, deep kiss on my lips. I drink in his taste and moan as he continues the sensuous caress. His tongue traces my lips, then tangles with my own. I whimper against the kiss, enraptured by his taste, and feel against me. He wraps his arms around me, pulling me into his chest as he nips at my bottom lip. He moves carefully, sitting us down in one of the remaining chairs, keeping me on his lap as he finally breaks the sensual kiss. He strokes the side of my face, watching me as I blink a few times as my eyes begin to itch. Vinny brings me in close, embracing me with a reverence that makes my breath hitch. He rests his face in the crook of my neck, remaining there as he breathes deeply.

"Vinny?" I whisper.

"I said you calmed me. More than you think," he whispers. "I don't need five hours of constant sex anymore. Not with you. I just needed...I needed..."

"To know I'm here." He nods into my shoulder, and I sigh, snuggling closer to him. We cling to each other in silence like nothing else matters within the world but us. He's okay. Vinny's okay.

Minutes tick by as I feel sleepy in his embrace, prepared to fall asleep in his hold. I am content to stay here, until he speaks in a broken whisper, "You trust me, right?"

"Always," I murmur.

He swallows roughly, gripping a bit tightly. "I need you to leave and don't come back until I tell you. No one else. You wait until you hear from me." I grip him harder as a small fracture cracks within my chest. "I'm sorry, sweetheart...but I have to take care of things for us. Or we may never have peace."

Tears begin to form in my eyes as my breathing becomes shallow, knowing what he has to do. What I have to do. The fracture splits further and my heart begins to shatter.

"Don't go to Topside, don't enter vampire territory," he demands. "They'll fucking kill you if you trespass. You said I made sure you knew vampires, then you know *exactly* what they're capable of. Stay with family, Beckham, or Rodney. *Don't* be alone."

The tears fall down from my eyes and cover my cheeks, dripping onto his shoulder. I listen to his instructions, doing my best to keep from shaking as my greatest fear comes to life.

"After what happened tonight, you'll be unsafe until I settle things with the Society and my father," he whispers. "I *have* to do this."

"They'll kill you," I choke out.

Vinny holds me closer. "I'm not leaving you behind...I

promised you, didn't I?" I nod against his shoulder. "Trust me to settle this, to make it safe for you. For us. Forever."

"Vinny," I choke out.

"Promise me you'll do as I say, Brenda."

"How long? How long until you come back?"

"I don't know." My throat closes up. He strokes my hair, cradling my head against his. "Promise me, sweetheart. Promise me."

I nod my head numbly. "I promise...I promise."

He kisses my shoulder and jawline, whispering, "I love you." He repeats this over and over again, catching the tears rolling down my cheeks.

My voice is on the brink of breaking as I whisper. "I love you...please come back. I need you... I need you...."

"Promised you years ago we'd be together forever. I intend to keep that promise." A sob catches in my throat while Vinny and I hold onto each other for what could be the final time.

CHAPTER 23
BAT OUT OF FUCKING HELL

Vinny's jacket is wrapped around me like a protective barrier as I walk home. I didn't want to let go of him, and it had to be him to separate us as the final look in his eyes was burned into my memory, fearful it'd be the last time. I numbly walked through the destroyed cigar lounge with fallen faces watching me leave. I could barely smell the relief, but I could sense the solemn warning as I left the broken lounge and vampire territory behind.

My eyes burn and itch as I approach *Unbound* in a numb state, stumbling through the backdoor. The club is in full swing tonight with loud sensual music. I clutch Vinny's jacket, breathing in his scent as I make it to the apartment door. It shuts, and I fall against the wall, my lungs burning against sobs pushing to be let out. After a few long moments, I shakingly walk up the stairs feeling dizzy and disorientated.

My head spins as I stop in the middle of the living room, hit by realization as my veins feel like ice. Horror overcomes me of what they may do to him for Claim Mating in secret and going into a bloodthirsty rampage. Stopping him or not, he still screamed for his Mate for all the Underground to hear and to know what we'd done. We hid the Claim Mating out of fear of my death sentence, but now we may have given him his.

I tremble, my fingers scraping against the leather. I may never see him again, hear his laugh, taste his coffee, have him hold me, or joke with me. Tears stream down my face as my worst fear comes to life. All I'd done to be careful and protect him sinks into the gutter. He'll be gone, and I'll be left to die without him.

"Baby?" Ma's voice reaches my ears as she comes out of the kitchen and halts with a towel in her hands. Her eyes widen, and the scent of cherry blossoms drift towards me. "Baby, what's wrong? Is that Vincent's—?"

"Is this what it felt like when they took you from Pops?" I choke on a sob, and her eyes widen, scent disappearing in dismay. I cry, "They're gonna kill him. They're gonna kill my Mate."

"Baby girl—"

"They can't...*I need him!*" I scream and fall to my knees, slamming into the hardwood floor, sobbing. I shriek in terror and pain as my mother cradles me as my entire world crashes and burns into nothing.

———

THREE DAYS. Nothing from Vinny in three days.

I wear his jacket on my bed, wrapping my arms around my legs as Ma walks in and sets chamomile tea on my nightstand. She sits beside me and gently strokes my hair. I've barely moved from my room since I returned from *The Lounge.*

I keep telling myself that they won't kill him for defying them or his father. Fear scratches under my skin, as I envision his blood on my hands and smeared across the ground. Unless I die before that happens, then it'll be mine on his.

"Do you want something to eat, baby?" Ma asks, and I

shake my head. She leans me into her side, soothing me with her touch.

It feels like all my walls have fallen, allowing the wave of fear to drown me. More than any of the nights I spent alone on Topside. More than finding the information about my past. Even more than the library being torn apart. I feel like those trashed books, waiting to be placed back together again by the one who knows me best.

Ma offers me my mug, and I oblige as she speaks, "You were like this the first time Vincent left. You'd only met twice, but you cried asking where he was for weeks."

"I don't remember that," I whisper.

"It was about two months after Pops brought you home. He had you below when Vincent came by and met you, and you growled at him because you thought he was threatening Pops. They both thought it was amusing."

"I *do* remember that," I say with a small smile.

"Well, he came by a second time before going north and didn't return for weeks, and you cried to Pops asking where the 'red eyes' went. Two months later, he came back, and you remembered him. Pops said you dragged him to a couch downstairs, telling him all about your artwork and books, showing him the braille alphabet. He stayed after that," she sighs.

My brows furrow, and I try to see her through the dark purple haze. "What do you mean?"

"He was planning to leave New York and go to Maine and leave the Blood Mafia due to a fight with his father."

"Why didn't he?" I rasp, clutching my mug close.

"He didn't want to leave you," she whispers softly, hugging me close. Why didn't Vinny tell me this? "He'll come back, baby. He always will for you. He's a good vampire like that. Even being a *vampire mafia boss*."

"I hope you're right...again, Ma."

Her hand comes to my face gently. "Your father found me. That's what Mates do."

I press my face further into her touch. "I want my best friend back."

"I know, baby," she says, kissing my head. "Now, there's no point sitting here in the dark crying. Why don't we bake your favorite pie? Help you feel better."

I nod, and she kisses my cheek, taking my free hand to guide me out of my room. I know she's right and there's not much I can do to argue against pie. Halfway through the apartment, I let go of her, clicking my tongue as I join her in the kitchen. We spend the next few hours baking, filling the space with the scent of pecans, berries, apples, and fresh clove. The aromas wash over me as a thick blanket, pushing back the drowning fears that lurk. As another pie goes into the oven, I hear the front door open and inhale Joey's scent as he reaches the kitchen.

"All done with business, sweetheart?" Ma asks him, and I hear them exchange kisses.

"Just about. Sis." Joey kisses me briefly on the cheek. "We need to talk."

"That's an uplifting tone," I mutter. "I can't even have pie yet?"

"Come out to the living room," he says, then turns to Ma. "Pops said he'll be late for dinner. There was a scuffle downstairs."

"I'll push the time back," Ma says, and pats my shoulder. "I'll bring some pie out to you later. Go talk with your brother, baby."

I follow behind Joey and pick up a familiar scent that sends reassurance through my body. I shove past my brother to the larger body with glowing pale, yellow eyes. Rodney's pine scent and warmth embrace me.

"Hey, lil sis," he whispers, wrapping his arms around me and kissing me on the head. He holds me for a moment as I take a few long breaths, then squeezes me and steps away as all three of us sit down.

"What's going on? You two starting a band?" I ask.

"Still got humor in you," Rodney comments.

"It's my specialty; terrible jokes at terrible times."

"Well, you may want some of that humor for this." A fantastic omen.

Joey takes a deep breath, grabbing my hand. "We found more on the ghouls."

Oh, *now* they do after shit's hit the fan. "Like what?" I ask.

"After we set up perimeters around the Bronx," Rodney explains, "my crew looked around and we did some background searches on the ghoul bodies we were able to obtain before they...well, turned to mush."

"We had a contact in NYPD who looked into a group of dead ghouls the police found," Joey says softly. "They were half-breeds before, too, but from years ago."

My eyes widen. "What?"

"Someone's been taking half-breeds off the streets for *years*, and none of us noticed. We fucked up," Rodney mutters. "And right now, the families under our protection *and* outside of it, aren't feeling safe." His voice is rough and tired, telling me he hasn't slept lately. "Not only are they terrified of Feral ghouls being loose, but now being kidnapped to turn into ones."

"We're looking further into it, but this is more than an Underground Mafia issue. And the NYPD and PSB are already pointing fingers at us, asking questions. Then there's..." Joey's voice vanishes, and his scent dampens.

"What is it, Joey?"

They shift in their seats as Joey answers, "I know you've been looking into more than just the missing people and ghouls. And, perhaps, against better judgement, with the help of that detective—"

"Not anymore," I scoff, and they both go still. "Don't ask. What are you getting at?"

"You need to stop searching altogether and let us take care of it."

"For your own protection, lil sis," Rodney continues. "Let us handle the situation. It'll get worse before it gets better and more dangerous. None of us want you hurt or taken, especially after those bloodsuckers who tried to nab—"

"Shit. You heard?" I ask.

"Saw the camera footage," Rodney chuckles low as I sigh. "You took them down quick."

"Element of surprise," I mumble, rubbing my eyes.

"We can compare shooting notes later," Joey says stiffly. "Blood Mafia is in an uproar, and the Vampiric Society is pissed they may be implicated for fault in the disappearances. It could bring the entire NIIA down here."

"Were they working for vamp Voldemort?"

"Bruno claims he had no idea why his lackies were taking people, but the security camera outside *BloodScape*, the footage that survived anyways, shows multiple kidnappings of half-breeds *and* humans," Joey explains as my chest starts to ache. "They're afraid any vampires who've gone rogue will diminish how the Society looks to Paranormals and humans. Or footage leaking on how quickly a half-breed took down five vamps."

Rodney snorts and grumbles, "Of course, those backward-ass Cullens care more about their reputation than actual people missing."

"They're also in an uproar cause everyone knows you and Vinny Claim Mated," Joey says carefully. I nod and wait for them to chastise me, telling me how stupid we were and should've thought it through more. They can't be any worse than Anita.

"Hey, lil sis," Rodney whispers, rubbing my knee lightly. "Can't be surprised you two would do something that sneaky, and kinda wish you'd said something. Could've had more material to jab at the bloodsucker, but we understand why you kept your mouth shut. Hell, most of the Blood Mafia likes you and didn't think the Society would be this furious. But when we saw Vinny—"

"You saw him?" I grip Rodney's hand as his scent dissipates, and he squeezes my hand back.

"Last night he called an emergency meeting with select people," Joey says.

"What was—?"

"Sorry, sis," He holds onto my shoulder, stroking his thumb over a scar. My stomach twists, and I suddenly feel sick. "Private information that can't be repeated until Vinny says. We gave our word. And he's stuck with a few hard…errands to take care of."

"Like what?" I ask. Rodney scratches himself and is about to speak when Joey's scent becomes harsh, causing Rodney to shut his mouth and adjust uncomfortably. "Fucking hell, tell me. I'll be a worse wreck if you don't."

"Baby sis—"

"Let Rodney go and tell me," I warn, and the scent of Joey's powers disappears.

Once released from Joey's hold, Rodney explains bluntly, "Vinny executed the five vampires who attacked you, including a few others who were in on the gig at *BloodScape*." Joey snarls lightly at him. "Don't use your hormone control on me. She'd find out sooner or later. She's not fucking blind to certain business dealings, Joey."

"Now who has terrible humor?" I ask.

Rodney pokes my knee. "You know what I mean."

"Did they find out who they were working for?" I ask, worried we lost our only lead.

"No, he needed to get rid of them quickly to regain control. They were loose cannons. Bloodsucker had to, lil sis. He's still the boss."

"For now," I whisper, rubbing my face as I sigh. "Fuck, this is a damn shitty mess."

"Watch your language, Ma might hear you." Joey pulls my hand down from my face.

"If I'm going out without Vinny, let it be by Ma's hands. It's a sweeter end than what awaits me."

Joey swallows hard. "There's one last thing, sis—"

"Damn it. What else is there apart from me basically starting a damn war within the Vampiric Society, which none of us can intervene because it'll start *another* war with the whole Underground. And if I enter their territory, they'll fucking try to kill me for making them look bad, which was why I moved to Topside three years ago!" I hiss under my breath. "Drauper warned me not to enter Topside or he'll arrest me, half-breeds are disappearing, ghouls are going Feral, I've got a judgmental daemon daddy who's prowling through clubs scaring succubi, and I'm positive Anita is planning to drain me dry after feeding her lead. And that's *if* I'm ever allowed near vampire territory again! Damn it!"

I grip into my hair and wish Vinny was here to hold me close, telling me we'll figure it out and then offer a bottle of scotch to share. A scream presses at my throat as Joey pulls me beside him, rubbing his hand over my back to help calm me as he whispers low, "I know everything feels difficult right now, sis. But we'll figure—"

"Joey it's not just that, you don't know—"

"Pops told me about Traloski."

I freeze against him. "What?"

Joey swallows hard and grips me tighter. "I talked to him about not letting you go back to Topside, and have you walk away from this. He kept saying you were looking for something. We argued about Vinny and you, that the timing wasn't right, and I was offering ways to help, about years down the line, and he...he broke down, Brenda. He broke down and told me why you were working with Drauper, searching into the half-breeds, and the ghouls. He told me about you...you dying."

A sob sticks in my throat, replacing the growing scream and tears form in my eyes. Joey holds me with trembling arms and presses his face into my neck. Rodney's scent dampens and I turn my head toward him, seeing only swirling dark shapes.

"Joey told me after the meeting," Rodney whispers. "I kept pushing to wait before going back up Top, get away from NIIA or PSB, and give the bloodsucker time to get his mess together first. I knew you'd hate being apart from Vinny, but I didn't realize that...that it could mean...fuck." He clears his throat and rustles in his seat.

"We know you didn't want us...us not to worry about you dying," Joey says quietly. "But, fuck, we'll find the bastard, Brenda. Vinny will finish his shit with the Society, and you'll give us headaches for another few centuries, and...and..."

The choking sound in my brother's voice almost breaks me. I wrap my arms tightly around him, hugging him close as I clutch his head against my shoulder. Tears stream down my cheeks as I whisper, "I'm sorry for hiding it from you. Both of you."

"I know," Joey whispers as he shudders in my grasp, and I feel a few tears land on my shoulder.

I reach my hand toward Rodney, and he takes it with a firm grip, stroking his thumb over my skin. I hold onto them both, feeling a weight coming off my shoulders but my stomach is heavy like lead. My secrets are out, and I'm still left racing against time.

All three of us stay there in silence, quiet until I break it with a soft, teasing voice. "You better continue telling embarrassing stories and such." Joey scoffs, then kisses my cheek finally pulling away.

Rodney gets up, sitting beside me on the couch and puts his arm around my shoulders. I can smell the fear wafting from him, and then it quickly disappears with the clove aroma from Joey. Rodney settles back and the couch groans. Oversized wolf.

"Well, you know my dirty secrets and latest expiration date, now what?" I ask.

"Wait until we find something," Rodney answers, and I

groan. Of course, another waiting game. "I've got people looking through Topside and the tunnels for the mad scientist. We'll find any trails that'll lead to him. We've gotta tread lightly with the ghouls prowling through most of the Bronx and upper Manhattan."

"We'll cover as much ground as we can, but it'll be difficult now that PSB is beginning to sniff around," Joey adds. "There's a lot of places to cover and not enough time."

"And the Blood Mafia?" I ask carefully. "Can you do anything for Vinny?"

Rodney lets out a long sigh. "I may dislike the asshole, but he's a smart vampire. He hasn't survived this long upsetting vampires without being conniving. He's just gotta convince the Society how dangerous Bruno is, and they may not kill him for 'betraying' them. If most vampires side with him, both Society and the Blood Mafia, he'll have a chance without much reper- cussion."

"They may still exile him... or..." My chin quivers and Joey grabs it.

"Hey," he says quietly. "His relations with the other mafia families will give him a leg up. And the last thing we need is Bruno taking the damn title back. Vinny can't give up being boss without putting you in danger or ripping the Blood Mafia in half. He can't just step away from all of that and his blood- line, but he'll do what he can to protect you."

There's a scoff behind us, and we all turn toward Ma as she walks in to set down a fresh apple pie on the coffee table. "Son, the day you find your Mate, you'll realize how much war you're willing to cause to keep them safe. Ask your father," she says sternly and begins to walk away. "Rodney, you're staying for dinner. You all can have some pie to hold you over since it'll be late. I'll bring out the plates."

Ma pats my shoulder and disappears into the pink haze of the kitchen. Rodney whistles low and chuckles as Joey sighs on my other side. Mother knows best.

BRUNO
IS A
Bitch

CHAPTER 24
THE HORSE'S HEAD

Eight days.

No Vinny.

I'm wiping down the bar at Joey's coffee shop, which should be up and running next month, delayed due to the chaotic circumstances of late. I've spent the last few days busy organizing all of it with Ricky. He and Gina have tried several times to get me to dance, hoping to help me through this depression and blow off some steam. I can't focus. My mind slips every once and a while searching for Vinny in every crowd I pass, hoping I'll see him alive and fine.

I stop and lean over the counter, sighing heavily. Fucking hell this sucks.

My throat tightens as I try to calm my spiraling thoughts, but I have no way of knowing if he's exiled, dead, or will waltz back like nothing's wrong. I thought it'd been bad a few months ago when Vinny and I had our fight, but it wasn't even close to what I felt now. I hate not knowing what to do and waiting as the clock ticks.

I toss the towel to the side, beginning to reorganize the coffee grounds, *again* when the back door opens. Just as I'm about to say we're closed, the unwelcome scent blows in of burnt wood, worn leather, and scotch. I grab the Desert Eagle under the counter, aiming at the figure as I click back the safety. I turn toward the doorway and my gaze meets his hateful, dark blood-red eyes.

"Bruno," I growl.

"That won't save you," he sneers under his breath.

"Sure, about that?" I tilt the gun slightly toward his head. It's not loaded with silver, but he'll have a headache for days.

He's wearing a dark blue pinstripe suit, a black button-up that's open at the top, and there's a shadow of a beard along his jawline and upper lip. His hair is slicked back like Vinny's, and I notice the family ring on his hand. Fuck.

I keep the gun steady, and I tilt my head. "What do you want?"

He approaches the counter, closing in until only the counter stands between us. Instinct screams for me to run, especially as his eyes darken and the bite marks on my neck pulsate. The memory of what if felt like with his teeth painfully sunk into me flashes. He cocks his head. "How much are you willing to give up for him?"

"More than you know."

"Interesting, he said something similar." His hand swipes up and clutches the barrel, twisting it away from my grasp. My wrist throbs as he flicks the safety and tosses it across the counter. "He said he'll give up his position for you. After I gave him *everything*, he's throwing it away for a deformed, stupid, half-breed descended from an outcast daemon. So, it appears my warning didn't get through to your...*neck*."

A part of me wants to taunt him, while the other is telling me to tread carefully. I ignore the latter. "I'm a pain to puppeteer."

"There are other strings to pull," he says venomously, then shows me the ring. "Other ways to remind my son who I am and get back everything he cost me. No matter what, *neither* of you will change the inevitable." His fangs elongate as he sneers, "*My* success."

My blood chills as I glance down at the elongated fangs before me and clutch the poor wooden counter between us. The scars on my neck throb harshly as I rasp, "Over my dead body."

Bruno's expression darkens as he cocks his head. "Easier said than done."

His scent intensifies, and I almost gag at the detection of old blood in the aroma. "Pity your human-snatching vamps couldn't finish the job for you. Including adding more half-breeds to your collection."

Bruno smiles darkly, and my spine stiffens as his scent worsens. "Fortunately, the truth died with them."

My stomach drops. "You admitting it then?"

"You always seem to forget where you don't belong, don't you?"

"And *you're* a bastard. When the rest of the Blood Mafia and Society find out—"

"They'll never believe you," he says, leaning forward. "You'll never be part of them, forever an unwanted *human*. Like the Cuorebellas, Vincent had an unfortunate bout of mercy for you; the blind, *defenseless* human found in the sewers they took out of pity. You're like other humans; powerless and dependent on *us*."

I swallow hard. "You're wrong."

"Am I?"

"You know *nothing* about family," I sneer.

He laughs with a malicious, sinister grin that pulls at his lips, and he stands to his full height, devouring my size. Terror pricks at my spine as I tighten my jaw and ask, "Unless you're just here to taunt me, what the fuck do you want?"

"For you to leave the Underground."

"Fuck, no."

"We had a deal three years ago, half-breed, and you broke it. But I can make an exception for you to leave now, and no harm comes to Vincent, your family, your precious wolves, and even a certain...*detective*." My breath shortens, and he smiles in victory. "Beckham has lived long enough...don't you agree?"

I struggle to focus, gripping onto the counter harder. "You wouldn't fucking dare."

"I take what's mine, and a rejected female won't ruin that," he snarls, his smile disappearing. "This city will be *mine*, just as Vincent always was. Not yours. Leave, or I'll destroy everything you love, half-breed."

Bruno turns to leave as his body bristles with contempt. The scent of old blood beginning to disappear with him. But, of course, my sassy ass has to get the last word in. "You're just pissed that Vinny didn't end up fuck-killing me, like how *you* licked your own crusty cum off your Mate's body after you murdered her."

He yanks his head around and snarls, his eyes glowing in fury, ready to pounce until the door swings open. The vampire freezes as the shop fills with the aroma of cold metal mixed with smoke and cinnamon, his expression dropping as he turns to face my father.

"You're on Cuorebella property, Dracultelli," Pops says with a low growl.

"Just having a simple discussion, *Alanzo*," Bruno replies. The cold metal smell becomes stronger, and Bruno's body stiffens.

"We both know you don't talk." Pops steps to the side, slamming the door open as his eyes flash violet. "Get out before I do something I may regret."

Bruno glances back at me, then approaches him near the door. "You already did the moment you found her."

Pops snarls as the vampire disappears through the door into the darkened alleys of the Underground. I loosen a long breath, slumping against the counter behind me as Pops closes the door. The shop goes back to smelling of coffee beans when he approaches me.

He grabs the gun, putting it away, and asks, "What did he want?" I scoff. "Baby girl."

"What do you think, Pops? For me to leave, or Vinny loses everything." I go back to cleaning.

"He won't, baby girl. Most of his assets belong solely—"

"Did you keep me out of pity?" The question leaves me before I realize it, Bruno's words searing through me as it combines with the fear of the past week. I can't pretend I never thought of it before or crossed my mind. Pity. That's what I always got living on Topside. Is that what's happening now because I'm dying?

I tightly clutch the towel in my hand and Pops' eyes widen. "Baby girl…"

"Out of all the survivors, children, people, why me? Why keep the child from the sewer?" I throw the towel down, running my hand through my hair roughly. "I know I shouldn't ask, but right now, it feels like I'm an unlucky charm for everyone. I'm so unsure, and maybe it's because—"

"Baby girl," Pops says, putting his hand on the side of my face, making me look at him. Bright violet eyes focus on me as his thumbs strokes my skin. "I won't say there wasn't some pity in my heart when I found you, and I can't tell you the exact reasons why it was you I brought home. What I can tell you is that the moment you called me daddy, there was no being who'd take you away from me. The way you clung to me, your laughter, smile, protective growling, everything about you made me love you more and more. You are *my* daughter because I love you unconditionally."

I grip onto his wrists while fear tears through me as a wave of guilt wrenches around my heart. The words of Bruno echo from years ago, Vinny forsaking his life for me, Rodney jeopardizing himself and his crew, Drauper being in danger, and Joey fighting for me, and all for what? Blame consumes me as I wrench Pops' hand off my face and grab Vinny's jacket, clutching it to my chest.

"Talk to me, baby girl," Pops says softly.

"You're all fighting for a dead female," I choke out. "I'll die, and you'll have nothing but blood, pain, and a worthless war that'll hurt everyone. I'm a ticking timebomb, and when I finally explode, there'll be nothing. Because of *me*. You'll have nothing but pain."

I start to leave the shop as Pops calls out, "No, baby girl, we'll find Traloski—"

"You don't know that!" I yell, turning toward him as tears well up.

"You *have* to believe we'll find—"

"All the leads have gone cold! Even if we do find him, there's *no* guarantee he'll have the answer."

"You can't give up, baby girl. Not like this." He shakes his head.

"Just face it, Pops, I'll be dead, and this will *all* be in vain. You'll have nothing."

"None of this was nothing," he argues, moving toward me. "You're worth more—"

"I'm a blip in everyone's lives, and I'll be forgotten in less than a hundred years." I yank open the shop door. "That's what I'm worth."

I run out of the shop, ignoring the tears in his eyes as he calls after me as I sprint through the darkened Underground. His only name for me echoes behind me. I go further north of the Underground and into werewolf territory, weaving past Paranormals and humans as my mind churns in chaos and hurt.

My fault. All of this will be my fault for fucking existing, because I was selfish. I'll lose Vinny, hurting him in the end instead of saving him. Everyone will go through all this just for me to one day not wake up. One day soon, fuck it could be tomorrow, or two hours, I won't be here. I wipe away tears as I slow down, growling in frustration and noticing an old familiar sign.

It's been forever since I've visited this bar. Only a few wolves sit inside as I walk in and head toward the main bar, setting down a couple of twenties. A young timber wolf comes around, eyeing the cash as I say, "Whatever fucking whiskey you have for this. Bring the bottle."

He turns and grabs from the bottom shelf a shitty bottle of whiskey, placing it in front of me and taking the cash as I pop it open. He sets a glass down, but I forgo it and down half the fucking bottle. I put it down with a long breath as it burns through my throat and insides. Maybe I can drink myself to death quicker, save everyone the trouble. Save me from seeing a dead Vinny, heartbroken Pops, or the devastation on Ma's face.

"Haven't seen you in a bit, lil sis," Garrick's familiar deep voice catches my attention. The older timber wolf sweeps his deep green eyes over me as he cleans a few glasses, tilting his head and nods toward the half-emptied bottle. "Been a while since you've been on this side of the Underground. Vampires piss you off, finally?"

"You could say that," I grumble, taking another harsh swig from my bottle.

"Slow down there—"

"Don't, Garrick," I snarl through my teeth. Fury burns through me, and my knuckles have that hard, sharp pressure against them again. Garrick's eyes widen at the snarling sound, and I wish I could've made it years ago. It would've made parts of college more bearable.

"Fine, if you want another, it's on me. You look like shit," he comments, walking away as I scowl, and continue to drink.

Usually this far into the bottle, I'd call Vinny, who'd come throw me over his shoulder and force coffee down my throat. He'd then tell me not to overdrink without a buddy, get my head out of my ass, and ignore his father who's a narcissistic bastard. But Vinny's not here, and he may never be.

My chin quivers, and before I know it, I finish the bottle in record time. I glance to the side, watching the wolves divert their gazes. Another bottle clinks before me, and I turn back to see Garrick disappear into the back. Opening the bottle, I hear the door open, and my hand twitches at my side, detecting his fucking stale scent. Edgar's feathers rustle beside me, and I ignore him as he sits and orders a drink from the young wolf. I swirl the scotch, focusing past his aroma, taking another gulp from the less shitty bottle.

"Why should I not be surprised you drink like that?" He asks.

"Because I have daddy issues?" I smirk.

"You're mouth, I swear—"

"Stick around, and you'll realize how bad my mouth gets." Suddenly, his scent scorches, and I smirk again. Pissing the daemon off is the first good thing to happen today.

"Those beings made you difficult."

"Those *beings* took care of me after you left me with a psycho, *dad*," I growl, looking at him.

Edgar's gray eyes flash, and I see he hasn't really shaved. He scowls deeply, his eyes roving down to assess me. I bring Vinny's jacket closer around me, hoping his lingering scent pisses the daemon off more. I haven't really mocked anyone in a week, and my snark game needs a work-out. I gesture toward him with the bottle in hand. "What the hell you want? Other than degrading me for my life choices, *again*."

"Can't we just talk?"

"Chastising, complaining, and grumbling isn't talking."

"I know what's best for you. None of—"

"You forfeited that fucking right decades ago, birdman," I snarl.

"I am *still* your father. You *will*—"

"Fucking nothing, featherbrain." I throw a tip down and

stalk out of the bar with bottle in hand, shouting, "See you later, Garrick!" The door slams behind me as a chair screeches.

"Brenda!" Edgar yells for me.

"Don't feel like talking or hearing bad news, and I *definitely* don't take direction well. Pro-tip, I hate authority," I say, drinking from the bottle as I walk. Do I look like a drunk? Yes. Do I care? Nope.

"I am trying to save you, or do you want to die, making *everyone* suffer because of your selfishness."

I spin and grab him by the neck as a snarl rips from my throat. "Don't you *dare* speak of them."

He seethes as his wings flare out behind him, and the aroma of worn leather, patchouli, and oil comes back full force, sickening my stomach. Damn, really pissing him off. I should choke him more often to shut him up.

"You left me," I hiss. "And because you didn't have the guts to find me sooner, I'll be leaving the ones who did care about me behind. All of them left in a *fucking* mess you helped cause—"

"Then do the right thing and leave with me before it gets worse."

I stumble back, letting him go as we stand in the deserted alley. Amber light illuminates the daemon as his wings rise above him, gray eyes flashing as he rubs at his throat. "What?" I ask.

"Leave with me. We'll find Traloski together and get what you need. I've watched your 'family' and seen how they haven't been able to help you. *I* know what you need. The others will just flounder—"

"They're *actually* trying to help me, whereas you—"

"Those degenerates know nothing!"

I point my finger at him, yelling, "*They* care about me! While you *stalk* clubs and judge—"

"*You* decided to live that filthy, immoral life," he growls, pointing back at me. "A life not meant for you as a daemon!

You don't belong with them and never have. Deep down, you know it. Don't act like they've accepted what you are. *They* used you, *kept* you when you did what they wanted and became something you aren't. You were a *project* to them, no different than Traloski—"

"Shut up!" My voice shakes as I grip my bottle. "Fucking shut up."

"And now they're fighting over you. Destroying themselves because the vampires know what's right. *They* at least understand the natural order of things. You are a daemon half-breed, not a succubus, vampire, or werewolf. You were *never* one of them."

I tremble, taking a step back, fury writhing under my skin as my hand flexes, wanting to choke him. Tears leak from my eyes as I sneer at him. "No…"

"This is what happens when daemons stay where we don't belong," he says, taking a step toward me. "Leave with me, right now, and be what you should be. Only *I* can give you what you need. Only *I* know your worth. They never will, and the last of your days will be in vain, keeping up this lie that you belong." Edgar takes out the folded newspaper clippings, showing them to me. "*They* tried and look where it got them."

I reach for the obituaries, but he clutches them tighter in his hand. He frowns at the crumpled papers, smoothing them back out with a reverence. He then takes a step closer toward me, and I move back before his hand touches my shoulder, frowning at him. I fight back tears that try to escape. "Tell me how to survive."

"I just told you, you need me—"

"No. *What* do I need?"

He glances at the clippings, peeling back one of the pictures with his thumb, stroking it and saying quietly, "To awaken your Paranormal abilities, of course."

"Is that how you tried to help them?" His eyes flash up to meet mine. "Tell me how, Edgar."

"Come with me—"

"Not happening."

He shoves the clippings into his jacket. "Then you'll die like the rest of your siblings. All potential lost."

I step toward him with a malicious snarl as his wings flare out, growling. "If you're not going to tell me, then what do you want? What's your fucking endgame, *father*?"

Edgar tilts his head, and the movement causes a shiver through my body, piercing ice through my veins. He flexes his hands and there's a flicker of blue lightning across his fingertips, while his face shifts along with his scent into a calm that makes me want to cower. "*My* daughter, of course. What's mine and what those *beasts* took from me. What I am *owed* after every sacrifice I made for *you*."

Suddenly, I'm the little girl left in the sewer. The air feels thin as his scent worsens, and he takes a step toward me, lightning sparking across his hands.

For years, I've been warned about the monsters who hide and strike in the shadows. They are the ones who Vinny, Pops, Rodney...all of them, protected me from. Edgar looks at me with a hunter's want, and I remember why daemons are feared as his eyes flash. There's a darkness to his face, a warning of how dangerous his vengeance can become, and I don't want to know how deep it may run after losing his children.

Caution coils in my gut and screams for me to stay away as I hear Vinny's warning, *"Don't be alone."*

I slam back more alcohol with a shaky hand, turning and walking away. I hear him follow after me, but people fill the alley, his footsteps disappearing along with his scent as my pace quickens.

My breath becomes ragged as I contemplate how little control I had in this world. I then realize why Vinny stayed all those years ago, why Rodney watched over me, why I had the emergency system on my phone, why people walked me everywhere, and why Pops kept me close to home. At the end of the day, I was a human without powers.

My soul cries out for Vinny; his touch, his laugh, his smell, *anything* to make the monsters disappear. I've never felt more alone as the pressure against my knuckles worsen, my own monster clawing to be let out.

CHAPTER 25
BOOKS FROM THE VINE

Twelve days.

I've been holed up in *The Vault* for almost four. I couldn't bring myself to face Pops. My mind felt like it crashed after seeing Bruno and Edgar, and still no Vinny. So, I did what I always do—hide in the library.

During my days of self-quarantine, I reorganized Beckham's history, biology, and genetic sections as I scoured for answers to awaken my Paranormal abilities. Beckham brought me food after Ma threatened him, and Ricky tried to give me new clothes, but I've stayed in the same ones.

I've gone through shelf after shelf for *something*, falling asleep in aisles, surrounded by books when I wake up in a cold sweat, plagued by nightmares. I ravage through the books on daemons for anything that may awaken my dormant side, but nothing. Nothing helps, and I can't find anything about Mating effects from vampires or daemons. More questions rise in me as I go back and forth searching through medical studies, but all the suggestions and theories result in more testing or just death. I find myself deep within *The Vault*, finding journals in crevices I didn't know about discussing antibody studies from the 18th century. No one got as far as Traloski, and he was the only one who bred his own subjects, past scientists focused on already living ones. Plain and simple, I shouldn't exist, and being a medical anomaly sucks.

I rip my glasses off with a growl as my eyes itch. I stopped wearing my contacts a day ago, which made it harder to read some books. I get up from the ground and search again for ghoul genetics and any connection between Paranormal abilities changing with the additive of their blood. I glean through the documents and inhale the aroma of peppermint tea and fresh biscuits. My stomach grumbles, and I look up to see Beckham at the end of the aisle, holding up a tray.

I take the documents with me, joining him in the small reading nook as he sits down across from me, putting the tray down and hands me some tea. "Thanks," I murmur.

"It appears you've not found your answers," he says, tracing a finger over the books on the coffee table.

"Being a librarian seems moot at this point." I gesture to the clutter.

"I thought I taught you, Little Sister, that not every answer comes from books."

"Except, it needs to be because there's nothing out there, Beckham. It's dead ends, dead people, dead *ghouls*, and...*me* dead." He sits back, slowly stirring his tea in silence as I slump back. I told him everything from the Claim Mating, Traloski, and my looming demise when I arrived four days ago. He's been quiet most of the time, giving what I need without a word, this is the most we've spoken in the last four days.

Beckham reaches over and picks up a book about daemon anthropology from India, then another over societal functions with daemons observed in the 1500s. He's a glowing portrait of grace with dark hues of greens and blues. "You are grasping many pens and dropping them it would seem."

I shake my head. "I'm covering all my bases. Whether it's antidotes from modern times or older, medical surgeries that failed, blood fusions, white blood cell research—"

"By now, you should understand you cannot find medical answers in these books because there's no solutions given. Yet, you're still looking for answers."

"It's the only thing I can do, Beckham. I've got nothing else."

He tosses the books on the coffee table and stares at me. "I do believe that is an excuse."

I gape at him in surprise. "An excuse?"

"Yes."

Maybe I'm not the only one off my rocker these past few days and Beckham fell off his, age catching up with him. "How is looking for a way to live an excuse?"

"Days here, you've not found the answer, yet you still pull at every string, hoping it will unravel the mystery. What if the answer is outside, and you're hiding from it instead?"

"Why would I hide—?"

"Did you speak with the daemon of what he knows?" He asks suddenly. "What he had discovered while in New York? Or what he might've found before you?" My jaw clenches, and I shake my head. "A source right there, and you didn't take it, very unlike you, my little librarian."

"I don't trust him."

"Yet, you've resigned your end to his words." He sets his own mug down and tilts his head, his long hair spilling over his shoulders. "What did he say that made you frantic? What was it that made you avoid a potential source?"

I swallow hard and shrug. "I...I...don't know."

Beckham heaves a long breath and picks up another book on the coffee table detailing the genetics of humans in comparison to Paranormals. "I've lived a long lifespan, little one. I'm aware the next day could be my last, and I thrive on the stories and people that I adore and care for. Even now, like you, my end races quicker to me each day, not knowing when. But I shall not falter over past mistakes, choices made, and guilt because I *lived*."

I'm silent as he picks up another book and stacks them off to the side. "What are you getting at?"

"I always thought you saw it the same, living your life without regret or fear, each day bright with anticipation with the need to learn and grow," he muses, smiling at me. "It may be one of many reasons we Paranormals of the Underground fell in love with the young child who giggled at our snarling. The child who lived amongst us without second thought, cherishing everyone and forgetting the shadows that originally made you. Now, you need to look into the past, Little Sister. Not in these books."

"The past? Beckham, that's what I've been doing, reading history."

"Ah, but you've been looking into the *wrong* history, avoiding the correct one," he says, placing a few books onto a shelf. "Memories are not written down, neither are moments created. You're a historian; you know that the past holds answers we seek, but not everything is written."

"You're still being cryptic, Beckham," I say as he disappears down an aisle. I huff, falling back onto the couch.

His chuckle echoes down the aisle and he comes back, collecting more books. "Do you remember the first time you came here?"

There he goes diverting the conversation again. "Yeah, why?"

"You were so young and blind," he muses, and I roll my eyes. "Your other senses were immaculate, practically born to be a succubus. You divided books by smell and touch, fascinated with how much there was here, running through the aisles as you clicked your tongue."

"I still ran into some shelves," I murmur.

Beckham chuckles. "Only three times, but in two hours' time, Alanzo had to barter with you to leave. You remember our agreement?"

A smile rises on my face as I remember the foggy darkness

of Beckham, allured with the smell of tea and books, shining eyes through the darkness filled with amusement. Such as now. "You'd be my teacher, letting me take home any book even out of my reading level. Once I got glasses, you helped me read with my eyes. In return, I'd have to help you transcribe books into braille when I was old enough. You told me I was *born* to read."

"I was certainly correct, wasn't I? Such the natural."

He sits down beside me, humming to himself as he offers me some biscuits. I take a few to munch on and ask, "Is there a reason you brought that up?"

"A loving family does not depend on genetics," he says.

"I know that—"

"Do you?" I stop mid-bite. "Knowing where you come from and who you are a part of does not change *who* you are. It does not negate the life that has been lived over the years and cultivated. You've survived that past, and it does not define you."

"Beckham, I've tried looking and…" my voice falters at the thought of trying to read the paperwork again, "…I already told you how that turned out."

"Then, what are you afraid of, Little Sister?" He asks gently as he places his hand on my shoulder. "Why are you avoiding the obvious choice for an answer?"

I stare down through warped colors, fisting my hands as I try to collect my thoughts. I'm afraid of a lot, from losing Vinny, bathtubs filled with water, children reading circles, including losing my family. Except, there's one that's always followed me since I left for Topside.

"I'm afraid of failing," I answer quietly. "I was already a failed experiment, and in the end, it wasn't good enough. *I* wasn't good enough. And everything that's been done for me will be a waste, and that I failed…failed my family."

Beckham lays his hand against my cheek, prompting me to look at him and I'm met with a shimmering gaze. "Your own history holds weight like these books you cherish, and your time with us is not *nothing*. You were *always* good enough, mistakes and all. Whatever you have done, no matter the outcome, has always been in the best interest of your family, and the *entire* Underground," he says tenderly, squeezing my cheek. "This is *why* we'll fight wars for you because we love you unconditionally no matter what runs in your veins. It is due to that love to which even I let you...*destroy* my library. You are more than enough."

My chin quivers, and he wipes away a stray tear rolling down my cheek. "I wasn't enough for him," I whisper. "For Edgar. What if I find out why and it makes things worse? Why I failed—?"

"When you learned of Alanzo losing your mother, did you think he failed?" I shake my head. "What about Vincent and his past decisions?" I shake my head again. "Just as you accepted them and their histories, the same will be given to you. Those memories and relationships are not nothing."

"You said look into history, not memories."

"Same thing, are they not?" He smiles. "Your roots may be seeped with pain, but you have gained new growth because you fought for a new life. And if you do not fear the histories or roots of those called 'monsters' then do not fear your own."

"But you all know who you are. You know where you belong, and I...I'm either a failure as a daemon or a succubus—"

"That is because you don't belong to one or the other," he says, tapping my nose. "You belong to *all* of the Underground... baby sis."

Words which haunted me, condemned me, or spewed hatred falls away like sand.

Fuck, I'd been listening to the wrong people. I should've believed each time Vinny said I was his everything, Pops calling me his "baby girl," Ma soothing me, Joey protecting me, and Ricky dancing with me. I always saw them as good enough, and I was to them, no matter what my past held or who created me.

Some moments in life you feel like a naïve idjit, and this is one of those times.

"You know, as your favorite librarian, sometimes I feel blind in a different way," I comment.

Beckham chuckles, stroking my hair back, and says, "You're book smart *and* street smart, Little Sister. A rare combination that can cancel out the other in dire circumstances."

"It's a terrible burden," I joke.

"Your adoration for others outweighs your own safety at times. Even after lessons of self-love from your family, you seem to forget your own worth."

"Alright, I get it, don't dig the hole deeper," I mutter, pushing the last of the books aside. "I'll look into my own past, but we already tried the paperwork. And that shit only seems to bring everyone pain. So, any advice on where to start? Everything's like a spider-web coated in maple syrup, and the spider who wove it is hiding."

"Sounds delicious," he smirks, and I grimace. He stands up, taking books with him as he peers through the pages. "Spiders usually hide in plain sight, right in the center of everything and the beginning they created." He goes still, pausing on a page. "It does appear you're the center of all this, though, are you not?"

"Let's not add 'god complex' to my list of grievances today."

"You *are* the only denominator," he muses. "And the only history *you* do not know or have investigated yet. So, if you were to begin your own self-discovery, where would your web begin?" Beckham disappears down the aisle into the quiet library, and I sit back, thinking over what he said. An idea grows as I recount his words and decide to start cross referencing outside the library.

I grab my phone, dialing the familiar Chicago number. It rings three times before Bill picks up, and I speak before he can. "We tried running my DNA for matches years ago and came up with nothing, *but* we didn't when daddykins came around. I need you to run his bloodwork and DNA through the public hospital records for humans and Paranormals." I try to remember what I saw the two times Edgar showed me the clippings. "Start in Iowa City and Denver, ages between twenty-six and twenty-eight, died about sixteen months ago. I know two more of my siblings were in New York; you can start there, too. I need to know every symptom the hospitals recorded, how they died, and places of admission. Edgar presumably had multiple children; one of them has to show up in the system."

If I can't find Traloski or medical treatments that already exist, then I'll make my own deductions. I can work with Charlene on what's found with those who died and maybe I'll find another solution to staying alive.

"One, good morning. Two, you have siblings?" Bill asks. "And you didn't think to bring this up beforehand?"

"I've been busy, vamp tramp."

"Well, now I have to think of a world filled with—" Someone screams, and doors slam in the background.

"You switch pomegranate juice with blood again?"

"They should know the difference by now," he says, and something crashes as car horns blare. "As I was saying, there's more of you out there?"

"You get anything I said? They're dead, Bill."

"Unfortunately, yes, I heard you."

"Can you find all that, then? Preferably in the next 48 hours?"

"Very time-sensitive, aren't we? Do I get a raise?"

"I want answers immediately, Billy Bob," I retort. "Or I'll send a candygram to your office."

"I'll need a hobby after this tiny *confusion* that's happening in the office anyways," he says, and I snort. "Push it to 72 hours. New York, Iowa City, and Denver, you said? Quite the spread."

"Fine. What'll it cost me, besides a headache?"

"Nothing, baby sis."

I furrow my brows. Nothing with him is free. "What's the catch?"

"It's widely known you and the boss have Claim Mated," Bill laughs. "It's causing waves I've wanted to see for *years*. This will be my Mating gift to you. In fact, I'll find every possible detail on any half-siblings of yours, maybe find their favorite color. I still want an invite to the official Mating Ceremony, though. I need a vacation after this past week."

"If there ever *is* a Ceremony," I mumble. "Alright, Sin City Wannabe, deal. And I'm sure my week was worse than yours."

Midnight snorts. "*You* try keeping all of Vincent's assets and his fail-safes together."

My breath catches. "What?"

"You didn't know?"

"I...I haven't seen him recently," I rasp. "What about fail-safes?"

"All the contacts in PSB and NIIA for the Blood Mafia are on his payroll, no one else," he explains. "Even our wonderful 'she-devil' on Topside, who I heard he has dirt on. I've always meant to ask him how he got—"

"Bill, what do you mean fail-safes? What did he—?"

"Apart from said 'she-devil,' he's collected blackmail on all the higher members of the Vampiric Society, including some secret locations that NIIA doesn't even know about," he snickers wickedly. "Basically, if they ever tried to get rid of him, I'd have no choice but to release the preverbal hounds on them. All information gets sent out to a server to the NIIA, PSB, and human governments, which the President of France would *love* to have. It's an impressive list. Want a copy?"

My jaw slackens. "When did he do this?"

"Just after he became boss. Few weeks give or take. He's been a busy vampire, like he knew this was coming." Someone shouts and a car screeches. "Gotta go; new partner caught up with me. I want front seats to the Mating Ceremony!"

The phone clicks, and I drop my hand to the side in shock.

Laughter suddenly erupts from me, echoing through the library and causing my stomach to ache. He knew. He fucking knew when we Claim Mated that we'd be fine because he was already prepared. Vinny has done the most Vinny thing ever, and I don't know why I ever doubted him.

CHAPTER 26
THANKS 4 THE PAINT AND MEMORIES

It's peak twilight as I stand outside *Unbound*. The neon sign flickers, and for a moment, I'm a child again who was first brought here. It was quiet that night, too, when Pops carried me from the sewers. I close my eyes and think of the memories surrounding this place.

It wasn't for nothing. I hadn't failed.

I take a deep breath and walk inside to soft music and lights as Bobby takes inventory behind the bar and the dancers move in and out of the changing rooms. I look up and smile when I notice my panties still showcased above the stage after almost three months now.

"Look who decided to leave that musty library." Ricky's voice carries over the music, and I turn to see him walk toward me. He's wearing a mesh shirt, dark slacks, and hair pulled back with a smile. He hugs me quickly and looks me over. "You doing alright, sis?"

I take a deep breath and ask, "You got those paints?"

He looks taken aback. "Yeah, wait, you serious? You actually offering?"

I smirk. "Overdue, don't you think? Or have you lost your artistic touch and don't wanna embarrass yourself?"

He laughs, putting his arm over my shoulder. "Okay, maybe you should hole up in *The Vault* more often," he says, squeezing me a little. "Don't tell Ma I said that. Let's shave your head while we're at it, getting shaggy."

"Alright," I chuckle.

We head to the back, and he shaves my head, telling me how Joey and Pops were gone most of the time while Ma worried at home. Then we move to the main lounge area, where I strip down to my underwear and lay down on a couch as Ricky sets up his paints. I tell him everything from searching for the ghouls, Traloski, Edgar, and more as he paints my torso. The guilt that's simmered in me dies as each word comes out, Ricky listening silently as he paints and blends the neon colors together.

He finishes my torso and legs, finishing up my arms into a canvas of bright violets and blues, which I can see with my glasses. I sit up to change positions, waiting for him as he mixes more paint, but he keeps his gaze away from me.

"Ricky?" I ask, my stomach twisting a little from his silence.

"I know it was hard for you to talk," he says quietly. "Thank you for finally telling me." I put my hand on his shoulder, and he grasps it, kissing a part of my unpainted wrist. "I really want to hug you right now, but it'll mess up my masterpiece before it dries."

"Can't have that, can we?"

"Do you really think you're dying?"

I swallow hard. "I'm gonna try not to, at least not soon."

"Spite-filled, stubborn, and prideful," he muses. "Pretty sure that's why you're still alive and kicking now." We chuckle awkwardly. "Guess you learned it from Pops and Joey."

I lean forward and grasp Ricky's neck, touching my forehead against his. He takes a long breath in, and I feel his powers shudder, reaching out to calm and ease. I whisper, "Sorry, I can be a shitty sister sometimes."

"No, you're not," he says. "You just forget to share the burden and talk. And I'll love you anyway, even if you were."

"Kudos, bro." I kiss him on the cheek, and he reciprocates.

He ruffles my hair lightly and clears his throat, ushering me to my next position. "Come on, gotta finish you up. Lean over the back, I need my workspace clear." He pats my shoulder. "I should've figured the stress was too much when you wanted to be painted."

"I don't ask—"

"Do, too."

"Do not."

"Do, too, and if you keep arguing, I add glitter," he warns, and I dramatically gasp.

"Conniving incubus."

"For glitter? Always." He sweeps my hair off my back. "Maybe I taught you spite."

I lay down and feel the soft bristles of the paintbrush sweep across my skin, and we continue talking about better things as his sweet rose aroma fills the space. Joey joins us with a tired huff, playing with my hair as he sits beside me, and I catch him up on what Ricky knows. I also tell them what I'm having Midnight do, but we don't stay on the sore subjects long. We talk like we did what seems like forever ago, just siblings, pretending the harsh realities of the outside don't exist. We laugh, toss jokes, bet how long my panties will stay up, and devise show routines. During the last part of my back being painted, we think of a name for Joey's coffee shop, which prompts Ricky and I to give some ridiculous ideas.

"*Underground Café* sounds too formal," Ricky pouts at Joey's suggestion.

"And I'm pretty sure *Creature Café* is already taken," I muse.

"I'm not calling it *Wings and Rings*, Ricky. It's horrendous." Joey grimaces.

"I doubt anyone's going to guess the rings mean donuts." I laugh under my breath.

"You two have no imagination," Ricky scoffs. "Especially you, *Diablo of the Underground*."

"You told him?" Joey asks as I turn around.

"I was not withholding that ridiculous shit to myself." I pull back my hair and Ricky hums about what color to paint my facial scars.

Joey moves beside me. "Why not violet to match her eyes?"

Ricky pauses, muttering under his breath. "Guess you have *some* artistic imagination, doesn't save you from that name."

Joey snorts and I push him a little as Ricky gathers the paint. I close my eyes as Ricky sets to work when Joey's phone goes off and he leaves to answer it. The sweet rose and clove scent drift over my senses, and I sigh as the small brush sweeps across a scar.

"You gonna talk to Pops?" Ricky asks.

"Yeah..." I mumble.

"He's been pretty worried, it makes more sense...well, it makes more sense now." I grab his free hand, and he nuzzles mine briefly. "I think you better show off this new paint to him. Help him feel better. It'll cheer you up, too."

"Not sure it'll help," I sigh heavily, squeezing his hand. "I was a real fucking dick, even if it was my tenth mental breakdown in twelve days."

"You thought you lost your Mate, sis. And on top of—"

"That doesn't excuse my behavior, Ricky. I deserve whatever—"

"He's our Pops, sis," he says, tapping my cheek and I open my eyes to shimmering blue ones against a dark background. "If anyone understands that kind of pain, it's him."

I nod numbly. "Yeah."

He ruffles my hair again, bringing a small smile to my face. "And come on, how many times did we almost destroy this place, and he never batted an eye?"

Ricky continues to paint me as memories filter back.

Unbound was my playground where I ran from my brothers,

hiding under couches until Pops would coax me out. I danced on stage with Ricky, played dress-up with Gina, colored with my brothers, showed-off glittering costumes to Ma and Pops, learned how to bartend with Bobby, and almost broke two stripper poles with Joey. I grin, remembering my brothers finding me in a puddle of lube and running away outside until Pops caught me. He would shut down *Unbound* and strap me to his back as he worked with the survivors or ran the club. Those early years, I never really left Pops' side, and he always seemed content with that. All of it was more than good enough of a life.

Damn it, why is that shifter always right?

"Hey, sis, you hear me?" Ricky interrupts my thoughts, and I blink harshly, bringing my attention to him. "You alright?"

"Yeah, just remembering."

"Such as?" Brushes clatter as he finishes.

"Random stuff." I touch my face, feeling the wet paint beneath my fingertips, smiling. Ticking timebomb or not, I belonged. I had people who made sure of it, and for some reason, I seemed to have forgotten that my family truly loved me. I'd been so intent trying to protect them, I hadn't stopped and seen they were there. Hard times or not.

Joey comes back to sit beside me, mumbling about a meeting later as Ricky sits on my other side, and I continue grinning. Both shift next to me, and Joey asks, "Why you smiling like that?"

"I hope you two know I love you very much," I say, and they become frozen next to me. "You're the best siblings anyone could ask for, and you'll *always* be my big brothers. Got it?" Joey's scent changes to sweet cardamom, balancing out with Ricky's rose scent. I'm not surprised as they pull me into a group hug, becoming stuck in their embrace, and gratefully accepting it. "You're still annoying."

"No, we aren't," they say in unison as a drifting scent of cinnamon mingles in the air.

"So, this is the hold-up." Pops says behind us.

"Sorry, Pops," Ricky says. "Baby sis wanted to be painted, and the bar was catching up on inventory."

"I had a phone call and baby sis clearly needed some cuddles," Joey adds.

"Throwing me under the bus there, huh?" I mutter.

"You can get away with it, *favorite*," Joey teases, tickling my side. I screech, almost falling onto Ricky's paints as he yelps in dismay. Joey doesn't relent as Ricky tries to fend him off.

"Uncle! Uncle! Stop!" I giggle.

"Alright, let her go," Pops instructs, and they immediately listen. "We'll open after dinner, and I'll see *all* of you upstairs ready when Ma is. Joey, you and I need to talk beforehand." My brothers get up, each giving me a kiss on the head before disappearing into the club. I'm left alone with Pops, and I walk up to him slowly, putting my glasses on. "You alright, baby girl?"

"Better. Had a…much-needed conversation with Beckham."

"He takes the role of grandfather quite seriously with you."

"Yeah, pretty much." I wrap my arms around me, feeling my throat tighten. His hands twitch at his sides as his scent dampens. "I'm sorry, Pops, I shouldn't have said those things or yelled at you back at the coffee shop."

"Baby girl, it's okay, you were hurting."

"No, because I was a gigantic dick to you."

"You were telling me your fears, and I didn't want to face my own. Being positive won't fix everything, and you were right to admit those fears. I should've listened. I'm sorry if I made you feel unheard."

"No, you have nothing to apologize for. I was taking all my frustrations out on you, because…"

"Vinny wasn't here," he says with a knowing smile, and my arms drop. "I understand."

"You were trying to be supportive, Pops. It's just that… fucking hell."

"Watch your language, baby girl."

I shuffle my feet, rubbing my hand across my undercut and avoiding his gaze. He takes a step forward, and I say, "I was afraid I wasn't enough for my family. You've all given me so much, and I'm scared I failed in returning that kindness to you. I didn't want you to...to regret giving that time. I already disappointed one father, and I didn't want to with another," I sniffle, looking up at his wide eyes. "You're everything to me, Pops, and the idea of leaving you behind tears me apart. I've felt lost these last few years, trying to do the right thing, and I didn't want you or anyone else to get hurt because of me. I never, *ever* want to cause you pain. I just wanted to be good enough, and for you to know that I tried, because I love you—"

A sob breaks in my throat, and Pops pulls me into his arms, holding me close to his chest as tears stream down my cheeks. He cradles my head against him, kissing the top of it with a gentle touch. "You were *always* good enough," he whispers. "And I'll never regret finding you that day. You are my daughter, and I love you with all my heart, baby girl."

"I love you, Pops."

He kisses my head and pulls away to trace a finger along one of my facial scars. "Matches your eyes."

"Joey's idea."

He hums, kissing my forehead and patting my shoulder. "Go change. Ma will be happy to see you, she'll be back home just before dinner. Don't make a mess of your room; she cleaned it about a day ago."

"I owe her. Pretty sure it was in worse shape than the city dump."

Pops clears his throat. "Now, go on."

I kiss him on the cheek, walking up the stairs to my childhood home and take my glasses off as I enter the apartment. I stop in the foyer and take a deep breath in. The first few months being home, Pops had most of the apartment bubble wrapped, afraid I'd bump into everything. I kind of did in the beginning, but within six months I had the apartment layout memorized and would skid across floors.

I remember when Pops would come home, I'd run into his arms to hear about his day or show him what I learned. Ma would cook as I sat at the kitchen table, sometimes baking with her, and other days I'd get tutored by Beckham. I'd fall asleep on Pops' lap on the couch, curled up while my family watched late-night television.

My hand runs over the walls as I pass the bathroom, remembering my first attempted bath as I screamed in horror, fearful of the water. It took Pops that first night hours to get me cleaned, using rags to scrub off all the grime on me. It wasn't until my first sleepover with Vinny that I tried a bath without screaming, and I was fifteen for my first full shower. I still hate them.

I come to my room and groan in embarrassment, realizing how much Ma cleaned up. The room smells fresh, and there are no clothes to trip over as I head to my closet, putting on a comfy dancing bralette and shorts to show off Ricky's painting. I put my hair up and notice my disorganized bookshelf, taking my glasses off when I reach the tiny mess.

I inspect the leather bindings and find one of my earlier braille books Pops gave me. It's a story about a bat and a mouse becoming friends, having adventures and causing mischief. I put it away and find the first braille book I received, *Alice in Wonderland*.

"Talk about timing," I murmur, opening the book and feeling across the first chapter, but realize it's the dedication page. I always skipped it, like the others, kind of forgetting the book had one. I run my finger over the sentence, and my breath hitches.

May you find your way through Wonderland, little one. ~ V. Dracultelli

I'm confused, distinctly remembering Pops giving me this on my first birthday when I was adopted. It was a private party with only my family, and I was excited to get my first book. My fingers trail over the page again and again, reading the line as my heart starts to ache.

"You *proved me wrong and became the starlight I didn't know existed.*"

His words echo in my head as I clutch the book tightly to my chest, realizing it had always been enough. Through a twist of fate, I had a lifetime with him that was worth it all.

Vinny would clear out clientele and have playdates with me at *The Lounge*, our favorite game being hide and seek with Samuel. He always let me win. I had my first sleepover at his place, falling asleep on his lap watching *Scooby-Doo*. He taught me how to shoot, practicing almost every day since I was eleven, while he taught himself braille to read with me and help with homework, sneaking me chocolate between study sessions. I first got drunk at seventeen, and he carried me home over his shoulder, warning me not to puke on him. He always walked me home, played pranks with me on Rodney and my brothers, and looked for books in *The Vault* during my research missions. Too many times he'd drag me home after finding me in a pile of books.

I ran to *The Lounge* the day I was accepted into college, him cheering, spinning me around before taking me out to get ice cream. He was the one who walked me to campus my first day at Columbia because I wouldn't let my family do it. He was the person I called my first night away from home and let me stay at his place when I was almost suspended after a few fights; I don't think my parents ever found out. We'd stay on the phone together for hours, and there were nights he'd fall asleep on my apartment floor, complaining how he hated my class schedule. He'd bring me dinner during finals, and always hated when my place smelled of wolf. He was there for graduation, my move to Topside, and wished me luck my first day with the Head Librarian position on Topside. He was always there.

And I was there for him.

I was the first to know when he got the title Boss, and then we got drunk together in *The Lounge* and destroyed most of his father's office. I cleaned him up after his father would retaliate and sat with him when he lost people or finished a 'job' he didn't want to talk about. He told me about his mom, living outside New York City, countries he's visited, and the shit that scared him. Only I know his favorite ice cream flavor, a sworn secret I promised to never tell. I'd make him laugh when he had shitty days and call to check he had blood on long nights, invent new nicknames for people so he can rate them, or pin up pictures on his office walls.

He'd always been my Vinny. He was many things to the world, but he'd been my constant companion no matter what. Always. And I loved him through every moment, shitty or great, because deep down he would forever be a part of me. I wasn't scared of not having enough time, but of it ending. I didn't want *us* to end.

There's a shift in the air as the familiar scent of dark spices and bloodlust drifts into my room. I instinctively grab the .22 hidden under my bed, aiming at the doorway. My arm trembles as I turn, catching a glimpse of ruby eyes against the dark blue and black haze.

"You're painted again," Vinny says in a rough voice. I nod, dropping the weapon to the ground. His eyes disappear as moves to my dresser, before walking over to kneel on the ground with me. He lifts my chin up gently, wiping away stray tears. "You're missing something, sweet cheeks."

Something clicks in Vinny's hand, and he holds my face still, circling dots along my facial scars as I focus on his intent gaze. My body is trembling as he finishes, putting the marker away. He strokes a finger down a facial scar, whispering, "There. Gotta have those silver flecks."

I choke out a laugh, swallowing back tears. Vinny cups my cheek, and I shudder at the touch I've craved for two weeks as I rasp, "Is it done? Are you back?"

"Yeah, sweetheart."

"I was afraid you'd never...come back. That I lost..." A sob escapes me, and I can't stop the overflow of tears that come as I hang my head and cry with my entire body.

Vinny pulls the book from my hands, bringing me into his arms to soothe me. "It's alright sweetheart. It's going to be okay. I'm sorry it took so long—"

"Promise me something, bloodsucker."

"What?" He asks, leaning back to stare down at me.

I look up into his crimson eyes, a lighthouse through the darkness. "You'll always be my best friend."

"Thought I already made that promise," he whispers, cupping my cheek.

"Then never leave me again," I rasp. "Stay with me."

He places both hands against my cheeks, kissing me briefly. "Always, sweetheart. And only ever for you."

I wrap my arms around him into a tight embrace, sobs racking through my body as relief floods my senses. The only sound is my crying, allowing the uncertainty of the last twelve days to melt away with each tear. Everything in me rejoices over his touch, smell, and voice, and I'm relieved to have him back, no matter how long that may be.

CHAPTER 27
ALL IN THIS TOGETHER

"You just had to call Midnight," Vinny complains.

"He said it's a Mating gift," I explain, waving him off. "And he needs to be invited to our supposed Mating Ceremony."

"More strings attached," he groans.

"*You're* the one who let him handle your assets."

"He's the only cousin who doesn't want to stab me in the back."

"Then be thankful he's fucking helping, bloodsucker. Stop being so damn picky."

"No one took soap to your mouth while I was gone, huh?"

"Well, figured you needed some sweet talking when you came back...*cuddle buddy*," I muse, throwing his jacket on.

"Never getting that back, am I?"

"Invest in new attire," I smirk, and Vinny blocks my path out of the bedroom. I grin at him wildly, my entire being elated to have him near me. "Were you ever gonna say anything about gifting me *Alice in Wonderland*?"

"I thought you knew?" I shake my head. "You never read the dedication?"

"I was too invested in the story."

"Is my smart librarian admitting she skipped pages?"

I fight a smile as I touch his face, feeling his upturned lips as he grins. "Never tell anyone."

"Secret's safe with me, sweet cheeks." He places a searing kiss on my lips, then places another on my forehead. "I've missed you."

"Ditto, bloodsucker." I slip my glasses on as he chuckles, putting his arm around my shoulders as we head for the living room. We spent the last half hour cuddling on the floor, crying my eyes out, and catching up. He was only able to get me up after saying something about talking with my family.

As we reach the living room, I notice there's no one in the apartment. "Where is—?"

"Baby sis," Joey says, walking through the front door.

"Joey, where is everyone?"

"Downstairs." His voice is gruff as he looks at Vinny. "You didn't tell her?"

"I was distracted," Vinny replies in rough voice, pulling his arm off me. My stomach drops and I instinctively grab for him. "It's fine, sweet cheeks. And before you curse me out..." I scowl, "...I called a meeting with select mafia members and your family. You all should hear from me what's happened and not from anyone else."

"Not comforting," I mumble. "What did you do, bloodsucker?"

"Fulfilling our new promise." He leans forward and whispers, "Not leaving you, *ever*."

"Midnight told me about your fail-safes," I say, and his brows raise. "Did they work?"

He chuckles. "More than you know."

"Something tells me I'm gonna need a drink," Joey says, leaving the apartment as Vinny scoffs.

"And Bruno?" I ask. Vinny doesn't reply, instead leading me out of the apartment. "Oh, fuck me."

"Later," he muses, and I swing, hitting him in the arm as he snorts.

We go down to *Unbound*, walking into the quiet club with dimmed lights, causing my senses to tingle. I see everyone's discolored outlines throughout the space; my family is sitting in the main seating area, Rodney is with Marcus and Gunther on the other side, and Beckham is sitting near the bar with Samuel and Anita.

"So...how pissed is Anita?" I mumble. This mafia meeting better not go like the last one I was in.

"You ruined her favorite slacks," Vinny answers. "Don't go near her without me for a few days."

"Noted," I say, glancing at everyone. "Really, wanted the *whole* family, huh?" Vinny sits me next to Ma on the couch, and she pats my leg as he stands next to me.

"Alright, Vincent," Pops says, clearing his throat. "What's happened?"

Vinny's hand brushes over my shoulder before placing them in his pockets; his business stance. "By now, all of you know that Brenda and I have Claim Mated," he begins. "We did so without the approval of *any* Paranormal community, and unfortunately the Vampiric Society has not taken it well with our decision. Even with the laws around Claim Mating, they've rejected the Mating, their defense being she has no vampire blood, no Paranormal abilities, no *blessing* from my father, and that she deliberately 'attacked' vampires on Topside in a non-neutral zone."

Growls emanate from all corners of the room, and Joey sneers, "She shot those bastards because they were kidnapping a *human* cop."

"They don't care," Vinny responds. "Even with my disposal of the *kidnappers* and those connected, they saw it as a...threat." He flashes a glimpse at me.

"Come off it, you knew they would never accept her, bloodsucker," Rodney snarls. "They made their intentions clear years ago—"

"Let him explain," Pops warns.

"Yes, they had," Vinny continues. "I already had plans in place to convince them to accept her as my Mate. However, when we learned about her...shortened lifespan, we made a decision. *Together.* It was a decision between her and I, no one else. We understood the consequences, and I won't apologize for it, no matter how any of you feel. She is *my* Mate."

Ma laughs under her breath as others murmur in the room. Beckham's voice rises above them, "I am quite certain our Little Sister feels the same way, do you not?"

I look up at Vinny, grinning as his ruby eyes catch mine, and say, "Forgiveness before permission is pretty much my life motto." My family chuckles as Rodney grumbles.

"We were planning to keep it a secret until we figured things out, but then those thieving leeches bit her," Vinny explains, stiffening next to me, along with a few others as I inhale their heightened scents of anger. I grip Vinny's arm, and he flashes his eyes to me, his scent of dark spices rising.

"I'm fine now, bloodsucker," I whisper. "So, calm your tits." His scent eases, and he places a hand at the nape of my neck, squeezing gently.

"Those vampires were taken care of," Vinny says roughly to the group. "What's done is done, but the Society has already decided that anyone without vampiric blood isn't allowed in vampire territories. For...*precautions.*"

"Good, make my life easier and have them stay there," Rodney mutters.

I give an exasperated sigh and point at him with a snarl. "Lassie, watch your mouth before I shoot your kneecaps. And Balto, you'll be next in line if you try to stop me."

Rodney's pale eyes glare at me, and I bare my teeth at him in challenge. We stay at this standstill for a moment, until he settles back into his seat. The scent of pine dissipates as I hear him grumble under his breath. Didn't mind us Mating, my ass.

"If you're upset with us, fine, but as Brenda said, forgiveness before permission," Vinny says, stroking his thumb over my neck. "You're all here because you care about her. I did what I needed to protect her after a decision *we* made."

"And what have you done to uphold that?" Pops asks.

Vinny glances over at Anita, shifting in her seat. "I did what I do best; I struck a deal."

"Oh, fuck," Joey mutters. This bloodsucker makes more deals than the damn devil.

"I'm abdicating everything I have in the Blood Mafia to Anita and officially stepping away from the Underground Mafia. She will take the title of Blood Mafia Boss. Everything now falls under *her* control, including shared territories I may have had with you all, except for *The Lounge*."

Fucking hell, he actually did it. He *left* the mob.

"And what does *Bruno* get out of this, if he didn't get the title back?" Joey asks.

"I relinquished my position within the Vampiric Society, handing it back to my father. And I've been completely disowned by the Dracultelli bloodline."

Everyone murmurs as I remember Bruno wearing the family ring, my heart clattering in my chest. Vinny said he was willing to give up everything for me, but I thought he only meant the Blood Mafia. He gave up his fucking *heritage*.

"Hold on, Vinny," Joey says. "Do you know how vulnerable that makes you?"

Ricky blurts, "They'll turn you over to the NIIA."

"NIIA would be a mercy," Rodney scoff. "Those vamps are gonna send hitmen after you. There'll be a target on your back."

"Abdicated or disowned, the Underground Mafia can't protect you," Joey adds. "And Anita won't be able to help you either. She'll be expected to side with the vampires."

"I've already handled the Vampiric Society," Vinny answers. "They'll have hell to pay if they even try to touch me." Thank goodness for his diabolical fail-safes.

"What about Bruno?" Pops asks. "He may send the NIIA after you still. It doesn't just endanger you, but everyone here if he decides to."

"Let's not forget any rival human mobs," Rodney adds. "They'd *love* to get their hands on you."

Vinny peers down at me and whispers, "One last fail-safe."

"What did you do?" I ask.

"Made a deal with the she-devil." My eyes widen as I stand, clutching his arm. "Freyja's wiping all my current records and pushing out a narrative that Vincent Dracultelli no longer exists. Every organization from NIIA to PSB and even the human governments will believe I'm dead by *tonight*. Anything that traces back to me will be destroyed, and I'll no longer exist. Everything I own now falls under your name, sweet cheeks. *The Lounge* is yours."

"Holy fuck," Rodney breathes out, and Gunther whistles low. Joey and Ricky swear under their breaths. Pops mutters, moving beside Ma as she grabs his hand.

Everything. He gave up everything.

I stare at him and only see unquestionable certainty. "No more deals until the fucking New Year," I rasp, and he smirks.

"Don't worry, baby sis," Samuel says from the side. "He still has to run the place. And pay for damages."

"There go my dreams of her staying as a librarian," Beckham sighs like I picked the wrong football team. And there goes the stripper librarian idea.

"Ballsy move," Joey rasps, getting up to grab alcohol from the bar.

"*That's* an understatement," Gunther mutters.

"Did you give your brother this idea?" Rodney asks Anita in a rough tone. "Make a deal with that *woman*—?"

"No, and she *always* follows through," Anita purrs. "As long as we hold up our end."

"It was the only way to get around Bruno," Vinny defends his decision.

"Or just tear the bastard apart," Rodney argues and stands, making the vampires shift. "I don't know why you haven't already."

"That's not the—"

Rodney snarls, "He's had it out for lil sis the moment the Cuorebellas adopted her. If you really wanted to protect her, you'd get rid of him for good."

"And what? Start a war?" Vinny questions.

"Wouldn't be the first fucking time."

"It'll bleed out into the rest of the Underground, jeopardizing everyone, including her. Do you want that? The Wolf Mob being dragged into it?" Vinny snarls back.

"We already are!" Rodney points at me. "I agreed to work civilly with the Blood Mafia because of her! I have complied with Alanzo's conditions and Brenda's, but like *fuck* am I gonna go back to working with Bruno. He gets beings *killed*."

Anita sneers. "Hey, *wolf*, I have the title, not him."

"Yeah, but you're never *here*," Rodney growls, and Marcus and Gunther join him. "Your *father* will take it as an opening—"

"Watch it, hound," Anita threatens, standing up as the smell of tainted roses climbs.

"Enough!" Pops shouts, blasting the scent of cold metal into the air, causing everyone to stiffen and settle back into their seats. The wolves gasp, Anita whimpers, and Vinny stops breathing as I hold him close to my side. Pops releases them all, soothing them with a cinnamon aroma to calm back down as I hear Joey take a shot. "Vincent's correct to avoid war. And believe me, if Bruno had laid a hand on my daughter, he'd be reminded who first erected this city. And it *wasn't* vampires or wolves."

The bite marks on my neck pulsate as Vinny tenses next to

me. A large part of me is glad I've kept my mouth shut these past three years, and another part wants me to tattle.

"We may not have gotten along in the past, but we do now because Brenda came along," Joey remarks. "We've worked well together outside of that. No point in starting a fight now."

The tension eases as the scent of cinnamon drifts away, bringing silence throughout the room. Ricky joins Joey for alcohol, knocking back his own shot as Ma speaks calmly, "If you're all finished with your tangents, I don't think Vincent has finished sharing his thoughts."

Vinny squeezes me a little, letting out a breath. "Most of my personal guards, like Samuel and Adrian, are leaving with me. There'll be new guards and runners on our routes in about a week. Even with these changes, we still need to find the missing half-breeds, stop Feral ghouls from spreading, and make sure the NIIA doesn't get involved."

"The Vampiric Society wants nothing to do with it, so we won't receive their help," Anita says as Joey and Rodney scoff quietly. Okay, I'll give them that one.

"We're covering as much ground as we can," Gunther says. "At least the buildings and tunnels in the Bronx are clear."

"Manhattan is next," Joey adds.

Everyone starts to chime in, suggesting next steps as Vinny holds me close to him. My own head spins with the new information, not paying attention as I try to make sense of everything. He made a deal with Freyja, the 'she-devil of Topside NYC.' I'm afraid to ask what his end of the bargain was. I can't blame Rodney for his outburst, given any deal made with her comes at a price. Vinny and his damn deals, this shit is gonna bite us in the ass later.

My phone suddenly vibrates, and I pull away from Vinny and the group, seeing that it's Bill as I answer, "Hey—"

"You alone?" He asks urgently.

"No, why?"

"Get alone."

I glance over and see everyone acting like adults. "Hold on." I sneak down the back hallway into the changing rooms, remaining in the dark as I lean against the counter. "Alright, shoot."

"Understand I may play pranks and delight in the occasional scare, but no way am I being the one telling your Mate or father what I found."

"Well, this is a great fucking start. What did you find?"

A door closes in the background, and I hear a keyboard clicking. "Brenda, I'm not allowed, as a PSB Agent, to run any form of someone's DNA without their consent. It's both a Paranormal and human law, by the way, so I put my ass on the line for you, and only for *you* would I do so."

"Okay, I'll up the ante and buy you a milkshake machine instead."

"I better get the newest model," he mutters, then continues. "I could run yours because you consented, but Edgar didn't outside of the paternity test. It's why I didn't think of running his shit through the system when I did that preliminary background check. When I ran *your* blood through the system, there were no matches apart from him. I've done some shady shit for Vincent but running someone's DNA without permission is something even I don't want to push the boundaries on, but I did because you seemed certain there were others who survived Traloski's testing. Then you gave me those cities to investigate, and now I'm upset I have morals."

"You're stalling."

"You would, too, if you found what I found," he says, and my stomach twists. "I only found matches through *Edgar*'s blood. Traloski must have cross-stitched your genetics or something to not match with your siblings. He created a fucked-up version of *Where's Waldo*, basically."

I shake my head, trying to make sense of what he's telling me. "Okay, wait, so you found them? And they're...*not* my—"

"Oh, they *are*; the science is next level," Bill comments.

"More like fucking lunacy. If I wouldn't get in trouble, I'd send this to a couple of guys to see how the fuck Traloski created all of you from the same parent without sharing DNA with each other."

"Then what *does* connect us as siblings?"

"Facial features, immunities, similar birthdays, blindness, scars, and more. If you put everything on a spreadsheet, it's *obvious* you're siblings, but only if you know where to look."

My stomach twists as I begin to pace through the changing room. Fuck, I thought Vinny's news was the most insane thing I'd hear today. "How many did you find, Bill?" He doesn't answer, his breath shaky on the other line. "Bill?"

"36."

I stop, my veins feeling like ice as I clutch the counter. I really am the last one. "Did you find their hospital records? How they died?"

"That's where this gets a bit more fucked."

"*Now* we're at the fucked part?" A door opens and closes again, and I hear Midnight's computer clicking. "Damn it, Bill...stop stalling and fucking tell me."

"Brenda, sit down." I do as he says. "They were *all* murdered."

I almost drop my phone. "What?"

"Some went missing for days," he explains as my breathing slows to nothing. "They were found dead, or taken to the hospital and died there. Their causes of death include blood draining, bullets, stabbing, but that's not even the worst of it."

"How can it be worse?" I grind out, wanting to hurl all over the floor.

"Ten of them were killed by daemon claws, slashed through the throat. And when they were found autopsy reports state they'd been...sexually assaulted."

The world shifts around me as the truth clangs through my body. I stare over at the costumes hanging on the wall, remembering conversations with the dancers and their worries, *knowing* their pasts. My mind flashes over encounters I had with Edgar; his scents, his reactions, and the cut-up obituaries. Dark realization sets in as the puzzle pieces begin to fit together, and the sickening feeling in my stomach is replaced by wrath.

"Bill...there were two in New York," I say slowly. "What happened to them?"

There's silence as I hear his keyboard again. He inhales sharply. "Slashed through the throat. They were two of the ones who were assaulted."

The rage builds in me as it feels like knives are piercing through my knuckles, and my vision begins to go red. I'd been manipulated to believe I was dying. Pops thought he was losing his only daughter. My Mate just gave up his *entire* life...all for a corruptive tale.

"None of the cases were solved, mostly written off as freak accidents by Feral Paranormals," Bill explains.

"No one connected the dots?" I ask as fury writhes inside me.

"Across the entire U.S., half-breeds just being found dead? No. Most of your siblings were unclaimed and grew up in foster homes or were homeless. They were hiding in plain sight, baby sis."

Something clicks inside me. "Bill, send every autopsy report and any news articles over their deaths to me, got it? Then wipe your computer clean."

"Probably for the best," he breathes out. "What are you gonna do?"

"Remind him whose daughter I am." I hang up as the fear I'd felt for weeks disappears.

I walk out of the changing rooms and down the hallway, everyone still discussing the next steps for the Underground Mafia. All of a sudden, Vinny is in front of me, dark spices clinging to me as he clutches my face. "What happened?"

"Bill called," I say in a low tone. "Trust me as I've trusted you."

"Sweet cheeks…"

I move around him, walking toward the bar with him close behind as I approach Beckham, who's stirring a cup of tea. He tilts his head and comments, "You appear determined, Little Sister."

"I need shifter teeth," I state. Vinny tenses behind me.

Beckham smiles, showing his long-pointed teeth as he brings the teacup to his lips. "How many do you require?"

CHAPTER 28
RELEASE...THE KRAKEN

Rodney glares at the metal door to the interrogation room. "You sure about this?"

"You chained him, didn't you?" I ask.

"Yeah, and the fucker zapped me," he growls. "Doesn't mean he won't try—"

"He can't hurt me anymore."

Rodney's gaze sweeps down to the folders, shifter teeth, and Edgar's jacket in my hands. "I'm not gonna like this, am I?"

"No. Stay near the elevator."

We're below *The Lounge*, beneath the gun range where Vinny does his "dirty work," which includes an interrogation room, viewing office, and clean-up area. Rodney moves away as I open the door into the interrogation room, locking it behind me.

Edgar is chained to a metal chair and table, seething as black blood trails down his forehead, lightning flickering at his fingertips. The burning scent of motor oil and leather fills the room, churning my stomach. Anger simmers under my skin, and I glance at the dark viewing glass. Edgar's growls pull my gaze to him, and I suppress my own as I drop his jacket.

"After our last talk, you almost had me," I say, taking off

Vinny's jacket and approaching the daemon. "You were *really* good at manipulating me with my fears, knowing what strings to pull. But that's what you did with the others, wasn't it?"

"I don't know what you're talking about," he sneers.

"Really?" I walk over, dropping the folder on the table, revealing the photos of my dead siblings and their autopsy reports. "Because it seems you lied about *how* they all died."

His eyes flick down, scanning over the photos with no remorse. Lightning lashes from his fingertips, but I step back before it reaches me, pulling out the shifter teeth and jamming them into his hands. Edgar shrieks as the electricity fizzles out and black blood spatters onto the pictures.

"Since you didn't give a shit about consent, I won't either," I hiss.

"I have nothing to do with—"

"I have my own Nancy Drew, fucker," I warn with a sneer. "And you gave me your DNA, so all I have to do is check the blood under *their* fingernails." I point at one of the photos, a crime scene showcasing a body found with stab wounds.

"You conniving, little bitch!" He lunges forward as his sickening aroma punches through the air, wincing as the teeth in his hands dig deeper.

"Coming from you, that's rich," I scoff. "You took advantage of my exhaustion, *knowing* I almost died from that sting and made me believe I was in trouble. But it seems the only danger I was in..." I snarl, leaning in close, "...was from you."

"No," he growls. "I was *protecting* you."

"Is that what you did with my siblings? Protect them?" I ask, walking back toward his jacket. He yanks at the chains wrapped around his wings and chest, the air becoming thick with his burning scent of oil. "Did you know I have a better sense of smell than even a werewolf?"

The chains rattle again, and I look behind me as his eyes darken. A malicious smile grows on my face as I pick up his jacket, and say, "That's why you hid in the back." I pull out the newspaper clippings from his jacket without him seeing. "You knew how to hide because of those you already killed. Daemons are good at hiding in the shadows, camouflaging. So, tell me, how many did you kill before you realized we could smell you coming?"

Edgar flicks his eyes down to the pictures on the table, and he looks up at me with a feral grin. "There's a reason he liked you best."

My body stiffens, and I clutch the clippings in my hand before putting them in my pocket. I loosen a long, shaky breath, strategically moving my hair to the side, showing off more of my shoulder. I walk back, leaning over the table to push some pictures aside as his scent intensifies, burning my nostrils. "Did you know anger and sexual arousal smell the same?" I ask, and his scent worsens. "Oh…you did."

I move around the table, allowing my cockiness to thrust me forward as I pull out the clippings. Edgar breathes heavily as I hold up the small pictures he kept, growling, "Those are mine."

"The dancers mentioned something about how you watched them, like you wanted to devour them. I didn't notice the pattern at first, confused why you were alone, congregating in places you assumedly despised. Daemons don't do that. It didn't make sense, but you played the disgusted father *so well* after so much practice." I frown, looking down at the photos he kept on his person. "I never really thought *why* you only had ten of them," I murmur, touching an obituary from Denver.

I separate the clippings, matching them with their autopsy reports and copies of newspapers detailing how the bodies were found. His heavy breathing slows as his expression becomes calm, looking down at his children; the two from New York City at the top. His victims. His scent worsens, making me want to gag as a grin forms on his face. I frown and shove the shifter teeth further into his hands, and he shrieks.

"They have similar features to some of the dancers you kept

watching, including me," I whisper. "I checked who you tried to grab at the other clubs, too. You seem to have a preference... *pervert*."

The only sound in the room is the dripping of his blood onto the floor. His scent disappears, leaving the interrogation room with a cold chill as he looks upon "his legacy." I watch him as he licks his lips silently and it takes everything in me not to rip his wings off. He tries to move his hands to nab at the photos, but I sweep them up, taking them out of reach and hiss, "You're *never* touching them again, you disgusting, excuse of a daemon."

He slowly looks up with a malicious warning, and my stomach twists as I stare into the eyes of the monster before me. The reason why my instincts screamed to stay away, years taught by my family to find predators in the dark.

A vicious smile rises on his face. "Coming from *my* daughter who willingly stripped before me? *Now*, who's disgusting?"

"Is that why you chose to work with a human scientist?" I ask, pressing forward. "You discovered a thirst he could help with as long as you turned your back on daemons?"

"He had no use of them if they didn't complete tests." I want to scream, tear out his lungs. "And of course, *he* never cared, as long as he got his precious results."

"Why were you trying to find Traloski?"

"He said I could have you," he muses, scanning over my skin. "Leather looks good with your scars."

"What were you planning to do?" I rasp as the pressure at my knuckles rises.

"Only *you* seemed unafraid of leather, *they* hated it," Edgar hums, glancing down at the pictures. "Did you ever fuck on stage?"

I growl, "What were you planning, Edgar?"

"You were supposed to be mine," he hisses, and bile rises in my throat as I step back. "But you were his *favorite* experiment, and *he* needed you untouched. The *good* one. But you wouldn't have screamed like them, would you? Not back then, not even now. No...*not 37!*" The glass from the window rattles as Edgar yells, and muffled shouting comes from beyond. I'm done, I don't want to hear anymore. I grab Vinny's jacket and cover myself in it, prepared to give him to the wolves as he screams, "You were *mine* from the beginning! Taken from me! All of you! Mine to use! Not for those *fucking stupid weaklings* you call 'family'!"

Oh, he did not just insult my family with his damnation on the table.

I turn toward him with a ferocious growl. "Watch it."

"Why, what are they going to do?" He taunts.

"What do you *think* they'll do to you?"

He pulls at the chains, laughing wickedly. "*Nothing!* They are a pathetic, soft-hearted, degenerate species!"

I quirk a brow at him and ask, "Soft-hearted and pathetic?"

"And you can send in that vampire to kill me, but it won't change that you were already mine—"

"You were part of a fucking program that specialized in genetics and never thought to do your research, knowing what those immunities were *for*?"

"Why the fuck would I care?" The glass rattles again, shouts sounding on the other side. "Vampires bite, werewolves claw, shifters change, and your pitiful family *dances*. They're all beneath daemons!"

I listen to the commotion outside, knowing I should open the door and let him destroy him already, but now spite fills me. And Beckham taught me that education is essential.

"Well, good thing your daughter is a librarian, we can remedy your *lack* of understanding," I smirk, walking over to collect the pictures and reports as he snarls at me. "You see, every being in the Noctis Immortalis is intriguing given how expansive their powers are, but you're right. Incubi and succubi are considered the weakest in comparison to the others. I mean, you have vampires and werewolves who could tear down buildings if they wanted. Hard to compete with." I tap the folder on the table, and the glass rattles again. "All seem to have excellent sense of smell, but those 'pathetic' ones can discern different scents for each emotion due to their ability to control pheromones and hormones. I learned that from my family...*not*, because I was Traloski's favorite."

He growls, yanking at the chains as I step away, putting the folder under my arm. "Yet, they still let me into their clubs. How good is that *father* of yours now?"

The door rattles with a thundering force. "You'll know soon."

Edgar's eyes flash to the door and back to me. "What's he gonna do? Sick the vampire on me?"

"I didn't finish about incubus powers, did I?" I say, cocking my head at him as vengeance calms me. "They're ability to control hormones like serotonin is how they get people happy and calm, but the more powerful ones can control part of the amygdala, giving broader access to all emotions, including fear. This is where it gets fascinating, because they can influence the amygdala to the point of people believing mythical monsters exist...like sea creatures," I muse, walking around him slowly. "Or they can manipulate people to kill themselves from perpetual horror over never-ending nightmares. Historical documents relay it's why people feared them in the 1600s, not because of orgies, but the horrors they created in the mind. I wonder what your biggest fear is...*father*."

BANG.

Edgar freezes, and the darkness in his eyes fades as I come to face him.

"Only ten incubi have been recorded to have complete control of the amygdala," I say calmly. "And five are still alive."

BANG. The door rattles.

"One is the head of the NIIA office in Germany, and two are deep in prison cells within Russia. I mean, where else would you keep a being who can create living nightmares at a fifty mile-radius?" I pause. "Well, maybe Texas."

BANG.

"Uncle Nick is in Africa, probably water skiing."

BANG.

"And the last one is just outside that door." I glare at Edgar, whispering venomously. "It's why your 'employer' sent you to get me. There's a reason why so many listen to Alanzo Cuorebella, notoriously remembered as 'The Kraken of the Red Sea.'"

BANG.

"He single-handedly destroyed armadas after they stole his Mate. And you just admitted to fetishizing and planning to kill your biological daughter. In a club *he* created; a safe space from beings like *you*," I say darkly, walking to the door. "And he'll only touch you when *I* say so because unlike you, he's serious about consent."

"No!" Edgar screams. "I'll give you *anything*! Don't you... fucking bitch... I AM YOUR FATHER!"

I stare at the metal door, unlocking it. "No. You're not."

The door slams open, revealing Pops and my brothers with wings unfurled. The air is thick, and I taste it—cold metal and smoke. Rodney is by the elevators, snarling with hackles raised. Speakers worked.

I look back at Pops, fury lining his expression as he breathes heavily, trying to maintain his powers. "He's yours," I say.

"*Joseph. Ricardo,*" Pops orders, and they move past, ushering me out of the room with the door slamming shut behind me. Edgar lets out a bloodcurdling scream for mercy before Joey rips the speakers out.

My body shakes as I walk toward the elevator, concentrating on the dark walls, not looking at Rodney as the doors open. "Make sure they dispose of the body correctly," I whisper. "Don't want titanium claws on the black market."

"No problem," he growls beside me. I walk into the elevator, punching the button. "How'd you stay so calm?"

A small smile rises on my face. "From you babysitting me."

Rodney snorts as a strangled scream echoes from the interrogation room. I slump against the wall when the doors shut, shivers traveling down my spine.

The elevator doors open, and I'm instantly in Vinny's arms, carried into his office as I bury my face in his shoulder. He whispers as I grip onto him, "Fucking hell, sweet cheeks, you okay?"

"I'm alright," I whisper, holding onto him as he stops us near his disheveled bar. "Sorry I kept you up here."

"I don't think my lounge could take another rampage," he murmurs. "Well, *your* lounge now."

"Given all my money is going towards Midnight's milkshakes, that's a relief."

We hold each other in silence, the clock ticking away on the wall. I concentrate on his aroma, letting it fill me with warmth. After a while, he asks, "Want a drink?"

"Finally, you ask, yes," He steps away, pouring both of us a large shot of scotch, and we knock it back. He pours another as I place the folder of evidence on a broken table. "Least you won't be rid of me that quickly. You could still be stuck with me for centuries," I say, smiling up at him faintly.

"I'll stock up on chocolate ice cream and scotch," he says, rubbing the back of my neck. "You'll have to help me take care of this place."

I look around at the destruction leftover from his unbridled pureblood rage. "What should be the first project? Besides a new desk?"

"Could repurpose the meeting room, given my recent *retirement.*"

"Library?" I perk up, knocking back the drink.

"Another one?"

"I just found out the sperm donor was a sexual predator. Give me this."

"You still can't put shelves on ceilings."

"Fine, but I could save those shredded books from the Topside New York Public Library."

"You adopt misshapen books like humans adopt ugly dogs."

"Don't talk about Rodney like that." We laugh lightly, but my smile falters. Vinny puts our glasses down and holds me to his chest again, kissing my head and stroking my hair back. I hear the elevator ding from the foyer. He keeps his arm around me as we walk out, the doors opening to reveal Rodney and the stench of fresh blood. Vinny growls deeply, pressing me closer to his side in a territorial manner. Rodney steps out, speckled with black blood.

"Your clean-up area is better than mine," Rodney mutters.

"It's open for use," Vinny mumbles.

"You got an extra fucking shirt?" Rodney asks. "Unless you want your place to smell as terrible as it looks."

"Watch it, Airbud." They snarl at each other.

"Knock it off; I am too tired to referee," I scold, smacking Vinny's chest. "Give him a damn shirt, bloodsucker."

Vinny rubs the back of my neck as the elevator gets called back down and offers, "I may have something to fit your over-sized chest, Krypto." Rodney scoffs, walking past us and flashing a look of compassion toward me before disappearing into the office. "Do you want me here?"

I shake my head, and he nods, kissing my forehead and following after Rodney. I watch in anticipation as the lights blink, the elevator dinging open to reveal my brothers. Both are covered in blood, their wings hidden, and their faces solemn as they approach. Ricky hugs me first, gripping me tightly. "I'm sorry, I shouldn't have pushed you to dance," he rasps.

"It's not your fault," I whisper, cradling his head against mine. "You took care of me. It's okay." He nods, gripping me harder.

"I'm gonna let Ma know. She needs...she needs to know." I nod, kissing his cheek before he walks out silently.

I turn toward Joey, who has tears streaming down his face

as we collide into a tight hug. His breath is shaky as he speaks, "He's not...Pops isn't okay, sis. That damn *daemon*...I'm sorry, I'm—"

"It's not your fault either, you hear me?" I say harshly. "None of you will take the blame for what he did."

Joey shudders in our embrace, then pulls back as I wipe away his tears. He exhales sharply. "He's not gonna want you to dance for a bit, okay?"

"Well, I own *The Lounge* now. Career change, I guess." He nods as the elevator is called down, and my chin quivers, knowing this part will hurt the most. "Get a shirt from Vinny. Any argument, tell him I'm hanging his underwear up with mine."

Joey presses his forehead against mine, then kisses my cheek and walks away, entering the office as he calls out, "Where the fuck is the alcohol, Vinny?"

My hands shake, and my stomach churns as the elevator lights blink. I'd rather confront Edgar's monstrous ways again and again than see the guilt or pain on my Pops' face.

Tears roll down my cheeks as the doors open, and he steps out, walking toward me covered in blood, his hand drenched, and his wings still out. He keeps his gaze from mine as he quietly stops a few feet before me. I step forward, but he raises a hand to stop me, and I start shaking, my throat tightening as my lungs burn against rising sobs.

"I'm sorry, baby girl," he rasps.

"Pops," I choke out.

"I'm supposed to protect you, instead I let a monster in."

"No, you didn't—"

"I agreed for you to dance. *I* agreed. It's *my* job to protect you, and I failed."

"You didn't, Pops." His eyes meet mine, blazing with rage and grief. "It's not your fault. You didn't know—"

"I should have," he states. "*Centuries* I've hunted his kind."

"He may have done this for decades; he *knew* how to hide."

"He killed your siblings, his…his own *children*. And then you…" he snarls, and the cold metal aroma lashes out, "…*you* were next, and I let him in *my* club, near *my* family," he grinds out, tears forming in his eyes, shattering my heart. "I promised to protect you."

"You did, daddy," I cry. "You never failed me, you saved me so many times, I've lost count. If it wasn't for you twenty years ago, *I'd* be in those photos. *You* protected me. Please, *please*, don't blame yourself for this…*please*." I step forward, gripping his arms as he hangs his head. "I'm safe because of you. I'm safe."

His throat tenses as he clenches his fists at his sides, tears streaming down his maroon skin as he whispers, "I don't want you dancing for a while."

"I'll stop. It's okay. I'll stop," I say.

"Only with family…only with—" His body shakes, and his wings flare out as he brings his gaze to mine. He slowly strokes the side of my face, his hand trembling as he grazes a scar.

"I'm safe because of you. And I love you, I will *always* love you." I give him a small smile and whisper, "You are more than good enough. You're *my* father. You always were."

His restraint snaps, and Pops yanks me into his arms as I sob into his chest. He hugs me tightly as he buries his face into my hair, tears dropping onto my skin as his chest rattles with sobs. His wings wrap around us like a cocoon, encasing us in darkness.

He cries against my skin, "My baby girl…"

CHAPTER 29
BURN MY LIFE INTO PIECES

Ma greeted us with a tearful expression when we made it home. She and Pops disappeared into their bedroom, repeating her endearment for him, *"Mio cavaliere"* with the scent of cherry blossoms trailing behind. My brothers and I finished prepping dinner quietly until our parents returned. Vinny tried to leave, wanting to give our family space, but Ma refused, telling him he was part of this one. Ma did what she did best as the ultimate caretaker. The air was filled with sweet aromas as we spent the hours together, not speaking about what happened and letting it remain in the past. At some point, I fell asleep on Pops' lap on the couch with Vinny at my feet.

It's been two days since then as I come down the spiral staircase, stopping at Beckham's front desk and holding up the maps. He smiles and says, "You found your last puzzle piece."

"Yeah, some shit hides in plain sight," I say, slinging the tube over my shoulder. "Should've heard you the first time."

"Some lessons take longer than others," he smirks. "Do I get my teeth back?" I grimace and he chuckles. "I'll acquire more."

The Vault doors open, and I catch her scent as I murmur. "Right on time."

Anita pulls off her dark sunglasses, placing them in her front pocket as she saunters toward the front desk and leans on the counter, grinning at Beckham. "Hello, handsome."

"Flattery shall get you nowhere, my young friend," he muses.

"Doesn't hurt to try."

"Could try reading, it's his favorite kind of foreplay," I joke, and Beckham slides a displeased look my way. I immediately apologize, "Sorry."

"I'm here as you asked, baby sis," she says, turning toward me. "Did you want me to read you a bedtime story?"

"Do not insult my protégé, remember the last Dracultelli who decided to do so, Anita." Beckham takes his mug of tea and heads for the second floor

Anita stiffens, narrowing her eyes at the shifter as he leaves with a sly expression. I suppress a chuckle, reaching into my back pocket for the spare phone and toss it to her. She catches it easily and raises a brow. "I reset the emergency system to only signal *that* phone. When I press it, you come to the location immediately."

She looks it over and scoffs. "Why should I?"

"You'll hate yourself if your brother dies of heartbreak."

Her eyes flash, the scent of mulled wine burning as she frowns. "What are you implying?"

"You probably won't grieve me if I die," I say, and she scoffs again. "You only ever gave a shit about me because of Vinny. It's probably why you agreed to be the Blood Mafia Boss. You don't want to lose him like you lost your mother."

She stalks toward me, breathing on my skin as her fangs elongate. "Don't speak about—"

"If anyone hates Bruno more than me, it's you. So, when you arrive after the phone goes off, you'll do what's needed to protect Vinny."

"And what would that entail?"

I smile defiantly. "You'll know when you arrive. Trust me."

Anita takes a step back, looks down at the phone, then pockets it. "You're learning to be more careful. Are we finally *thinking* things through, Brenda?"

"Careful, Beckham the Grey, may hear you," I smirk.

She smiles, taking out her sunglasses and walking away. "I don't necessarily dislike you. You're just predictable with your irresponsible impulses, just like any human."

"Newsflash, Elvira...I'm not human." I cross my arms, and she chuckles, leaving *The Vault*.

"Ah, what cards do you have up your sleeves, Little Sister?" Beckham asks from the balcony above me. I look up, grinning and he smiles back, disappearing into the darkness of the library.

I grab my things and leave *The Vault*, heading toward *The Lounge* for the meeting I called with Vinny, Rodney, and Joey. I'm ready to be done with this whole mess, ending everything that's threatened me, my family, and Vinny. I stop abruptly, looking up at the lights flickering faintly above for the evening, and realize there's one more score to settle first.

I turn for *Unbound*, marching my way down the paths with resolve straightening my spine. I walk through the front and aim for the bar, emptying a metal bucket and heading to the changing rooms, ignoring Bobby's confused stare. The dancers are getting ready in the back, and I walk toward the costumes as Gina asks, "Baby sis?" I fling back the clothing, searching until I find the outfits I'm looking for, stuffing them into the metal bucket and snatching the boots. They all watch with wide eyes as I walk out.

I weave through patrons, heading for the apartment door not bothering to take my shoes off, dropping the bucket once I enter the foyer. Ricky jumps in the dining room and watches me walk into Pops' office. I open his desk drawer and see the folder stare up at me, nestled against everything I printed of my dead siblings and the clippings Edgar had. I take it all, leaving the room to see Ricky and Ma's gaping stares.

"Baby, what's wrong?" Ma asks as I walk into the kitchen.

"I need lighter fluid," I say, rummaging through drawers until I come across a bottle and some matches. "Never mind, found it."

"Sis, what are you doing?" Ricky asks as I move past, snatching the bucket and boots.

"Destroying what's left of him." I go down the steps and stalk out the back of the club.

I drop the bucket in the back alleyway, and it clangs loudly against the brick as I shove the boots on top of it. I pour the entire bottle of lighter fluid over the clothes Edgar watched me dance in and light a match, tossing it onto the pile. It starts slow, consuming the fake leather before igniting into a raging inferno.

I stare down at the pictures covered in black blood and toss them into the fire. Next, I fold up the clippings and drop them in with the burning pictures. Then I look at the folder of paperwork, the title no longer mocking me. I flip open to the last page, pulling out the picture of me and four of my siblings. The label marks #37-#41. I hadn't been the last. Grief swells within me, knowing all my siblings had their lives stolen so young, born into this world by monsters. Rage rises for those who never got a chance.

"Enjoy hell," I sneer, clutching the picture in my hand as I toss the paperwork into the flames, burning the scars of my past. The folder is consumed, turning to blackened ash.

Cinnamon, sweet rose, clove, and cherry blossoms fill my nose, and I turn to see my entire family standing behind me. Pops with his arm around Ma, Joey next to him with a solemn expression, and Ricky staring wide-eyed. I glance down at the picture of me in my hand. The first picture of me.

I look at Pops and hold the picture up as I say, "I never had a choice in the beginning, but you gave me the chance to have one. Sometimes I wondered where I belonged, but there's one thing I knew for certain." One last look at the small child with the violet eyes and scars, and I toss the picture into the fire. "I belonged with this family, *our* family."

Ma shakingly touches her mouth with a gasp as Pops whispers, "Baby girl."

I glance over at Ricky and say, "I'll pay you back for the costumes."

"No worries," he breathes out, staring at the inferno behind me.

I look over at Joey's violet gaze, and he nods with a small smile, beginning to walk down the alley. I glance at Pops and say, "It's time we remind them what happens when you mess with the Cuorebellas."

Pops smiles, and Ma's eyes well up as Ricky steps beside her. Joey and I leave for *The Lounge* as I grab the maps off my back, glancing down at the final piece. "You're next."

CHAPTER 30
CUOREBELLA'S ELEVEN

I toss the maps onto the splintered bar, rolling them out to reveal the territories of the Underground Mafia. I brush off wood splinters, looking down at the red dots and lines I replicated from Vinny and Rodney's maps. I saw the answer weeks ago when I researched Traloski at *The Vault*; I just didn't know what I was looking for. I never completed my original investigation, but traumatic events, depression, and being gaslit by your predatory father will distract you.

"Joey, hand me that bottle," I say, and my brother walks up behind the wet bar, giving me the whiskey. I flick off the top and knock back a few gulps. He chuckles, taking it back to drink from as well.

"Starting off strong I see," Rodney comments, walking into the disheveled lounge.

The Lounge is a disaster zone of Vinny's rampage from two weeks ago, filled with shattered glass, wood, shredded carpet, broken bulbs, and empty bottles. Inheriting the place by name seems like a cruel joke now. If he makes me pay for any damages, I'm shooting him again.

Rodney walks up, cocking his head. "You actually remade the old route maps. Are those the new ones, too?"

"Yeah, told you two days ago, Lassie," I smirk, and he looks over my shoulder, growling a little. "Calm down. None of you are gonna remember routes or shit anyway. Besides, Vinny's retired."

He grumbles, settling against the bar and taking the whiskey Joey offers. "Why even bring them out at all?"

"I'll explain when Vinny gets here. Which should be…" I pull out my new Desert Eagle and aim at the door, clicking off the safety, "…now."

The door opens, and Vinny strolls in, chuckling darkly when he sees the gun. "You were gone long enough; thought you fell asleep in the books again."

"Some of us work, twinkle toes," I say.

"New nickname. Come up with that while I was gone?"

"No, I was busy thinking about other things."

"Did it involve toys, finally?" He asks, leaning in next to me.

I shift the gun, pressing it into his groin. "Guess I won't need this."

"You'll miss it, sweet cheeks."

"Wanna find out?"

We smile, and Rodney groans next to us. "You're already Mated, so quit it. It's nauseating."

"Jealous, *Lassie*?" Vinny asks as I put my gun away.

Rodney glares at him, crossing his arms over his chest. "Some of us aren't meant for it."

The alpha wolf keeps his face stoic, turning his attention to the maps as I give him a questioning look and grab the whiskey again, then begin to explain. "Things started clicking when Midnight mentioned 'hiding in plain sight,' and I remembered Rodney proposing the idea of a third party wanting us out of the Bronx," I say, pointing at the routes they used to run. "We all cleared out, and then the ghouls went missing, and *no one* noticed."

"Because we were gone," Rodney says.

"Yes, but even with us giving up those territories, NYPD or

PSB should've noticed sooner. They were already up in arms; how could they not see the ghouls leave *or* bodies being dumped? Then I got to thinking. What if the ghouls never left?"

"Except, we checked everywhere," Joey answers.

"It's empty apart from dead ghouls," Rodney adds. "Like you said, cleared out."

"Yes, *but…*" I pull out a current map, circling some routes, "…our *new* routes oversee every exit out of the South Bronx. We should've seen them leave."

Vinny peers closer. "Shit, you're right. Someone should've noticed."

"And then the second attack at the center got me thinking." I point at the center. "Ghouls would never leave their dead behind, but they would guard them."

Rodney grabs the whiskey back from me, taking a swig back. "We walked into their fucking nest basically, but that doesn't explain where the others are. We still have dozens missing."

"And those buildings and tunnels are clear, we triple-checked," Joey adds.

"Not all of it." I unfurl a map of tunnel systems from thirty years ago and circle my finger around Traloski's old center and the tunnels beneath. I point at the newer maps that don't show the same tunnel systems.

"What are those?" Joey asks.

"Bomb shelters were built underneath the buildings in the 80s, after the terrorist attack. Some medical centers, public buildings, and government-owned facilities had them, but the bomb shelters were deemed too unstable by the city. Traloski used it beneath his own facility because he was government-funded," I say, pointing to the tunnel system that connects to the sewers where I was found. "And that community center has it, too." I move across the map, pointing to the bomb shelter beneath the center.

"Holy shit," Joey exclaims, grabbing the map from me. "Does Pops know about this?"

"Maybe, but as I said, they were categorized unstable, wiped from any map for decades. I only knew because I looked up where Traloski's old center was and missed it the first time."

All three stare at the old map, silent as they look at each other. "They were hiding under our noses and the ghouls were distracting us," Vinny says.

Rodney peers closer at the center on the map. "Who owns the building now?"

"Freyja."

"Fuck," Rodney snarls.

"You're gonna owe Midnight for this one, I'm running out of milkshakes to give him," I tell Vinny. "He had to dig deep, but he traced it to one of her dummy companies she rents to feds. Cross your fingers she doesn't realize he hacked her."

"Black ops hire her again?" Joey asks.

"To be in the Bronx?" Vinny asks.

"If the fucking she-devil is involved, it could be. And it explains how we were compromised during that sting," Rodney says.

Joey knocks back a shot of vodka. "The government has gone through her before to do shit they want hidden, but do you think she's *really* involved with whoever's there?"

"No," I say, and Rodney glares at me. "Look, she may be a bitch in more ways than one, but she has particular priorities. You really think she would *willingly* help people get turned into ghouls? If anyone hates people changing species, it's her."

"She's right," Vinny says. "You know her history."

"Bill said she has plenty of red herring companies," I explain. "They help maintain her client's secrecy and being anonymous. He couldn't even trace who. She probably doesn't know either...hopefully."

"So, it's whoever knows these tunnels exist, has Freyja's

contacts, and motive to turn people into ghouls," Rodney growls.

"Don't forget targeting half-breeds," Joey adds.

"Sounds like a fucking federal government operation to me," Rodney states.

"Maybe," I mumble, and he glances at me. "Most of the medical experiments I've researched these past few weeks were mostly government-funded."

"Except, wouldn't Bill or any of our contacts in PSB or NIIA know they were doing this?" Joey asks. "I doubt any Paranormals working within them would stay quiet. We would've heard *something* about it."

Rodney shrugs. "Rogue agents? Not the first time going to Freyja. Remember those agents from Boston?"

"Rogue agents creating Feral ghouls to clear out the Bronx by hiring a mad scientist to test on missing half-breeds?" Vinny grumbles. "Yeah, it sounds like something a human would do."

"*All* great theories," I say, rolling my eyes. "Whoever got a hold of that center, we need to stop them from taking more half-breeds and starting an undead plague. They could use the forgotten tunnels to send the hoard out without being caught."

Joey smooths out the maps, peering down at them. "We can scope out the center. See who's below."

"Feds, Freyja, Traloski, fucking Pete the Magic Dragon, I don't care, we take them out," Rodney says, crossing his arms. "They fucked with our people and territories, so there's only one thing we should do." He and I share a grin. "We blow it up."

Vinny scoffs, pointing at the zone line. "We'd be starting a war with the feds *and* Freyja if we do."

"She deserves it," Rodney shrugs. "And we don't let her know we did it."

"One day, I want the story between you two," I say, pointing at Rodney's chest and he scoffs.

"We'll end up kicking off the terrorism alarms," Vinny says.

Joey shrugs. "It could work. We take the emergency exists Pops put in place. After the first blast or two, it'll take about fifteen to twenty minutes before everything shuts down between Topside and the Underground. Plenty of time to escape."

"We set the explosives underneath," Rodney points at the center. "My crew can tamper with nearby lines, make them think it was faulty gas lines. It's an old, condemned building with a forgotten bomb shelter. Easy to manipulate a story that shit finally malfunctioned underneath."

"And none of the tunnels are connected to ours. We'll be safe."

Vinny rubs his temple in aggravation and mutters, "You all are serious. You wanna blow up a building in the Bronx."

Rodney grins ruefully. "Fucking mob, bloodsucker. Remember? Why not destroy everything, take back our fucking territories, and get rid of what's down there?"

I stare at the map as Vinny grasps my shoulder, while all three go silent. Joey says in a quiet tone, "We can send someone down there first. See if there's a way to save whoever may be left. Even the ghouls—"

"Forcefully being turned Feral or not, there's no saving them," I say, grabbing the whiskey to take a long drink. I spent an extra day in *The Vault* looking for ways to save them, and nothing. Once a ghoul goes Feral, there's no turning back except for an agonizing death if not shot or pierced with daemon claws. I already knew Rodney would suggest blowing it up, whether Traloski was down there or not. It's a nest of Feral ghouls, a potential for a miserable undead outbreak. "We could try getting any who haven't gone Feral out, but from what we found last time, we may be too late."

"I can add something to dissolve what's left of them," Rodney murmurs. "Give them a proper burial."

"And if no one is down there?" Joey asks. "If we're wrong?"

"Fucking blow it up and move on," Rodney says. "Place is a

hub of bad luck, get rid of it. Maybe it'll scare whoever's taking people to show themselves."

"You're riled up tonight, huh?" I ask.

Rodney gives me a dark expression. "Three nights ago, I had to listen to you confront a predator because of that program. And in the last few weeks my Pack hasn't felt safe, and we've lost over a hundred half-breeds being turned into ghouls. This shit needs to end *now*."

I take a deep breath and nod. Vinny squeezes my shoulder gently, and I look up to his comforting gaze as he says, "Whether it's him or not, we'll stop any more beings from suffering."

"It'll only take a few hours to evacuate the area," Joey says. "Make it fast before NYPD or PSB notices. How long for explosives?"

"Six hours," Rodney answers.

"Well, I'm a ghost already," Vinny sighs. "They'll go after your ass, instead, hound."

I stare at the maps, tracing a finger from where I was found to the center. It's only a hunch that it's Traloski, but in my gut, I know it's him. And even if it isn't, I'm stopping the monster who *is* down there.

"It's gonna be you, isn't?" Vinny asks me. "To go into the center." I nod.

"Whoa, what?" Joey asks.

"If ghouls are guarding the center," Vinny explains. "She's the only one to get past if she gets bit and maybe slip in easier being a half-breed." That, and because like hell I'd let anyone else do it.

"She's also our best shooter," Rodney mumbles.

"Oh, fuck no," Joey growls. "Our family's been through enough, sis."

"Then don't snitch on me," I counter.

"Unless you don't make it out," he growls.

"Believe in me a bit more, damn."

"Don't try that on me." He points at my face.

"I'll see if I can get anyone out and if not, I'll run out like a rabbit," I say, trying to placate him. "I'll take weapons, so no worries. I've looked at the schematics the most. I know the layout."

"Brenda—"

"She needs to do it, Joey," Vinny defends me. I look up to see his hardened crimson gaze, jaw muscles tense. "It's that, or she'll go without our support."

Joey rubs his head, sighing and knocking back the last of the liquor as Rodney says, "Tomorrow night we'll do it and I suggest only our closest personnel be part of it."

We spend the next fifteen minutes discussing the set-up and my route into the backway by using our tunnels while they watch the west and east side of the center's block. They'll keep the blast radius clear of people and will be close enough to Entrances to scramble. Rodney and Vinny head into his office to talk about who to involve, leaving me with my brother at the bar.

"Of course, you find out you're not doomed to an early death, so you decide to do this instead," he groans.

"I won't have peace until he's gone," I say gruffly. "He'll suffer for causing so much pain, not just me, but *everyone* involved. I want him to know it was me that ends him."

"And if it's not Traloski?"

"Then I'm stopping who *is* doing this and making sure they join Edgar in hell."

Joey walks around the bar, leaning with a huff next to me. "You know, Pops and Ma tried hard to keep you out of the business, but…you fall in pretty well."

"Learned from the best," I smirk, looking at the destroyed lounge.

"Vinny the Vampire?" He chuckles, and I shrug as he glances down at my gun. "Is that why you always greet him with a gun?"

"Who? Vinny?"

"Nah, Rodney," he snorts. "Yes, Vinny. I noticed you started in your teens, but never explained why."

I pull out the gun, smiling. "We made a deal."

"Him and his damn deals. Sure he's not a devil?"

"Nah, just a territorial bloodsucker."

"What was the deal, then?" Joey inclines his head, and I know he's trying to distract himself from what happens next.

I put the gun away and smirk. "I was fifteen, and after four years of shooting, one day I couldn't make a fucking shot even with glasses. I was livid. Vinny, in his usual style, took my glasses off, told me to aim and to use my other senses. He used himself as a target, making noise or using his scent for me to track him, and he'd adjust my aim then move again. All afternoon we did it."

"He was training you to see without your eyes," Joey muses. "That's how your echolocation got so good."

"Yeah," I say, grinning. "The times I'd been attacked, I was vulnerable without my sight. He knew that. He made me train like that more often, but targets don't make noise or have aromas. We made a deal; every time he entered a room, I'd aim using my other senses. Just aim, no matter what and without hesitation. I started without a gun and just never stopped after I started carrying. It's one of his few ideas that I'll actually admit worked."

"What was his end of the deal?"

I look at my brother with a smug expression. "He buys me ice cream."

Joey scoffs, and glances back at the office. "He really has done his best to protect you, huh?"

"Yeah, he has."

"Apart from the ice cream and you being better than any of us now, why keep up with it?"

I grin ruefully. "Cause it's fun. And I'm never gonna admit I'm slacking to the bloodsucker."

Joey kisses me on the cheek. "Never tell him I said this, but I'm glad you have him as your best friend and Mate."

"So am I."

———

"Is this the part where I make you do the hula?" I ask.

Rodney grins, handing me the last of the explosives. "Only if you buy drinks after," he says. "We'll provide enough distraction without skirts. Just tell me if we gotta abort the mission."

We gathered in the tunnels a few blocks west of the center. Rodney's crew is spread out and prepped to distract ghouls surrounding the area, Joey's people cleared out the last of the buildings and tunnels from the blast radius, and those loyal to Vinny are set to play backup for ghoul control. Everyone will scatter once I blow the building, but I have the longest route to get below. I just gotta sneak through the back and get out before being blown to smithereens or being caught by police. Easy peasy.

At least I know I look good in orange.

The tunnel is lit by emergency lights with me, Rodney, Vinny, Marcus, and Samuel prepping below before going to our next destinations. I strap on the last of the explosives to my hips, along with weapons, and finish my to-go coffee as Rodney hands me my radio, pats my head, and disappears down the tunnel. Marcus follows him, stopping to look at me with a stiff nod.

"Keep an eye on Lassie," I say, seeing a glint in his eye.

"Better than yours," he retorts.

"Ouch!" I give him the middle finger, and there's a hint of a smile on his face before disappearing down the tunnel.

Samuel comes up and pats me on the shoulder. "Be quick; don't hold back punches. Still gotta show you that Jersey Shore shit."

I fake gag, and he laughs, disappearing next and leaving me

with Vinny, who's wearing a black tank, slacks, and gun holster over his shoulders. Crimson eyes meet mine as I toss the empty cup with the rest of the trash. He walks up to me and clutches the side of my face as his jaw ticks with worry. I hold his hand against my cheek and ask, "How much of your territorial side is fighting you right now?"

"All of it," he rasps, placing his other hand on my hip, above the weapons.

"Wow, you have better control than me."

"A bit," he smirks, looking to where my exit is. "I told you I'll never tell you what to do. And after everything, you need to finish this. Not me." I squeeze his hand, and he grips my hip. "You trusted me to handle my shit, and I'll trust you to handle yours."

I stroke his hair and smile. "You know, we should take a long honeymoon after this."

"Any ideas?"

"There's always Vermont."

"That's the best you got?"

"I could say Utah, land of sunburns and not enough lotion."

"Grand Canyon sounds like a great place to toss you."

"Reminder: you're afraid of heights."

"Am not."

"Empire State building scares you."

"Too many humans taking pictures, and that stupid fence isn't enough to keep anyone in, especially hangry werewolves."

"Yeah, sure," I say, rolling my eyes. There's a shout and a beep from my radio, and I press a button, signaling I'm ready. "Wanna make a deal?"

"That's my line."

I press my lips to his with a bruising force, and he cradles my face, moaning at the contact. The kiss deepens into a searing hold as I breathe in deeply, shuddering as my veins fill with fire and steel. I break what could be the last time kissing him and say, "If I finish this in less than three hours, I get two weeks' worth of 'Vinny coffee' and ice cream. Any longer than that, you can repurpose the meeting room into a sex dungeon."

"Good thing you'll do anything for coffee," he whispers with a half smirk.

I force myself to let go, stepping back as cold develops over my skin, his touch leaving me. I throw on my old leather jacket, keeping my gaze from his as I leave, his scent lingering behind me before I breathe it in one last time, disappearing into the tunnel. I feel no fear, only resolution and determination to be done with this. Tonight, monsters will learn that messing with the Underground Mafia comes with a steep price.

CHAPTER 31
KILLER DAEMON QUEEN

I close the secret tunnel behind me and slip onto the back street behind the center as twilight passes. Streetlights spill shadows over brick buildings as I check for signs of movement, then move for the center. I run the layout of the building through my head as I approach the back door, pushing it open with a smile. Vinny slipped through the walls earlier and unlocked the door. "Thank you, Matey," I whisper, entering the building.

Emergency lights flicker inside as I gag at the rotting stench of flesh and venture through the hallways with a gun in each hand until I find the door leading to the basement. Bingo. I kick it open with a bang. No movement, only rancid aromas I can taste on my tongue. Not my choice for a palette cleanser. I make my way down the hall toward the basement stairs, bare light bulbs buzzing as the air gets colder. The scent of dead flesh shifts, and I flick back my gun safeties, concentrating on the shuffling near the steps. I take a deep breath, turn around the corner, and fire.

The sound of bullets and screams ricochet as I hit three ghouls, unloading on more coming down the hallway for me. Shrieks echo around me as I tear through the ghouls. Before I know it, I have twenty of them prone in the hallway and seven more on the stairs. I reload both guns, listening for any movement from them. I've got about thirty minutes before they revive—*if* they revive. I move down the stairs, coming to a small landing where the door to the hidden bomb shelter should be. I brush my fingers over the brick, finding the door crack and pushing it to reveal metal stairs. Bright lights greet me as I make it halfway down, my gut clenching as they remind me of nightmares, memories, and that damn hospital.

I hear a low growl around a corner and fire a bullet into a ghoul's head. Three more appear and thud to the ground as I shoot my way to the bottom. I'm met with lime-tinted light as five more come from above, each falling with a shot to the head. No point wasting bullets.

Once cleared, I observe the long hallway that smells of chemicals and bleach, seeing three metal doors on the right and two more on the left, separated by a darkened glass panel. There's a final metal door at the end with brown streaks on the floor before it. A ghoul growls behind me, and I aim at the sound, but the body slumps before I fire. I glance behind me seeing them crumpled on the steps. "What the—?"

Suddenly, muffled screams sound through the hall, and I run to each door, trying to open them. I come to the last one on the right and kick it hard and it gives a little with a groan. I kick again until it swings open, and I want to hurl my coffee. Tiles are covered in bile and brown liquid, reeking of burned flesh and rotting organs. I move my gaze up and see where its coming from. Bodies. Ghoul bodies.

I move closer, noticing the brown liquid that seeps out of the ghouls from their noses, mouths, and ears as they lay in cages or chained to walls. I choke back a gag, kneeling by one of them and swiping a finger through the brown liquid. It wasn't acid or sludge. It was ghoul blood.

My heart shatters as I realize the ghouls we found hadn't died from being Feral or being changed wrong; they were deliberately killed by the Head of the Hive, a rare ability that few have or will use because...they'd never kill their own. It's only been recorded twelve times in history at this magnitude. Fuck, I should have tried harder to see the bodies. If I'd seen them, I would've known they were never Feral. I sweep my gaze over the bodies and find the young ghoul I saw weeks ago, their eyes spilling with brown blood. If the Head took their own out just now, they know I'm here.

I set the explosives and their detonators on the far side of the room and near the exit. I crack the door behind me as I leave, heaving in breaths of bleached air as I reload my guns. I look at the ghouls on the stairs and see the brown blood drip onto the floor, then turn toward the end of the hall. Metal clangs and machines beep as I ease open the final door, sneaking into a viewing room. I come to the glass and see a laboratory, my stomach twisting in horror and rage.

The Head of the Hive is chained to a metal slab against the wall, slumping against their silver shackles. Syringes and scalpels are lined on a workbench next to three metal tables stained in dark blood and leather restraints. Machines line the wall, riddled with long tubes connected to glass containers, next to see through refrigerators filled with vials of numerous colors. Glasses clink, and I turn my gaze to see my target wearing a white jacket filling a syringe.

Quietly, I place the explosives and detonators under the viewing plane and grab one of my handguns. A low snarl rips from my throat as I slam open the door with my boot, and Traloski turns with wide eyes and vials in his hands. I shoot his kneecaps, and he falls to the ground screaming, vials smashing open as he grips the tiles.

"I was gonna sneak up, take my time, and give a big speech, but...fuck that," I say as I walk in, keeping my gun trained on him. Dark brown eyes meet mine as he slides back toward the wall, reaching for a scalpel. "Oh, no, you don't." I kick the scalpel away and jam my boot into his leg. He screams, and the ghoul flinches.

I kneel next to him, pressing the barrel to his head, and he stops, staring at me. He rasps, "How did you—?"

"It's Traloski right?" I ask, cocking my head. "Or do go by John or cocksucker?"

His eyes widen. "How did you find me? They said...how do you know—"

"Even with memory loss, it's hard to forget the eyes of the one who ripped you apart. It's like knowing not to enter certain shadows or to stare out at the harbor too long; you just don't forget that kind of terror."

He stares at the scars on my face then across my chest. His eyes widen in shock and a twinge of delight as recognition moves over him. "37."

"Hey, Frankenstein." I grin as my fist comes full force across his jaw. He spits blood as I step away and look around the laboratory for anything helpful, noticing the expensive-ass medical equipment. "Got the full scholarship ride, huh?"

"You're supposed to be dead. You can't be alive."

"I'm stubborn."

"He got rid of you—"

"Who? My father?" I ask. The Head ghoul watches us quietly as I look over similar scars across their face and body.

"Edgar?" He rasps. "He's...he's alive?"

I hear the confusion in his voice and give him a wicked look. "Not anymore." Our eyes meet and I see worry come across his gaze. "So, he lied to you, too, huh?"

He clutches at his wounds, shaking as he shifts further back against the wall. "What did you do?"

"Learned new hobbies, such as reading and stripping," I say, flicking open a cabinet of jars filled with dark liquid. "But you restarted yours. So, who funded you this time, fucker?"

Traloski sneers, "My employers are none of your concern."

"You were stealing half-breeds off the streets and pissed off the entire Underground Mafia, so yes, it is," I say, deliberately knocking over some vials.

"Stop!" He shouts, reaching toward where I am. "You don't know—"

"What I'm doing? I'm not stupid, *John*..." I scowl with a low snarl, "...*you* created me and should know that."

"37...you will listen—"

"When are you males gonna understand, I hate being told what to do." I leave to grab the explosives from the viewing room, bringing them in to set near the machines.

Horror lines his expression as he begs. "Wait, wait, wait... I'll tell you why I created you!"

"Yeah, don't care."

"He's still alive, the one who—!"

"Oh, I *know*," I say, and he freezes. "Monsters like him come out of the woodwork when their plans burn, like rats escaping the nest as it turns to flame."

"He'll kill you," he warns. I cock my head, smiling at him as quiet rage trickles through my veins. He's got nothing for me. I aim the gun at his head, and he holds up his bloodied hand and screams, "You're incomplete! He wouldn't let me finish you! You need me! I can complete you!"

"Careful, Finkel."

"You'll die as a human without me!"

"Edgar already tried that line."

"Then you'll die—"

"Better than in here," I snarl, and it echoes through the laboratory.

The Head ghoul calls out to me, "Daemon! I know how to awaken it! Daemon! I know!"

"Shut up, beast!" Traloski screams, and they flinch.

I meet the ghoul's dark violet eyes as they remain still in their chains. I see the recognition and understanding of similar pain in their eyes.

Traloski pleads in a pool of his own blood as if he doesn't

deserve to suffer, after years of never having mercy in mind for the children he created and ghouls he tortured. Rage fills my veins, overriding every emotion as I realize how done I am. Utterly, completely done. His actions not only brought me pain but to my siblings, my family, and innocent half-breeds. No more.

"You need me!" He begs loudly, dragging himself toward the door. "I created—"

"So, did others and their creations killed them, too. Welcome to the big leagues." I lift the gun to his head. "*Monster.*"

Two shots ring out, hitting him squarely in the forehead. I put the gun away as the Head ghoul speaks quickly, "Refrigerator, blue vial, drink it. It activates the...the..."

"Hold on, let me—"

"Take it now! Before you release me!"

I follow instructions, opening the fridge and see three blue vials, showing one to the ghoul. They nod, and I look at it and then the dead scientist. "Well, come on, Alice," I mutter, snapping the cork off and I glance back at the ghoul, and they nod again. I'm not the only one with an insane escape plan.

I knock back the vial and swallow the contents. Nothing happens as I wait a few moments, feeling no different. Fuck. I assume it didn't work until I take a step. My body suddenly feels engulfed in flame and ice, screaming as electricity flashes through my bones. I clutch my head as my eyes burn, yelling and tearing my contacts out from the intense agony. My spine stiffens, and I breathe deeply as the pain fades, leaving as quickly as it came. I swallow hard against burning lungs, opening my eyes to similar dark hues and contorted shapes as before, but then I see the ghoul glowing a faint orange. I glance at the lightbulbs, seeing an odd reddish glow.

What the fuck, am I Predator now?

"Only daemons can cut through silver," the ghoul says.

I look at them, cocking my head at the new vision and walk

over to them, mumbling, "New sight to get used to, great. And I ruined my contacts."

"Daemons once had specialized heat vision."

"Most were supposed to have died out in the 18th century."

"His experiments revitalized the abilities," they rasp. "Don't go into daylight with that vision."

"Noted." I look down at my hands. "Advice on turning *off* heat vision and, maybe, getting claws to get you out?"

"You can control your abilities by thinking it."

I concentrate, remembering what Joey said long ago about his own wings. The familiar feeling of knives suddenly presses at my knuckles, and six-inch titanium claws punch out, wrapping around my fingers. They glow a dim amber mixed with violet. Cute.

"How long did he have you?" I ask, swiping through the shackles before willing the claws away.

"Eleven years." They fall forward, and I catch them, wincing at their answer. "Taken from Raleigh and they killed my...my family."

"You were a half-breed?" They nod numbly. I hook their arm over my shoulders, carrying them toward the door. "Who were the ghouls who came to town months ago?"

"People turned over the years," they rasp. "Brought back here to continue his research for experiments...to make a serum."

"For what?"

"Change people into ghouls without biting. The ability to control a hive."

"Fucking great," I grumble.

"They targeted half-breeds with immunities...trying to bypass anything that could fight off the serum." I lead them through the viewing room, clicking my tongue to find my stuff and place the explosives. The hall lights burn my retinas as we leave Traloski's lab, and I groan, blinking harshly until I'm back to my old sight. Thank goodness switching isn't difficult.

"You said 'they.' Do you know who hired him?" I ask.

"People with badges...don't know who..." Their words falter as I place another explosive by the door, my hand brushing against the ghoul blood.

"Why did you kill your own?" I ask, leaning them against a wall as I set to finish with the rest of the explosives and detonators.

They shudder and shake their head. "Turned against their will, in agony. I could feel it all, their pain. I was trying to...give them peace, end their suffering. I saw you through their eyes and...and..."

"You saw your chance to liberate them and yourself. Mercy."

"Suffering...they were suffering. Do...do you remember?"

"Enough." I come back, swinging their arm around my shoulder, practically dragging them to the stairs.

"I hoped...someone knew about the connections breaking... did you?"

"I hadn't seen the bodies until just before I kneecapped Traloski. Otherwise, I would've known."

"You know...ghouls?" They rasp as I weave us through bodies.

"Would you believe me that I'm a librarian?"

They choke out a laugh. "You came just in time."

The stench makes my stomach churn as we move up the stairs, and I switch to heat vision again. This is gonna become a fun party trick. "In time?"

"The work was almost ready...to fully use."

"Well, shit."

The aroma of death hits worse as we make it to the top of the stairs, and I notice the bodies' dimming glow of faint green against dark hues. My radio starts to go off as we reach the back hall.

"Brenda! Fuck, answer me!" Rodney yells on the other end. Damn it, must have lost reception.

I place the ghoul on the ground to rest, grab the radio, and answer, "Signal was lost."

"Change of plans! Abort mission!"

"Why?"

"Police were contacted too soon! They've surrounded the center, fighting off ghouls!" Shots echo behind the radio static.

I look over at the Head ghoul, "You left some alive?"

"To get out," they rasp. "They had...an escape plan...using police."

"The badges who hired Traloski?" They nod. "Explains the police busts weeks ago," I mutter. "Keep those ghouls alive. Stay here."

I run up the stairs and make my way into the center, and my vision warps from piercing, flashing pink and green lights coming through windows. I barely make out the orange heat signatures of people against the glowing light of car engines.

"Whole circus is here," I murmur, then speak into the radio. "I can leave through the back."

"They have the place surrounded, lil sis!"

"Everything's set, and I got dead ghouls who need to burn."

"We won't be able to get you out!" Vinny's voice yells over the comm.

"Distract the police. I'll find a way out. There are tunnels I can take to the Underground before they shut down the Entrances," I say, hearing shots ring out from outside the front. "You *have* to scatter when the building blows, you hear me?"

"They'll fucking arrest you!" Vinny argues. "Even with—"

"This place isn't falling into *anyone's* hands."

"Brenda!"

"Start moving out now. You got five minutes tops. Scatter and get below before they close off everything," I order, walking back to the hall. "I've got business to finish."

"Lil sis...*fuck!*" Shots ring out.

"Sweet cheeks, don't you—"

"I love you, bloodsucker. Now *run*." I turn off the radio,

tossing it aside as I go down the hall and approach the Head ghoul. "I can get us—"

"No," they say. "Give me the trigger...my life is done for, not yours."

"There's no way—"

"It's that or your claws to end me. Which is it?" I stagger toward the ghoul, and almost imagine their violet eyes. I can smell it. They're already dying. "Ghouls out there will have peace when I'm gone...finally. Please. For all of us...give us peace." I kneel beside them, and they wrap their hands around the trigger. "Live for us."

Shouts and gunfire echo from outside, and my heart aches as I let them take it. "Press this in one minute, and everything will chain react." I show them, letting go completely and placing a kiss on their cheek, feeling the moisture of their tears and diminishing flesh against my lips. I pause and ask, "What's your name?"

"Genevieve."

"I promise you...you won't be forgotten. I promise." I kiss her cheek again as she nods, and I run for the stairs and down the hallway to the backdoor.

I bite back tears as I pull my guns out, kick the back door open, and shoot at the glowing shapes of cop cars, turning away before the blasting light blinds me. I run past the burning vehicles, using the exploding sounds to run down the alleyway. The ground shifts and rumbles as the first blast hits deep below the center. Another rumbles, and I slam against a wall as heat rises at my back. Sirens go off as people scream, including the ghouls who die with the Head. Righting myself, I sprint down the alley, adrenaline pumping through me as I race to an exit for the Underground. I had to get below and destroy one last piece of my past...before it's too late.

TNT
Boom

CHAPTER 32
I'M LATE, I'M LATE FOR A MURDEROUS DATE

Chaos implodes and echoes collide behind me as I focus on the glowing shadows bouncing off the walls. Each step gets easier using the heat vision as I zig-zag through alleys to get to an Entrance on the east side of the center. I hear yelling, sirens going off, helicopters fly high, and explosions continue, shaking the city around me. I come around a corner and inhale a familiar scent, stopping when I hear the click of a safety going off.

I pull my gun out, aiming at Drauper's muted amber form with red outlining him. He points his gun at me a mere 20 feet away. Easy shot.

"Brenda?" He asks, stepping toward me at the intersection of an alleyway. Officers shout in the distance for evacuation as another blast echoes. "Did you do this?" I step toward the alley on my right, having less than ten minutes to make it to the Entrance. "Stop!"

I pause, taking a deep breath. "You were right about the ghouls being a distraction. It was him...all of it."

"What are you talking about?"

"The half-breeds, ghouls...it was because of Traloski. Those ghouls were brought here against their will." I hear him shift as his scent lightens, his shoes scuffing the pavement. I lift my gun up, showing my hands as I put it behind my back. "This isn't over, Louis. There's one more left, and this city isn't safe until—"

"Did you kill him? Traloski?" I nod my head. "Don't trust the system to give him justice?"

"Do you?" I ask, and he steps back. I'm losing precious time as I hear voices beyond him. "We're on the same side, Louis. Please believe me when I say that we *both* want this city safe. For *all* people."

The voices close in, and I'm half a second away from taking my gun back out, scared of what I may need to do. Drauper shouts, "This way is clear!" He drops his aim and says, "Run."

I sprint down the streets to the main Entrance as police cars come rushing past and people scream. I glance back to where the center was and only see bright red and yellow light bursting above buildings. I run through the thrall of people, dodging past the bright figures until I hear the wailing siren. The first warning that the Entrances are shutting down.

I rush past people and drop a gun into a trash can and another into a dumpster, taking a shortcut toward the Entrance when I see glowing engines of police cars. Shit. I turn and run back to where I came, hearing shouts ahead.

"Hey! Stop!" An officer yells behind me as I sprint down an alley.

I drop my last gun into a trashcan around the corner and strip my jacket off, racing toward the subway. I toss the jacket to a hunched over person as I clear a corner almost to the subway, hearing a "Thanks" as I run. People scream around me, helping me see what my new infrared vision can't.

Firetrucks, ambulances, and police cars wail from a nearby street as I reach the subway, run down the stairs, jump over the handrails, and land on the bottom. People shout as I race through, jumping over turnstiles and reaching the platform to see the bright lights of the stopped train. Bingo.

My lungs burn as I push past people onto the train, darting through the cars as officers close behind. Just as they announce departure, I make it through the closing doors and watch two heated figures pound on the closed glass. Smiling, I turn and run down the platform to the other side and jump down onto the railway as an incoming train echoes. I charge towards it as people shriek. Bright lights engulf my vision as the oncoming train lets loose a loud horn, telling me where my exit is.

Lights blur my vision, and I blink a few times to will away the infrared vision. I land in darkness with two bright pink lights coming for me and jump to the right, feeling the wall for the door and pushing it open just as the train passes. Air whooshes past as I descend the spiral stairs toward the emergency exit of the Underground.

I smack the wall, determining my steps as I make it to the bottom and hear the last warning wail of the Underground going into lockdown. I freeze as the alarms go off, and the clang of the barrier goes up over the exit ten feet away. Shit.

Think Brenda. Think.

I breathe in deep, and a whiff of sewage reaches my nostrils. "Oh, fuck me. Just had to be *that*."

The alarms keep blasting as I follow the stench to a doorway that leads to the sewer system. I inhale deeply, finding another scent buried in the sewage. I turn, continuing down until I feel the crack of a hidden door and push. The rush of stale air meets me, and I know I found one of Pops' old tunnels.

"Thank you, Pops; I did not want to wade through sewage today," I mumble as I slip through.

I bang my fist against the wall, and it echoes around me with a wet slosh. I keep a hand on the wall, following the tunnel and listening to the subway trains above until I reach a divide in the tunnel. Wrong direction, and I'll be upstate. I inhale deeply with a gag. That's it, I'm not eating for two days. The left has a mustier aroma, and there's the drift of old blood. Left it is.

I keep going down, hearing the trains stop above me as the subway systems halt for the next step of the Underground shutdown. I bang the wall again and notice a change further ahead. Once I get to the end, I'm met with a metal grate door, locked with multiple chains. I can smell the scent of brick from the Underground, just beyond.

"No!" I shake the door, the only thing separating me from freedom. I pull at it again, but it doesn't budge. No, I *can't* go back. This is my only chance.

Frustration builds, and my veins tick with ice as my knuckles become pained with a pointed pressure. I pause and look down, willing my long titanium claws to punch out, almost slicing my clenched fists. Keep hands open. Noted.

I furiously swipe at the chains, cutting clean through. I grin wildly, glancing down at the long claws, switching to infrared to see their light amber violet color. "You just became my new favorite toy."

I rip the grate away, continuing down until I reach the last doorway. I slice through the handle, and electricity skitters over my hands. The feeling disappears quickly, and I grin again. My chances of survival just went up.

I push through the door, stumbling out a wall and into the Underground as people rush to get inside their homes. Sirens wail through the Underground as I will my claws away and take in my surroundings, knowing where I am. Sprinting down a path, I weave through people as the alarms echo until I reach the bar, slamming open the doors to hear the television broadcasting the "attack" happening.

Something thuds and glass breaks as I look over to see the glowing figure of Garrick. "Shit, lil sis, what are you doing here?"

"I need a drink," I say, pulling out the only surviving item on me—my phone.

"Right now? Seriously? While—" A reporter talks on the TV about damages and casualties.

"Blown up for a reason. Just business."

"Which mob?"

"All of us." I grin, gesturing for that drink. "And I've got a favor to ask."

Garrick pauses, cocking his head and I notice his heat signature is a darker orange. He grabs a bottle, putting it before me. "Something tells me I'm not gonna like it."

"Maybe, but it'll be entertaining." I reach for the glass, and miss. Really? *That's* what I miss? I growl and grab the whiskey, knocking back the bittersweet taste.

"Alright, I'll bite, what are you planning, lil sis?"

"How badly do you want to see the vampires squirm?"

"Depends," he says with a lilt of excitement in his voice. He's ex-Wolf Mob, they'll never dismiss a chance to jab at the vamps. He fills a glass and clinks it against the bottle in my hand. "How do I play into it?"

I hold out my left hand, and my claws punch out against the counter. Garrick doesn't budge, but his heat signature flashes red as he grabs the bottle from my hand. He takes a long drink and clanks it against the bar. "You've got my attention."

"Call Dracultelli and tell him #37 sends her fucking regards."

CHAPTER 33
BBEG

"Any damages, put it on…fuck it, Rodney's tab."

"If you pull this off, you get free whiskey for life, lil sis," Garrick responds as he loads his shotgun. "Sure you don't want silver bullets?"

"I never carry, and he knows that," I say, pouring one more shot of whiskey. "He'll sense something is up."

He growls, setting the shotgun under the bar within reach for me. Everything is quiet outside, cleared of people and the alarms have stopped. The smell of rain falling on Topside drifts to the Underground as I watch the news reporter get soaked.

"Get outta here; no point in starting a turf war," I say, pushing the bottle away, babying my shot of whiskey. "Press the button when he arrives."

He holds up my phone and a remote. "Good luck, lil sis. Put the bastard in his place. And don't die."

"Will do," I snort.

He leaves, and I'm left with the television rambling as I adjust to my new sight abilities, catching things I didn't know had heat. I flex my hand as they report a bad gas line exploded, saying the Entrances need to stay shut throughout the night.

Speculation of drug operations by the ghouls is the next story. No bodies have been recovered.

I knock back my drink and get a whiff of his damn scent. I slip my hand forward, grabbing the shotgun as the door clicks open and whip around, aiming and firing it off twice. He easily avoids both shots, and I use the shotgun to swing at the fast-moving body. It slams into his fist, shattering into two pieces. His hands are soon around my neck, pinning me to the counter.

"Hello there," I grunt against his biting nails.

Bruno's heat signature rises to a bright red, darkened at the edges, and his scent burns my nostrils as he snarls through his teeth, "You *bitch*."

"Wrong line. Try again."

"You fucking *killed* him."

"Thought you wanted him dead?"

"Not before *I* needed him," he growls, and the counter vibrates beneath me. My bones ache, screaming against the pressure of the wood. I struggle a little for air as the pressure tightens on my neck. "*You* were supposed to die."

"You really think *Edgar* would've succeeded?"

"He easily took out the others."

"You forget my *real* father?" I sneer as he snarls back at me.

"Damn Alanzo and his bleeding heart."

"You hired Traloski. Why?"

A sinister laugh leaves him. "Control over *my* city." Not enough. Give me more, fuckface.

I gasp as my throat tightens. "It was for you...the serums. You knew Pops would stop you."

"Like father, like daughter," he snarls, shaking the room as lights flicker. "With that serum I would've *murdered* him."

"What about the Society...how—?" I wheeze, beginning to feel lightheaded as his grip tightens.

"Traloski's serum would've given me the power to destroy them *permanently*. But that fucking human got caught, and everything needed to disappear. *Everything*. Including you."

Bruno throws me hard against the wall, knocking the air out of my lungs.

I moan, standing on wobbly legs as Bruno stalks me, and I pull out the other gun Garrick gave me from my boot. I aim for his head, but he dodges the bullets, slamming me into the wall again as he grips my neck.

"Edgar was supposed to finish you like the rest," he snarls, and I thrash against his hold. "Don't worry, you'll join them *and* that delusional freak soon. Then *no one* will know."

I gasp for air, clutching at his hand around my throat. "Vinny...will kill..."

Bruno's eyes grow black against his glowing features, heat dissipating as a cold, dark scent seeps from him. "He's outlived his purpose officially since I have *my* position back. And after I make him watch your blood fill my cup, he'll join you...*half-breed.*"

Rage courses like fire through my blood, and the roar of fury in my head destroys any other thought. The image of Vinny's blood on my hands comes back like a tidal wave, pushing me over the edge. My restraint snaps.

My titanium claws punch out, and I swipe them across his face and into his stomach. I kick forward, and he flies back into the other wall. I run toward him, punching him again and plunging my claws forward. He dodges the blow and grabs me from behind, tossing me through the window as glass shatters around me.

I roll away on the pavement and hear a gun cock, moving to dodge the bullets. One skims my side, and I scream, swiping up as Bruno charges for me. Claws slice through his skin, making him howl. I attempt to keep ahead of him, twisting around to grab a gun at his back, and aim for his chest. He moves away swiftly, and my bullets hit a water pipe and lamp. Water sprays over us as we go fist to fist. A snarl rips from my throat as water practically steams from our bodies.

"You let the others go! Why was I left in the sewer?" I scream.

"You were a failure!" He growls, punching me across the face.

I stumble back and swipe with my claws again, aching as we prowl around each other. "I have all the immunities. What more did you need?"

"All?" He taunts. "There was *one* vital immunity you failed... 37."

I snarl as realization hits me, yelling, "*You dumped me because vampires can heal me?*"

"I needed control, not *your* survival." He runs forward, and I twist out of the way, slashing my claws down. We move around each other, fighting with slashes and fists. He pivots and gets behind me, grasping my throat and grazing my neck with his teeth. Not again. NO. I struggle against his hold, thrashing to get him off me.

He whispers darkly, "After I kill you, perhaps I'll use my son to finish what you failed."

All I see is red as the hatred of two decades combines with pure territorial, primal wrath. I growl loud enough that it echoes against the alley walls, and I reach back at Bruno's head, focusing all energy on him.

Lightning blasts from my hands and into his skull, and he howls against the electrocution and stumbles back. With strength I didn't know I had, I flip him over my shoulder into a puddle and thrust my hands onto his chest, electrocuting him again. His body spasms as the dark lightning courses through him. My infrared vision is gone, replaced by only crimson as territorial vampiric rage takes over. I throw him against the brick wall and plunge my claws into his chest, blasting the electric lightning straight into him.

"*You will never touch Vinny* again," I snarl low. "*He...is...mine.*" I burn him from the inside out as he screams.

"Brenda, stop!" Vinny's voice reaches my ears, and some of the red I see fades as the lightning dies from my hands. Bruno's breath is shallow as I smell burning flesh and bone.

"He was going to use you!" I scream back at him. "Make you bleed again!"

"Let me finish this," Vinny coaxes, coming closer.

"No...I can't let you..." No, there's already too much blood on his hands.

"Sweet cheeks," he whispers, placing a hand on my shoulder, easing my entire being with his touch.

Bruno chokes up a cough, laughing darkly as he slowly heals. "Tell me *Vincent*, how does it feel to know you *failed* to protect her? Or did you ever notice the bite marks on her neck while you fucked—"

Vinny rips my hands from his father's chest, piercing his nails into Bruno's neck with a gurgling sound. He slams Bruno to the ground and snarls, "I warned you *never* to touch her."

Adrenaline begins to leave my body as I slump against the brick, hearing Vinny rip into his father. He hurls Bruno into the ground and brick flies up with a rumbling force. Bones snap and blood spills as Bruno screams in horrified agony, drawn and quartered by his son. His limbs thump to the pavement as I blink for my infrared vision to come back, concentrating on the shape of Vinny tearing his teeth into his father's neck. Bruno gurgles, flailing a half arm as he's slammed into the ground.

Bruno chokes and warns, "You kill me...and you'll never get back—"

"I gave it up for her, and I'll do it again," Vinny snarls. "I'll forfeit *everything* for her."

"Vinny, stop!" I yell, wincing at my side. "Garrick's place was bugged. I got his confession. The Society will—"

"He deserves to die!" Vinny yells as he rips back Bruno's head.

Bruno begins to laugh, gurgling out blood. "Like father, like—"

Gunfire blasts, and Bruno's head implodes into orange flecks.

Vinny steps back as Bruno's body slumps to the ground, and I smell mulled wine. He turns toward the source of the gunfire and rasps, "Anita?"

She walks forward, her figure a glowing white ember, lined in dark violet as she puts her gun away. "Sorry, baby sis, but there wasn't a chance of me not telling Vincent your little plan," she says to me. "He wasn't supposed to beat me here, though."

"Anita...what have you done?" Vinny asks.

"Keeping a longtime promise," she says quietly. "I'm returning the title of Blood Mafia Boss back to you. It seems no one else can take it. It was always meant to be yours. Never mine." She steps toward Bruno's body and flicks a lit match, setting the body to flames. "And as the only *official* Dracultelli alive, I am pardoning your exile from our bloodline."

"Anita—"

She raises her hand, and he quiets as she approaches him. "Don't worry about the Society. Once they realize they won't survive without us, they'll agree to anything we want. They should be reminded who *actually* makes the decisions, don't you agree? And I doubt they'll fight you now since you've become too valuable, brother. No name to track by the government? And all that blackmail you've curated over the years? The one thing our father did right...he made you the perfect boss. And now you have a Mate who can electrocute people to death. Amusing, by the way. He should've let you do it longer."

I snort at her. "For once, I agree with you."

She reaches Vinny, and he cups her face as he asks, "Why?"

Anita places her hand against his as her tone becomes a deadly calm. "It's my duty as your older sister to protect you, baby brother. I promised our mother."

Footsteps sound from across the path, and I turn to see Garrick's figure as he whistles at the carnage, then gives a small, thrilled growl. Vinny stands still as Anita walks away toward Garrick, who comments, "You work fast."

"Garrick, I'll need the footage from your bar. The Society will want proof of who to trust," she says, pausing to look back at me. "And who they should fear from now on."

I grin slowly, willing my claws away finally with some ache. "I'm too expensive to hire."

Anita chuckles and pulls out her gun. "I'll need more silver bullets to enforce those reminders. Care to help?"

"Only if you promise to clean up *that* mess and my bar," Garrick says, walking down the wet alley with her.

I bring my gaze over to Vinny, who stalks toward me with purpose. He stops and grabs my face, crashing his lips against mine into a searing kiss. I gasp, tasting and breathing in his wonderful scent. His tongue sweeps over my mouth, and I reach up to pull him closer, placing his body flush against mine. My chest expands with a deep breath of relief, the dark emotions leaving me into a fully settled calm.

He grips me, holding me close until he pulls away and warns, "*Never* scare me like that again."

"Do I get kisses like that afterward?" Cause *worth it*. Vinny growls, crushing his lips to mine again. His chest rumbles with a snarl, and I moan at the vibrations and snarl in return as I clutch his hair. I pull away, breathing raggedly. "So, about that honeymoon?"

"First, some ground rules for this *evolving* relationship... *sweet* cheeks."

"Aw, shit."

"One."

"Fuck, there's a list."

"One, *sweet cheeks*, quit sacrificing yourself to protect me."

"You started it."

"Two." I roll my eyes. "You're not allowed near explosives for a month." I grimace, okay, he's got a point. "Three, no more secrets, even though I knew about him biting you." My eyes widen. "I was waiting until you were ready to talk."

"I really thought I got away with that."

"Not that dumb."

"Never said that, bloodsucker. And since we're going off the whole 'no more secrets,' well, I have some left."

"Go on," Vinny grumbles.

"First, I stole your toothbrush when I was eight and used it to clean your sink." He barks out a laugh. "Second, I stole that 200-year-old bottle of scotch you were saving when I was sixteen and gave it Rodney. I think he still has it." His chest rumbles with more laughter. "Third, it was actually me who put itching powder in your underwear the second time."

He cradles the side of my face. "What am I gonna do with you?"

"No clue, since I'm also the main reason both our fathers are dead." We glance over at the smoldering ashes of Bruno.

"Better late than never," Vinny muses. "Our fault for raising you in the mafia, I guess."

"It seems like a horrifying, terrible flex." My face scrunches. "Beckham's gonna make me record this for the library."

"As if you'd hate that."

"True, and I have a promise to keep," I whisper, thinking of Genevieve. Vinny grips my face a bit tighter. "All reasons are morbid at this point."

"That's an understatement."

"But good news! I took a magic potion from the mad hatter, and you're probably gonna have to deal with me for a very, *very* long time," I say, putting my arms around his neck and willing my vision to go back to normal. I soon see ruby eyes staring down at me, glowing with warmth, love, and most of all, amusement.

"Oh, I'm counting on it...*bestie*." He kisses me, and I melt into his touch, moaning at the contact. Suddenly, he breaks the kiss and throws me over his shoulder as I screech. "Deal's a deal, sweet cheeks. You did it under three hours, so it's time for ice cream and your 'anti-murdery juicey-juice."

"Fucking finally!" I yell as he walks us away from the carnage toward home.

TO WONDERLAND
TOGETHER

— BLOODSUCKER

CHAPTER 34
VINNY THE VAMPIRE & ME

I was grounded for a month.

Vinny took me home as I became a laughing fit, almost hysterical from the aftershock of the night's events as my adrenaline wore off. My parents didn't scold me for being reckless until the next day, allowing me to fall asleep on Vinny and it was the hardest I'd slept in six months.

I lean back on the brick wall, sipping my thermos filled with "Vinny Style" coffee as I watch the sunrise over the New York City skyline. I adjust my glasses to the spilling of light over the horizon and sigh. It's odd seeing it without Vinny waking my ass up.

It was reported that the explosions came from the unstable gas lines beneath the forgotten tunnels after Rodney's bombs incinerated any evidence. NYPD and PSB were deterred from their investigations with a bit of help from Midnight and other contacts. Vinny's already told Bill to head anyone off the pass who tries to dig further on the real reason, including Freyja. There was nothing left of Traloski, his lab, or the ghouls…well, except one thing. Me.

Beckham and I are recording the whole ordeal for *The Vault*, detailing what was found and who was lost, including

Genevieve. Every single half-breed who went missing, my siblings, and the ghouls will be remembered not just as experiments anymore. They'll be written down and remembered as living beings.

Last week I was retested, my daemon side blossoming full throttle. My lifespan now outmatched Vinny's, ironically. I gained titanium claws, lightning, infrared vision, and slight super strength, but Charlene thinks that's from the Mating. No wings. Damn it. I'm still showing traits from pureblood vampires, which she thinks is from the experiments. She has a theory that I'll develop other Paranormal abilities over time due to the "magic potion" I took. We'll see. And despite all that, I'm still technically blind.

"Had to choose the top of a building at 6 AM?" Drauper's voice disrupts my thoughts.

I turn and smile as sunlight skims across the roof of my old apartment building. "What? It's a really good view and better than any bar."

"I thought you'd stand me up."

"And miss the sunrise?" I gesture toward the skyline. "Not a chance. Mufasa knew what he was talking about."

"Pretty sure he was talking about *owning* everything the light touches, not its beauty."

"I wasn't talking about beauty either," I smirk as Drauper walks up beside me. He's wearing his leather jacket with his detective badge hanging over his chest. His hair is cut short again, faded on the sides with a clean shave. He adjusts his sunglasses, remaining quiet as we look out at the brilliant light. "Alright, I've seen my kingdom. What did you want, Drauper?"

He continues watching the sunrise. "You were right."

"Must be hard to admit that."

"Don't make this harder than it already is. I'm guessing you know how the investigation ended?"

"Pretty much."

"I couldn't find the names of those who controlled that

center," he says suddenly, and I still. "But during my video footage search for those missing, I came across something."

"Such as?"

He exhales loudly, looking over at me as his scent grows stronger. "There was one camera that worked down the street from the center. Three PSB Agents were seen multiple times walking toward it."

"Do you have the footage?"

"No, because practically five blocks of the Bronx exploded and incinerated any to all hardcopies," he says, eyeing me. "And someone wiped all the software ten minutes after the...*gas lines* went up."

"Did you ID them?"

Drauper pauses, looking away. "No."

"You hesitated. Hiding something from me?"

"Coming from the one who *did* hide information from me."

"I did it to protect you," I mutter.

"You expect me to believe that?" He scoffs.

"Surprisingly, I give a shit about you and didn't want you getting killed." He takes a step back, and I smell the drift of dark spices from the other side of the roof. "Why do you think I agreed to meet you? I cared, even after you insinuated that I was working with the bad guys and questioned how I saved your ass from vampires almost *kidnapping* you."

"You were the one who called me in the first—"

"I went to the Bronx *twice* for you, and nearly died both times because of it. I jeopardized a shit-ton the moment I went to help you, but I'd do it again because you were my *friend*." Drauper goes still. "I came back up here to find answers, and you were the *only* one on Topside who ever listened to me. The only one, like me, who wanted to help those missing half-breeds. And who read the fucking books. I *trusted* you."

The scent of dark spices grows, and a growl loosens from my throat, making it dissipate. Nosy, territorial bloodsucker.

Drauper adjusts where he stands, turning away from me. I

sigh, "I fucked up, Louis. But I honestly never wanted to see you hurt."

"I thought we agreed we shouldn't be friends," he murmurs.

I take a sip from my thermos. "Yeah, well I suck at professional relationships. Ask Janice."

He snorts, turning back to me and pulling out a small travel-sized liquor bottle, placing it on the brick wall. "You got to the ghouls first," he says.

I take the bottle. "Look, we're not perfect, and our track record for being in the field...isn't spotless, but we could get better. And I really did consider you a friend."

"I think we deserve a gold star for sharing information... without the mob bit," he says, and I chuckle. "I considered you my friend, too."

I pocket the alcohol, leaning against the short wall. "Guess I'll take the liquor as your apology." Drauper snorts. "I'm a dick, but I'm a forgiving dick most days, especially if you get me the good whiskey."

He leans against the wall with me, both of us gazing out at the rising sun. He rubs his face and says, "If I knew the Agents' identities, I'd tell you." I quirk a brow at him, and he shrugs. "Something doesn't add up, and if it's PSB, I need info outside of the government."

I smile softly. "You'll need more reliable resources then, and I know just the people for that."

He stills and stares at me. "You are *not* suggesting—"

"You're gonna be my NYPD contact," I say as he groans loudly, and I hear a snicker from the far side. Shut up, Vinny.

"This can't be happening." Drauper starts pacing. "I already almost lost my job. If I'm caught, I'll lose my badge forever!"

I shrug. "We control the courts, including parts of NYPD; you'll be fine."

"You'll put me out of my jurisdiction."

"Learning opportunities. Education is good for the soul."

"I'll be helping the bad guys!"

"To get the *real* bad guys."

"They're still criminals."

"More like morally-gray-fucked-up-sense-of-humor guys." There's a distant snicker again, and I scowl. "With no sense of preservation from their *partners*." The sound stops and Drauper groans, pinching his nose. "You'll be safe under our protection."

"And whose protection is that?"

I steady myself. "Vincent Dracultelli, Blood Mafia Boss."

Drauper's jaw drops. "He's gone. NIIA made a statement—" I shrug, and he steps back. "How?"

"We'll call it 'family drama.' And you can't say anything. Otherwise, you may have another *wonderful* talk with my brother."

He stares at me for a moment. "If I say no, they gonna kill me?"

I snort. "Course not; too much paperwork. If you don't want to, fine. But anything regarding those Agents and stopping them, you *have* to stay out of the way. Leave it to us."

"How will you find any information—" He stops himself; mouth still open in realization as I grin.

"You're *my* first contact in the NYPD." He folds his arms over his chest and looks out to the city as light streaks over skyscrapers. I glance back to the door and see a pair of crimson eyes gleaming before disappearing into the wall. "Drauper, I was only ever trying to protect my family. They're everything to me, including Vinny. I won't apologize for doing that, but I *am* sorry for lying."

He leans over the wall, gripping the brick and whispers, "You know, if someone had told me two years ago this sarcastic librarian with a bad sense of humor would turn my life upside down, I'd tell them they're high."

"If I was told I'd be friends with a human detective, I'd ask for stronger alcohol."

He scoffs, nodding as he looks back out to NYC. "Alright. Few ground rules first."

"These damn rules and lists of late," I grumble.

"I trust you for some reason within this...bizarre friendship," he says, and I snort. "And you've been right when it comes to Paranormals, but I want nothing to do with Dracultelli. I'll only speak with you."

"Seems reasonable."

"And *not* your brother."

"Don't blame you there."

"And if you ever ask me to go to the Underground, I take at least a clip of silver."

"Okay." He raises his brows in surprise. "What? If anyone knows there are assholes below who deserve to eat silver, it's me. You want hollow points?"

He laughs, genuinely laughs, making me smile. "Lastly, you and I get a drink once in a while...as friends. You still have to try drinking me under the table."

"Heads up, I'll win. But I'll buy the next round since I made you come up here at sunrise, Mordecai."

"What happened to Sherlock?"

"You have to earn it back." I pat his shoulder and start walking for the door.

"Wait? Are we starting now?"

"Might as well," I say. "I'll contact you in a few weeks. The number you had will be disconnected in two days, and I'll have a separate phone sent to you."

"*Weeks?*"

"Yeah, I was grounded and need to finish out my sentence." He snorts loudly as I wave my hand, opening the door. "Enjoy the rest of the sunrise and wait until it hits the Empire State Building. It's comforting."

I leave through the door, finishing my coffee off as I head down the stairs, walking the familiar steps I climbed for three years. I come to the bottom as Vinny slips out of the wall and leans against the doorway. "He fully agreed?" He asks nonchalantly.

"Funny enough, yeah. For a moment, didn't think he would."

We walk outside, skirting around the sunlight spreading across the sidewalk. I look over at him wearing a new leather jacket while I wear his old one. He lightly shoves my shoulder with his as we head to the Entrance. "Heard that preservation comment."

"Good, you nosy, busy-body."

"You asked me to come."

"We both know I never ask," I smirk.

"Let's check that theory. We could sneak off—"

I push him, but he doesn't budge as he puts his arm over my shoulder. "We're already gonna be late. Or do you want both our hides ripped off?"

"They can't start without us if we're late...we'll say you were taking hours to get ready. Getting *perfect* for me."

I slip my arm around his waist and snort. "No one's gonna believe that, and I'm only wearing that damn thing *with* heels because of Anita and Ma."

"Not for me?"

"I could wear a burlap sack, and you'd be happy, bloodsucker."

"Not that picky."

"Except with blood."

"And guns," he adds.

"And who to fuck, but that's a recent development." He begins to put me in a headlock, and I laugh. "Kidding, Gomez!"

He lets go, leaning down to brush his lips across my earlobe. "And *you* prefer that I am, or I could—"

I grip his hair tightly, growling. "Don't finish that sentence."

"Now, who's territorial?"

"Learned from the best."

"That you did, sweet cheeks, that you did."

THE RECEPTION HALL buzzes with everyone we know, and somehow by luck or mercy, all Paranormals are getting along. Ricky and I threatening to shoot kneecaps if they ruined anything did help. The place is filled with candles, diamonds, velvet, and red and black flowers. A jazz band plays as people dance, drink, and talk around the tables.

I've finally gotten a moment away from talking, moving toward the back and catching a glimpse of myself in a mirror. Gina put my hair up in an intricate updo with crystals that accentuates the long black satin gown held up by thin straps with a deep plunging neckline, showcasing the scars Ricky painted violet to match my eyes. I look down at the black metal ring on my right index finger.

I'm officially Mated to Vinny the Vampire by the eyes of the Vampiric Society and the Underground Mafia.

They caved pretty quickly with Bruno gone. Probably helped that I could electrocute purebloods to the brink of death, plus Anita threatened to take away their blood supply. Vinny's records were expunged, which means the outside world of the Underground thinks he's gone. For now. Technically, he's still abdicated from his bloodline to hide the truth of his existence, but he's still the Blood Mafia Boss and last male of the Dracul-telli line. *The Lounge* is still under my name, along with the rest of his assets. I was always gonna keep the Cuorebella name anyways.

"How are you doing, baby?" Ma asks, handing me another drink. Thank goodness for my Ma and whiskey.

"These always so boring after the blood ritual and ceremony?"

"Your father's and mine was filled with more dancing…and poles," she giggles, brushing a hair behind my ear. "I'm so happy and proud of you, baby."

"Thanks, Ma."

"And I know you'll take care of him," she muses, kissing my cheek. "Just as he always took care of you."

I shrug. "It's what friends do."

She laughs, her scent blossoming as Pops approaches us. "*Mio cavaliere*, have you seen Gina?"

"She's with Joey and Midnight on the other side," he says, and Ma kisses his cheek before leaving us alone.

I knock back the shot of whiskey, and Pops chuckles, taking my empty glass to set aside. He comes back, cupping my face as I smile. "You're not moving out until you're a hundred." A laugh bursts out of me. "If it's a rule with your brothers, it's the same for you, too. Mated or not."

"Sure, Pops, *that's* why," I laugh, grabbing his hand. "Vinny's place is still a mess. It'll probably take him decades to clean it up."

Pops kisses my forehead, and the rush of cinnamon I inhale loosens the tight muscles across my shoulders. Leave it to my Pops to ease my nerves still. He caresses the scars down my face, then turns as we both notice Vinny talking with Samuel.

"You did a good job with that center, baby girl."

"Am I still grounded—?"

"Oh, you are, mainly for giving your brother a heart attack and going after a pureblood vampire by yourself," he scolds lightly, and I grimace. Yeah, not my best move of late. Pops suddenly chuckles under his breath, "But you reminded me of how I was centuries ago, when I was young starting out. I tried to keep you away from the business, but you're a strong, stubborn Cuorebella."

Tears start to prick my eyes. "Pops, what are you getting at?"

He looks down at me, his eyes glowing dark hues through my glasses. "I know you're going back to work with Beckham, but I may need a…sharpshooter to accompany Michello out to *Silver Paw*. He mentioned something to Joey about you seeing the mountains." My heart swells as a large smile grows on my face. "Think about it, baby girl. Right now, I need to go dance with my beautiful Mate."

He kisses my cheek and strolls up next to Ma, taking her into his arms as I hear her laughter chime. I chuckle softly at the idea of being one of Pops' guards. A librarian enforcer seems like a nice gig to add to my resume, right under ex-stripper. I inhale the scent of bloodlust and make a finger gun, jabbing it into Vinny's stomach as he comes up behind me.

He chuckles deeply, nuzzling his face in my shoulder. "We should leave."

"Party's for us, bloodsucker."

"They have enough alcohol, they'll be alright. And they saw the main bit." I stroke my hand down his arm, clutching his hand as I feel the metal ring on his index finger. "By the way, I prefer this dress over the burlap sack."

"What about your leather jacket?"

"Oh, there's *nothing* better than you in leather, sweet cheeks."

"Only for you, bloodsucker." I smile as he kisses my neck. "You know what, I know a place for us to disappear to."

"Vermont?"

"Too far away."

"My bed, then?"

"*Our* bed, bloodsucker." He laughs. "But no."

"Is it fun at least?"

"When is it not with us?"

Vinny grabs my hand, leading me out toward the back of the reception hall, his eyes glowing with mischief. "Let's escape then, Mate."

I kick my heels off, and we hurry away, grabbing our leather jackets from the coat check and throwing them on as we sneak out the back door. I start to run down the brick path, laughing with Vinny close behind. We race through the twinkling evening of the Underground like a couple of maniacs in our black-tie attire as people stare at us. I lead him to our escape, stopping before the marbled steps and Vinny lets out a boisterous laugh.

Fifteen minutes later, we're sitting in the dim lighting of a back corner in *The Vault,* our leather jackets folded over an armchair. I drape my legs over his while he lounges back on the sofa, one arm along the back with the other holding a mug of coffee. I have my own "anti-murdery juicy-juice" as I grab one of the books I collected, trailing my fingers over the braille with a smile.

"What are you *regaling* me with today, sweet cheeks?" I hold out the book, and he traces the bumps on the spine. "*Cthulhu, Krakens, and The Leviathan: The Noctis Immortalis Myths of the Deep.*"

"It's a good read," I say, bringing it back into my lap.

"Couldn't have picked out a fairytale?"

"Technically, these should be."

"Except, all of them exist."

"*You* told me Cthulhu was a shifter with anger issues obsessed with Davy Jones."

"You were twelve and had a fear of water."

"Yep, and if you *ever* take me near the bay, I'm shooting you in the foot with a spiked bullet," I warn. "Those don't exist, but I'm certain Rodney would make it happen."

"Your foreplay is unrivaled."

"I know," I say with a smile.

Vinny's eyes glow against the darkness, putting his coffee down to trace his fingers over my painted facial scars with silver flecks. He kisses me softly. "I love you, sweet cheeks."

"I love you, bloodsucker," I whisper against his lips. We settle in, and I start reading aloud, both of us exactly where we need to be. Best friends forever, whether it's mob shit chaos or in the quiet of our favorite reading spot.

Just sweet cheeks and her mob boss.

ANOTHER MOB BOSS, ANOTHER DAY...

The series continues with Rodney McLycan
The Wolf Mob Boss in:

<u>The Wolf Boss & His Darling</u>

BOOKS BY ELM JED

Mafia, Murder, and Mayhem Series

Vinny the Vampire & Me

Sweet Cheeks & Her Mob Boss

The Wolf Boss & His Darling

The Werecat & Her Lone Wolf

Memories of the Underground: Volume One

Contemporary Mafia Series

My Dear Watson

My Forgotten Demons

My Emerald Fire

My Dear Leo

ABOUT THE AUTHOR

Elm Jed is an award winning author, who mostly writes mafia, paranormal, and suspense romance. They are a disabled, queer, Marine Corps veteran, who's been writing since they were ten years old with a degree in Theatre. Their books focus on mental health awareness and giving readers a space to feel seen in different ways from disabilities to understanding their queerness.